You're Still the One

By Darcy Burke

CONTEMPORARY ROMANCE

Ribbon Ridge
Where the Heart Is (a prequel novella)
Only In My Dreams
Yours to Hold
When Love Happens
The Idea of You
When We Kiss
You're Still the One

HISTORICAL ROMANCE

Secrets and Scandals
Her Wicked Ways
His Wicked Heart
To Seduce a Scoundrel
To Love a Thief (a novella)
Never Love a Scoundrel
Scoundrel Ever After

Regency Treasure Hunters
The de Valery Code
Romancing the Earl
Raiders of the Lost Heart
The Legacy of an Extraordinary Gentleman

The Untouchables
The Forbidden Duke
The Duke of Daring
The Duke of Deception
The Duke of Desire

You're Still the One

RIBBON RIDGE BOOK SIX

DARCY BURKE

AVON IMPULSE

An Imprint of HarperCollinsPublishers

An excerpt from *Serving Trouble* copyright © 2016 by Sara Jane Stone.
An excerpt from *Ignite* copyright © 2016 by Karen Erickson.
An excerpt from *Black Listed* copyright © 2016 by Shelly Bell.

EPub Edition APRIL 2016 ISBN: 9780062443533

Print Edition ISBN: 9780062443557

Avon, Avon Impulse, and the Avon Impulse logo are trademarks of HarperCollins Publishers.

AM 10 9 8 7 6 5 4 3 2 1

Chapter One

HAYDEN ARCHER DROVE into the parking lot at The Alex. The *paved* parking lot. He hadn't been home since Christmas, and things looked vastly different, including the paved lot instead of the dirt he'd been used to. The project to renovate the old monastery into a hotel and restaurant was nearly complete, and his siblings had done an amazing job in his absence.

He stepped out of his car, which he'd rented at the airport when his flight had arrived that afternoon. Someone would've picked him up, of course. If they'd known he was coming.

He smiled to himself in the summer twilight, looking forward to seeing his brothers' surprise when he burst in on Dylan Westcott's bachelor party. Hayden glanced around but didn't see anyone. They'd all be at the underground pub that Dylan had conceived and designed. It was fitting that its inaugural use would be to celebrate his upcoming wedding to their sister Sara.

Hayden could hardly wait to see the place, along with the rest of the property. But he figured that tour would have to wait until tomorrow. Tonight was for celebrating. And shocking the hell out of his family.

He made his way to the pub and immediately fell in love with what they'd done. He'd seen pictures, but being here in person gave everything a scale that was impossible to feel from half a world away.

They'd dug out the earth around the entrance to the pub and installed a round door, making it look distinctly hobbit-like. He wondered how much of that design had come from his brother Evan, and was certain Kyle's fiancée, Maggie, the groundskeeper of the entire place, had tufted the grass just so and ensured the wildflowers surrounding the entry looked as if they'd been there forever. A weathered, wooden sign hung over the door, reading: Archetype.

As he moved closer, he heard the sounds of revelry and smiled again. Then he put his hand on the wrought-iron door handle and pushed.

The noise was even louder inside, and it was nearly as dim as it had been outside. There were recessed lights in the wooden beams across the ceiling and sconces set at intervals around the space, all set to a mellow, cozy mood.

Hayden recognized most of the twenty or so people here. A few tables had been pushed together, and a handful of guys were playing some obnoxiously terrible card game while others were gathered at the bar. Kyle, one of his three brothers—the chef with the surfer good looks—stood behind it pouring drinks.

Hayden made his way to the bar, amused that no one had noticed him enter. "Beer me."

Kyle grabbed a pint glass. "Sure. What were you drinking?" He looked up and blinked. "Shit. Hayden. Am I drunk?" He glanced around before settling back on Hayden.

"Probably. Longbow if you've got it."

Kyle came sprinting around the bar and clasped him in a tight hug. He pulled back, grinning. "Look what the cat dragged in," he bellowed.

The noise faded then stopped completely. Liam, his eldest brother, or at least the first of the sextuplets born, stood up from the table, his blue-gray gaze intense. "Hayden, what the hell?" Like Kyle, his expression was one of confusion followed by joy.

"Hayden?" Evan, his remaining brother—the quiet one—leaned back on his stool at the other end of the bar. Like the others, he registered surprise, though in a far more subdued way.

"Hayden!" This exclamation came from the table near Liam and was from Hayden's best friend, Cameron Westcott. He was also the groom's half-brother.

The groom himself stood up from where he sat next to Evan. "What an awesome surprise." Dylan grinned as he hugged Hayden, and for the next several minutes he was overwhelmed with hugs and claps on the back and so much smiling that his cheeks ached.

"Why didn't you tell us you were coming?" Liam asked once things had settled down.

Kyle had gone back behind the bar and was now pulling Hayden's beer from the tap. "Do Mom and Dad know you're here?"

Hayden looked at Liam. "Because I wanted to surprise everyone." Then he looked at Kyle. "And no, Mom and Dad don't know." Hayden took his glass from Kyle and immediately sipped the beer, closing his eyes as the distinct wheat flavor his father had crafted brought him fully and completely home.

Kyle leaned on the bar. "Mom is going to be beside herself." He slapped the bar top. "Now this is a party!"

Cam, who'd been Hayden's closest friend since elementary school, sat back down on his stool and gestured for Hayden to sit next to him. "Tell us all about France. Still hooking up with that French hottie?"

Leave it to Cam to ask about Hayden's love life first and foremost. He'd transformed hooking up into an art form.

"France is good, but it's nice to be back." He should tell them about the job he'd been offered—assistant winemaker at the winery where he'd been interning the past year. The winery owned by his "hook-up's" father. But he didn't want to bring it up tonight. He wanted to drink Archer beer and settle back into the only home he'd ever known.

Liam clapped his hand at the back of Hayden's neck and gave him a firm clasp. "It's good to have you here."

Hayden peered at him, his brow arched. "I can't believe you're here, too. Permanently." Liam had moved to Denver after college and become a successful real estate developer. He'd never planned on returning to Ribbon Ridge. "What the hell happened?"

Everyone laughed, and Liam shrugged. "What can I say? The woman I fell in love with is a diehard Ribbon Ridger."

Hayden knew Liam's fiancée. Aubrey Tallinger had been their brother Alex's attorney. She'd set up and now administered Alex's trust, which had funded everything around them. Before his death, Alex had used his trust fund to buy a dilapidated monastery and left instructions for all of his siblings to return to Ribbon Ridge and renovate it into a premier hotel and restaurant. Everyone had a designated job—Tori had been the architect, Sara was the event planner, Kyle was the chef, Evan was supposed to do the technology, but was instead the creative director, and Liam was now handling all of the development aspects and apparently overseeing the hotel management. There wasn't really a job left for Hayden, which was fine since he planned to make wine. He was done serving the family businesses.

"I suppose Alex got what he wanted," Hayden said.

Kyle nodded. "Yep, now that you're here."

Except Hayden didn't know if his move was permanent, like Liam's. The opportunity in France was amazing—making wine alongside one of the best winemakers in the world. After that Hayden could probably take his pick of wineries to work for back here. Or maybe he could start his own label.

Dylan leaned his head around his half-brother. "What hottie was Cam talking about?"

Hayden took another drink of beer, unsurprised that he was almost ready for another. He'd missed his family and his hometown, but damn, he'd missed their beer nearly as much. "No one, really. She works at the winery."

Aside from her father owning it, Gabrielle was also the event manager. She was up to her eyeballs in weddings all summer long, not that he would've invited her to come here with him. Their relationship, which was *not* the right word, was extremely casual. He knew she saw other guys, and the only reason he didn't see anyone else was because he didn't have time.

Hayden was more than ready to change the subject. "Speaking of women, where are the strippers? Isn't this supposed to be a bachelor party?" He didn't really expect there to be strippers, but it effectively diverted the topic away from France.

"No strippers," Evan said, shaking his head. "The girls are only over at the Ridgeview."

The Ridgeview was the special event venue that Sara had designed and had been the site of Derek and Chloe's wedding last summer. Hayden looked around the pub again. "Where's Derek?"

Kyle frowned. "We sent him over to the restaurant to get another couple bottles of tequila. That was a while ago though."

"Should we send a search party?" Cam asked.

Liam chuckled as he finished off his beer. "Nope. My money's on him going for a booty call." Liam slid his empty glass over to Kyle for a refill. "Come on, like you guys haven't thought of doing that?" He looked pointedly at Kyle and then Evan.

Evan scowled at his beer. "I actually *hadn't* thought of it. Damn."

Kyle grinned. "Sure, but I didn't act on it." His gaze fixed on the back corner of the pub. "Ah, here comes our guilty brother now."

Derek wasn't actually their brother, but had come to live with them at seventeen when his mother had died of a brain tumor. He was also Kyle's best friend, except for the years they hadn't spoken following Kyle's departure from Ribbon Ridge due to trouble stemming from his gambling addiction. Derek walked past the table of card players and came toward the bar, a bottle of tequila in each hand. He didn't seem to notice Hayden as he walked around and set the liquor down in front of Kyle. "Ready for shots."

"Dude, how long were you gone?" Hayden asked.

Derek's head snapped up, his dark blue eyes widening. "Hayden, you're back!" He smiled and came back around the bar to embrace him.

Hayden hugged him tight—they'd become close over the past five or so years, before Hayden had taken the internship in France last spring. They pulled apart, and Hayden sniffed. "Dude, you smell like perfume."

Liam grinned. "Told you. Booty call."

This was met with whistles and taunts.

Derek rolled his eyes. "Whatever. You guys are just pissed because you didn't think to do it."

"As a matter of fact, I didn't." Evan sounded resigned. "I doubt Alaina's even awake. She can barely stay up past nine." And it was well beyond that.

Hayden was looking forward to meeting his new sister-in-law, who just happened to also be one of the most famous actresses in the world. She and Evan had gotten married in April but it had been a rapidly planned event since she was pregnant, and Hayden hadn't been able to come home.

Derek briefly put a hand on Evan's shoulder. "Sorry, bro. But this too shall pass, and then you can look forward to changing diapers." More laughter ensued.

Hayden could still scarcely get his head around the fact that come November he was going to be an uncle, let alone that Evan would be the first of them to have a child. Once upon a time, Hayden had expected that would be him…He shook the memory away and thought of his brother instead. Evan had Asperger syndrome and had always told Hayden he'd never planned to have kids. Just like Liam had sworn he'd never come back to Ribbon Ridge. Just like Hayden had said he'd never leave.

But he *had* left. He'd had to after Alex had died. Before that, Hayden had been the only one to stay after college, aside from Derek. It had fallen to him to support Dad in the family business as well as help look after Alex, who'd suffered the brunt of the health problems that typically came with a multiple birth. There'd been six babies, and one of them had to be the smallest, the sickliest. Others had their issues—primarily Evan with his Asperger's and Sara with her sensory processing disorder—but none had been as impacted as Alex. He'd battled chronic lung issues his whole life, spending long periods hooked to an oxygen tank. He was Liam's identical twin, but you could always tell them apart because Alex had never looked as vital and robust as Liam.

"Thanks for the reminder," Evan said. He pushed his empty glass over to Kyle. "Aren't we supposed to be doing shots with that tequila?"

Liam nodded. "Absolutely. And Hayden needs to catch up."

"Uh-oh, how many am I behind?" Everyone seemed a bit tipsy, but not outright drunk.

Kyle started lining up shot glasses on the bar. "Two, which means he gets three." He threw Hayden a grin. "Ready, little brother?"

Hayden finished his beer and set it on the other side of the shots. "Refill that, too."

Kyle arched a brow at him.

"Hey, I need a chaser, right?"

Kyle refilled the pint then poured out the shots. He doled out limes and set out a saltshaker. "Hayden first."

They all chanted, "Drink, drink, drink!" while Hayden downed the three shots in quick succession. He licked the salt from his hand and sucked the lime wedge then chased it with a good third of his pint. Cheers answered his efforts, and he grinned. Damn, it was good to be home.

Conversation broke off into smaller groups then, and Hayden was content to sip at his beer and just enjoy the camaraderie of being back with family and friends.

Cam gave his bicep a light punch. "It's great to have you back. But for how long?" He kept his voice low, which was good. There were things Hayden would share with his best friend that he wouldn't with his family.

"You want to take a walk?" Hayden asked.

Cam held up his mostly empty pint glass. "Sure, let me top this off." Kyle had moved down the bar to chat with someone, so Cam went around to the tap and helped himself. "You want a full glass?" he asked.

"Sure, why not?" Hayden was beginning to feel tipsy, but there was apparently pizza on the way from the restaurant, cooked by one of Kyle's new staff, and a quick jaunt outside with Cam would clear his head a little.

They stepped out into the darkness, and Hayden inhaled deeply, loving the scent of his home. Burgundy was gorgeous, especially in summer, but nothing compared to the rolling hills, verdant vineyards, and delicious berry and flower smells of Ribbon Ridge.

Cam shook his head, but smiled. "Dude, you could've told me you were coming."

Hayden gave him a sly look. "I could've, but where would be the fun in that?"

"You're a dick."

"For surprising you guys?" Hayden laughed. "I can do better, just wait."

"Uh-oh, I don't like the sound of that. Don't tell me this is just a visit, that you're going back to France, because that would be a *total* dick move."

"I need you to keep this between us," Hayden said, knowing he could trust Cam more than anyone.

"Of course. We've got a vault, right?"

Hayden nodded. "They offered me a job as assistant winemaker. I'd be stupid to say no, but it's a minimum two-year commitment."

Cam winced. "Damn. I'm happy for you, of course, but bummed for myself. I miss my wingman."

Hayden laughed again. "As if you need me."

Cam liked to go out, and before Hayden had taken the internship, they'd spent their fair share of time carousing in Portland bars. Cam also spent plenty of time carousing in other cities within his sales territory. He was an account manager at one of the largest wineries in the valley.

"Anyway," Hayden continued, "I haven't decided."

A light breeze stirred Cam's brown hair. "You know what my vote is. If you're taking input."

"Thanks. It's good to know I'm wanted." Hayden knew what it felt like to be an important part of his family, but sometimes he thought they'd taken his presence for granted—like he'd always be there. Until he'd left. And now that he was back, he was curious to see what that felt like.

"You're at least home through the wedding next weekend, but what about the opening?" Cam nodded toward the hotel rising in the darkness behind the pub.

The soft open was in just under four weeks. Even if he took the job, he didn't have to get back to Burgundy until the second week of August. "I'll be here for the soft open for sure. But if I take the job, I'll miss the grand opening."

"Your family's going to be disappointed."

Hayden knew that, but he was resolved to make his decisions independent of what they wanted. He'd spent far too long considering everyone else's feelings and his place in the family. He was finally pursuing *his* dreams, and he wasn't going to compromise them for anything or anyone ever again. "They'll get over it. It's not like they'll miss me. Ribbon Ridge is crawling with Archers now."

Cam chuckled. "Good point. I'm going back in to hit the head."

"I'll follow you—to the bar, not the bathroom." Hayden threw him a snarky smile before taking a long drink of beer.

He heard the door close and then heard voices, but not from the pub. Maybe it was Kyle's staff bringing the pizzas. Except they'd take the underground tunnel that joined the pub with the restaurant kitchen. And the voices were coming from the opposite direction—the track that led to the Ridgeview. He pivoted and squinted in the darkness. There were lights on the property that allowed him to see his sister Tori walking alongside Maggie, whom Hayden had met last summer when he'd come home briefly for Derek and Chloe's wedding. They were heading toward the hotel with a couple of other women.

He was about to turn and go back into the pub when he recognized another face. He took a few steps forward, but the women were already filing into the hotel.

It couldn't be Bex.

But it *could*. His sisters were still in touch with her, still counted her as a friend. But close enough to invite to Sara's bachelorette party?

He blinked and dropped his head, shaking it. He was drunk. He was seeing things. But no, he wasn't that drunk, and maybe that was the problem. Hell, he'd been back in Ribbon Ridge all of five minutes, and he was already hallucinating his ex.

Damn it, he'd spent a long time—way too much time—getting over her. It had taken Alex's death and Hayden's subsequent departure from Ribbon Ridge to truly flush her out of his system. He'd started fresh with his life, and it had been remarkably liberating. He didn't want to go back to feeling tethered. Frozen. Hollow.

So he wouldn't.

Even if it *was* Bex, she was the past. His future didn't include her, whether it was here in Ribbon Ridge or back in Burgundy.

He took a pull on his beer and decided he definitely wasn't drunk enough.

Chapter Two

BEX HOLMGREN OPENED her eyes and stretched. As the first person to sleep in this bed, she could attest to its comfort. She didn't really want to get up, but her need for coffee was overwhelming. Last night's bachelorette party for Sara had been a doozy.

Throwing off the covers, Bex slipped from between the pristine ivory sheets and padded to the bathroom to freshen up. The hotel rooms weren't quite ready, and one of the missing elements were the coffeemakers, which meant she had to go downstairs where a breakfast buffet, including coffee, would be laid out. Or so Tori had said last night when they'd come over from the Ridgeview for the sleepover portion of the party. They'd eaten popcorn and drunk pinot noir until the wee hours.

Bex was glad she'd been invited. She'd missed the Archer sisters since leaving Ribbon Ridge five years ago. Now she supposed she'd have ample opportunity to see them, and that made her happy. Also maybe a little bit apprehensive. Though she'd broken up with their brother five long years ago, the wound felt somehow fresh. Likely only because she was back in town for the first time since their brother had died seventeen months ago.

She looked around the hotel room. It was sumptuous—or would be once it was completed. It featured all the elements of posh elegance: a stone fireplace, a balcony with a view of the valley, a marble bathroom with both a shower and a tub, and a sitting area with a table. Missing were the chairs and the appliances—besides the coffeemaker, there would be a fridge and a television hidden in a cabinet. The window seat with its velvety soft cushion was the icing on the cake for Bex. She could curl up with a book and happily spend her day there.

The Archers should be very proud of what they'd created. She was only sorry it had come about because of their brother's death. One of the famous Archer sextuplets, Alex had committed suicide in February of last year. Bex could picture him sitting in that window seat. He'd have his oxygen tank, which typically wasn't far away, a book, and maybe a beer. She'd known him very well when she'd lived in Ribbon Ridge, and she still couldn't quite believe he was gone. Being here made his absence more real. Living somewhere else she could almost pretend he hadn't really died. But now she'd be living here again, and she wouldn't be able to hide behind that lie any longer.

As she slipped on a pair of flip-flops, she wondered for the umpteenth time if she'd made the right decision in coming back to Ribbon Ridge. Not that she could change her mind. She'd already left her job in Eugene, and she had to be out of her apartment by Monday.

She was being silly. This was a good move. She'd have her own brewery and would be making some of the finest beer in the state. Rob Archer had created an incredible brand, and she was fortunate to have studied under him after college. Now she had the chance to not only brew his legendary recipes, but also craft her own. Rob calling her personally and expressing his support had been the deciding factor. It seemed that things wouldn't be awkward for her with Hayden's family.

Ready to face anyone she might encounter, she stepped from her room on the third floor and made her way to the elevator.

Anyone?

She pressed the button and waited. Okay, not *anyone*. She wasn't sure she was ready to run into Hayden. Luckily for her, he wouldn't be back in town until early next week. The Archers had assured her he would be prepared for and fine with her being here.

Thinking about it still made her nervous, however.

The doors opened, and she stepped onto the elevator then pressed L for the lobby.

Don't be nervous, she told herself. *At least not today.* She gave herself permission to be a basket case on Tuesday when Hayden was due back.

The elevator slowed, and she glanced at the numbers on the panel, thinking it couldn't be the lobby. Nope, this was the first floor—she'd thought they'd all stayed on the top floor. Maybe it was one of the guys. Or maybe the elevators weren't working right yet.

The doors opened, and every fiber, every nerve, every sense inside her came alive. Standing there in khaki shorts and a dark blue T-shirt, his light brown hair slightly mussed with a bed head she recognized all too well, was Hayden Archer.

Her ex-boyfriend. Her former best friend. The love of her life.

So far. She still hoped she'd fall in love again. As of yet, no one had come remotely close.

His light blue eyes widened upon seeing her. "Bex." He sounded as surprised as he looked. *Damn it.*

"Hayden, I didn't expect to see you." Instinctively, she smoothed her hand over her hair, but she'd already tamed the overnight tangles and pulled it back into a ponytail.

"I flew in early. As a surprise."

Oh, it was a surprise all right. But she couldn't say it was a bad one. Just awkward. "It's really great to see you. You look fantastic."

And he did. She'd seen him just once in the last five years—at Alex's funeral—and he looked different. He seemed broader, more muscular, and his skin was bronze, as if he spent a great deal of time outside.

His gaze dipped over her, and she wished she'd changed out of her pajama shorts into something a lot less...short. "Thanks. You, too."

The door started to close. She reached out to press the open button just as he put his hand in front of the door.

He stepped onto the elevator and turned toward the door, keeping his gaze fixed straight ahead. "You're here for the bachelorette party?"

It was a polite question—small talk—since the answer was obvious. "Yes. I bet your brothers were stoked to see you at the bachelor party last night."

He nodded. "It was a fun surprise." He sent her a glance that made her wonder if, for him, this encounter was a *bad* surprise. "Are you still living in Eugene?"

Did his question mean he didn't know that she'd accepted a job here at The Alex as the brewer? Oh shit, this wasn't good.

She nodded and answered tentatively. "Yes." Technically she was. Until Monday.

The doors opened, and he gestured for her to precede him. "Are you coming back for the wedding?"

There was no way he knew about her working here. Otherwise, he would know that she was starting this week and that she would already be in town for the wedding. She didn't want to lie to him, but she also didn't think he'd want to hear this news from her in this way. He'd already been shocked to see her. Crap! Why hadn't the Archers prepped him like they'd said they would? They'd hired her three weeks ago.

"Yes," she finally said. *And for my new job*, she mentally added. They walked toward the large seating area off the lobby where the buffet was being set up.

"Cool." It was a monosyllabic utterance completely devoid of emotion.

She couldn't tell if he was fine with her being here or pissed as hell. And given the way they'd broken up, she had to think it would be more of the latter.

They approached the table with the coffee, and again he gestured for her to go first. With each step, she'd felt wobblier and more uncertain. Anxiety threaded through her even as logic tried to gain control of her mind. She reminded herself that this was Hayden and that they'd known each other as well and as deeply as two people could. She could never hate him, and she had to think he couldn't hate her either. But she also couldn't bring herself to ask.

She did the next best thing and tried to at least address the elephant. "Is this weird?" She focused on filling her cup with coffee so she wouldn't have to see his expression in case his dislike was evident.

"Should it be?"

She flicked him an uncertain glance before stepping to the side and adding cream and sugar to her cup. "You seem... Uh, never mind."

He filled his cup. "I'm so jet-lagged. Sorry." He yawned as if to punctuate his claim.

That made sense. She preferred that explanation anyway, so she'd take it. "I bet. How long are you home?"

She had no idea when his internship was done or if he'd be staying on over there. He'd worked for the family business since graduating from college until he'd taken the internship after Alex had died. Sara and Tori had given her a brief overview last night.

"Three or four weeks," he said, answering her question. "Something like that. My ticket's open-ended."

That sounded a little bit like an escape clause. Or maybe that was just *her* perspective. As an only child with two parents who'd never much cared what she did, she'd found his large family a bit oppressive at times. She liked them all, loved them really, but someone was always there. She cherished her solitude and preferred her independence. Not that they demanded dependence—they were just super helpful and concerned and attentive. They offered unsolicited advice where Bex's parents' counsel had been strictly limited to "don't get in trouble" and "clean up after yourself."

The Archers also had family dinners on Sundays, while the closest Bex's family had come to such a thing had been pizza night on Mondays. Even those had been family optional since her mother was often traveling, and her father was working at the ER. By age ten, Bex had pizza night by herself. And a lot more often than just on Mondays.

It might sound sad and pathetic, but to her, it had been reality. She just hadn't known any other way. Until she'd met the Archers and taken a crash course in Family Perfection 101. Given that she'd practically run from town, she considered her grade a total fail.

"So you *are* going back then?" she asked, thinking it would be so much easier if he wasn't here. When considering the brewer job, she'd asked if he'd be living here, but his siblings hadn't known. Maybe they still didn't.

"Have to. All my stuff's there. Well, not *all* my stuff."

Right, she'd learned last night that his brother Kyle and his fiancée, Maggie, were living in his house. Kyle had returned from Florida last year, and Hayden had conveniently needed a tenant. Kyle was also driving his car.

She tried not to look too hard at his chiseled arms or the sexy stubble along his jaw. "I bet it's weird being the visiting Archer."

He chuckled. "A bit. Strange, for sure."

She relaxed a bit with his show of good humor. Maybe this wasn't as bad as she thought. They were grown-ups, and their relationship was ancient history. Even if he wasn't going to be living here, she wanted to be on good terms since she'd be working for his family. For him, really, since he still owned part of this entire business.

Good terms meant being honest, so she decided to take the plunge. "So, uh, I don't know if you heard, but I'm going to be working here. As the brewer."

His eyes flickered with the same surprise as earlier. No, not quite the same. His lashes fluttered briefly, and his irises darkened to cerulean. "Really? That's great." He said those three words so slowly that she had more than ample time to wilt inside. Nothing about his demeanor or tone reinforced what he said.

She couldn't keep from wincing. "Sorry. I thought you maybe knew." So much for honesty—there was no way he'd known. Ugh, this was so awkward! After five years, she'd wanted to think they could be normal. Or at least not weird. And maybe they could. If they'd ever talked about things. But they never had. The wound had lain

open and untreated, and she realized now—too late—
that maybe it had never really healed at all.

She suddenly wished she hadn't taken this job.

"No, I didn't know. But it's cool." There was that word
again. And *that* seemed to go with his attitude—chilly.

That was it. She couldn't take anymore. Not right
now with a mild hangover making her head ache and her
stomach roil. Not standing here in short pajamas without
a bra. Oh God, she wasn't wearing a bra. Yeah, past time
to go.

"I'm sure I'll see you later," she said weakly. "Bye."

She turned and walked very quickly to the elevator.
She pushed the up button about fifty times in her haste to
get away. And she didn't dare turn around.

The door opened, and Tori, another of the sextuplets,
and Hayden's oldest sister, smiled at her. "Morning! I see
you have coffee. Thank God." Her smile immediately
faded. "What's wrong?"

Bex considered trying to play it off, but why bother?
As soon as Tori went to get her coffee, she'd see the problem. "I ran into Hayden."

Tori's jaw dropped, and her eyes practically goggled
right out of her head. "What?"

Bex stepped onto the elevator, and Tori pushed the
close door button several times. She looked through the
closing doors, craning her neck in an effort to see her
brother. Bex pressed the number three for her floor.

"Bex, I'm so sorry. I had no idea he was going to be
here."

"He flew in early as a surprise."

"Wow. That's great, but…We blew it." Tori leaned back against the wall and looked up at the ceiling. "We completely blew it."

Bex sipped her coffee, but its medicinal purposes were grossly inferior this morning. "Why didn't you tell him I'd be working here?"

"We wanted to tell him in person."

That sounded like it was a big deal. Like they were worried about his reaction. "You told me it would be fine. Liam told me it would be fine." Their father, Rob, had even told her it would be fine, but she didn't throw him into the mix. "I'm not sure this is fine," she said quietly.

Tori stepped away from the wall. "I'm so sorry. Let us fix this."

Classic. Archers loved to fix things. Bex knew that from personal experience. Liam had been the first to leave Ribbon Ridge—just a few weeks after graduation. Rob had tried to entice him to stay and work for the real estate division of Archer Enterprises, but Liam wouldn't have any of it. Then Tori had taken a job in San Francisco. Emily Archer, their mother, had pulled in a favor and arranged for an interview at an architecture firm in Portland, but Tori had left anyway. Yes, Archers tried to manage things, and Tori was perhaps the most managerial of them all—at least of the children.

"What do you mean by that?" Bex asked as the elevator door opened. She stepped into the hallway, and Tori followed her. "I hope you aren't planning to run interference between me and Hayden—we don't need that."

Alex had tried doing that when she and Hayden first started having problems after living together a few months. They'd argued about where to live—she'd wanted to leave Ribbon Ridge and have some adventures before they settled down, and he'd said he couldn't. With all of his siblings gone, he'd felt it was his responsibility to work for the family business and also support his brother, who'd been chronically ill.

"I know you don't. I didn't mean it like that." Tori blew out a breath just as Sara came out of a door across the hall.

"Hey, what's up?" she asked, a sunny smile brightening her face.

"Hayden's home, and he ran into Bex downstairs," Tori said darkly.

Sara's smile died. "Oh crap." She looked over at Bex. "What did he say?"

"Not much," Bex said. "Listen, I don't want to make a thing out of this. I just wish you'd told him." She'd known it would be awkward. But this had been a level of discomfort she hadn't anticipated.

"We should have." Tori looked at her sister. "We really screwed this up."

Sara nodded and turned back to Bex. "We all talked about it and thought it would be best to tell him when he got home. We had no idea he'd show up unannounced. Totally our bad. We'll fix it."

There was that damned word again.

Once more she thought about their responses and how they'd planned to wait until he'd come home to tell him, like it was really bad or at least earth-shattering news. "Do you think Hayden is going to have a problem with my working here? I thought you all said it would be fine, but now it seems like you were worried about his reaction."

Tori seemed to pick her words somewhat hesitantly. "I think he'll be fine. We don't know too much about your breakup, but you said you were good, right?"

Yes, she'd said that, but seeing him again, she didn't really know. She'd have to find out. It would suck to have to back out of this job, but if it would be best for Hayden, she'd do it. "Look, let's not make this into more than it is. We haven't seen each other in a long time, and we weren't expecting to run into each other this morning. I mean, look at me. I didn't realize the guys would be downstairs at all." Or she would've put a bra on. At least she'd brushed her teeth.

Tori snorted. "They shouldn't be given how late they were up. Sean was drunk-texting me at four this morning."

Bex couldn't suppress a smile. Sean was Tori's husband.

"But Hayden's in a completely different time zone," Sara said. She gave her sister a sheepish look. "How pissed is he going to be at us?"

Tori exhaled. "Let's go find out. Bex, again, we're so sorry." She pushed the down button, and the elevator immediately opened.

As the Archer sisters disappeared behind the doors, Bex turned and made her way back to her room. How she hated family drama. No, *hate* wasn't the right word. Back when she'd been with Hayden, she just hadn't known how to handle it. The entire concept of family and relationships had been completely foreign. She'd done her best, but ultimately had pulled away from it as much as possible. She'd started skipping the family dinners and other events. It was just so much easier to be alone.

And she'd absolutely perfected that.

HARDY BURKE

Chapter Three

HAYDEN STOOD STARING into the massive fireplace that dominated the center of the wall in the sitting area off the lobby of The Alex. A few members of Kyle's staff had set up chafing dishes and asked if Hayden was ready to eat, but he was fine with just coffee. Which he probably shouldn't be drinking since he hadn't slept. But hell, his internal clock said it was cocktail hour, not breakfast time.

Tired and turned around as he was, he hadn't been hallucinating last night after all. He *had* seen Bex.

She looked as beautiful as he remembered, even without makeup this morning and her dark hair scooped into a messy ponytail. No, she was even more stunning. Her pale jade green eyes were the same, but her legs seemed somehow longer, shapelier, her curves more pronounced. But he could just blame the fact that she'd been wearing summer pajamas, which hadn't left much to his imagination. And given their three-year relationship, he had plenty of *memories*, which were a step better than imagination anyway.

Damn, he'd hoped to be immune to her.

He didn't want to go back to missing her, to feeling like there was a hole in his heart. That hole had finally healed, and he wasn't going to let his body's reaction to his former lover open any old wounds.

But he sure as hell wished he'd been prepared for it.

"Hayden?"

He turned at the sound of his sister's voice and saw that Tori wasn't alone—Sara was beside her. They wore matching expressions of contrition. Good.

Sara launched herself forward and wrapped her arms around him. "I missed you so much."

He hugged her back. "I missed you, too."

She stepped aside and let Tori have her turn. "Wow, how much do grapes weigh?" Tori grinned as she looked up at him. "You've put on some serious muscle."

"It's a lot of grunt work." And it had felt good after years toiling behind a desk.

He thought about whether to ask about Bex now or save it for later when his brothers were around. But the decision was made for him when Liam and Kyle walked in. Okay, it wasn't everyone, but it was close enough. Evan would hate the confrontation anyway.

Ultimately, Hayden didn't have to say anything.

"Hay, can we talk to you for a second?" Liam asked, running his hand through his dark hair, which was standing completely on end. In fact, both he and Kyle looked as though they'd just rolled out of bed. Literally.

Hayden casually sipped his coffee, but on the inside his emotions had begun to seethe. The shock he'd felt at seeing Bex and hearing about her job had transitioned to anger and hurt.

He gestured toward his sisters. "Let me guess, you two ran into Bex. Then you texted these two"—he pointed toward his brothers—"to meet you down here. That sound about right?"

"Nailed it," Kyle said. His blond hair was just as tousled as Liam's. More so, since it was a bit longer. "Look, we're really sorry we didn't tell you. We'd planned to when you got home. You know, on *Tuesday*."

Hayden's anger got the better of him. "I'm terribly sorry my surprise fucked up your plans. Guess that'll teach me to try to be the fun one." He sent a pointed look at Kyle since he seemed to have the market on fun. But that's how it was in their family. Everyone had a place, a role, an identity. And forget trying to break out of that.

"We deserve that," Tori said softly. "And you *are* the fun one. So much more fun than these losers." She rolled her eyes at Liam and Kyle.

Hayden appreciated her saying that, but knew it wasn't true. Kyle was the life of every party. And while Liam wasn't fun, he was exciting, what with his daredevil adventures and playboy attitude.

Meanwhile, Hayden was dependable. Friendly. Boring.

Geez, he was seriously jet-lagged. He shook his head and worked to gain control of his emotions. But it was hard. As the unplanned seventh kid with sextuplet siblings who'd had their own freaking reality show, he'd always felt like the odd kid out.

Liam threw an irritated glance at their brother. "Kyle didn't mean to say it like that. He meant we wanted to tell you in person. We thought we owed it to you."

Hayden wasn't buying it. "I'd think you'd owe it to me to talk to me before you actually hired her. Tell me, Liam, how would you feel if we'd hired Whitney Parker?"

She was the woman Liam had hooked up with for a while and who had tried to extort him for sex a few months ago when her father had filed an appeal against their zoning change for the hotel. She'd offered to make the legal battle go away if Liam would sleep with her.

"You can't compare her to Bex," Liam said, frowning. "Please, for the love of God, don't compare her to Bex. We *like* Bex. We always have."

That was great, but Bex hadn't dumped them. If she had, maybe then they wouldn't like her. Hayden hadn't, but at the same time, he hadn't been able to stop loving her either. Not until Alex's death had given him the wake-up call he'd needed to finally put his life in motion.

He didn't want to be bothered by Bex working here. But was his anger about her, or was it about his siblings leaving him out of a decision and once again making him feel like the odd one out? He realized he didn't want to address either one. It was too damn much effort.

"You know what? It doesn't matter. I'm not here for the day-to-day anymore, so what you decide to do hiring-wise isn't my business."

"Of course it is," Sara said, her blue eyes crinkled at the edges with concern, making her look so much like their mother. "You still own your equal part. We should've consulted you."

She wasn't really helping their cause, but he wouldn't put it past the others to have talked her out of contacting him about this before hiring Bex.

"If you have a problem with her working here, just say the word," Kyle said. "We completely screwed the pooch here, and we'll make it right, bro."

By rescinding their job offer? Whatever history he and Bex shared, she didn't deserve that. Even if it was surprising that she'd accepted it in the first place—she'd been eager to leave Ribbon Ridge five years ago and had done so in a hurry. "Did she apply for the job or did you guys ask her?" The answer mattered to Hayden, and it shouldn't have.

Liam answered. "We contacted her at Dad's behest. He's ready to lighten his load, especially with Archer splitting into separate entities."

Liam was taking over the real estate arm and wrapping it into his Lion Properties, which he'd started in Denver with great success. His company would now be headquartered here, where he planned to live with Aubrey. The brewery side was going to be overseen by Derek, and they were expanding the operation from their chain of ten brewpubs to bottling, something Dad had been resistant to in the past.

"Dad wanted her?" It wasn't the answer Hayden had expected, but it was probably the most palatable. And he shouldn't be surprised. Bex had interned with Dad after college, and he would've offered her a permanent job if there'd been anything open at the time.

"Adamantly," Kyle said. "This is a good step for him. With everything he's gone through the past year and a half, we've been hoping he'll at least semiretire. If we don't keep Bex, we'll have to find someone else he approves of."

In other words, they needed Bex. And just like that, Hayden did what he always had: He rolled over and let his family rule. "It'll be fine. You offered her the job, she's here, Dad wants her, it's all good." Good? She'd be living here in Ribbon Ridge, working with his family, a constant reminder of the haze Hayden had lived in for four years as he'd struggled to get over her. The job in France was looking more attractive by the minute.

Oh fuck it anyway. They didn't need him here. They were running things fine without him, and back in Burgundy he *was* needed.

"I wasn't going to mention this until later, but it might relieve you to know that I won't be here, so it doesn't really matter that Bex will be working here."

"What do you mean?" Sara asked.

"I've been offered the assistant winemaker position, and I'm going to take it." He hadn't decided until that moment, but yeah, it seemed the right choice. For someone who once thought he'd never leave Ribbon Ridge, he now wondered what it would take to lure him back.

Kyle shook his head. "Wow, that's crazy." He smiled and reached over to clap Hayden on the bicep. "Congrats, that's awesome. I'm so proud of you."

"Thanks, but keep it quiet for now. I haven't talked to Mom and Dad yet. I'm heading over there now."

Tori flinched. "Uh, just so you know, Bex will be staying in the garage apartment for a few weeks until she finds a place. The rental market is pretty tight around here just now."

Hayden had been well aware of the real estate market in Ribbon Ridge before he'd left, and it didn't sound much different now. Real estate was a good portion of their family business—the one *he'd* actually worked for while they'd all been scattered to the four winds. He swallowed a snarky comeback and blamed his jet lag again. He needed some air.

"Thanks for letting me know." He tried not to sound sarcastic, but acknowledged he hadn't been completely successful.

Tori came toward him and touched his wrist briefly. "Hayden, I am so sorry. You have every right to be angry. I guess we were busy getting everything ready after the zoning was finally cleared. We were in a rush to fill all the positions, and we made a bad decision."

Hayden wanted to shrug it off and be okay with it. And eventually he would. But right now he needed to get out of here. "Thanks, Tori. Really, I'll be fine. You guys look like you need to go back to bed." He summoned a smile and shook his head at his brothers, who had to be nursing brutal hangovers. Given that, he appreciated how quickly they'd come downstairs. At least pissing off Hayden was a fire they wanted to put out. Wouldn't it be worse if they didn't give a damn?

"Good call," Kyle said. "See you later, sisters." He clapped Hayden's arm again, this time letting his palm linger a second. "Later, bro."

He headed out, and Liam nodded toward Hayden. "You always were a good sport. About everything."

Yep, that was Hayden. And he could live with that. Especially since it would be for only a few short weeks. Then he'd be on his way back to France.

AFTER RETURNING TO her room to put on real clothes, Bex enjoyed a fun, if slightly nerve-racking, breakfast with the women from the bachelorette party and the men from the bachelor party—at least those who were able to rouse themselves. Now she was on her way to the Archers' house, which she'd call home for a few weeks. It was also where Hayden was staying, and, as Sara had informed her, he was apparently already there.

As she drove up the long driveway toward the house, butterflies flitted in her belly, and anxiety nested in her spine. She hadn't been here in so long, and yet it still gave her the sensation of home. She supposed that made sense because she'd lived in the garage apartment one summer in college while working at The Arch and Vine. Then, after college, she'd interned with Rob Archer while working shifts at the pub. She'd stayed in the apartment again until Hayden had bought a house after about six months. They'd moved in together, which had sparked all sorts of excitement as his family believed an engagement was forthcoming. And she supposed it would have if things hadn't gone completely and horribly off the rails.

Was it any wonder she was nervous as hell to be back here?

She clutched the wheel as she drove into the turnaround in front of the house. The waterfall fountain in the center was on, and if her window was down she'd be able to hear the gentle sound of the water and smell the pine trees dotting the land. The Archers had two hundred or so acres, including an old homestead built by the founders of Ribbon Ridge. Or their kids. Something like that. The area was rich with Archer family history.

She drove through the porte cochere and parked outside the garage apartment, on a patch of pavement between the garage and the main house. She grabbed her purse and stepped out of the truck, closing the door.

Bex pushed her sunglasses up onto her head and stared at the back door that led to the mudroom. Presumably Emily Archer was just inside—in the kitchen probably. Bex's anxiety kicked up a notch. She and the Archer matriarch had been close once, but Bex dumping her son had pretty much severed their relationship. Bex had fled Ribbon Ridge and hadn't looked back, aside from keeping in moderate touch with Tori and Sara.

She shook the thoughts away from her brain. Revisiting that painful time just as she was about to step inside the Archer stronghold was *not* what she needed to be doing.

Taking a deep breath, she started toward the house. Back in the day, she would've let herself in, but that had been a long time ago. Instead, she knocked.

A moment later Emily opened the door. Petite and blonde, with bright blue eyes and the warmest smile Bex had ever known, she was everything Bex's mother had never been—present.

Seeing Emily again stirred feelings of longing and love, and the tension that she couldn't seem to shake since running into Hayden that morning.

"Bex!" Emily held her arms out and embraced her.

Bex held her tight for a long moment. "It's so good to see you."

Emily patted her back. "You too, dear. Come in!" She glanced at her purse. "Is that all you brought?"

"Oh no, I have more in the car." She had a small load of clothing and toiletries and would bring another when she returned on Monday after cleaning out her apartment in Eugene. The rest of her belongings—furniture and house-hold goods—were going into storage pods until she found a place to live. "I'll take them up to the apartment in a bit."

Emily winced. "About that…I'm so sorry, but it's not habitable just now. I contracted some work, and it's not finished. There's no flooring anywhere, and the plumbing in the bathroom isn't even working." She shook her head. "That'll teach me to hire someone other than my almost-son-in-law!"

Dylan, Sara's fiancé, had his hands full as the contractor in charge of The Alex. "He *is* pretty busy right now."

"Which is why I hired someone else." Emily waved a hand. "It's not their fault, really. They're doing their best, but the materials haven't come in yet. And anyway, between the house and the rooms that are ready at The Alex, we have plenty of space for out-of-town guests. I thought you could stay in Tori's room."

Right down the hall from Hayden's room. Awesome.

"Thanks, that'll be great. When do you expect the apartment to be ready?" Bex would be looking for a place immediately anyway, but she wanted to know how long she'd be bunking so close to her ex.

"I wish I knew," Emily said with regret. "You'll be the first to know! Now come into the kitchen and tell me what you've been doing."

They walked down the short back hallway and as she rounded the corner, she was struck with her biggest dose of nostalgia yet. She'd spent so much time in this kitchen, with its cozy gathering room and view of the pool below with the backyard stretching out behind it to the forested area beyond.

Rob Archer popped up from behind the beer tap, which was situated in a second kitchen island. "Bex!"

He looked older than the last time she'd seen him—at Alex's funeral. So did Emily. Rob's hair was grayer, and they both had a few more lines. Bex couldn't imagine what they'd gone through and was glad they seemed to be happy now.

How could they not be? One of their children was about to get married, one was having a baby, and the rest were already settled down or on their way.

Except Hayden. Why did he keep invading her thoughts?

Rob came around the island. "I'm just hooking up a new keg." He had an incredible home-brewing facility downstairs where he conducted all sorts of mouthwatering experiments.

She hugged him, and the sense of home was nearly overwhelming. Home? Oh man, did that give her system a start. She hadn't thought of Ribbon Ridge as a permanent home, and she hadn't thought of this move as coming "home." But she also hadn't realized how much she'd missed these people. "What is it?"

"Loganberry with some honey. I made something fruity and smooth for Sara since it's her wedding week." He stepped back and glanced at the clock on the microwave. "Too early for a sample?"

It wasn't noon, but that had never stopped Bex. When you made beer for a living, you tasted at all hours. "Never."

With a chuckle, he went back to the keg and drew a small pour then handed her the glass. "Remember, this is for Sara."

Sara didn't particularly care for beer. The more bitter the brew, the more she hated it. Bex expected something light and flavorful, with an edge of sweetness. She sampled it and wasn't disappointed. "She'll love it," she said.

Rob rubbed his hands together, his gray eyes sparkling. "I think so, too. I bet you can hardly wait to get started on your own."

At her new state-of-the-art brewhouse. Rob had designed the facility, which was attached to the back of The Arch and Fox, the restaurant at The Alex. Bex was beyond excited to begin work. "Thanks for convincing me to come."

He laughed. "Ha! Did it really take that much? You've wanted your own brewpub for as long as I've known you.

And it was you who presented me with a well-researched and thought-out plan for expanding the operation into bottling."

Yes, she *had* done that. And she'd been disappointed when he'd declined five years ago. That had been one of the many things that had contributed to her leaving Ribbon Ridge. Professionally, it had been a dead end for her at the time.

"I'm so excited you're finally doing it. And I appreciate the opportunity to maybe bottle some of my own." The Archer kids—Tori and Liam, specifically—had offered her the brewer position initially, but she'd waffled because of Hayden. Then Rob had called her personally and talked to her about bottling. He was finally ready to expand his production and mass-distribute his beer. And he'd said there was every chance he'd include her creations for special and seasonal lines.

He'd made it pretty much impossible for her to refuse. So here she was surprising and probably horrifying her ex. And sleeping about thirty feet from him.

"We have so much to do," Rob said. "Derek's already working on securing some space for us to use in Portland while we build our facility between here and McMinnville."

"Sounds exciting," Bex said.

Emily smiled and shook her head. "It's all he talks about."

Rob held up his hands, palms out. "Hey, I can barely compete with wedding mania."

Emily gave him a playful punch in the arm. "It's not that bad. Sara is about the farthest you can get from a Bridezilla."

That made sense because she was a wedding planner. She knew firsthand what it was like to deal with a nightmare and wouldn't want to be That Bride.

Emily walked to the fridge. "Can I get you something to drink besides the beer sample, Bex?"

"No, I'm good." Bex finished off the small glass and set it back on the counter. "I should probably get settled. I wanted to drive into town this afternoon and poke around before making the thank-you baskets tonight."

All of the girls were getting together for dinner at the house followed by assembling the baskets of goodies Sara and Dylan were giving to the guests. They were a whole new level of wedding favor, but Bex expected nothing less from an Archer who was also a wedding coordinator. The Archers did everything big, especially when it came to their generosity.

"I imagine you're tired," Emily said. "I'm sure last night's party lasted into the wee hours."

"Yes. It was a lot of fun. It's great seeing everyone."

Emily crossed her arms and leaned back against the counter, smiling. "Tell me what you've been up to in Eugene. You're not breaking some poor guy's heart by moving back here, are you?" She laughed softly, but Bex wondered if it was masking something else. Was she harboring a grudge about Bex leaving Hayden?

"I was seeing someone, but we broke up a few months ago." She'd dated a guy over the winter, but it hadn't lasted. He'd finished his graduate program at the University of Oregon in March, and they'd called it quits. Like every other relationship she'd had since Hayden, it hadn't been serious.

Bex considered saying something about her and Hayden's breakup, but maybe Emily's question hadn't been loaded. *Maybe* Bex should work harder to leave the past where it belonged.

Rob picked up Bex's empty glass and took it to the sink. "We're so glad you're back. This job was meant for you. It seems like it was just the right time for you to be back in Ribbon Ridge."

He was making it sound like some sort of fated occurrence, as if the stars had aligned or whatever. She wasn't sure she believed that. Life was what you made it, which was one of the primary reasons she'd wanted to leave five years ago. She hadn't been ready to settle down. But now...Hmm, it seemed she'd just proven his point about it being the right time. Except she wasn't ready to say she was here forever. As much as she loved this family, and she did, they scared the hell out of her sometimes.

On the one hand, she envied their camaraderie and these two amazing, engaged parents. On the other, she had no idea what to do with those things. She'd had to rely on herself for so long—forever, really—and sometimes being with the Archers was a bit like wearing a pair of shoes that were a half-size too small.

And on that note, she was ready for some alone time. Emily was right about one thing—she was exhausted. "I'm just going to run out and get my bags."

"I'll help you," Rob offered.

He helped her with a trip up to Tori's room, and Bex was able to get the rest on her own on the second trip. She hefted the last two bags into her temporary digs and turned to close the door.

But she couldn't move. Standing there, leaning against the doorframe, his sky blue eyes watching her, was the only man she'd ever loved.

Chapter Four

HAYDEN FELT A jolt when her jade green gaze connected with his. When he'd seen her earlier, he'd experienced the same awareness, but had chalked it up to his shock at running into her so unexpectedly. So what was his excuse this time?

History. It had to be their shared history. He couldn't afford to let it be anything else.

He crossed his arms, still trying to decide how he felt about her being here. He was annoyed with his siblings, but not necessarily with her. He didn't want to be bothered by it—by her—at all. He wanted a nice clean break. "How've you been?" he asked.

She blinked, and those long, inky lashes he'd loved grazed her cheeks. "Good, thanks."

"I have to admit I'm surprised you took this job. You couldn't get out of Ribbon Ridge fast enough."

Her eyes darkened, and she crossed her arms over her chest. "You knew I had to leave after what happened."

He shrugged, not wanting to dredge up an old, painful argument but unable to stop himself. "I know you thought leaving was the only way you could deal with losing the baby, but staying was the only way that I could."

She glanced away and blew out a breath. "Right. I get it. We don't have to do this."

He shook his head, glad that she didn't want to rehash it either. "We definitely do not. Looks like we're both in a good place. Things turned out all right."

Her answering stare was long and hard. Had he said something wrong? He was happy making wine, hanging out with Gabrielle from time to time, living a chill lifestyle in France. And Bex was about to start her dream job as a brewer in charge of her own facility. "Are you not in a good place?" he asked.

She dropped her hands to her sides and shook her head. "Sorry. I'm great. Just really tired after last night. And you're right, things did turn out fine. As they were supposed to, I guess."

Supposed to. The old "things happen for a reason" bullshit or "this was meant to happen," excuse. He didn't buy any of it, and Alex's death had reinforced that. There was no reason or meaning in his death or in the car accident that had caused Bex to miscarry. It was tragic and terrible. Period. End of story.

"It wasn't easy," he said quietly. They'd stupidly had unprotected sex while she'd been taking antibiotics, which had negated the effects of her birth control pills.

Upon learning she was pregnant, she'd been upset. For her, the timing had been bad because she'd had *plans*. For Hayden, however, the timing had been fine. He'd had a great job, a supportive family, and he'd just bought a house in the town he planned to grow old in. The stage had been set for a happily-ever-after. "I was pretty broken for a long time."

She took a step forward and looked as though she wanted to touch him, but that wasn't who they were anymore. "I know. I was, too. I know you didn't think that I was."

Of course she would think that. In his anger and grief, he'd accused her of wanting to lose the baby, even after they'd decided to have it and get married. But he'd been so upset. "I was young and stupid. And I felt guilty."

The night of the accident, they'd been arguing about where to live. It was dark, rainy, and the road had a vicious S-curve. Though he'd driven it hundreds of times, he'd miscalculated. The shoulder was unforgivingly slender and he'd driven right over it and into a deep ditch. It hadn't been a serious accident, and the doctor had said she might've miscarried anyway. But the hell of it was that they'd never know. He hadn't driven that road since.

"You don't feel guilty anymore?" Her expression softened into a smile. "I'm glad."

She'd told him then that she didn't blame him. Which was maybe why he'd been so hard on himself. When the person you loved most in the world gave you a pass for something terrible, it was hard to let go of your own culpability. Or shame. Whatever. He'd had a hard time living with himself for a while after that.

Hadn't they both agreed they didn't have to discuss this? "This conversation is taking a real turn into the maudlin." He infused his tone with as much levity as he could. "Completely unnecessary, especially as you're about to embark on the career of your dreams."

She brightened. "Yes! And you're already doing your dream job, right? How are things going over there?"

He may as well continue the lie he'd told his siblings earlier—that he was taking the job in Burgundy. It was only part lie, he reasoned. Chances are, he *would* be taking the job.

"Really well, actually. They offered me a position as assistant winemaker, and I start next month."

Her eyes widened. "Oh, wow. That's great. Congratulations." She squinted briefly. "How'd your parents take it?"

He chuckled. She knew them—and him—so well. Or at least she had once. "I was just on my way down to tell them. Wish me luck."

She laughed, and the sound was so familiar, so filled with fond memories, that it was like smelling gingerbread and instantly feeling like Christmas. "Good luck. And now I won't worry about staying here. I was afraid that my being here in the house might be weird—the apartment isn't ready, and your mom doesn't know when it will be."

"I see. Well, I'm still going to be here three or four weeks." He studied her expression, but couldn't quite read her. Five years was a long time, longer than they'd been together, and she'd likely changed just as much as he had.

They really didn't know each other at all anymore. "Does it matter to you if I'm here?"

She seemed to hesitate before she answered. "Should it?"

He laughed. "Look at us, trying to be so respectful of each other. We've known each other too long and too well not to be completely honest. You need to do what's best for you. I'll do the same. Deal?"

She came forward and held her hand out for a shake. "Deal."

He shook her hand and felt…warmth.

"So we're friends then?"

"I think so." But not typical friendship. More like Friends With History. If that was a thing. Yeah, it was definitely a thing.

She exhaled then smiled. "Tell me about France. I was so happy to hear about your internship. I'm not the least bit surprised you parlayed that into something permanent."

"Thanks, it's been pretty spectacular."

"And the internship came at the perfect time. Because of Alex dying…" Her voice trailed off, and she winced. "Sorry, I didn't mean to throw the conversation off a cliff again."

He shook his head. "It's okay. Yeah, it was perfect timing." He didn't tell her Alex's death had been the catalyst that had finally pushed him out of Ribbon Ridge. That had been such a bone of contention for them, why revisit that conflict? She believed that his family was more important to him than she was, but that hadn't been true. She just hadn't understood the bond they shared, not when her parents were so messed up.

Maybe things with them had improved. He hoped so, for her sake. "How's your dad?"

"Still working at the ER. And with Joss, though they continue to live apart. It's so weird." Joss was the woman her father had started dating when Bex had been in community college. The woman who had prompted Bex to leave Bend and move halfway across the state to go to Oregon State. Hayden had met Joss—she was incredibly intense—so he understood Bex's difficulties with her.

"And things are still rosy between you and her?"

Bex rolled her eyes. "Totally. She's such an enabler, but whatever. I can't fix my dad and his various issues. He's her problem now."

Hayden doubted Bex could turn her back on him so completely. She'd been looking out for him since her parents had divorced. "Is he still self-medicating?"

She shrugged. "I guess. Like I said, I stay out of it."

He took the hint. Bex had never liked talking about them too much. She preferred a laissez-faire approach, which was the exact opposite of what his family would do.

"How's your mom?" he asked.

Her lips curved up. "Still living the high life in Seattle. We e-mail periodically, see each other now and again. It's blissfully low maintenance."

Yuck. Hayden couldn't imagine having that kind of relationship with his family. They'd always been pretty close, even when they'd been sprawled all over the place. "How was Eugene? Tough place to be for a Beaver."

Eugene was home to the University of Oregon, and the state rivalry between the Oregon Ducks and the Oregon State Beavers was epic. Hayden was the only Beaver in the family, while both Liam and Tori were Ducks and pretty much everyone else rooted for the Ducks. It was just another way he was the odd man out.

She laughed. "Don't I know it? Didn't stop me from wearing my Beaver gear, especially during football season."

Hayden smiled. They'd gone to every home game together. So many happy memories were wrapped up in Bex. So many painful ones, too. "I missed going to the games last year while I was in France." And he'd miss them for at least two more years, assuming he took this job.

"I bet. Their version of football just doesn't cut it, I'm guessing."

Hayden shook his head. Not that he followed the sport. He'd been too busy immersing himself in the winery. He'd wanted to soak up all he could.

She winked at him. "Maybe you should try to like it since you're going to be living there for the foreseeable future."

He laughed. "Yeah, I guess. I'm still wrapping my head around it." That was the truth. He'd thought of little else since spilling it to his siblings earlier. Well, that and Bex.

"I get it," she said. "I imagine it would be a hard choice for you to leave Ribbon Ridge in the first place, not to mention stay away."

Her empathy on this topic surprised him. But it *had* been five years. He couldn't cast her as the young woman who'd broken his heart anymore. At least, he shouldn't. That might be a tough adjustment. But it was one he'd have to make if he truly wanted to be friends.

"Thanks, I appreciate you saying that."

She looked away for a moment, and when she made eye contact once more, there was a depth of emotion in her gaze that he'd never expected to see again. "I'm sorry about the way things ended."

The wound had been raw for so long, but now it just felt...tired. "Like I said, it seems we've both come out all right."

"Yes, it does."

"I'd go so far as to say thank you. I think you did me a favor when you broke up with me."

Her dark brows rose high on her forehead. "I did?"

"Sure. Can you imagine how different things would be? The experiences we would've missed out on?" It had taken him years to get to this place, but it felt good. "Anyway, I should get downstairs and break the news to my folks. I'll see you later, Bex."

She reached out and touched his arm as he turned. "See you, Hayden."

The contact of her hand against his bare flesh, though brief, rocketed through him, leaving a blazing trail in its wake. What the hell? He'd just shaken her hand with no problem. He'd also braced himself before doing it. This touch—this caress—had taken him completely off-guard. Even more than when he'd seen her at The Alex earlier.

He'd been startled, that was all. It didn't mean a thing. He shook the sensation away and went downstairs.

His parents were sitting together at the bar in the kitchen talking in low tones. Hayden felt like he was interrupting them. He briefly considered skipping this chat altogether, but knew one of his siblings would inevitably slip when they came around later.

He cleared his throat, and Mom turned, her face lighting up. "Hayden, I just love seeing you come in here."

And, here he was about to drive a stake through her heart. No, he couldn't think of it like that. This wasn't about her. It was about him. "I need to tell you both something."

"Uh-oh, this sounds serious," Dad said, his mouth pulling into a slight frown. He turned on the stool and gestured to one of the chairs at the long farmhouse table. "Do you want to sit?"

"Sure." Hayden took one of the chairs and instantly felt like a kid again. With his parents on bar stools, he had to look up at them. Not ideal when he wanted to feel like the master of his own destiny, but he'd make do. Might as well rip the bandage off quickly. "Antoine offered me a job as assistant winemaker, and I'm going to take it."

Mom's mouth opened then closed. Her eyes widened, but she schooled her expression pretty quickly. "That's wonderful."

He heard the tightness in her voice. "It is, but you don't have to act enthusiastic, Mom. I know you'd prefer I moved back to Ribbon Ridge."

She relaxed and let her frown take over. "To be honest, I didn't think there would be a choice. I thought you'd be more than ready to come home."

"Don't get me wrong, I miss you all, and I miss Ribbon Ridge, but right now this is a good decision for where I am. I'll gain so much experience. When I come back—and I will at some point—I'll have a much better chance of competing with the rock-star winemakers around here."

"You could compete with them now," Mom said quietly.

"Actually, I can't. There aren't enough jobs for everyone looking, and I'm the low man on the totem pole. The Archer name has a lot of cache, but not in winemaking."

"I told you to make beer," Dad said.

Hayden bristled, but also heard the lightness in his father's tone that said he wasn't serious. Yes, Dad had suggested he make beer, but he'd also understood Hayden's passion for grapes, not hops. "Too late." He smiled at Dad to take any sting out of the words.

Dad reached over and clapped his hand on Hayden's knee. "I know. I'm so proud of you, son. How long will you stay over there?"

"Antoine's asking for at least a two-year commitment, which I think is more than fair."

Mom's frown deepened. "That's so long."

"It'll go fast, you'll see." Hayden could scarcely believe he'd already been gone more than a year.

"Or you could think of it in terms of age," she said. "Your niece or nephew will be going on two by then. You'll miss all of that."

Now it was Hayden's turn to frown. It wasn't as if Evan's kid was Hayden's. No, Hayden's child would be almost five now. Damn. He hadn't thought about that before. Maybe he'd prefer to skip watching Evan's kid—right now, he had an ache in his chest that he'd never imagined.

Dad patted Mom's hand. "Emily, leave him alone." He looked at Hayden. "She'll be fine."

Hayden knew she'd had a rough time after Alex died. She'd seen a therapist and had taken medication off and on. Then she'd gone with Hayden to France for a couple of months, and that had finally seemed to help her make some progress. She and Dad had been at odds before that, and they'd reconciled when she'd come home. That didn't mean she—and Dad—didn't struggle. Their child was gone, and they had to live with that every day. Hayden thought he understood, at least a little bit.

He leaned forward and took his mother's hand. It had softened with age, but was still strong, and he could feel it stroking his back as she tucked him into bed at night. "I'm going to be here for a month, and I'll be home again at Christmas for a couple of weeks, okay?"

She sniffed and wiped at her eye before a tear fell. "What about Kyle's wedding in September?"

Right. That. Everyone was getting married, for crying out loud. "I'll be here, don't worry."

She nodded, sniffing again. "I'm sorry. I didn't mean to make you feel bad."

"It's okay. I love you, Mom."

She smiled. "I know. We'll just have to make the most of you being here."

"Deal." He squeezed her hand then let go. "And now I think I need a nap before I head out to dinner with the guys later. This time change is brutal."

He stood, and Dad got up, too. "I meant it, Hayden. I'm so proud of you." He gave Hayden a fast but fierce hug.

Hayden nodded at him then turned and went back the way he came. As he left the kitchen, he heard them whispering and could've sworn he heard Dad say, "Don't worry, we have time."

Yes, they had time, but he wasn't going to change his mind.

Chapter Five

EMILY HAD PUT out a spectacular salad bar for all of the women, and after they'd stuffed themselves, they moved into the great room. Two stories tall, it featured windows overlooking the pool and backyard, a massive fireplace, and was currently sporting two long worktables in the middle of the room.

Chairs were set at intervals around the table. Sara had set up stations earlier. There were bottles to put labels on, little boxes that needed ribbons, and several canisters of long, finger-thick pretzels next to a stack of plastic bags and ribbons, candles, and pint glasses etched with Sara's and Dylan's names as well as the wedding date.

"These have to be the craziest favors I've ever seen," Bex said, laughing.

Alaina Pierce, the superstar actress who'd needed no introduction when Bex had met her last night at the bachelorette party, rolled her eyes. "Right? I feel like a slacker now. But that's what happens when you have a shotgun wedding, I guess." She rubbed her hand over her curved, but still small, belly and winked.

Bex knew it hadn't been that sort of wedding—Alaina and Evan loved each other and while the baby hadn't been planned, he or she was very wanted. It was the opposite of what had happened to Bex and Hayden, and Bex couldn't help but feel a pang of sadness. No, it was more than that. She hadn't wanted that baby, not then, but she would've had it anyway. And for the first time, she realized she wouldn't have regretted it. Maybe it was being back here, seeing Hayden again, but the loss felt somehow magnified.

She took a deep breath and told herself to suck it up. It was natural to think of what might have been when faced with your ex and a pregnant woman. Wasn't it?

Sara went to stand at the end of the tables. "Let me explain the tasks and then you can pick which one you want to do. Except the ribbons on the chocolates. No one ties a ribbon like my mom. Mom, you're doing those."

Emily chuckled as she took the chair at the opposite end. "Happy to, dear."

Sara smiled at her. "Thanks, Mom." Sara walked over to the chair on Emily's left. "This person is going to put the labels on the cider. Bex, Dad made special batches of beer and cider, because I don't really like beer, if you remember."

"I do," Bex murmured. She knew so much about this family. But it had been five years, and she was no longer the close-knit almost-member she'd once been. No one would recall precisely what Bex knew and didn't know, and she didn't expect anyone to. The other women in the room—*they* were the Archer women. Bex was just an old friend and now an employee. She'd expected a little awkwardness, but she hadn't been prepared for the baby thing or for how she'd felt when she'd seen Hayden. That afternoon things had seemed charged between them, but maybe that had just been her perspective.

Sara moved on down to the center of the table. "And this is for labeling the beer." She took a few more steps. "Here are the pint glasses." She held them up. "Aren't they cool? Each basket gets two. Whoever sits here will slide them into Bubble Wrap sleeves." Sara circled to the other side of the tables. "Next come the pretzels. This is a two-person station. One will put five pretzel sticks in each plastic bag and the other will tie it with a ribbon."

"I don't know if I want that job," Alaina said. "I'm worried your bow standards are too high."

This was met with laugher, and Sara grinned. "These will only require a simple bow, like tying your shoes."

"Which I won't be able to do in a few months." Alaina glanced past her barely showing tummy at her feet.

"You have plenty of sisters-in-law and sisters-in-law-to-be to help you," Emily said, smiling. "Not to mention a mother-in-law."

Bex's heart twisted, and she internally chided herself. She had to find a way to be here without thinking of the past or what might have been. She walked toward the table. "What's next?"

"The last job is putting stickers on the lids of the candles."

Bex looked at the circles printed in navy blue, sage, and pink. They were decorated with a twirling vine and said, "Thank you for sharing our day. Love, Sara and Dylan." Adorable.

Chloe, Derek's wife, and the artistic director for the Archer pubs and The Alex, glanced around the table. "That's only seven stations, and there are eight of us."

"I'm going to start assembling as you finish the items." Sara gestured toward several boxes, one of which was open to reveal the baskets. "How do you guys want to decide what to do?"

"I'm taking candle stickers," Alaina said. "No bows for me, thanks."

"I'll do the bows," Bex offered, which put her next to Alaina. She'd been intimidated by her last night—it was hard not to be when she'd starred in some of Bex's all-time favorite movies—but now she just seemed like another one of the gang.

Maggie took the chair to Bex's right. "I'll take the pretzels."

The other three went to the opposite side of the table, where Aubrey took the glasses, Tori went for the beer, and Chloe claimed the cider.

Everyone sat and started in on the tasks. "This is going to be such a fun wedding," Chloe said.

Maggie handed a bag of pretzels to Bex for tying. "Yours was pretty awesome last summer."

Chloe smiled at her and nodded. "That was your first event as an Archer significant other. Good times."

"Yeah, after Kyle sprung her on us at your rehearsal dinner," Tori said. She looked at Bex. "That could've been a major disaster."

"Wait, I don't think I know this story," Alaina said. "What happened?"

Sara answered. "You know that Maggie had been Alex's therapist, right?" At Alaina's nod, she continued. "She was sort of persona non grata around here since, you know, she'd failed to see that Alex was suicidal." She gave Maggie a warm, sympathetic look. "But Alex fooled even those of us who knew him best, so poor Maggie hadn't stood a chance."

"But what happened at the rehearsal dinner?" Alaina pressed. She grinned at Bex. "Sorry, I love a juicy story, so long as it's not about me in a tabloid."

Everyone laughed, and Tori finished the story. "Kyle had been seeing Maggie in secret—something Sara might be familiar with." She coughed and gave her sister a pointed look. Sara blushed, and Bex knew it was because she and Dylan had carried on a secret friends-with-benefits relationship for a while before finally going public. Much had been made of that at last night's party.

"Anyway," Tori went on, "we had no idea he was seeing Maggie, and then he up and brought her to the rehearsal dinner, shocking the hell out of everyone in the process."

"Don't forget the part where he told us he was a gambling addict," Chloe said, her blonde brows arched.

"Yeah, that, too," Tori said. "It was an eventful night." She gave Chloe a sheepish smile. "Sorry about that."

"Not your fault, and not yours either." Chloe looked at Maggie. "I remember thinking how happy I was to be joining such a wonderfully close and supportive family. I didn't have that." She smiled at everyone around the table, and Emily blew her a kiss.

Bex hadn't had that either. She could've, but she'd walked away. It had seemed the right decision at the time, and she didn't want to regret that choice, but damn, it was hard with all of the love and camaraderie in the room. They *were* an amazing family, and she wasn't a part of it. Nor would she ever be.

The conversation turned as Maggie asked Tori how her new house was coming.

"The foundation's dry," Tori said. "They're due to start framing tomorrow."

Bex looked over at Tori. "Did you design it?"

Tori nodded. "We're pretty excited. So are Sean's folks. They can't wait to come visit from England. We're looking forward to having them here for a month or so."

"Sounds fun." For them maybe. Whenever Bex had thought of her parents commingling with the Archers, she'd practically broken out in hives. The Archers were so well-adjusted and *normal*. And her parents were so…*not*. She couldn't imagine the level of awkwardness that would've ensued, and she didn't want to. Thankfully her mother had never wanted to visit her in Ribbon Ridge, and Dad preferred to be a homebody.

Maggie shuddered. "Sure, if your parents aren't weird like mine."

Bex instantly felt a connection to Kyle's fiancée. "What's wrong with your parents?"

Maggie gave her a gimlet eye. "What *isn't* wrong with them?" She shook her head and smiled. "That's not fair or true. They're good people. Loving. They're just…odd. They have an open marriage and have since I was a kid. It was a strange way to grow up."

"But you had love," Aubrey said. "As opposed to the cold fish I grew up with." She grimaced as she slid a glass into its Bubble Wrap.

Another kindred spirit, Bex thought. Maybe *cold* wasn't the best word to describe her mother. No, *absent* or *oblivious* were both more apropos.

Maggie passed off another bag of pretzels. "True. And as weird as they are, I wouldn't trade them."

Bex wasn't sure she'd trade hers either. As self-absorbed as her mother was and as distracted as her father was, Bex had enjoyed a freedom most kids would've killed for. Which wasn't to say it had been the best upbringing. It was, however, the only one she had.

"I can beat all of you," Alaina said, arching a brow to the table at large. "Raise your hand if your dad was a felon." She paused. "Anyone? No? How about a mother who was literally once a crackwhore?"

Bex stopped in the middle of tying a bow and looked at Alaina. She couldn't recall if this information was common knowledge—given that most of Alaina's life was plastered in the media it probably was—but Bex hadn't known that about her. "Yikes, that couldn't have been easy."

"Especially when you throw in my pastor grandfather, who we might as well nickname Grampa Judgy."

Bex winced. Alaina might have a seemingly perfect life, but you never really knew the truth behind someone's façade.

"Sorry we can't contribute to this pity-fest, but we have the best parents ever," Tori said, smiling, in a clear attempt to lighten the mood. Not that it had turned dark, but Bex didn't know these people well enough to say for sure.

Emily's mouth quirked into a satisfied smile as she focused on tying a bow. "I can't disagree there." She set the box of chocolates in her done pile and glanced around the table. "And I certainly hit the jackpot when it came to children and children-in-law." Her gaze hit Bex last before going back to the task in front of her.

Bex didn't for a minute think that short look meant to include Bex in anything. She and Hayden had never even been engaged, no matter how much they'd all expected that to happen.

Emily wrapped another pink-and-navy-striped bow around a box of chocolates. "If Bex and Hayden had gotten married, everyone here would be an Archer or Archer-to-be."

Every muscle in Bex's body tensed, but she tried not to show any reaction. She calmly tied the ribbon around the bag, ignoring the surreptitious glances sent her way.

Alaina slid her an inquisitive glance. "I didn't realize you guys were that serious."

"Yeah, for a while."

Alaina's eyes flickered with something—understanding maybe. "That was a long time ago, right?"

"Five years."

"I'm sorry, I didn't mean to cause any awkwardness," Emily said.

Bex chanced looking at her and was relieved to find that her gaze was sympathetic. "It's fine. That *was* a long time ago."

Bex realized she was the lone single woman in the room. Which was fine with her. Her relationships since Hayden had been...short. Granted, she'd moved around enough to make a long-term relationship difficult, but it hadn't been a challenge to keep things casual. In hindsight, she realized that not one of the men she'd dated had held a candle to Hayden. Had she subconsciously compared them all with him?

Tori's forehead puckered slightly as she slapped another label on a beer bottle. "Anyone know anything about the girl he's seeing in France?"

Bex messed up her bow and had to start over. He was seeing someone? She felt like she'd been kicked in the gut, which was stupid.

"They're not serious in the slightest," Emily said. "Otherwise she would've come."

Sara gathered items and arranged them in a basket. She was way behind the rest of them, but when they were all done, they could pitch in and help with the overall packaging. "Are they even seeing each other, really?" she asked, glancing at Tori. "I thought they were just friends—they work together after all."

"Well, not together-together," Tori said. "I don't think they interact much at work. But yeah, I guess they're maybe just friends. I was sort of hoping he might be dating her. He could use a girlfriend."

Tori tossed Bex an apologetic look, and Bex responded with a nonverbal "it's okay" smile. Except her insides were twisting into knots.

Chloe glanced around the table. "Why aren't we drinking? Or are we still feeling the effects of last night?" She chuckled.

Alaina waved a hand in between stickers. "Don't mind me. I'm just suffering the effects of this." She glanced down at her belly then smiled. "Not that I mind."

This was met with laughter around the table.

"Beer or wine?" Tori asked, standing.

The consensus seemed to be wine, so Tori went downstairs to grab a couple of bottles from the Archers' impressive cellar.

When Tori returned, she wasn't alone. A pack of testosterone trailed behind her, led by Kyle.

"What are we drinking to?" he asked, going directly to Maggie then leaning down and kissing her cheek. "Hey, babe."

He was followed by Liam, Evan, and two men Bex had met that morning at breakfast—Sean Hennessy, Tori's husband, and Dylan Westcott, Sara's fiancé. Hayden brought up the rear. All the men went to their significant others and greeted them with a kiss or a caress, or both. She and Hayden sat and stood there awkwardly. Or maybe the awkward was all her.

"You need wineglasses." Hayden turned back and went into the kitchen. Sean went with him, and a moment later they returned with stemware.

Liam shook his head. "Oh, we're going to need more than that. Come on, Derek." He and Derek left, presumably to fetch more of everything.

Evan stood next to Alaina's chair and massaged her shoulders. "Can I get you anything?"

She pointed to the table. "I've got my water bottle."

He smiled down at her. "Never without it."

They were a striking couple, and obviously very in love. They all were. It made Bex feel…lonely.

Crap, what had she done agreeing to move to Ribbon Ridge? She'd expected a little weirdness, but not this total assault of nostalgia. Or maybe it was more than that. Maybe it was regret.

Would she do things differently now? She wasn't sure.

She'd already wanted to leave Ribbon Ridge before she'd even learned she was pregnant. Then she'd felt trapped, her future completely decided for her. When she'd miscarried, that weight had been lifted. Suddenly the dreams she'd had—of running her own brewery and spreading her wings—had become possible again, and she hadn't been able to get out fast enough. She'd felt like she'd dodged a bullet, but now she had to wonder if she hadn't lost something else entirely.

Sara stood next to Dylan, who had his arm around her waist and had pulled her tight against him so he could kiss her temple. "If you guys are going to hang out, you have to help," she said.

Dylan loosened his hold on her. "Put us to work."

She did just that and when Liam and Derek returned, they had double the hands completing the tasks.

Hayden stood near the doorway as all the other men went to help their significant others. His choices were to help Bex or his mother tie bows. Bex sensed his uncertainty. He likely knew his mother didn't need help—or more accurately that Sara wouldn't allow him to help her. Which meant he could help Bex, and she didn't think he wanted to do that, so she rescued him by saying, "Hayden, you could help Sara and Dylan with the basket assembly."

"Good idea."

Bex stood, intent on grabbing a glass of water from the kitchen. She passed Hayden on her way and got a whiff of his shower gel for her trouble. She closed her eyes briefly, recalling the scent of Hayden. That smell aroused so many memories, so much joy.

She swallowed and reminded herself they were as dead as disco. Why then, did she feel like a junior high kid with her first crush? Because she'd either never gotten over Hayden Archer or her feelings had been rekindled in a huge way. Whatever the reason, she was completely screwed.

Chapter Six

MONDAY NIGHT HAYDEN walked into the arctic interior of The Arch and Vine in downtown Ribbon Ridge. His internal clock was still a bit off from the time change, but he'd gotten over his jet lag. With every day at home, he felt a little more connected and a little less sure about his decision to take the job in France. Maybe that was why he hadn't yet notified Antoine.

Coming here wasn't helping that cause either. His family's flagship pub was like a second home. It was cozy and comfortable, welcoming like an old friend. Especially when there was an actual old friend behind the bar.

George Wilson, the bartender and an old friend of their father's, came out from behind the bar situated in the center of the pub. "Hayden Archer, I heard you were home. Took you long enough to come see me." He grinned, and his eyes, framed by a pair of wire-rimmed glasses, lit up like a Christmas tree.

Hayden gave him a bear hug. "Good to see you, George. I've been busy acclimating. And sleeping." He'd gone to bed early Saturday night and had pretty much slept straight through yesterday, with the exception of the family dinner.

They stepped apart, and George sized him up. "I'm sorry to say it looks like France agrees with you." He frowned. "I hope that doesn't mean you're staying there."

Hayden chuckled. George had never made a secret of his desire for every Archer kid to stay in Ribbon Ridge. He'd understood why Hayden had left, but he'd also made it clear he expected Hayden to come right back home when he was finished with his internship.

"Not forever, but yes, I'm taking a job as assistant winemaker." Hayden winced at the disappointment in the lines on George's face. "Don't look at me like that!"

George scowled. "You darn kids. Makes me glad I never had my own." He shook his head, but there was a ghost of a smile haunting his mouth as he went back to the bar. "You want the usual or have you given up beer entirely now that you're Mr. Wine Guy?"

Hayden slid onto a stool. "That's one of the things I missed most when I was over there—the beer just isn't as good."

"Ha!" George pulled him a pint of Crossbow, an unfiltered wheat beer that was one of their primary brews and Hayden's favorite. He slid the glass across the counter. "Maybe you should rethink that job."

Hayden took a drink and closed his eyes in rapt appreciation. Maybe he should. But he supposed he was since he hadn't actually committed yet.

George leaned against the bar and studied him. "What's France got that we don't?"

After one more sip, Hayden set his glass down. "A world-class winery where I'll be the assistant winemaker."

George waved his hand as if Hayden had just told him France had something as mundane as daylight. "We've got world-class wineries."

True, but Hayden didn't work for any of them. Winemaker jobs were hard to come by, especially for someone like him. His internship was a good resume builder, but he had a long way to go to compete with the winemakers in the Willamette Valley.

"I have a great house with a garden and an amazing view of vineyards." He rented a 150-year-old two-story stone cottage that looked like it was straight out of a travel show. What it lacked in a few modern conveniences—a rather small fridge, no dishwasher, and the bathroom off his bedroom was a closet—it more than made up for in charm and ambience. He was living the rustic French lifestyle and loving it.

George looked unimpressed. "You have a house here, and the vineyards are close by."

He *did* have a house here. The house he'd bought after college and lived in with Bex until she'd left him. Upon leaving that house himself, he'd realized it had been part of the reason he'd been unable to get over her. It reminded him of her, of them, of the plans they'd made and the future they'd lost. He planned to ask Kyle if he wanted to buy it from him since he and Maggie seemed to really love it.

Hayden took another drink of beer. "There's a girl in France. That's a good enough reason to go back, right? Even for you."

George folded his arms over his chest. "Ah. Got a picture?"

Hayden pulled his phone from his pocket and found a photo of Gabrielle. She smiled in the photo, her dark eyes sparkling against the cloudy spring sky, her feet in rain boots because they'd been trudging around the vineyard surveying the bud break.

Hayden handed the phone to George. "This is Gabrielle. Her father owns the winery where I work."

George looked at the picture then gave the phone back to Hayden. "Pretty. Can you communicate very well? I don't remember you being fluent in French."

Hayden laughed. "She speaks great English, actually, but I've become quite conversant. It's hard not to when you live there and hear the language all day long." In fact, it had been a bit of an adjustment coming back to English twenty-four/seven. He realized he'd started thinking in French.

"She could always move here," George said.

Hayden shook his head. She'd never move away from her family winery, not when she was poised to inherit. And anyway, they were *nowhere* near that serious. They hung out, they occasionally had sex. It was extremely casual. Perfect for the lifestyle he wanted right now. "She's locked into her family business."

George gave him a pointed look. "So were you."

One of the servers, a young woman Hayden didn't recognize, which felt weird, came up to the other side of the bar. "George, can you pull a pitcher of Longbow and a pitcher of Shaft?"

"You got it, Kelsey." George nodded toward the door behind Hayden. "Looks like your buddies are here." He waved toward them before going back to work.

"See you later, George," Hayden said, turning on the stool to see his man-dates for this evening: Cameron and his two younger brothers, Luke and Jamie.

Cam came forward, grinning, his familiar green eyes glinting with humor. "Well if it isn't my favorite Frog."

Hayden turned to Luke and Jamie. "Glad you guys could join us."

Luke, the middle brother and two years younger than Cam and Hayden's twenty-eight, rubbed his hand against his stubbled cheek. "Hey, I'm free every night this week. I haven't been home for so long since I moved to Cali, and our mother is beside herself." He lowered his voice. "She's driving me nuts."

Hayden chuckled, feeling his pain since his own mother was simultaneously thrilled to have him home and upset that it was only temporary. "I'm sure she's even more excited to see Jamie since he lives even farther away."

Jamie had been busy earning two master's degrees from the London School of Economics over the past two years. He and Hayden had finally managed to get together for a long weekend in Paris this past spring.

"Don't you know it," Jamie said. "So yeah, Luke and I are more than happy to go out every night this week. We could even spend a night in Portland—maybe relive some of the fun of our Paris trip." He winked at Hayden.

Hayden laughed. "That was an epic trip." Two guys, Paris, good food, good drink, and a night at a dance club that Hayden could barely remember.

Cam glared at them both, but it was clearly meant in jest. "You guys are pissing me off. Next time, I'm flying over. Come on, let's grab a booth." Cam led them to the corner with their favorite table.

Hayden slid onto the seat next to Cam. They were barely situated when the server, Kelsey, came to the table and tossed four coasters onto the wood. "Welcome, guys. George tells me you're regulars, and you"—she looked at Hayden—"are an Archer."

"That's right," Hayden said. "And these jokers are soon to be Archers-by-marriage."

Cam laughed. "Sort of." He looked at Kelsey. "Our half-brother is marrying Hayden's sister this weekend."

"Right, that's the big wedding that half the staff are going to."

Cam looked at Hayden in mock distress. "What, you didn't invite the *entire* staff and shut the place down?"

Hayden held up his hands. "Don't look at me. I have nothing to do with it. I don't even live here anymore. Besides, there's no way we'd close the pub on a Saturday and lose all that wine-tasting traffic, let alone the people going to and from the beach." Ribbon Ridge was a popular destination, or stop-in point, for weekend travelers from Portland and beyond.

Kelsey laughed as she tucked a lock of wavy brown hair behind her ear. "It's fine. I'm new to town, and I don't know very many people. It wouldn't make sense for me to come to your sister's wedding."

Hayden arched a brow at Cam and gave him a look that said, *see?*

Cam exhaled. "All right, but is it my fault if I'd like to include an attractive young woman on the guest list?" He winked at Kelsey, who only chuckled.

"Aren't you the smooth talker? I've seen you in here a couple times," she said. "Now I know to steer clear."

Everyone but Cam laughed. "Ouch," Luke said. He looked at Kelsey. "Don't judge us by our brother's obnoxiousness. He's never met a pretty face he hasn't flirted with."

Cam rolled his eyes. "You guys are totally ruining this for me."

"Don't sweat it," Kelsey said. "I've got a boyfriend anyway. Sorry. You guys want some beer, or do you need a minute?"

Luke picked up his coaster and ran his thumb along the edge. "Pitchers of Crossbow and Longbow."

"And nachos," Jamie said. "I've missed them so much. You just can't get decent nachos in England."

Hayden nodded. "Or France. Onion rings too, since Walla Wallas are in season. God, I missed those last summer."

"You got it." Kelsey turned from the table, leaving them alone.

Hayden sat forward and set his elbows on the table like his mother had always told him not to. "Luke, what's new in Napa? I'm sure it was tough to get away this week."

Luke was the vineyard manager at a midsize winery. He'd worked his way up since graduating from UC Davis four years ago. "Yep, but I've got a good crew. I fly back Sunday night. How's France? I was sorry I couldn't make it out after harvest last fall. Maybe this year. Assuming you're going back."

Hayden shot Cam a grateful look since he'd clearly kept his mouth shut. "Yeah, I'll head back next month. As assistant winemaker."

Luke grinned. "Congrats."

"Good for you," Jamie said. "I'm mulling what to do next. Might head back to England. I've got a couple job offers."

Kelsey returned with their pitchers and three pint glasses. She looked at Hayden. "I didn't bring you a new glass. Do you want a fresh one?"

"No, I'm good, thanks."

She left with a nod, and they served themselves.

Hayden topped off his pint. "With Jamie in England, I'll have family on that side of the world—we can keep each other company." He raised his glass toward Jamie.

Jamie responded in kind, and they drank.

"That blows," Cam said morosely. "I mean, I'm happy for you, but it sucks when your best friend and your brothers live so far away."

Jamie set his glass down on his coaster. "It's kind of funny, if you look around the table, we could pretty much start a winery tomorrow. If we had, you know, grapes."

"Yeah, those are kind of important," Luke said wryly before taking a drink of beer.

Hayden looked around. Luke would be the vineyard manager, obviously, Cam would be in charge of sales, and clearly Hayden would make the wine. "What would you do, Jamie?"

Luke laughed. "Anything he damn well pleases! He's smarter than the three of us put together."

Not quite, but Hayden knew what he meant. Jamie was Mensa-level genius.

"I wouldn't just want to do sales," Cameron said, sounding far more serious than normal. "It's kind of interesting you brought this up, Jamie. I've been getting tired of sales."

"What, you want to run the business?" Luke asked.

Cameron shrugged. "Maybe. I just wish I didn't hate accounting so much."

"I can do that," Jamie said. "I love numbers. And wine." He grinned as he lifted his glass. "*And* beer."

Kelsey returned with the food, and they all dug in. It was quiet, and Hayden wondered if they were seriously pondering this idea. They needed more than just grapes; they needed a vineyard for Luke to oversee. And starting a vineyard from scratch would mean at least five years before a worthwhile vintage. Five years of investment with zero return. Hayden had a trust fund, and he'd have income from The Alex at some point, but the other three didn't. He doubted they could afford that scenario.

Luke swiped a napkin over his mouth and took a swig of beer. "We'd need a vineyard."

"I was just thinking that," Cam said, answering Hayden's question as to whether they'd all been mulling this venture. "And there's actually a vineyard or two in the area to be had."

"Are they decent, though?" Luke asked.

Cam plucked another onion ring from the basket. "Probably decent enough."

Jamie looked around at all of them. "Wait, are we actually serious about this?"

Luke blew out a breath. "I'm stuck where I am. I can't leave them in the middle of summer."

"Well, it's not like we'd find a working vineyard we could take over in midsummer either. But after harvest…" Cam shrugged. "Just something to think about, I guess." He looked over at Hayden. "Or not, actually. We wouldn't have a winemaker for at least two years."

Hayden suddenly felt like a buzzkill, which was stupid. They were just shooting shit. They weren't *really* serious. Even so, he had to admit that working with Luke would be a hell of a good time. He was great at vineyard management. "Would you consider coming back to Ribbon Ridge?"

Luke leaned back against the booth. "Sure. I always figured I'd end up here at some point." He smiled. "I just keep getting jobs in Cali."

Cam wiped his fingers on a napkin as he looked at Hayden. "The question is, would *you*?"

"Sure, if the timing was right." Which it wasn't just now. Give him two more years in France then he could come home. Bex would probably be gone by then, and he could settle back in. Wait, this was all about Bex? No, it was more than that. It was him following his dreams and not caving in to his family's desire for him to come home. This was *his* time.

"So, uh, we saw Bex at breakfast the other morning after you left," Jamie said. "How's that going?"

Cam had texted Hayden as soon as he'd seen her—three simple letters: *WTF*. Hayden had responded that it had been a surprise, but they hadn't talked about it in depth.

Hayden shrugged. "Fine, I guess. I've barely seen her." He'd expected to run into Bex at the family dinner last night since she was staying in the house, but had learned that she'd gone back to Eugene first thing Sunday morning to finish moving out of her apartment. She'd been due back today to start at the brewery, but something had tripped her up and she wouldn't be back until tomorrow.

Cam sat back and blinked. "No shit?" He looked over at Hayden. "I can't believe you're cool with that."

"Kind of have to be, don't I?" Hayden took a drink of beer, feeling a bit uncomfortable discussing this, but refusing to acknowledge the sensation. He wasn't going to let Bex get under his skin. Not after he'd worked so hard to finally move past her. "It's cool, really."

Luke finished his beer and poured another. "You were hooked on her for a long time."

"Hooked as in past tense," Hayden pointed out. "Her being here is...weird, sure. But it doesn't affect me. I'm only here a few weeks anyway."

Cam exhaled, and Hayden could hear the disappointment in the vocalization. "Right."

"I guess that means the winery plan is just a pipe dream." Jamie also sounded disappointed.

Hayden couldn't really blame them. The entire scenario was not only possible, but damn enticing. Could he consider it? He'd rushed into telling his family he was staying in France, but acknowledged—to himself—that it had been a knee-jerk reaction to their underhandedness in hiring Bex. If that hadn't happened, he'd be seriously thinking about this plan.

But it *had* happened, and Bex was here. For good. Or at least for as long as she could stand it. He gave her a year. Two, tops. He could put up with her for that long, couldn't he? Ribbon Ridge was a small town, but surely it was big enough for both of them.

Oh, he was being stupid. This wasn't some Hallmark Channel movie that his mom and sisters liked to watch at Christmastime. Maybe he could think about the winery for a few days at least. He figured he could tell Antoine he was taking the job after the wedding next weekend—he knew Hayden wanted to think about it for at least a week. In the meantime, he'd see how things felt.

The winery idea could be postponed anyway. Luke was tied to his job in Napa for the short term at least, and Hayden wouldn't be gone forever. Unless this job turned into something even more phenomenal. Could he turn his back on Ribbon Ridge?

He wanted to say no, but realized he'd somehow come to learn that nothing was certain. No matter how badly you wanted it to be.

BEX LET HERSELF into the back door of the Archer house on Tuesday night. Even though she'd done it hundreds of times, it still felt strange to be doing it now. Things were different. *She* was different.

But how? More guarded and more tentative, she realized. When she'd been younger, she'd jumped into life here in Ribbon Ridge, into the Archer family really, and she'd been in way over her head. They shared things she'd never dream of sharing with her parents. There was a closeness she just hadn't understood, and it had made her uncomfortable. Oh, she supposed they'd tried to include her, but she hadn't wanted it. She hadn't wanted that level of intimacy. Did she want it now?

It didn't matter. She wasn't a part of this family just because she worked for them. And was staying in their house. Good grief, she needed to find a place of her own, stat.

She trudged toward the kitchen, exhausted after driving up from Eugene that morning and working all day in the brewery. She'd stopped here briefly to drop the last of her stuff off this morning, but she'd been anxious to get to work, especially since she'd missed yesterday due to a mix-up with the storage containers.

As she rounded the corner into the kitchen, she stopped short. Emily was dishing up ice cream next to the fridge. She looked up at Bex with a warm smile. "Hi there, are you just getting in?" She glanced at the clock, which said it was after nine.

"Yes, long day. I'm wiped out."

"I bet. Are you hungry?"

Bex's stomach growled, answering for her.

Emily laughed softly. "There's some leftover pasta salad and a chicken breast if you're interested."

Bex would've settled for well-seasoned cardboard. "Sounds great. But, I'll get it. You need to eat your ice cream before it melts."

Emily put the container back in the freezer. "I suppose I do. You want some company?"

It was a casual, simple question, but complicated just the same. Bex could say no, that she was too tired and would eat in her room. That would establish some necessary distance between her and the Archers.

But *was* it necessary? She wasn't in danger of anything. She was a houseguest, nothing more. Okay, and an employee. Though, not of this woman.

"Sure." What would be the harm? Besides, Bex liked Emily. She just didn't know what to do with this family's…*inclusiveness*, for lack of a better word. Bex opened the fridge and found the chicken breast and salad. She considered whether to heat the chicken up and decided she'd rather just chop it and eat it with the pasta salad. Easy and fast.

Emily sat down on the other side of the counter at the bar. "There's some fresh lemonade in there, too."

Of course there was. "You are the only mother in the world who could have fresh lemonade on hand four days before your daughter is getting married."

Emily chuckled. "It's important for everyone to stay hydrated. It's been so hot. I hope it cools off a little before Saturday. The wedding and reception are both outside." She ate a bite of ice cream while Bex prepped her salad and asked, "How's your mom? Is she still in Seattle?"

Emily had never met Bex's mother, and Bex had shared the bare minimum. She hadn't wanted to talk about her parents' inattention and self-absorption. Looking back, she realized she'd been embarrassed. And she still was to a certain extent.

"Yes, still in Seattle and still shilling big pharma." Bex's mother lived in a high-rise condo with her eight-years-younger boyfriend. "I lived up there for about eighteen months before I moved to Eugene."

Bex had taken a job at a brewpub in Seattle thinking she and her mother might have a better relationship as adults. She'd been wrong.

"And how'd that go?" Emily's question wasn't just polite. There was a genuine note of concern and interest. It had taken Bex a little while to figure that out because in her experience it was a mother's job to instruct, expect, and ignore. And even then, the instructions and expectations were pretty minimal.

"It was fine."

"I hope you don't mind my saying this, but I've always wondered why your parents never visited you here, particularly after you and Hayden moved in together."

It wasn't a question, but Bex couldn't ignore the statement. She could, however, deflect and rely on the same excuse she'd given for her parents her entire life. "They're both really busy."

Emily spooned another bite of ice cream. "That's too bad. And how's your dad?"

Bex finished making her salad and poured a glass of lemonade. "He's good."

Her relationship with him was far better, despite his general anxiety and being a workaholic who depended on alcohol and other medicinal supplements to help him "relax." She'd gone to live with him after her parents had divorced when she was twelve. That her mother had given full custody to her father had been upsetting at first, but every time Bex had visited her mom in Seattle, she'd seen how much better off she was in Bend. Dad ignored her too—when they'd been married they'd both ignored her, so it made sense that they would continue—but he at least made sure she had food and clothes and whatever else she needed. "He's still working at the ER."

Emily's eyes flickered with surprise. "Really? I would think he'd want to take it a bit easier at some point, maybe go into private practice."

That would require him to establish lasting relationships with patients. Bex nearly laughed. He and his girlfriend didn't even live together, and they'd been dating for nearly a decade.

Emily shook her head. "Sorry. I don't mean to butt in. You've always been very private about your family." She gave Bex a meek smile and went back to her ice cream.

Bex stood there for a moment, her hands full with the salad bowl and the glass of lemonade. She sensed Emily felt bad for her, and she'd always hated it when people pitied her—teachers, coaches, her friends' parents. They'd seen how alone she was and either made "supportive" comments or outright tried to intervene by including Bex in their events. It wasn't that Bex hadn't appreciated their efforts. She just didn't know how not to be alone. She *liked* being alone. Except for the first time she wondered if being alone had somehow, somewhere become feeling lonely instead.

She'd thought about retreating upstairs with her dinner but found herself circling the bar and sitting down next to Emily. "My family is pretty messed up."

Emily turned on the stool and looked at her. "What do you mean by 'messed up'?"

"Well, let's see. My mom never took me school shopping, taught me to make my own dinners when I was seven, and attended exactly one parent-teacher conference."

Emily stared at her, but her gaze was sympathetic. "I don't know what to say. What about your dad?"

"He was marginally better. He made sure I had school supplies and clothes to wear, even if they weren't the most stylish." She laughed, which she could do now. "When I was eleven, I begged him to just drop me off at the mall for a few hours so I could buy my own clothes."

"And he let you?" Emily looked horrified.

Bex smiled at her. "It's okay. I grew up pretty fast. I had to. And I turned out okay." She hoped she'd turned out okay.

Emily finished her ice cream and shook her head. "I had no idea."

Bex looked down at her food and thought she maybe should've eaten upstairs after all. "Yeah, I didn't like to talk about them much. I still don't."

In fact, the only person she'd ever told these things to had been Hayden. He'd actually met both of her parents, accompanying her on a few trips during their relationship.

It had seemed necessary to prep him for their narcissism, since his family experience was completely different. His reaction, particularly upon meeting them in person, was much the same as Emily's.

"You turned out just fine," Emily said firmly. "But who knows if that's a credit to them or to you. I would venture to say it's the latter. I was always impressed with your independence. You reminded me a lot of Tori. Not that you're just like her," she clarified. "There are differences."

Yeah, Bex lacked the nurturing instinct that Tori seemed to have. Bex could take perfectly good care of herself, but that was about it. Once, she'd been alone here at the house with Alex, and he'd needed help changing his oxygen tank. He'd walked her through it, but she'd felt awkward and nervous and had accidentally let a lot of oxygen out of the tank. In the end, he'd laughed, but she'd sensed his frustration along the way. Probably because it hadn't been the first time she'd botched something to do with him. On another occasion, she'd taken him to a doctor appointment, and she'd caught his oxygen tube in the door, creating a hole. She supposed that made her seem more klutzy than anything, but in her mind, it reinforced the idea she'd cultivated since childhood—alone was easier, better.

Bex stuffed a bite of salad in her mouth before she decided to keep oversharing.

Emily exhaled. "I'm always surprised when offspring turn out so different from their parents, but I shouldn't be. Kyle isn't really like either one of us, and for a while there, we wondered if we'd lost him for good."

Bex briefly compared herself with her parents and was surprised to find she wasn't that different. She cringed. Maybe she'd never opened herself up to the Archers because she was too self-involved. She'd been incredibly focused on chasing her own dreams, but maybe deep down she hadn't wanted to connect with these people.

Emily smiled at her and rested her elbow on the counter. "How was today at the brewhouse?"

Grateful for the change of topic, Bex swallowed the bite of salad she'd just taken. "Great. I spent the day getting organized so I can start brewing tomorrow."

"You must be so excited. Like Hayden when he went to France. I was there with him last summer for a couple of months. After Alex, things were difficult."

Bex had seen Emily at Alex's funeral. She'd been pale and withdrawn, a shell of the vibrant woman Bex had known before and nothing like the woman who was sitting here now. "Was it good for you to get away?"

Emily nodded. "Spending that time with Hayden might have saved me, actually. Watching him immerse himself in his dream was very cathartic."

Bex felt a mixture of emotions—happiness that it must have been a good respite for both of them and discomfort because here again was the family intimacy she wasn't used to. This was when she'd typically change the subject or leave the room. But she found she didn't want to. The awkwardness she was feeling didn't have to be a bad thing. Maybe it was a challenge worth fighting.

She wanted to know how Hayden had been after Alex's death. One of the primary reasons he'd told Bex he couldn't leave Ribbon Ridge was Alex—he hadn't wanted to leave the brother who was stuck here. The brother everyone else had abandoned. But then Alex had gone and abandoned Hayden, and that had to have been brutal. "I imagine it must've been very hard for Hayden." Bex rushed to add, "For all of you," lest Emily think she had a special interest in Hayden. She *did*, but she didn't need to advertise that.

"It was difficult for everyone in different ways." She frowned. "I just wish he wasn't staying there. Everyone else has come home, and now he wants to stay away?" After a pause, Emily shifted on her stool, turning toward Bex. "I hope you won't find me overly intrusive, and of course, you don't need to answer, but can I ask why you left exactly? It seemed to happen so quickly, and Hayden wouldn't say much."

Bex's insides twisted into tight, painful knots. She and Hayden had made a pact to not tell anyone about the baby, and for her part, she never had. Apparently Hayden had done the same. Still, that hadn't been the only reason for their breakup. "We were just immature, and we wanted different things. I wanted to see what the world had to offer away from Ribbon Ridge, and Hayden didn't want to leave." She smiled. "I was young and silly." And she'd thought ultimatums would net the right result. She'd been wrong.

Emily seemed to hesitate before saying, "I always wondered…That is, I wondered if we maybe drove you away. I imagine we're a bit intense, especially for someone with your background."

Her insightfulness carved a wedge into Bex's heart, making her feel more vulnerable than she had in years.

Maybe in forever. And she wasn't sure she wanted that—
not with these people anyway. They weren't her family,
and they never would be. "Like I said, I was young and
silly. You all might've been a little scary, but with more
maturity, I think I would've handled it better." Crap,
what the hell did that mean? She immediately wished she
could take those confusing words back. She was making it sound like she'd handled it *badly* when she'd really
done the only thing she'd known how to do—deal with
her pain alone.

Emily seemed to brighten. "Does that mean you'd
change things if you could go back? Maybe you and
Hayden would still be together."

Whoa, was she hoping they'd reconcile? Bex wouldn't
have thought that was possible, hadn't even entertained the
idea. But now that she was back and her feelings for him
had apparently only gone dormant instead of disappearing
entirely, maybe she *could* think about it. "I don't know." She
did *not* want to get this kind woman's hopes up, if she did
in fact have hope, and it sounded as if she did. "It doesn't
really matter since I *can't* go back. None of us can."

"I know." Emily stood up and took her bowl around
the island to rinse it before putting it in the dishwasher.
She looked over at Bex with a sad smile. "I'd always
hoped you and he would find your way back together.
You seemed so happy."

They *had* been happy. Until Bex had messed everything up by wanting to get away from Ribbon Ridge with
him. The need to be away from his family—to have him
to herself—had felt so important. Now, in hindsight, it

seemed immature and selfish. Bex's chest felt hollow. She didn't know what to say, so she said nothing.

Emily wiped her hands on a dishtowel. "I will gladly settle for having you back here in our lives. I hope you know how much we all love you, Bex. You'll always be an extended part of our family."

Emotion scalded the back of Bex's throat. She took a long drink of lemonade to ease the ache. "Thank you." She didn't deserve that at all, but she'd accept the sentiment anyway.

"I'm off to read for a bit," Emily said. "Good night!"

Bex watched her go then finished her dinner and put her dishes away. She set the dishwasher to RUN and made her way upstairs. As she touched the doorknob to her room, she heard a click down the hall and turned her head. Hayden appeared in the hallway, dressed in athletic shorts and an OSU T-shirt, his hair wet from the shower. It could've been eight years ago at his apartment in college, the first time she'd spent the night with him. He'd showered and put on one of his favorite college tees. Not the one he was wearing now, but the image was almost identical.

Except it wasn't eight years ago. He was different now. The angles of his face were harder, the length of his hair shorter, the breadth of his shoulders wider. He exuded a magnetism and a confidence she'd never sensed in him before. It was unbelievably sexy and literally made her weak in the knees.

She wondered if she could slip into her room without him noticing her. Ha, right. He was looking straight at her. She couldn't have moved if she wanted to.

Chapter Seven

HAYDEN STOPPED SHORT as he walked out of his room. Bex stood in the middle of the hallway wearing Bermuda-length ripstop shorts and a yellow T-shirt sporting a beer logo. Her dark hair was swept into a ponytail while her pale green eyes stared at him, unblinking.

He swallowed the compliment that sprang to his lips. What good could come of him telling her she looked amazing? "Are you just getting in?" he called down the hallway.

She smiled. "Your mother asked me the same thing."

He walked toward her. "She did?"

"We had dinner together downstairs. Rather, I had dinner and she had ice cream."

"Mmm, ice cream sounds pretty good. I was just going to head down for a snack."

He wondered what they'd talked about, but decided he was better off not knowing in case it was him. There was something unsettling about being the topic of conversation between your mother and ex-girlfriend.

"You start at the brewhouse today?" he asked. He'd spent the day on a variety of errands and on starting the process of selling his house to Kyle and Maggie. They'd offered to give him back the entire contents, but he didn't want most of it back. He wanted his wine collection and a few odds and ends, but they could keep the furniture and décor. He idly wondered if he should ask Bex if she wanted any of it, but figured she'd already taken what little she'd wanted when she'd left.

She nodded in answer to his question. "Just getting organized and stuff. I can hardly wait to start brewing tomorrow. I imagine you feel the same way about getting back to France and making wine."

He *had* been, but since last night's dinner with Cam and his brothers he'd been thinking more and more about starting a winery with them.

She put her hands behind her back and leaned against the doorframe. "What are you up to while you're home?"

"Not much, really." It was strange to be here and not have work to do. Kyle had taken over his job as COO at Archer until last month when he'd relinquished his duties so he could focus on The Arch and Fox and his burgeoning reality show chef career. "Tomorrow I'm heading up to The Alex. Next week I'll probably spend some time at Archer Enterprises to see what's up with the transition. You heard all about that, right?"

"I think so. Your dad's splitting the brewing into a separate company now that he's going to bottle, and Derek's running that, right?"

"Yeah. Dad says he's going to semiretire."

She tipped her head to the side and her ponytail grazed her shoulder. "You don't believe him?"

Hayden shrugged. "I think he wants to do that, but we'll see if he can. He's pretty passionate about his beer."

She smiled, revealing the dimples he'd loved so much. "I know. But this will free him up to actually brew more, especially here at home."

Dad had an incredible microbrewery on the ground floor, which he kept pretty busy with home brew. "Yeah, just when I think he can't possibly come up with new varieties, he does."

"Isn't it the same way with wine? Can't you think of a thousand ways to blend it?"

He blew out a breath. "I don't know about a thousand, but a lot, yeah."

"I'm so happy for you, that you've found your place."

Did she mean his place was halfway around the world while everyone else, including her, called Ribbon Ridge home? That was absurd. She meant he'd found his calling. Or something like that.

"Thanks," he said. "You, too. Funny that it's back here in Ribbon Ridge, though, right?"

"Yeah. The timing was just right, I guess. Everyone's been so welcoming." She gave him a look that seemed to hint at gratitude, as if to thank him for being cool with it, too.

And he was cool with it. In fact, this conversation was surprisingly normal for a couple with their history. It felt good to be able to do this. It meant he really was over her.

"It's different, isn't it?" he asked. "Everyone's married or getting married. Weird."

She laughed softly, and the sound heated dormant places inside him. Places he chose to ignore just now. "Is it weird?"

"Totally. I was the Ribbon Ridge guy with the live-in girlfriend. And now it's like Opposite Land."

Her laugh was stronger this time. "You're right. On all counts. I can't believe Liam's engaged or that Evan's going to be a dad." She gave her head a quick shake. "He and Alaina are the craziest pairing. If you'd told me he would end up with a famous actress, I would've bet my annual salary against it."

Now he chuckled. "No kidding. On paper they make absolutely no sense, but in reality, they're perfect for each other."

"I guess you just never know what will stick and what won't." Their gazes connected for a moment, and he knew she was thinking the same thing he was—they were supposed to stick. That was something everyone would've bet on. Yet, they'd fallen apart.

"Sean told me he might film you brewing. Has he talked to you about that?"

"Very briefly. We're going to talk more about it after the wedding." She looked down at the carpet and drew a shape with her big toe. "I'm not sure if I want to be on film. It's a little strange, right?"

"Yes, and I speak from experience."

Her lips curved into a smile, and once again her outrageously cute dimples peeked out. "Of course you do. If I decide to do it, do you have any tips?"

He thought back to the show they'd done as kids—*Seven is Enough.* The show had focused on the sextuplets, but Hayden had made them the seven. That he'd come as a surprise after his parents had undergone so many fertility treatments had been a recurring theme. As if he could ever forget that he wasn't one of the core six, the ones his parents had wanted more than anything. It wasn't that they purposely made him feel left out, he just *was.* "I don't think I can tell you anything helpful, sorry. Just hit your mark."

She looked at him in confusion.

"When they tell you where to stand for the camera shot, be sure to get it right or they'll have to shoot it again. That can make them cranky." At least that had been his experience. "Ask Kyle about it—he was always the star of the show, and look at him now."

She nodded. "Good idea."

They fell silent, and Hayden figured they'd run out of safe, mundane topics. Time to go before he said something stupid like, "What did you and my mom talk about over dinner?"

She pushed away from the doorframe. "I'm going to hit the shower and then maybe watch an episode of *Sherlock.* I just started it recently, and it's very addictive. Do you watch it?"

He shook his head. "I have, but not in a long time. I haven't been watching much TV the past year. Too busy."

"I can imagine. It must be cool to experience another culture like that. How's your French?"

He grinned at her. *"Trés bon."*

"Now, that's sexy." She sounded playful, joking, but there was something in her gaze that rekindled a desire he preferred to suppress.

And just like that they were on the edge of the danger zone. This shouldn't be possible. She'd dumped him and never looked back. He'd finally moved on. What was this—residual attraction?

"Enjoy your show. Maybe I'll see you tomorrow." He turned and headed for the back stairs.

Knowing she was a short walk from his bedroom gave him all sorts of inappropriate ideas. So he wasn't in a committed relationship. That didn't mean he wanted to take up with the woman who'd broken his heart.

He frowned, growing angry with himself for forgetting, even for fifteen minutes, what she'd put him through. He walked into the kitchen and poured a beer.

He exhaled and let his ire fade. It wasn't fair of him to put all the blame on her. He'd caused that damn accident, and if he hadn't, she never would've left. The baby would've kept them together. Maybe. But then Hayden wouldn't be where he was today, making wine, following his own path.

He just wished he knew where that path was leading. Fantasizing about that winery with the Westcotts had made him second-guess his desire to stay in France. He'd spent the evening researching winemaking facilities and thinking about how a year from now he could be watching his first vintage grow fat on the vine.

It was tempting as hell. Just like the woman upstairs.

BEX'S FIRST BATCH of beer for the day, an IPA, was already in the fermentation tank. Next up, she planned to make a blonde ale and add some loganberry puree.

Last night's almost-platonic conversation with Hayden had made her feel good about taking this job, especially after talking with Emily, who clearly hoped she and Hayden still had a chance. But they didn't. As soon as things had gotten the teensiest bit flirty—thanks to her inability to keep her mouth shut after he'd spoken French—he'd bailed. Who knew two little words uttered in a foreign language could be so unbelievably sexy? It wasn't like *he'd* said anything flirty. Her French was practically nonexistent, but she knew he'd just said, "very good." As in he'd learned to speak French quite well.

Even though she'd only heard him say two words, she didn't doubt his skill for a second. One thing about Hayden, when he put himself into something, he went all in—heart and soul.

How had she turned her back on that? More important, why?

Because she'd been young and shortsighted and emotionally stunted. Hopefully she was making progress on the latter. Her conversation with Emily had shown her that she was at least more open to a closer relationship, not that she ought to pursue that with her ex's family.

Bex hefted the bag of barley to carry it to the mash tun. It was heavy and bulky, and she adjusted her hold to lift it higher. But it was too much and she dropped it, splitting the bag so that barley scattered all over the floor.

She put her hands on her hips and stared at the mess all over her gorgeous brewery floor. "Hell's bells."

Laughter reached her ears, and she recognized it immediately. She mock-glared at him over the mash tun. "Hayden, are you laughing at me?"

He walked toward her, his expression amused. "You still say that."

She was momentarily confused then realized what he meant. *Hell's bells.* She'd said it her whole life. She'd heard it somewhere and decided to try it out at school one day. Her kindergarten teacher hadn't been impressed, but when she'd called Bex's parents to inform them of their daughter's misconduct, they'd found it cute. From then on, she'd had permission to say pretty much anything she wanted at home. It was one of the many ways in which they'd allowed Bex to steer her own ship.

"Of course I do. It's my signature phrase."

He chuckled and looked around at the barley littering the floor. "What happened here?"

"I'm trying a new decorative scheme. You don't like it?"

He laughed again. "No, it's great. But since you're making beer, you should add some hops."

She couldn't keep from smiling anymore. "Good idea."

His eyes glinted with humor as he looked at her. "You want some help cleaning this up?"

"Sure, but I don't want to interrupt whatever you're doing."

"You're not interrupting anything. I was just helping Kyle with the wine cellar. The sommelier he hired decided to take a different job, so Kyle's scrambling."

That must've been the reason for Kyle's yelling that morning. The door to the corridor leading to the kitchen had been open, and she'd heard him swearing. "Good thing you're here—at least for a while." She went to the corner and took a broom from a hook then handed it to him.

He started sweeping. "Yeah, it feels good to be needed."

Did he not feel needed? She knew he often felt like the odd man out in his crazy family. He'd opened up to her about it on several occasions, but it always seemed as if he held something back. Every time, he'd ended the conversation saying he was just being oversensitive or that it wasn't really that big of a deal. Looking back, she probably should've pressed him about it, but she'd been the last person who would've asked for more details, especially of the emotional variety.

Bex grabbed a second broom. "You kept the home fires burning for years while they were all gone. Of course they need you."

He moved around the mash tun as he swept. "Eh, I don't know. When I left for France, they managed to make do."

She didn't quite believe him. "Wait, Kyle took over for you as COO. He can't have just stepped into that job."

"He had to, but yeah, I gave him a long-distance hand."

Bex concentrated on sweeping the outliers toward Hayden's pile. "Sounds like you were needed to me."

"I was, but he picked things up pretty quickly. I've just missed being a part of The Alex." He paused to look at her. "But I knew moving to France would take me out of it. I can't regret that decision." He went back to sweeping.

She wanted to say something about not having regrets and about making tough decisions, but knew it would sound like she was justifying why she'd left five years ago. Best to leave that alone. "No regrets is a good policy."

He cast her a quick look, maybe trying to determine if she had regrets. Before coming back to Ribbon Ridge, she would've said she didn't—well, very few—but now she'd have a different answer. No, that was stupid. She couldn't regret the choices she'd made because they'd all led her to right here. And she was exactly where she wanted to be: sweeping up barley from the floor of her brewery.

"This good enough?" he asked, sweeping the last of it into a pile.

She grabbed a dustpan and knelt while he swept it into the pan. "Looks great."

When it was full, he looked around. "Garbage?"

She nodded toward the corner. "Over there."

He went and brought the can over for her to dump the dustpan. Then he grabbed the broom and swept more into the pan. They did this several times until the floor was clean.

He scooted the garbage can back to the corner. "So I guess you have to start over?"

She hung up the broom and dustpan. "Just that part, so while it's a loss of ingredients, it's fixable. Not like if you lost a bunch of grapes."

"Yeah, that would be catastrophic. Or not. If the wine turned out to be really good and the quantity was lower, we could just charge more."

She smiled over at him. "Good point."

"You want help with this?" he asked, looking around the brewery.

She cocked her head to the side. "I don't know. A winemaker in a brewery?"

He rolled his eyes. "Do you know how many batches of beer I've brewed? My siblings and I were home brewing our own stuff at fifteen."

She'd known that of course. "I always wondered why none of you wanted to take over for your dad."

"For a while, we thought Liam might, but he was bored with it by the time we were out of high school. He likes negotiating too much. He probably should've been a lawyer. Except I think he makes more money from real estate."

"And now he's marrying a lawyer, so he can still armchair quarterback."

"Ha! Somehow, I doubt Aubrey will put up with that. It's one thing for him to provide input when we were fighting the zoning appeal, but I think she'd probably give him the smackdown any other time."

Bex laughed. "The fact that any woman can give Liam the smackdown is awesome."

"Right? When Kyle turned out to be such a good cook, Dad asked if he wanted to brew instead of go to culinary school. Kyle said he'd think about it while he started classes, but I'm pretty sure the chef bug bit him hard and fast. Beer didn't stand a chance."

Bex shook her head. "Your poor dad."

His eyes glinted with humor. "Why do you think he was so excited when we were dating? You were his only hope."

She laughed but then felt a pang of that nasty emotion again—regret.

"Sorry, I didn't say that to make you feel bad."

"I know you didn't. It's fine." She went over to the stack of barley-filled bags. "You really want to help?"

He followed her. "I offered, didn't I?"

Yes, and in her experience, he was a man of his word. "I had trouble carrying this bag over to the hopper."

He picked the top one off the pile and hefted it. "Too heavy?"

"Too awkward."

He carried it over to the mill on the mash tun, where she opened the corner of the bag, and he poured it in. "What are you going to do when I'm not around?"

Feel bereft? Be eaten alive with regret? She was beginning to hate that word and decided to try to banish it from her vocabulary.

She turned the mill on. "I'll figure it out, don't worry."

"I never worry about you, Bex. If there was a woman who didn't need anyone, it's you."

He had to mean that as a compliment, right? Except he knew her better than maybe anybody, and one of their points of conflict had been her acute independence. "I need people," she said, sounding kind of lame.

"I didn't mean that in a bad way, you know."

She took the empty bag to the garbage. "I know." It was still nice for him to clarify that. "But I get what you're saying. I've mellowed a bit in the past five years. I'm more likely to ask for help than I was."

He laughed softly. "I find that surprising, but I guess we all change. I figured you had to have changed to come back here. You were so gung-ho to leave."

Did he really want to go there? She supposed they had to at some point, but they could keep things pleasant and reflective. It would be good for their friendship. "I was, and I won't say I didn't have second thoughts about coming back now. So far, though, it seems to be the right decision." Did he hear the uncertainty in her voice? She hoped not.

"I'm glad. I hope I've made the right decision for me."

Her pulse quickened at the thought of him staying. How in the hell would she manage her inconvenient feelings then? "About going back to France?" She thought of Emily and how thrilled she'd be to hear that he was having second thoughts.

He hesitated. "Not really. It's just my family. They'd like me to stay. And I *have* missed them."

"Your mom would be ecstatic if you decided to stay." *And I wouldn't mind either.*

"I should head out," Hayden said, ignoring her comment. "I'm meeting my dad for lunch over at Archer, and I need to swing into town to pick up sandwiches from Barley and Bran. Have you been back there yet? They have new owners since you were in town."

"Yeah, I went there on my first day to have lunch, and I was so disappointed that their menu was different." She laughed. "My bad for expecting that nothing would change in five years."

And here she was five years older, feeling the same attraction toward this man. Only it wasn't the same. There was something different about this. Something she longed to explore, thinking it could be deeper and better than what they'd had before. But she wouldn't. Not unless he put up a flashing bright green light. Somehow she didn't see that happening, especially since he wouldn't even be on the same continent.

Chapter Eight

AFTER HAVING LUNCH with his dad, Hayden went back up to The Alex to continue helping Kyle set up his wine cellar. He saw Bex's truck parked outside the brewhouse and considered walking in that way.

But why? He could walk in through the main entrance of the restaurant or the back way next to Kyle's office. There was absolutely no need for him to enter Bex's sphere twice in one day, and he shouldn't want to.

Shaking his head, and hopefully clearing it of thoughts of her, he walked into the restaurant and beelined back to the kitchen where Kyle and his staff were working on a test meal. They'd been practicing the past week to prepare for Friday's rehearsal dinner, which would be held here.

"What's cooking?" Hayden asked.

Kyle looked up from the fish he was filleting. "Salmon. It's our last practice before we do a run-through tomorrow night."

That was Thursday, the day before the rehearsal. "You're making the same meal two nights in a row?"

"Three, actually. The staff's families are coming up tomorrow night to be our guinea pigs, and then we'll serve it for real at the rehearsal dinner." He finished up with the fish and nodded at one of his employees to come and take over. He went to wash his hands. "Thanks for coming back. That shipment came in while you were gone." He'd been expecting several cases of wine from a distributor, and Hayden was going to inventory and stock them.

Hayden nodded. "Sure thing. Gives me something to do."

Kyle wiped his hands and laughed. "Like you wouldn't be up to your eyeballs in work over at Archer Enterprises if you wanted to be. Just say the word and anyone in this family would put you to work."

Hayden had always jumped in to help. When he'd been the only one to stay in Ribbon Ridge after college, he'd wondered if he was alone in feeling a responsibility to the family business. "Probably true."

"Come on, I'll walk down with you for a bit." Kyle led him down the stairs to where the passageway led to Archetype. They'd use it to deliver food from the kitchen to the small pub.

Hayden followed him into the wine cellar, which Dylan had converted from a root cellar, enlarging the space and installing floor to ceiling racks as well as a temperature control system. They'd inventoried and stocked several cases already that morning, and after Hayden finished with the shipment, he'd determine what else they needed to fill in the blanks. He already knew there was only one sparkling variety, and they'd need more than that to call themselves a respectable restaurant.

The cases were stacked in various towers around the room. There was a worktable in the middle, on which sat the laptop they were using to log the bottles. Hayden opened the first case and whistled. "Nicely done." It was a set of library vintages from a local winery. Kyle had to have called in a favor to get them.

Kyle went to the table and opened the laptop. "Thanks. I've been working all angles. You can thank Cam for that batch. He knows everybody."

He did, and damn that would be an excellent asset for their not-happening-right-now winery. "Cam is very good at what he does."

"True dat. I'm ready whenever you are," Kyle said.

Hayden did what they'd done earlier that day—he read out the winery, variety, vintage, and any tasting notes he could recall. He'd tasted a lot of this wine, but not all of it. He'd have to look some up later. Or tomorrow.

When they'd finished logging the case, which held three different wines, Hayden went about finding the appropriate location to store it then reported it to Kyle, who noted it in the program. Each slot in the rack had a specific address so they could find and pull the wines easily.

"I really appreciate you helping me out like this," Kyle said. "Once again, you are the lifesaver."

Hayden finished putting the bottles away and went to open the next case, which held just one kind of pinot noir. "Is that how you all see me?"

Kyle chuckled. "I don't know. You've just always been responsible."

"So's Liam, and you don't call him that."

"Hell no, he was way too self-involved for too long—not like you. You've always looked out for everyone." He looked up at Hayden and blinked. "Why do you think you're the most well-liked?"

Hayden laughed. "Is that it? You don't think it was selfish of me to bail on The Alex when I did?"

"I can't speak for anyone else, but I didn't think so. But then I'm the last person to fault anyone for getting out of Dodge." He was referring to his own departure several years ago, following a nasty situation in which he'd gotten in over his head with his gambling. Derek had found out and told their father, who'd paid off Kyle's bookie. Kyle had been pissed at Derek for breaking their confidence, and it had taken years for them to patch things up.

"Anyway," Kyle continued, "leaving when you did was good for you. Wasn't it?"

"Yes." For so many reasons. Dealing with Alex's death, getting over Bex, allowing himself to be exactly what Kyle said he wasn't: selfish. But was pursuing your dreams selfish? It didn't feel that way, but he'd blamed all of his siblings for being just that after they'd done the same thing.

Maybe he'd been too harsh. Or immature. Or both. It was nice to know they didn't think badly of him—or at least Kyle didn't. "I have to admit I wondered why no one else felt a responsibility to stay here like I did. Maybe I'm just weird."

Kyle shook his head. "No way. I thought about it—briefly—but I wanted to cook."

"Didn't Dad offer you a job at one of the pubs before you went to Florida?"

Kyle cleared his throat. "Uh, yeah. I just needed to get away. Like I said, I'm the last person to burn anyone for needing to leave. I was a mess back then, Hayden. I'm only slightly less of a disaster now."

"That is not true!" Maggie declared as she came into the wine cellar. She went directly to Kyle and kissed his cheek. "You're not a disaster. Maybe a small nuisance from time to time, but totally manageable."

Kyle grinned down at her, and their love and companionship filled the dim cellar, making Hayden feel like a third wheel.

"Hello?" Liam's voice echoed in the passageway. "I heard there's a party in here." He walked in with Aubrey, and it suddenly seemed it might be heading that way. He stopped to look at what Hayden was pulling out of the box. "Definitely a party. I love that pinot."

Aubrey peered over his shoulder, her chin nudging his shirt. "Yum, me too."

Liam picked a bottle up and took it over to the table where there was an opener. Glasses for tasting hung beneath the tabletop, and he reached down to grab a few.

"Hey, what are you doing?" Hayden asked, despite knowing precisely what his brother was doing. "We're in the middle of inventorying."

"So inventory this one out." Liam peeled the foil off then paused as he noticed Hayden staring at him. "What? You've got at least eleven more, right?"

"Yes. Fine. Whatever." Hayden wasn't used to his siblings—or at least Liam—interrupting his work.

"You good, brother?" Liam asked. "Didn't mean to overstep."

"No, it's good. It's just weird having you here."

Both Liam and Kyle laughed. "It is taking some getting used to," Kyle said.

Liam looked at Kyle as he pulled the cork from the bottle. "Like you being here isn't damned bizarre. Or the fact that you've managed to pull this restaurant together."

"And star on TV," Maggie put in. "Sorry, Liam, but you can't cast Kyle in the role of slacker anymore."

Liam poured out wine into five glasses. "Nope, I guess I can't." He held up his glass. "To my brother, the *former* slacker."

Kyle lifted his glass. "Gee, thanks. Next we'll drink to my brother, the current asshole."

This was met with laughter, including from Aubrey, who winked at her fiancé. "Sorry, babe, he's got you there."

Liam winced, but grinned nonetheless. "Ouch."

"What the hell's going on down here?" Dylan walked in and looked around. "Don't you people work?"

"Too damn much," Liam said. "But still not as much as you. I'd tell you to sit the hell down and drink with us, but there aren't any chairs." He poured another glass. "You can drink though. Here." He handed him the pinot.

"Dude, I just stopped in on my way over to Archetype. I have to finish installing the lighting."

Liam rolled his eyes. "*Dude*, you can take a fifteen-minute break. I'm pretty sure I'm your boss, so consider that an order."

Liam was the boss? Rather, *a* boss. Hayden supposed they were all "bosses" on this project. Was *he*? He had been before he'd left for France, but he felt completely disconnected, and he didn't like the sensation.

"I don't know, jackass," Dylan said. "The only guy down here who was around when I was hired was Hayden. I think he's more my boss than you."

Hayden couldn't help but smile, both at feeling included and at his future brother-in-law burning his most arrogant sibling.

"This is where you all are?" Tori asked as she walked into the cellar followed by Sara.

Damn, this really was turning into a party. A party in which everyone had a date except Hayden. And Tori, he realized. Except Sean took that moment to walk in.

"Who wants to know where we are?" Maggie asked, sipping her wine.

Sara shrugged. "I was just looking for my fabulous fiancé." She smiled at Dylan as she walked up to him and curled her arms around his waist. Dylan held her close for a moment and kissed her forehead. He whispered something to her, and Sara's smile broadened.

Hayden looked away. *Third-wheel status confirmed.*

"I think we need more wine," Liam said. "You cool with that, temporary sommelier?" he asked Hayden.

"Fine with me. It's not my restaurant." He looked over at Kyle, who waved a hand.

"I've got two more cases of this somewhere around here, so open away."

Hayden handed a second bottle to Liam, who pulled out more glasses. He stopped. "Wait, I shouldn't be opening this." He turned and moved to the side, making a grand gesture for Hayden to come forward. "You should do the honors."

Everyone was staring at him, and things had grown quiet. Hayden wasn't used to being the center of anything in this family. He went to the table and took the wine opener from Liam. "Thanks." He felt simultaneously happy to be singled out and odd to be the focus. He opened the wine and poured glasses for Tori, Sean, and Sara.

Conversation picked up again, and Hayden couldn't help but notice the couples all stood together. They were either very close to each other or touching in some way. Hayden had never felt more alone in his life. His siblings had all found happiness—love. And in the wake of Alex's death, Hayden had been excited to immerse himself in his new life in France, and he realized it had allowed him to bury everything else—Alex, Bex, his family, and this project that was really just an extension of Alex.

He liked being home, but it meant he couldn't bury anything anymore, especially with Bex living here. Going back to France ensured he could compartmentalize everything. He could leave all of these issues in Ribbon Ridge, where life seemed to be moving along quite well without him.

BEX DROVE INTO the mostly full lot outside The Arch and Fox for Sara and Dylan's rehearsal dinner. Plucking her small clutch purse from the console between her seats, she slid out of the cab and locked the truck before heading to the door of the restaurant.

She was immediately greeted by the hostess, whom she'd met the other day. "Hi, Lisa," Bex said as the door swept closed behind her. "This looks terrific."

Flowers and decorations in the wedding colors of sage green, pink, and navy adorned the interior, and the tables were organized in a special layout with the bride and groom sitting in front of the massive fireplace, which wasn't running tonight. Even though it was quite cool in here, a fire in mid-July would be silly.

"Thanks," Lisa said. "Come on in. Servers are circulating with appetizers, beer, and wine. If you'd like a cocktail, just head over to the bar."

Bex flashed her a smile. "Will do." A cocktail sounded good, so she headed to the bar where Miguel was pouring and chatting up a storm. He was going to be a fantastic bartender. They'd spent a good half hour discussing beer the day before, and Bex was stoked to work with him.

He grinned when he saw her. "Hey, Bex. What can I get you? I've got a great thing going with mojitos tonight." He winked at her.

"Sounds terrific, thanks."

Sara came toward her and gave her a quick hug. "Thanks for coming!"

"I wouldn't miss it. Thanks for letting me crash. The rehearsal was beautiful." Bex had watched them practice the ceremony in the backyard before coming over. All the tents and tables and chairs were set, the decorations in place; all they needed was the day to dawn.

Sara smiled. "You are not crashing at *all*. I'm honored you could be here with me. Sit wherever you like. I'm not a fan of assigned places." She gave Bex's arm a rub before moving on to welcome the next guest. Dylan was nearby, talking with one of the Archer cousins. Blake Archer, Rob's brother's son, was also staying at the house. Bex had eaten dinner with him and his sister, Laurel, last night. Neither lived in Ribbon Ridge, but said they never ruled out a return. Ribbon Ridge, it seemed, had a pull on all of them.

"Here you go." Miguel slid the mojito over to her. "Enjoy!"

She picked up the glass and took a sip. Oh, this guy knew how to mix. "Fantastic. Careful, Miguel, or I'm going to need a designated driver."

He grinned in return. "The Archers have that covered, if necessary."

Of course they did. They thought of everything. Bex turned from the bar and was approached by one of the servers bearing a tray of lobster puffs. Bex helped herself and nearly moaned in delight. Kyle was a wicked chef.

Suddenly, people started moving to the tables to sit down. Nothing was announced, but Sara and Dylan sat, and everyone knew to follow suit.

Bex looked for the nearest table, which had six chairs, and found a seat. Cameron Westcott came up beside her. "Mind if I sit here?"

She glanced around, wondering if it meant Hayden would sit there too, but she didn't see him. "Sure."

A tall redhead walked up to the chair on Bex's other side, at the end of the table. "Is this seat available?"

Bex didn't know the woman, but that didn't matter. "Yes."

"Hey, Sabrina," Cameron said. "Do you know Bex Holmgren?"

Sabrina sat down and offered her hand to Bex. "No, we haven't met. Hi, I'm Sabrina Davies, Dylan's sister. Half-sister."

Bex knew the basics of Dylan's family. His parents had divorced when he was very young, and each had remarried and started new families. His dad and new wife had raised three boys—the Westcotts—while his mom and her husband had just one child, Sabrina. Sabrina and her folks lived in the nearby town of Newberg, while the Westcotts lived in Ribbon Ridge. Bex had met all three Westcott boys, and had gotten to know Cameron quite well since he was Hayden's best friend, but she'd never met Sabrina.

Bex shook the younger woman's hand. "It's nice to meet you. You're a snowboarder, right?"

She nodded, smiling. "Yep. Training for the X Games in January, and of course South Korea."

Bex recalled hearing that Sabrina had missed the last Olympics due to an injury. "How's that going?"

"Great. I'm training up on Mount Hood right now. Best summer skiing in the country."

Bex knew that of course. But she'd done all of her snow sports on Mount Bachelor since moving to Bend after her parents' divorce. She loved being outdoors, and Oregon's climate pretty much allowed her to be year-round. "Sounds awesome. I haven't gotten to ski or board as much as I'd like the past few years because of work."

"Come up to Palmer this summer," Sabrina offered enthusiastically. "It's a great time."

"I'd love to." But she was pretty sure she'd be too busy working. It would be hard enough to pull off the hike she wanted to do at the end of the month.

"Don't plan on keeping up with her," Cameron said. "I've tried. It's impossible. And I'm no slouch."

Bex remembered. She'd been skiing with him once before. She, Hayden, Cameron, and his then girlfriend had spent the weekend at the Archers' cabin on Mount Hood. Bex tried to recall Cameron's ex's name, but couldn't. She could see her short, dark hair and sassy smile—she'd been a lot of fun. Crap, now that she thought about it, they'd broken up not long after that ski trip, and it had been messy. Messier than hers and Hayden's, in fact. She decided not to mention that trip.

Tables started to fill up. Liam and Aubrey took the two seats on the other side of the table, which left one lone chair at the other end, between Cameron and Liam. Naturally, it was Hayden who appeared behind it. He looked extra sexy tonight in a French blue button-down shirt with the sleeves rolled to midforearm and crisp khakis. "Looks like this is my seat."

Bex glanced around, and it did appear as if there weren't any others available. Her pulse sped a little faster at the prospect of having dinner with him, which was dumb. Nevertheless, she seemed unable to quell her excitement, interest, awareness...whatever it was that she felt when he was near.

Cameron picked up his beer to take a drink. "Have a seat, bro."

Dylan stood and thanked everyone for coming then encouraged the group to enjoy Kyle's delicious food. Servers appeared and began distributing salads. Bex took a drink of her mojito as their table was served.

"Looks good," Liam said. "But then I expected nothing less from Kyle."

Everyone dug in for a moment, and there seemed to be a collective sigh followed by a stream of compliments. Bex could hardly wait to add her contribution to the menu here.

As if he'd read her mind, Cameron asked, "So, you're making the beer here now?"

"Monday morning. I can't wait to get started."

"How long does that take?" Sabrina asked between bites of salad. "I mean, what's the time frame on brewing the beer?"

"It depends on whether it's an ale or a lager—ales ferment at a higher temperature and finish faster. Lagers are made cooler and take a bit longer." Bex purposely kept her description basic. She could delve into an hour-long lecture about brewing, but this wasn't the appropriate venue. "Ales can be done in under two weeks."

Aubrey had listened to her intently and now asked, "How many varieties do you think you'll have for the opening?"

Bex had spoken to Rob about which beers would be brewed down at The Arch and Vine and trucked up here and which ones she'd brew on site. "I'm going to get Crossbow, Longbow, and Shaft from The Arch and Vine because they have a larger facility. Plus, as long as they're making it, they might as well brew enough for us. I'll make some of the other Archer varieties up here—Robin Hood, Arrowhead, Will Scarlett, Feather, and seasonals."

"But you're making something special for the opening, right?" Hayden asked, sparking a thrill in her belly.

She'd seen him only in passing since he'd helped her out in the brewhouse the other day. "I am."

Hayden had his right hand wrapped around the base of his pint glass. Her eye went to his right ring finger. It was now bare, but once he'd worn a silver band she'd given him on their first anniversary. It hadn't really carried any sentimental meaning. He'd mentioned once that he might like to wear a ring, so she'd bought him one. She had no idea what had happened to it and wondered if he'd thrown it away after she'd left. Whereas she still had the arrow necklace he'd given her on their second Christmas together as well as the gold and opal bracelet from when they'd moved in together—not that she'd dare wear them. She'd considered selling them a time or two, but could never seem to part with them.

Hayden's lips curved into a half-smile, and she was glad her reaction was completely internal. At least she hoped it was. He was as attractive as ever, maybe even more now. He had a different air about him, something very masculine and incredibly sexy. "Are you going to tell us, or is it a surprise?"

What had they been talking about? Her beer, right. "I'm not quite ready to share, but I have a few recipes I'll be cooking up."

Liam laid his hand against his chest and arched a brow at her. "May I present myself as a tasting guinea pig?" He grinned before touching his fiancée's shoulder. "I think Aubrey would probably like to volunteer, too."

Aubrey nodded vigorously. "Absolutely. Just tell me when and where."

Bex laughed. "You got it."

"No fair," Sabrina said. "I'll be back on Mount Hood."

"Well, that's closer than France," Cameron said, casting a look at Hayden. "Bex, I'll also throw my hat in the ring for tasting help."

"Thanks." She glanced at Hayden. "Hayden, you're welcome to taste too—you're staying through the soft open, right?"

He nodded. "Yep."

Almost three weeks. She could bury her reemerging feelings for three weeks.

Sabrina took a sip of her wine and set the glass back on the table. "Hey, Liam, I invited Bex to come up to Palmer this summer. You should come, too. No heli-skiing though." She flashed him a teasing grin.

Bex was confused for a moment then recalled that Liam had been injured in a heli-skiing accident last winter. He was a total adrenaline junkie. She'd always wanted to go skydiving with him. Maybe now she could since they were both living in Ribbon Ridge.

Aubrey put her arm around Liam. "Ha! I don't think so. Liam's cut back on his thrill seeking by half."

Liam turned a grin on her. "Had to. I've got plenty of thrills right here." The look they exchanged was hotter than the asphalt in the parking lot this afternoon. Bex felt a pang of envy.

Cameron coughed, and it sounded suspiciously like, "Get a room." This was met with laughter, especially from Liam and Aubrey.

The servers picked up their salad dishes and quickly brought out the main course after obtaining everyone's preferences. They had to choose between a mushroom gnocchi, salmon with prosciutto butter, and pork with gorgonzola polenta. Bex had a hard time deciding, but ultimately went with the salmon. She consoled herself with the fact that she'd eventually taste everything on the menu—assuming these dishes made it past tonight's trial.

Aubrey tasted her pork and closed her eyes. "Oh my God, this is amazing. Liam, I hate to admit this, but I'm only with you because your brother makes such fantastic food."

"I think I'm going to marry this salmon," Bex said. Marry? Really? She flicked a glance at Hayden, but he was busy eating his pork.

Liam swiped a napkin over his lips. "So Bex, Tori tells me you've become quite the hiker in the past few years. What are you up to this summer? Maybe Aubrey and

I could tag along. We decided that's an activity we can both enjoy, since she sort of hates the idea of flinging herself out of a plane."

"I'd love to do that," Bex said. "I'll take you guys hiking if you take me on a jump."

"Deal."

Hayden looked at his brother. "Yeah, I heard you took Kyle, Derek, and Sean. I feel kind of left out."

"I'll take you up tomorrow, just say the word."

Aubrey gently elbowed Liam. "Duh, your sister's getting married tomorrow."

Liam winked at the table at large. "Right. Not tomorrow then." He leaned toward Hayden and stage-whispered. "Sunday's good."

Hayden chuckled at Liam. "I'll think about that."

Liam flicked a questioning glance toward Bex, nonverbally asking if she was in for Sunday, but she didn't say anything. Going skydiving with Hayden seemed like a bad idea, given this crush she seemed to have going. Crush? Were they twelve?

Liam swallowed a bite of salmon before asking, "Bex, what do you recommend for our first hike?"

"Depends on what you're up for. I'm going to do Slide Mountain, that's west of McMinnville, at the end of the month if I can squeeze it in."

Liam looked at Aubrey, who lifted a shoulder in response. They seemed to have a conversation without saying a word. Liam smiled at Bex. "Would you mind if we joined you?"

Bex preferred to go with a group. "Not at all."

"Is there a place to camp?" Aubrey asked. "We could make it an overnight."

Bex had researched the hike, and it seemed there was a primitive site with a fire ring, but nothing else. "Yes, but we'll have to pack everything we need, including water, tents, *everything*." She was prepared for that, but didn't know if they would be. Who was she kidding? If anyone was ready for that, it would be Liam Archer.

"If it's warm enough, we may not even need tents," Liam said. "Might be fun to just sleep under the stars."

"Well, now I might have to come down off the mountain for this!" Sabrina said.

Cameron nodded in agreement. "Yeah, this might need to be a group excursion."

Hayden cleared his throat. "I hate to be Debbie Downer, but that's right before the soft open here. Will there really be time for an overnight camping trip?"

Liam flashed him a smile. "Listen to you, being all responsible. I think we can manage. It'll be good for us to get away before the craziness really starts anyway. Besides, isn't this supposed to be your vacation? So far we've put you to work! You need to have some fun, too."

"An excellent point," Cameron said, glancing toward Hayden. "You deserve a weekend of fun with your family and friends. And anyway, I have no problem going at the end of the month." He winked at Bex.

If she'd been anyone else, she might've thought that Cameron was flirting with her. But there was no way he'd do that with his best friend's ex, even though they'd broken up five years ago.

Bex finished the rest of her mojito and decided to have one more. "Be right back. I need a refill." She stood and turned toward the bar.

Cameron joined her a moment later with his empty pint glass. "I needed another, too."

Bex looked back toward the table. The others were engaged in conversation. Hayden laughed at something Liam said. Did he suddenly look more relaxed now that Bex had left, or was that her ridiculous imagination seeing things that simply didn't exist?

"Uh-oh."

Startled by Cameron's utterance, Bex turned her head to look at him. "What?"

He studied her for a moment. "Nothing." He nodded toward Miguel. "Another pint of Robin Hood, please. And she'll have another mojito."

Miguel smiled at Bex. "Glad you liked it." He went to take care of their drinks, leaving them alone.

Bex stared at Cameron. Why had he said "uh-oh?" She'd been looking at Hayden…Did he see something she'd been hoping to conceal? Gah, no! There was nothing. Just a haunting sense of nostalgia about a relationship that was long dead.

Cameron rested his hand on the bar and gave her a sidelong look. "I don't know if you're aware of this, but Hayden was hung up on you for a long time."

Bex's insides curled. He'd been devastated when she'd left. But she hadn't been able to stay after losing the baby. Factor that in with Hayden's guilt and disappointment and his family's overwhelming closeness, and Bex had packed up and left within a week. It hadn't been easy. She'd still loved him on some level. But sometimes love wasn't enough.

Even so, knowing he'd carried a torch gave her a burst of hope. Maybe this could be more than an unrequited crush she was experiencing.

"What do you mean?" Bex asked softly. "How long?"

"Until Alex died, and he decided to go to France."

Shit. Almost four years. Bex had started dating less than a year after she'd left. She'd been trying to dull the memories and the pain, to move on. She inwardly flinched. "Why are you telling me this?"

He shrugged. "I figured it was something you should know since you're going to be living here. You don't need to *do* anything with that information, however—nothing needs to be discussed or resolved." His look seemed to ask if she understood.

She nodded.

"I just saw the way you were looking at him. Maybe I read it wrong, but you seemed...I don't know...*interested*." He looked her in the eye, and his gaze was full of compassion. "He's in a good place now. A great place. You have to give him his space. You have to let him go."

Oh, she'd let him go five years ago. But now, it seemed, she wanted him back.

Which was incredibly unfair to him. After everything he'd suffered—the guilt of driving the car when they'd slid off the road, losing the baby, her breaking up with him. She'd not only let him go, she'd pushed him away.

Miguel returned with their drinks. "Here you go!"

Cameron passed him a twenty. "I know we aren't supposed to tip you, but whatever. You're working your tail off, and I appreciate it."

Miguel chuckled and took the bill. "If you insist."

"I do."

Bex picked up her drink. "That was really cool."

Cameron tipped his head to the side. "I have my moments."

They walked back to the table, where the conversation had turned to issues surrounding the soft opening. Sabrina looked a bit bored, so Bex started to talk to her about training for the Olympic team. Thankfully, Bex became so immersed that she didn't think about what Cameron said.

It wasn't until much later, when she climbed into bed to go to sleep, that she began to doubt her decision to return to Ribbon Ridge.

Chapter Nine

HAYDEN STOOD WITH his brothers, sandwiched between Liam and Evan, as they posed for a picture around the groom. The ceremony had been absolutely gorgeous. Sara was a stunning bride, and Dylan was a thoroughly love-struck groom.

The photographer thanked them and moved on as the reception was just starting to get going. It was a warm evening, thankfully not quite as hot as the past few days, and the party would undoubtedly last into the wee hours.

He watched Derek and Kyle laugh at something one of them said and thought of Derek's wedding last summer. Hayden had come home from France to be Derek's best man. They'd become close over the past several years as they'd worked together at Archer and formed a friendship that went beyond the brotherly affection they'd developed when Derek had come to live when them.

Still, he and Kyle had been best friends since they were twelve—until their falling-out when Kyle had left town.

Hayden had understood why, when Derek and Kyle had patched things up just before the wedding, Derek had wanted Kyle to be his best man instead. Understanding, however, wasn't the same as being okay with it. And if he were honest with himself, he'd admit he'd felt like a runner-up, the placeholder until the real deal showed up.

Hayden shook away the old hurt. It didn't matter. He had his own best friend. Cameron had been there for him through thick and thin since first grade. All of Hayden's siblings shared a special one-on-one bond with each other: Liam and Alex, Kyle and Sara, Tori and Evan. He'd had to find his kindred spirit outside of the family. And he'd found it in Cameron. Then he'd found it in Bex.

Right away they'd bonded over their love of Harry Potter and beer. Their relationship had grown quickly from a close friendship to sexual intimacy. From the start, she'd always made him feel special and unique, like a valuable individual and not just one of a greater whole. That she'd been unimpressed by his family name or his role in a reality show when other girls had been typically starstruck had only added to her allure.

He stopped himself from looking for her amid the crowd. It was hard to avoid her since she was staying in the house, so he certainly didn't need to search her out now.

He'd seen her earlier, before the ceremony. Dressed in a pretty aqua dress with a flared skirt and strappy silver heels, she'd made his breath catch. But just for a moment. Did you ever stop finding your first love attractive?

He almost laughed at the thought. He'd thought her plenty awful when she'd left him. But angry and hurt as he'd been, he'd still loved her.

Finally, though, he could say he'd moved on. He exhaled and embraced a small sense of relief. Appreciating her good looks was fine. Emotional investment was not.

A clap on his shoulder made him turn. Liam inclined his head toward a server holding a tray of glasses filled with beer standing to his left. "You want a drink?"

Hayden picked a glass off the tray. "Sure. Thanks." He nodded at the server, who continued on.

Liam held up his glass and clacked it against Hayden's. "To everybody marrying off. Well, except you." He took a drink and Hayden did the same. "Kind of funny since everyone thought you'd be the first one."

Yep. But Hayden didn't want to talk about that. "This wedding beer is pretty damn good." Dad had crafted a light, wheat beer, perfect for a hot summer day.

"Agreed." Liam took another drink. "Is Bex being here weird for you?"

"Certainly no weirder than your ex-fuck-buddy trying to keep The Alex from opening because you dumped her."

Liam winced. "Yeah. That wasn't weird. That was completely messed up. I'm sensing you don't want to talk about Bex. That's cool. I just wanted you to know I'm here. You know...If you did want to talk."

What the hell? Hayden stared at his brother. "Since when did you become the caring big brother type?"

He shrugged. "I don't know. Blame Aubrey. She's softened me up."

Hayden laughed. He'd been home only a week, but he could see that Aubrey had completely transformed the arrogant playboy into a, frankly, rather pleasant, family-oriented dude. *That* was weird. "She's good for you, clearly."

"I'm a lucky son of a bitch." His gaze turned serious. "I mean it. If you ever need to talk—about what to do next or whatever—I'm here."

Hayden narrowed his eyes at Liam. "Did Mom put you up to this?"

Liam chuckled. "No, but I totally understand why you'd think that. Honestly, this is all me. I've been absent—and not just in the physical sense—for way too long. I missed my family. I'm only sorry it took me so long to realize it."

Huh. Well that was...unexpected. Or not. Even though they'd lived far apart, they'd managed to keep a tight bond, particularly the sextuplets. Is that what this was about? With Alex gone there was an opening in their club? Especially with Liam. His counterpart, or whatever you wanted to call it, was gone. Was Hayden his replacement?

Whether there was any truth to Hayden's thoughts was irrelevant. He needed a change of scenery. "Uh, thanks. See you later—I'm heading to the hors d'oeuvres tent." There were servers with trays, but there was also a central location so you could grab what you wanted.

Hayden found the canopy and went straight for the shrimp, which was being kept on ice. He loaded a plate with four tails and a dollop of cocktail sauce and moved to the edge of the canopy.

"Hayden!" His cousin Laurel approached, eyeing his plate. "Yum, shrimp. Hang on." She went and helped herself then joined him. "You guys sure know how to throw a party."

"Hey, I had nothing to do with it."

She grabbed a tail and dipped the meat into the sauce. "You know what I mean."

"I do. My family does everything big."

"No kidding. I still remember that insane birthday party that was filmed for the TV show. Carnival rides, ponies, craziness!"

Hayden remembered that, too. Along with everything else to do with the show. It had been surreal enough to have television crews filming at your house, but even more so when you realized they weren't really there for you. Hayden had figured that out partway through the first season when he'd been completely edited out of an episode. His parents had ensured it had never happened again, but Hayden had never forgotten that he was only along for the ride.

Laurel brushed her long hair back over her shoulder. "Man, I wish I'd worn this up. It's kind of muggy." She dipped another shrimp tail as she spoke in a low tone. "You hated that show, didn't you?"

He laughed. "*Hated* is a strong word. It wasn't my favorite thing. *Evan* hated it." With his Asperger's syndrome, he'd found the intrusiveness challenging. Hayden had always wondered if their folks had pulled the plug because Evan just couldn't take it anymore.

"I can imagine. You've been back in Ribbon Ridge for a bit now. How is it?"

He arched a brow at her. "You thinking of coming back?"

She shrugged. "You never know. It doesn't really feel like home for me. Not like I'm sure it does for you."

Leaving had been hard, and a part of him wasn't looking forward to doing it again. He'd enjoyed the past week—being back with his family and helping out, even if he did feel a little disconnected. They were all engaged and interwoven, part of the tapestry of Ribbon Ridge, while he was merely a visitor now. Still, he hadn't realized how much he missed his hometown. He loved the short drive to the beach, the smell of the spring rain, and the mist in the valley on fall mornings, which he wouldn't see if he went back to France in August.

If.

That little two-letter word blared through his brain. Somewhere over the past week he'd gone from taking the job in France to maybe not. Ever since he'd talked about it with the Westcott brothers, the lure of starting a winery had burrowed into his mind. But at the same time, he wasn't sure he fit in here right now, particularly with the presence of Bex.

A young woman, probably the same age as Laurel and Hayden, walked up to them.

Laurel greeted the new arrival. "Hi, Kayla, do you know Hayden Archer?"

Kayla shook her head. Average height, she had long, brown hair with blonde highlights, bright blue eyes and a great smile. She held out her hand to Hayden. "Nice to meet you."

"Kayla lives in Newberg," Laurel said. "We used to go to the same dance studio."

"Yep, and I lived across the street from the Davieses so I knew Dylan growing up."

"Cool."

She nodded and tipped her head in such a way that pinged Hayden's radar. She was exactly the kind of woman he'd normally dance with tonight and maybe hook up with later. That had been his life after Bex. Well, at first it had just been a solitary funk, but after nearly a year, he'd tried to date. That had resulted in a lot of first dates and some pretty meaningless sex. Not that meaningless sex was a bad thing when both parties were on board. Looking at her subtle body language, he sensed she'd be down for that.

Hayden finished his last shrimp, and his eye caught an aqua dress. Bex. She stood with a guy—he looked familiar, but Hayden couldn't quite place him—her face tilted up, eyes sparkling, lips curved into a smile. Then she laughed and touched his sleeve. Hayden had a ridiculous urge to throw the plate in his hand like a Frisbee and take the guy out.

Okay, he found her really, really attractive. He always had—and there was nothing wrong with that—but damn, she seemed even prettier now. There was something different about her—a maturity, a confidence, something he couldn't quite describe. But hadn't he just told himself that anything more than finding her attractive was bad news?

Hayden set his empty plate on one of the tables. "You guys want to get a beer?" He'd ditched his empty glass on the way over.

"Definitely," Kayla said, briefly lowering her lids in the universal language of flirtation.

Yes, focus on Kayla and ignore Bex. He glanced over and saw that Bex was laughing again. Once more, the urge to knock down the guy she was standing with swept through him. And once more, he chastised himself.

Surely, this…whatever it was…was only due to seeing her again after so long. There wasn't any emotional attachment between them now. When he was used to seeing her on a regular basis, the uneasiness—that's what he'd call it—would pass.

He arrived at the beverage tent with Laurel and Kayla, who were discussing what to drink. There was the special Archer beer and cider of course, plus a full bar, wine, and later there would be champagne.

Hayden opted for wine instead of the beer. They had a nice, cold pinot gris from a nearby winery, and that sounded pretty good right now. As he sipped the wine, he thought of what he'd do when he made his own. But when would that be? In France, he'd be making Antoine's wine.

If he opened up that fantasy winery here, he'd be able to make his own.

Except it was just that—a fantasy. Coming back here meant more than living in the same small town with the woman who'd broken his heart. It meant returning to the life where he'd never felt like the lead in his own movie.

Bex had been right. He'd needed to leave, as his siblings had, even if it meant he ultimately came back.

And he *would* come back. He just didn't think it could be right now. He had too many things to see and do. A voice in the back of his head added, *and maybe too much to prove.*

BEX WAS GLAD she didn't have to drive anywhere after this reception. She wasn't drunk, but she was a bit buzzed after beer and wine and finally champagne. The quantity of food she'd consumed helped maintain her equilibrium. A friend of Kyle's from culinary school had catered the event, and the food was just about as delicious as Kyle's.

It was good to have a moment's quiet. She'd been dancing for close to an hour and was happy to simply sit at the edge of the dance floor and watch. Or zone out. Or try not to look for Hayden. Because that had worked well for her today. It seemed everywhere she went, she couldn't help but see him. Standing with his brothers outside the beer tent. Chatting with Laurel and some knockout. Dancing with that knockout maybe a half hour ago. Where had they gone?

Ugh. That was absolutely none of her business.

She took another sip of water from the bottle she'd grabbed from one of the tubs stationed in the corners of the dance floor. The band was currently in the middle of a slow country song that had apparently been playing the night Sara and Dylan had first gotten together. Although they'd met in high school a decade earlier, they hadn't found love until after they'd encountered each other in a bar. Because that's how it was done, right?

Bex had met her post-Hayden boyfriends in a bar— brewpubs more specifically—because that's where she'd worked. She'd met Hayden at the college equivalent—a fraternity party.

She'd been a new transfer student at Oregon State, having spent two years in community college. She'd been eager to get out of Bend after Dad had started dating the She-Witch. She'd known a couple of people whom she'd gone to high school with, but had pretty much started over. The party flyer she'd been handed on her third day on campus had been just the invitation she'd needed. And Hayden, with his love for IPA and his lovably nerdy Gryffindor scarf, had caught her eye immediately.

The music changed to something faster, and Bex found herself swept onto the dance floor by Chloe, Aubrey, and Maggie. It was a Pink song, a rock anthem that demanded they sing along and stomp their feet. By the end, Bex was panting and laughing and wishing she'd worn different shoes. The silver sandals were super cute and went great with the dress, but after a hot night of dancing, they were like little torture chambers.

"Dude, I need to lose my shoes." Maggie giggled. "I just made an inadvertent rhyme!"

Bex was not the only person flying a little high tonight. "Me too. Can we?"

"Why not?" Maggie asked. "Especially you. You live here."

Well, she didn't *live* here, but yeah, this was where she was currently resting her head at night.

They went to the table at the edge of the dance floor where Bex had been sitting and, sighing softly, dropped into the chairs. Aubrey and Chloe sat too, but didn't seem to be suffering the same footwear trauma as Bex and Maggie.

Maggie's shoes were slip-ons, so she just kicked them off. Bex would have to unbuckle the straps on hers, but first she needed more water. Thankfully her bottle was still on the table.

Liam and Derek strode up to the table. They'd doffed their jackets long ago and loosened their ties. Kyle came up behind them, looking similarly disheveled. Nope, not disheveled. There was nothing messy about any of them. They all looked like they belonged in a photo shoot for J. Crew.

Liam held his hand out to Aubrey. "Hey, babe. You ready for another spin?"

She grinned up at him and twined her fingers through his. "Sure."

Chloe stood up next. "Come on, sexy, show me what you've got."

Derek let out a low growl. "You sure you want that?"

Chloe laughed low in her throat. "Bring it."

Though Bex smiled at their banter, she couldn't help but feel envious. Kyle looked between Maggie and Bex, his brow furrowed.

Maggie massaged her toes. "What's wrong?"

Kyle eyed her feet. "Well, we all came over to dance, but you look like you need to sit."

Maggie bounced up. "I'm good. I just won't be putting those back on." She pointed at the offending footwear she'd kicked aside.

"I liked those shoes," he said. "A lot." He grinned and kissed her cheek.

She chuckled. "Great, they're yours."

He laughed with her then turned to Bex. "You want to come dance with us?"

Bex didn't want to intrude on all the coupledom. "Thanks, but I need to rest my feet."

Kyle took Maggie's hand. "Okay, but if you change your mind, we'll be the ones with no rhythm."

Maggie socked him in the shoulder. "Speak for yourself!"

They laughed all the way to the dance floor where he pulled her into his arms for a slow-ish dance despite the upbeat tempo of the song.

Bex bent over and pulled at the strap on her shoe. With a flick of her fingers she freed her poor right foot and exhaled with relief. Moving on to the left, she tugged the strap back. Only the little metal toggle wouldn't come out of the hole. It was stuck. Crap.

She worked at it for a minute and, when too much blood had gathered in her tipsy head from being bent over, she sat back up with a huff. Standing in front of her was Hayden wearing a perplexed half-smile.

"Problem?"

She groaned. "Yes. My strap won't come loose, and I'm dying to get this shoe off." She brought her foot up to show him.

He leaned forward. "I see. Here, let me see if I can help." He sat down in the chair Maggie had vacated. "Give me your foot."

She envisioned handing him her severed foot like she would a hammer or a pen and promptly giggled.

His eyes narrowed briefly, and damn was it sexy. "What?"

"Nothing. Just buzz giggles."

He smiled. "I remember those."

That's what they'd called them in college. The uncontrollable laughter at things that maybe weren't that funny unless you were under the influence of alcohol.

She lifted her foot and wasn't sure where to go with it. Putting it on his lap seemed too...intimate. But the table was too tall and there wasn't another chair in close proximity.

He solved the problem by gently clutching it and setting it on his knee. Not quite his lap. This was okay. Safe.

Until he started in on the strap. His fingers grazed her flesh, sparking all sorts of inappropriate yearnings. She willed him to hurry up before she did something stupid. Like moan.

"Wow, this is really stuck." He frowned at her. "Your foot's kind of swollen."

"Thanks, Captain Obvious. It's hot, and I've been on my feet all day. I wonder why."

"Well, I'm going to have to tighten it"—he did just that as he said the words, making her cry out—"to get it off." The strap came free, and he tossed the shoe aside. "Better?"

His right hand was still on her foot, his thumb gently caressing her reddened flesh. Did he realize what he was doing? That he was stroking her? He couldn't possibly know how it made her feel, how she wished he would slide his hand up to her ankle, keeping up the massage, and to all points north of that.

She tried not to sigh and completely failed. "Yes, thank you."

Like his brothers, he'd ditched his coat. He'd also completely removed his tie, and his shirt was unbuttoned at the neck with the sleeves rolled up. Both places bared tanned flesh that contrasted sharply with the pure white of his crisp shirt. He wore a bracelet on his right wrist—brown leather with a slender silver rectangle.

God, he was sexy. Had he ever been this sexy?

"Cool bracelet. What is it?"

He lifted his hand from her, and she immediately regretted asking him the question. "Oh, I picked it up in France. It's Latin. It says *in vino veritas*."

Bex reluctantly slid her foot from his knee and sat up straight in her chair. "It looks great on you."

"Thank you." He stared at her a moment. "You seem…different."

She was surprised to hear him echo the thoughts she'd been having. "So do you. But I guess that's to be expected after all this time. We're not the same people we were."

"Nope. Is this strange?"

Bex relaxed against the chair. Maybe it was due to the alcohol, but she didn't want to put up a façade with him. "A little. Is it strange for you?"

"Yeah. A little," he said.

Yikes. Bex grimaced. "I want you to know that I thought long and hard about coming back here. I almost didn't."

"What made up your mind?"

"Honestly, it was just too good of an opportunity to pass up."

"I get it. And I understand." He looked at her pointedly. "*Really*. Do your thing. We'll settle into a groove, and this won't feel bizarre anymore." He rested his arm on the table and leaned back in his chair. "Anyway, I'll be out of your hair by the middle of next month." He adjusted the bracelet on his wrist, and it seemed a subconscious action, like when he'd twirl the ring she'd given him.

He looked off into the distance at something then stood. He looked down at her, the hint of a smile curving his lips. "You good now?"

Bex nodded. "Thanks again."

He gave her a gallant bow. "You're welcome."

As she watched him walk away into the night, she felt a pang of longing so strong that she almost went after him and asked him to dance. Would that be so wrong? They seemed to be getting along so well.

Okay, Bex, pull your head out. You just had an open conversation and acknowledged any weirdness. That wasn't the bright green light she needed. Time to move past him and live your life. The life you chose to pursue here in Ribbon Ridge, aka Archer Central.

That she now had an unexpected desire to rekindle things with her ex was a bummer. She thought of what Cameron had told her—that Hayden had taken years to truly get over her and was in a great place now. She couldn't mess that up. He deserved every happiness, and she needed to leave him the hell alone.

Come next month he might be out of her hair, but she didn't think he'd exit her thoughts so easily.

Chapter Ten

THE WEDDING BREAKFAST on Sunday was a bit subdued compared with the wedding the previous day, but still joyous as everyone celebrated the newlyweds. Hayden had never seen Sara so happy.

Dylan and Sara were opening gifts in the great room while people milled about—either sitting with them, nibbling on the buffet in the dining room, or hanging out downstairs. A lot of guests would be leaving today, and he realized that meant the house would be almost empty.

Almost. Bex would still be here.

Hayden went into the kitchen to refill his coffee. Even though it was past noon, he needed the caffeine after last night. He'd stayed up into the wee hours drinking with his brothers and the Westcotts. Several of them had spent the night in various places at the house. He'd been reminded of college days when they'd had parties here occasionally. Nothing major, just fun times with family and close friends. Times he couldn't have in France.

Dad came into the kitchen. "Hayden, how's it going?"

"Good, you?"

"Excellent. I'm getting the hang of this wedding business. Derek's was a good introductory lesson last summer, then Evan's in April, and now I'd say we're in the swing of things." He grinned and went to the tap to pull a beer. Dad eyed the mug in Hayden's hand. "You still drinking coffee?"

"For now." Hayden was also still thinking of the weddings. Kyle's was in late September, which would be tough for Hayden to make with harvest. Hayden would have to fly in Friday morning and leave Sunday. He basically wouldn't sleep for an entire weekend. No problem.

Then Liam was getting married on New Year's Day. That would be far easier to manage, and it made sense for Hayden to just come home for Christmas and stay a week or ten days. He'd flown home for just a few days last Christmas because his mother had wanted all of her children with her during the first holidays after Alex's death. And Hayden had wanted to be with them.

Alex's absence had been very strange because he'd always been there—the one brother who had never left home. The family had talked about that, of course, but there was still a disconnect between Hayden and his siblings. He'd lived near Alex, had seen him regularly, had known him in ways they hadn't, and had been there for him when just about everyone else had gone.

Dad leaned back against the counter and sipped his beer. "What's on your agenda today?"

"Not much. I might take a nap."

Dad chuckled. "I think that's going to be a popular theme. We're skipping Sunday dinner tonight. I think everyone's wiped out."

"Sounds like a good plan."

Dad looked him the eye. "It's great to have you back. We really missed you here."

Hayden sensed a hard sell coming. He and Mom had made no secret about wanting him to change his plans, dropping hints at every possible opportunity. "I've missed you, too."

"I've been thinking." He flicked Hayden an apologetic glance. "It's hard not to. You really could start up your own wine label. You have the same entrepreneurial spirit that pretty much runs in all of us Archers."

Hayden *could* start his own label. He didn't need a vineyard or even a winery. He could buy grapes from a producer, rent space from a facility, and use a bottling truck. The valley was full of small winemakers looking to establish a name for themselves. Unlike most of them, Hayden had enough capital to make a serious go of things.

"I've thought of that, but I like working with a crew. I like the vineyard aspect, the camaraderie of the winery."

"So start your own winery," Dad said.

Hayden laughed. "Yeah, I'll get right on that." Little did Dad know, he actually *could*…

"I'm serious. Why *couldn't* you do that?"

"I could, but right now I have the opportunity to rack up some terrific experience most people would kill for." That was a bit melodramatic, but he wanted Dad to understand how important this was to him. Making wine at a Grand Cru winery in Burgundy would gain Hayden an international audience for his own wine, when the time came.

"I get it." But he didn't look happy about it.

"I'm not going to be gone forever," Hayden said.

"You say that, but you never know. Liam said he'd never move back here, and now look at him."

He'd relocated his life here and was now as involved in The Alex as anyone. Anyone but Hayden.

But Hayden.

He sensed a common theme here. Except he had to remember that he'd removed himself from everything on purpose. If he wanted to come back, to participate, he'd be welcomed with open arms. That wasn't the point, however. Maybe he wanted them to ask—and not like Dad just had, for emotional reasons. No, it would be nice to be wanted. Needed.

Which he was in France.

"Dad, if you thought I'd come home and make wine, why'd you offer me a position at Archer Brewing with Derek?"

Dad shrugged. "I don't know. Out of habit maybe? I loved working with you at Archer. I'd always sort of hoped you'd develop a passion for beer the way you did for wine. And when you were with Bex it seemed that might happen since she was so passionate about it." He nodded once. "But I realize now that it was never your calling."

Hayden appreciated the sentiment and understood Dad's disappointment that not one of his kids had inherited his love of brewing.

Hayden's back pocket vibrated, signaling a text. He pulled his phone out and glanced at the screen. It was from Cam, which was silly since he was downstairs playing pool or something.

Cam: *Luke scheduled a walk-through at a vineyard in thirty. You in?*

In? For what? A tour? Or something more?

He cautioned himself not to get ahead of things. He was asking for a tour, nothing more.

Hayden: *Where?*

Cam: *Quail Crest.*

That was up in the hills over Ribbon Ridge. Hayden couldn't remember for sure, but thought they had about eighty acres. They didn't produce wine, but sold the grapes to area wineries and winemakers. It had a fantastic elevation, and in the right hands, the grapes produced some sensational wine. Hayden's interest was piqued.

What would be the harm in looking?

Hayden: *Sure.*

Cam: *We'll be right up!*

Presumably by "we," he meant Luke and Jamie, who were also downstairs last Hayden knew.

A moment later, the trio spilled into the kitchen. "You ready?" Cam asked.

Dad looked between them. "You guys headed out?"

Hayden threw them all death stares and hoped they understood: Do *not* say a word.

Hayden set his mug on the counter near the sink. "Yeah, we're going to stop in and visit a friend while Luke's still here." He cast another look toward the brothers, silently telling them to nod or at least not say anything contradictory. His primary concern was Jamie, who sometimes got lost in his own head.

"Have fun." Dad smiled at them and left.

Hayden led them out through the back door. "Who's driving?"

"I will," Cam said.

They all piled into his Range Rover—Hayden in the front seat, Luke and Jamie in the back.

Hayden gave all three of them a pointed look in quick succession. "I would appreciate it if you guys would keep this reconnaissance, or whatever it is, on the down-low for now. If my folks found out there was a chance I was thinking of starting my own winery, I'd never hear the end of it."

Cam looked over at him as he drove through the porte cochere and around the fountain. "Understood."

"They giving you a hard time about not moving home?" Jamie asked. "I'm getting the same guilt trip from my mother. When I point out the fact that Luke lives in California and Cam travels all the time, she said I at least needed to live in the same country like they do."

Hayden chuckled, glad that his mother wasn't the only one with unreasonable expectations.

Cam glanced at the guys in back in his rearview mirror. "So are we serious about this?"

"We're just looking at a vineyard," Luke said from behind Hayden's seat.

Hayden turned to look at him. "That *you* set up. Why would you do that if you weren't serious?"

Luke cracked a lazy smile. "Same reason you'd come to look at it if you're not serious."

Cam laughed. "I think we're all cautiously optimistic at this point. If it works out, great, if not, no harm done."

Jamie leaned forward. "Hayden, is there any chance you could turn down the job in France?"

He'd planned to contact Antoine late tonight, when it was Monday morning in Burgundy. But he supposed he could delay at least a few days if he wanted to seriously consider this enterprise. Hell, this was not what he'd expected to be doing. He'd wrapped his mind around going back to France. Sure, but he'd also fantasized about making his own wine.

"Maybe," he finally answered.

Luke thumped the back of his seat. "Vague much?"

Hayden laughed. "Yes, there's a chance I could turn down the job. But I have to be damned sure. How'd you just happen to hear about this place anyway—if you aren't serious?"

"I always keep my options open," Luke said. "After we theorized this thing last week, I did a little poking around and found out that Amos was planning on selling. I wanted to get a leg up before he put it on the market. Here we are."

Cam pulled into the small gravel drive leading up to the ranch-style house where the vineyard owners lived.

They all bailed out of the car, and Luke took the lead going to the house while the other three waited in the driveway.

A few moments later, Luke returned with a man in his sixties. "This is Amos French," Luke said. "Amos, these are my brothers Cameron and Jamie." He shook hands with each of them. "And our kinda-sorta-but-not-really-brother-in-law Hayden Archer. His sister is married to our brother."

Amos chuckled. "That's a mouthful. Pleased to meet you. Let's take a walk through the grapes." He beckoned for them to follow him into the vineyard, which started maybe fifty feet behind the house. They had a stunning view of the valley beyond and a hillside of neatly marching vines.

He spent a good ten minutes telling them when the grapes had been planted and what farming methods he used. Then he covered production yields for the past five years—he'd owned the land for nearly twenty; it was his retirement project—as well as where the grapes were promised this year. He hadn't signed any new contracts and had decided it was a good time to downsize.

"Are you planning to live in the house or are you going to put that on the market, too?" Cameron asked.

"Nah, you can have that, too. Well, not *have* it." He laughed.

Luke and Hayden spent about fifteen minutes exploring, discussing the plants, sampling the very young grapes, and falling into long bouts of silence. Hayden knew his mind was traveling at about a thousand miles an hour and suspected Luke's was doing the same.

Hayden ended up wandering off away from them and wasn't sure how long he'd been on his own tramping through the vineyard when Cameron caught up with him.

Cam wiped the back of his wrist over his forehead. "Should've brought a hat."

Hayden put his hands on his hips and looked up the hillside toward the house. He envisioned it transformed into a tasting room and next to it, a brand-new, state-of-the-art facility designed by Tori.

"What do you think?" Cam asked.

Hayden's mind was churning with possibility. "Too much."

Cam quirked a smile. "Luke said the plants are fantastic. Amos runs a good vineyard."

"I agree. And I've drank enough Quail Crest varieties to know the grapes will make good wine." Or great wine. Hayden's pulse thrummed with excitement.

"The three of us can't afford to buy the property and start the winery," Cam said matter-of-factly. They'd been friends long enough not to mince words. "And of course none of us can actually make wine."

Hayden turned toward him. "You're saying you need me." *And my money.*

He knew it was more than that. He *hoped* it was more than that. Hadn't he just thought about wanting to be needed?

"Of course we need you. This project doesn't happen without you. I mean, it could, I guess. But we'd have to find some second-rate winemaker with enough money to put in his quarter stake."

Hayden's brain tripped up. "You only want me to put in a quarter?"

Cam frowned slightly. "Yeah, what did you think? With three of us, we can't quite afford it—according to the numbers guy." That would be Jamie. "But with four of us, it's doable. Did you think we wanted you to front the money?"

"I wasn't sure."

"Wow, did France turn you into a dick? For as long as we've been friends, you've been rich, affluent, well-off, whatever. Have I ever expected you to be my sugar daddy?" When Hayden shook his head, he added, "Yeah, didn't think so."

"Shit, I'm sorry. I didn't mean to be a douche. I'm just...I've just been feeling like a fifth wheel since I came home. Like I don't really belong."

"That's ridiculous. Especially with me." Cameron took a step forward and while Hayden couldn't see the expression in his eyes behind the sunglasses, he could hear the genuine concern in his friend's tone. "We're good, right?"

"Absolutely. It's me. I'm off-kilter. Can I still blame jet lag?"

Cam lifted a shoulder. "Blame whatever you want. Blame your siblings, your parents, hell, blame Bex."

"Why would I do that?"

"Because she's back in your life fucking things up."

Hayden dropped his hands to his sides and started walking back up the hill. "She's not fucking things up."

Cam fell into step beside him. "She's not the reason you're maybe off your game or whatever?"

That could be part of it, he supposed. Okay, yeah. Last night he'd had every intention of meeting up with Kayla, his cousin's cute friend, but then he'd gotten caught up with Bex and her shoe and stroking her damned silky flesh, and he'd completely missed the opportunity. And he hadn't felt bad about it. At least not about Kayla. About Bex…he didn't like that he still found her attractive, that she distracted him in ways he didn't want her to.

"I'm going with jet lag and the fact that I've missed out on a ton of stuff the past year." That was completely true. So much had happened while he'd been gone. It's like life had been catapulting forward while he'd been sitting still. Which wasn't true at all. He'd been busy, he'd been moving forward, too. Then how come he felt left behind?

"So what do you think? Really. Don't give me any bullshit answers. I'm your best friend and hopefully your business partner."

Hayden paused. "Would that be okay? Us being business partners?"

Cam lifted a shoulder. "I think so. I can't make wine. You can't market it."

"Well, I *can*…"

Cam punched him lightly in the bicep. "Shut up. You get your area of expertise, and I get mine."

Hayden grinned at him. "I thought yours was philandering."

"Ha ha. I'm still waiting for your bullshit-free answer."

Hayden was afraid to say it out loud. He'd been ready to commit to France, to the next chapter in his life away from Ribbon Ridge. Coming back meant dealing with whatever issues he had with his family, and then there was Bex. He hated that she factored into this decision at all. He'd spent so long getting over that whole situation.

He chose his words carefully. "I'm not saying no. And that's not a bullshit answer. I'm...intrigued. I have a lot to think about. We need a business plan before we can talk seriously."

"Jamie's going to start working on it ASAP."

"Luke's going back to California tonight."

"Right, but we can talk things through over the next week or so. Amos isn't putting the property on the market until at least next week. We have a little time to crunch numbers and process everything."

They continued walking up the hill, the afternoon sun beating on them. Hayden took a deep breath. He loved being out here, rain or shine. The smell of the ripe grapes in September would be amazing. *His* grapes.

"Admit it," Cam said softly. "This would be pretty incredible."

It would be more than incredible. It would be everything he ever wanted.

Maybe not quite *everything*.

Chapter Eleven

OVER THE NEXT four days, Hayden was thrown into a whirlwind of activity as things got busier up at The Alex in preparation for the soft open. Plus, the annual Ribbon Ridge Festival was starting tonight and would run through the weekend, and he'd volunteered to help out with that, too. In his spare time, primarily late at night, he e-mailed and texted with the Westcott brothers as they discussed a business plan. This pipe dream seemed more viable every day.

Being so busy meant Hayden had little time to think about or even see Bex, which suited him just fine. It also meant his parents weren't badgering him about his plans. He'd sent off a note to Antoine, telling him he needed a little more time to decide. But what had seemed a runaway decision to return to France and take the amazing life-altering position had somehow shifted into a dead heat between Burgundy and Ribbon Ridge.

It was seven o'clock—time for Hayden's shift at the festival booth to conclude. He had plans to meet up with Cameron and Jamie later to talk about the winery. Jamie had put together a top-notch business plan, and based on that, Luke was working on pulling money together, while Jamie flat out said he'd have to borrow some to put in his share. Hayden wondered if Jamie would take a loan from him, but didn't know if that would muddy the waters.

Sean was working the booth with Hayden and Ford, one of Archer's employees whom Hayden had worked with for years. Both Sean and Hayden were done in a few, while Ford was staying on to close the booth. It was a beautiful evening, and even though it was only Thursday, the stream of thirsty festivalgoers that afternoon had been steady.

"Hey, guys!" Another Archer employee, Trish, arrived at the booth. "I'm here to relieve somebody."

"That would be me," Sean said.

Hayden sent him a look of mock offense. "Hey, it could be *me*."

Sean clapped his hand on Hayden's bicep. "True, mate."

Hayden had spent some time with Sean this week and liked him a lot. Tori had chosen a spouse who not only fit into their family, but also stood up to it. Marrying into the Archer clan was not for the meek.

Tori came toward the booth, dressed in cutoff shorts and a paint-stained T-shirt, and her hair in a ponytail. She smiled at Sean, and he stepped out to meet her, kissing her cheek.

Hayden looked at her. "Did you get drafted into painting?"

"Yeah. Helping Chloe with some accent stuff in the spa. It's not going to be ready the same day as everything else, but it'll be close."

The soft open was in two weeks, so it was crunch time. There were a myriad of last-minute things going on, many of which Hayden had helped with all week long, aside from taking care of a bunch of wine stuff and trying to find a sommelier for the restaurant. He had settled into a groove, finding at least a temporary place within this project. It felt great to be a part of it and to be working with his siblings. Maybe that had helped tipped the scales in favor of returning to Ribbon Ridge.

Everything was coming together—the rooms were decorated, the staff was mostly hired and trained, the grounds looked spectacular, and the restaurant was cooking every day to practice. And now their food was getting center stage at a booth that Kyle was running as a preview to advertise the restaurant.

A young guy came running up. "Am I late?" he panted. "Sorry. I'm Andy."

"Hey, Andy, you're not late. Go on in." Hayden stepped out of the booth as he called out, "See you later, Ford." He went to join Sean and Tori.

"Everyone came down for a quick dinner," Tori said. "I said we'd bring beer. There'll be eleven of us—assuming you're coming, Hayden—but Sara wants cider of course."

Hayden was hungry, and Cameron and Jamie were going to meet him here in a bit. "Sounds good."

They filled a couple of growlers, grabbed some cups, and snagged a cider for Sara then made their way to the eating area where there were picnic tables as well as extra tables and chairs set up for the event. Food booths, including the one for The Arch and Fox, and carts ringed the area. "Guess we're not eating at Kyle's," Hayden said. That line was easily the longest.

"No kidding," Sean said. "Bummer because I was looking forward to the pork sliders."

Tori flashed them both a smile. "Kyle's making ours. It'll be ready in a few." She nodded toward Liam and Derek, who were loitering near the side of the booth. "They're picking it up." She looked over the tables and pointed. "There's Aubrey and Chloe."

Hayden handed his growler to Sean, who carried the other. "I'll give them a hand with the food."

Tori and Sean went and sat at the table while Hayden walked up to the booth. He looked at Derek and Liam. "You need help transporting?"

"Probably, thanks," Derek said. He and Liam were both dressed in work clothes, and had clearly just come from The Alex.

Kyle poked his head out of the doorway. "Food's about up. Everybody here?" he asked.

Liam pushed his sunglasses more firmly on his nose. "Sara and Dylan are on their way. Evan and Alaina aren't coming. Too many people for his comfort, and she'd just as soon keep a low-ish profile since she suddenly looks pregnant."

"Cool," Kyle said. "Ah, here we go. Open the door, will you?" He turned while Liam held the door open. Kyle handed a tray with food stacked on it to Derek and then another to Hayden. "One more." Liam stuck his foot in front of the door as he took the last one.

"That it?"

"Yep. Maggie and I'll be over in a sec."

They went to the table and deposited the food, which was a variety of what the booth was offering: pork sliders, a mixed green salad, and chicken cilantro tacos. Hayden helped himself to a couple of sliders and a taco then poured a beer.

Kyle and Maggie joined them, still garbed in their aprons. "We have a bit of a reprieve!" Kyle sat down next to Hayden. "Beer me, *please*."

Hayden obliged. "You guys are swamped."

"No kidding. I had to call in reinforcements here." He nodded at Maggie next to him then blew her a kiss.

She caught the kiss and flashed a smile. "I can only stay another hour or so. I need to get back up to The Alex and check on the irrigation."

"I can help you out here if you need it," Hayden said to Kyle, thinking he could probably get Cam and Jamie to pitch in if necessary. Although, Cam was arguably the worst cook ever. Next to Tori.

Liam, who was sitting next to Hayden, grinned at him. "Aren't you the jack of a thousand trades?"

Hadn't that pretty much been his role since birth? Hayden bit his tongue before he said that. It was fine. He didn't mind that role.

Kyle lifted his beer. "And I appreciate the hell out of it. To Hayden being back and saving our collective asses."

Hayden hadn't saved anything. They'd been doing just fine without him. "I wouldn't go that far. You've all done a great job. I'm just coming in at the finish line—the credit is all yours."

Tori looked at him, her lips slightly pursed. "Don't discount your contributions. This project launched because of you."

Sara and Dylan walked up then, the latter looking more tired and frazzled than Hayden had ever seen him. He felt bad that Sara and Dylan wouldn't get their official honeymoon until next month. But then they were taking two full weeks in the UK, including a brief visit with Sean's parents.

Tori patted the seat next to her. "Sit, you guys. I'm glad you made it."

Sara sat and pulled Dylan down beside her. "I had to practically drag him."

Kyle looked at Dylan. "Everyone has to eat."

"I can eat at the job site," he muttered.

"Dude, it's all coming together." Kyle grinned. "Don't sweat it."

Dylan ran his hand through his brown hair and reached for a pair of pork sliders situated in a small paper dish. "It'll get there."

Sara smiled at her new husband as she patted his knee. "We know. Besides, we had to come down to the festival, at least for a little bit. You can't miss it."

Tori looked around the table, smiling. "It's so nice to have everyone here. I wish Evan and Alaina had come."

Conversation broke off around the table, as it usually did with so many of them in one place.

Kyle leaned over toward Hayden. "How's it going? You ready to blow back to France yet?"

Hayden gave him a teasing stare. "Are you asking if I'm sick of you guys yet?"

Kyle raised a shoulder. "I might be if I were you. You held down the fort for a long time. I don't blame you for wanting to be off on your own."

Hayden took a drink of beer and set his cup back on the table. "What's you're motive here, Kyle? I'm already selling you my house, which you love."

Kyle chuckled. "No ulterior motives. But I do appreciate your selling us the house. We *do* love it. I still can't believe you're willing to give it up."

Hayden shook his head with a laugh. "It's a commitment I don't need. I don't know when I'll be back in Ribbon Ridge." *Or if he was even leaving,* but he didn't say that.

Kyle sat back a little, understanding sparking in his gaze. "I get it. You want to be loose and free. Taking a page from my book now, are you?"

"Minus the part where I alienate people."

"Ouch. But I totally did that." He sighed. "I was a complete dick."

Hayden picked up his beer again. "Wow, you're, like, so grown up now."

"Have to be. It's easy when your life clicks into place. But you know what that feels like. You've been grown up and responsible for as long as I can remember."

Ha, right. Unfortunately it *was* right. Boringly, disappointingly right. That was one of the reasons he'd left. It had been past time to stretch his wings and stop being the go-to guy. Maybe he *was* following Kyle's lead—to a point.

Yet here he was, home for just a couple of weeks, and he was right back in that role of stalwart, dependable Hayden. Hell, he didn't know what he wanted. He wanted to feel needed, he wanted to be free. What the fuck?

Screw it, maybe he should go off and do something like Liam would've done before *he'd* fallen in love and returned to the fold.

Hayden swigged his beer. "Which is maybe why I want to unload the house and, you know, be irresponsible for once."

Kyle looked at him without his usual swagger. "Well, whatever the reason, Maggie and I are thrilled. Thank you."

Hayden smiled. "It makes me happy to know you guys love it."

"Are you sure this doesn't mean you're out of here for good?"

Hayden looked him in the eye, but let his mouth quirk up into a smile. "Isn't 'never say never' one of your mottos?"

"Maybe. Sounds more like Liam though."

Liam looked over at them upon hearing his name. "What does?"

"Nothing," Hayden said. He leaned toward Kyle and spoke a bit lower. "Did you talk to Aubrey about the sale?"

"Yep. It'll be super easy since we're paying you cash thanks to Dad giving me my trust fund back." He said this without animosity. He truly had put all of his darker days behind him. Hayden was glad.

Now he'd be even more liquid to make this winery start-up work. *If* he was going to do it.

Liam turned in his chair to face Hayden. "Hey, stop talking about me over there."

"Not talking about you at all, jackass. But I did want to ask you something. When are you taking me skydiving?"

Liam sat back in his chair and crossed his arms. "Damn, I forgot. Next weekend?" Liam shook his head. "No, that's the hike and campout with Bex."

Hayden had been so busy that he'd forgotten about that entirely, but clearly Liam hadn't. He'd remembered Bex's hike but not Hayden's request for a skydive? Irritation pricked at his neck, but he worked to ignore it. "Is that happening?"

"It is for us. I talked to Bex this week. We're all set to hike up. We're going to watch the weather, but right now we're planning to just sleep under the stars so we won't need to haul tents. Just basic cooking stuff and water."

Sounded complicated. But fun. Except it was with Bex. Could he do that?

Why not? They seemed to have formed a tenuous friendship. Like boring grown-ups.

He glanced around, wondering where she was today. Since she was living at the house right now and working at The Alex, she seemed as much of an extension of his family as she had five years ago. Only she wasn't.

"Is Bex at the brewhouse today?" he asked no one in particular.

"Yeah, she was up there this morning," Dylan answered. "But I haven't seen her in a while." He threw

Sara an apologetic glance. "I guess we should've invited her to come with us."

"Actually I saw her an hour or so ago," Sean said. He looked toward Hayden. "You'd stepped out of the booth for a few minutes."

Hayden almost asked why Sean hadn't told him that, but why would he have? The better question was why did Hayden think that was something Sean ought to share? He and Bex had no connection, especially to someone like Sean who hadn't ever known them as a couple.

"Well, this is a sorry-looking lot." Cam's voice carried around the table from where he stood behind Kyle's chair, grinning with his hands on his hips.

Kyle turned his head. "Where'd you come from? I must've missed the cat that dragged you in."

Cam winced as he blew air between his teeth. "Dude, that was kind of a whiff. I think you're losing your touch."

Kyle threw up his hands. "What can I say? I've been working my face off the last week. Hell, the last year."

Liam cocked his head to the side and gave Kyle his most condescending expression. "Poor Kyle. Wife in the weal world is so hawd," he said in a singsong voice.

Kyle stood then leaned over Hayden and patted Liam's knee in a thoroughly patronizing fashion. "Yeah, well, next time you work for a multimillion-dollar corporation, start up a restaurant, and appear on multiple television shows, let me know."

"Burn!" Derek said, laughing. Others joined in. Liam shook his head, but smiled widely.

Jamie joined them then, but the group was breaking up. Which was fine since Hayden didn't want to talk to Cam and Jamie with his siblings around.

Sara and Dylan took off, while Kyle and Maggie headed back to the food booth.

"We should head back up to The Alex," Tori said to Sean. They said good-bye and left.

Aubrey and Liam took off next, holding hands as they threaded their way out through the tables.

Once they were alone, Cam stepped toward Hayden. "Did you see that Butter Creek Cellars is here? They have wine from Amos's grapes."

Hayden's interest was instantly piqued. "Do they? Lead the way."

Cam took them to the booth where they were pouring. They each paid the tasting fee—five bucks for three wines, only one of which was from Amos's land. Hayden asked for a pour of just that and studied it before tasting, letting the wine linger on his tongue. He thought of what he'd do differently, of how he would've left it in the cask a few weeks longer.

They walked off to the side, and Jamie tasted the same variety. "This is good." He looked at Hayden expectantly. "Is it, or do I have no idea what I'm talking about?"

Hayden smiled at him. "Everyone is the arbiter of their own taste. You like what you like. Period."

Cam had tried the pinot blanc and just finished it. "Sure, but you've got the nose and the palette to understand what's really good and what's not. You tell schmucks like us what to drink so we don't waste our money on crap."

"Like you can't tell for yourself. You've spent enough time shilling wines that you know good from bad from phenomenal."

Cam grinned. "True. Guess that makes me qualified to be your assistant winemaker or something."

Hayden laughed. "Don't push it. You market, I craft, remember?"

"So what are we thinking?" Jamie asked, looking between his brother and Hayden. "Amos wants to list the property next week."

Cam nodded. "I know. We need to make a decision. What's your money situation, little brother?"

Jamie tossed his tasting cup into a nearby trashcan. Actual glasses would've been a disaster at an event like this. "I'm short, but I can get a loan. I'm in."

"I could maybe spot you—as a loan," Hayden offered. "If you're open to that."

Jamie exhaled. "It'd be a hell of a lot easier than going through a bank. Yeah, let me think about it."

Cam pulled his sunglasses off and looked at Hayden. "Does that mean you're in?"

"I want to be…I'm not sure yet. It's a huge commitment. I sort of like being free at the moment." His voice had trailed off as he'd finished his statement.

Jamie's cell phone rang. He pulled it from his pocket and looked at the screen. "Excuse me, guys, I need to take this." He answered the call and strolled a little ways away from them.

Cam moved closer to Hayden. "What gives? What's holding you back?"

Hayden shrugged. "There's no need to be dramatic."

Cam rolled his eyes. "Dude, I've known you forever. I can see how excited you are about this, how much of your mind it's occupying. You sent me an e-mail at two a.m. the other night."

That was true. "I don't know. I'm just…unsettled."

Cam's mouth turned down into a sort of grimace. "Is it Bex?"

"No, why would you think that?"

"Because she lives here now. She works with your family. She's currently more attached to Ribbon Ridge than you are."

That needled him. And Cam knew it. He wanted Hayden to commit to this idea. "That's not going to work, so knock it off."

"This is the chance of a lifetime. It's a great vineyard, we have all the right people together, the timing's great—"

"Is it? Luke's not free right now, and neither am I, really."

Cam's mouth dove into a full-on frown now. "Luke *will* be free, and you could be, too." He pivoted and took a step then went back to where he was standing. Sometimes he had a hard time keeping still. "What can I say to convince you?"

Hayden stared at his best friend. "You really want this."

"I really do. What I don't understand is why you don't."

But he did. He wanted it like crazy. So yeah, what the hell was his problem? Bex? His family? Did he feel like he was letting Antoine down if he didn't take the job in France? Yeah, that was part of it. Antoine was depending on him, and Hayden hated disappointing people.

"I do want it. Just give me some time to figure things out, okay?"

Cam turned his head toward the hills surrounding the town before looking back to Hayden. "That's the problem—we're running out of time."

ON SATURDAY, BEX worked in the brewhouse in the morning and then helped Maggie in the garden in the afternoon. They'd taken an all-hands-on-deck approach to get everything ready for the soft open. She'd more than earned the quiet dinner by herself followed by a long soak in the tub. Exhausted as she was, she decided she needed a nightcap.

She slipped downstairs to the daylight basement, intending to grab a glass of whiskey from Rob's collection. The bar was in the party room, where they also had a foosball table, pool table, and card table. So many tables. Plus couches, TVs on which to watch sports, and a killer bar.

The TV was on when she walked in, and there sprawled on one of the couches was Hayden. He was dressed in athletic shorts and an Archer beer T-shirt. And she was immediately transported to five years ago…She shoved the thought away even as her stomach did little flips.

He looked over at her. "Hey, Bex." He turned the volume down on the TV a few notches. He was watching a rerun of *Saturday Night Live*. *So* five years ago.

Bex forced her mind back to the present and made her way to the bar. "Who's the host?"

"Amy Schumer."

Bex opened the glass door behind which Rob kept a variety of liquors. "Love her. That's a great episode."

"I wouldn't know since I was abroad."

She selected a single malt whiskey and pulled a glass down from the cabinet. "There's this thing called the interwebs."

He paused the show and sat up, swinging his legs around to the floor. "There's also a thing called spare time, of which I have very little."

She poured the whiskey into the glass. "You're really that busy?"

He got up and joined her at the bar. "Where's my glass?"

"Oops, my bad. Sorry." She turned back to the cabinet and grabbed another glass. "Still neat?"

"Of course."

After splashing whiskey into his glass, she slid it across the bar to him and raised her own. "To being busy?"

"Sure, why not?" He tapped his glass to hers and took a sip. "Yes, I'm really that busy. Not just with work, but with life. I've taken a lot of weekend trips. If I'm going to live in France, I might as well make the most of it, right?"

Bex blamed the whiskey lighting a fire in her belly for the warmth spreading through her. It couldn't be Hayden's presence. Except the heat had started the moment she'd seen him laid out on the couch. How many times had they snuggled in that very spot watching *Saturday Night*

Live of all things? Ugh, she had to stop dwelling on the past. It was over. *They* were over. "You have to. What's been your favorite place to visit?"

Bex had been to Europe once in high school with her mother on a guilt trip—as in her mother had felt guilty after not seeing her for almost a year. It had been an odd vacation, with Bex spending most of her days doing touristy stuff while her mom worked. Looking back, she had to wonder what her mother had been thinking allowing a sixteen-year-old girl to wander around European cities by herself.

He sat on one of the stools at the bar. "Florence. It reminds me a lot of home, actually. Just a gorgeous place."

Bex's only stop in Italy had been Rome. "It's on my bucket list."

"It should be. Barcelona's pretty amazing, too."

"Wow, you *have* been all over. Where haven't you gone?"

He chuckled. "I'd really like to visit Copenhagen. That's next on the list. And the UK, but that's a longer trip."

"And did you do all of this alone?" She hoped she didn't sound too nosy.

"Occasionally, but sometimes I go with a friend—a gal I work with."

Jealousy snaked through her, and she took another sip of whiskey. "How fun to see it with a local. Or at least a European." She set her glass down, realizing she was white-knuckling it with her annoyance. "Are you looking forward to getting back?"

Hayden took a longer sip of whiskey and kept his gaze on the glass after he set it back down on the bar. "I was.

I *am*. It's just…I feel like I've got a foot in both places, if that makes sense."

She could see why he'd feel that way. For her, she'd be able to make the break. When her parents had divorced, she'd gone to live with her dad without a backward glance. Then when she'd left home to go to college, she'd done the same. Home wasn't related to a place in her mind. It was a feeling. A state of mind. "It does. Just remember that Ribbon Ridge—your family—will always be here."

A slight smile played about his lips, and even that small thing was enough to make her chest tighten with emotion. "Yep. There will always be Archers in Ribbon Ridge."

It seemed like he wanted to talk to someone, or maybe that was just her wishful thinking. She picked up her glass and walked around the bar, taking the stool next to him. "You can tell me to butt out, but I've known you a long time and we're friends now, I think." She hoped. "Your family is tough."

He tipped his head up to look at her. "Tough?"

"It's just…big. Complicated. Competitive."

His brow furrowed. "Is that how you see us?"

"That's how I see *them*. How do you see them?"

He smiled. "Complicated. Competitive." He looked at her with appreciation in his gaze, which wasn't helping her campaign to shelve her feelings for him. "It feels off being back now. I've always been the one to be here—you know that."

He'd felt it was his responsibility to stay. Except maybe responsibility wasn't what he'd felt. Maybe it was the desire to be the one who was necessary. Not martyrdom—nothing that self-serving—but a true need to feel...needed. Why had she never seen that before?

"I did know that, but I don't think I really understood it until now. I shouldn't have asked you to leave."

He sat up and pivoted the stool so he was facing her. His knee brushed hers as he turned, and she felt the connection everywhere. He, on the other hand, didn't seem to notice.

"Whoa," he said. "This is a total one-eighty. I'm not sure I can wrap my head around this." There were lines of humor around his eyes, so she knew he was at least half-joking.

"I know, right?" She brought the whiskey to her lips and drank.

"What happened?" he asked softly, his gaze intense. "Why do you say that now?"

Oh, this was dangerous territory. This intimate conversation, the dimness of the room, the familiarity and its pull—at least for her. "You seem out of sorts now, like you maybe can't find your place, whereas before you knew what it was. You were Hayden the Dependable, the one everyone counted on."

His stare pierced her. There was a bit of admiration there. She fidgeted with her glass, unsure where this was going.

"You get it. No one gets it."

She wasn't sure that was true, but maybe it was just that he hadn't talked to them about it. And maybe he didn't want to. Maybe his place *wasn't* here. "I get it *now*," she said, smiling. "But I didn't before. And I'm sorry."

"You said you shouldn't have asked me to leave. Do you…do you regret leaving?"

Damn, that was the worst question ever. Yes and no. "Until I'd come back here, I would've said no. Now…I'm not sure. It's hard to regret things, isn't it? Because we are who we are today because of the choices we made. And I like who I am." For the most part.

He hadn't broken eye contact with her the entire time she'd spoken, and she wondered if he felt this connection, this bone-deep longing that she'd truly never experienced before. Then he leaned in, and she did the same. Did he realize how close they were? If they both leaned just a bit more, their lips would touch.

"Maybe that's it." His voice was soft, sexy, but dark, too. "Maybe I don't like who I am."

That shocked her. He'd always been the most affable, the most generous, the most *likeable* person. Her fingers itched to caress the day's worth of stubble along his chin.

He shook his head, and she blinked. "Never mind, that was a dumb thing to say." And there went any chance she had of figuring out what he'd meant. Or of kissing him.

He finished off his whiskey. "It doesn't matter if you'd wanted to stay or go five years ago. Once we lost the baby, all bets were off." The look he gave her then was the most bare and vulnerable she'd seen him. He blinked and dropped his gaze to the empty glass in his hand. When his eyes found hers again, the intensity had lessened, but she still felt a connection and wondered if he did, too. "It was a terrible situation. I'm not sure if…at that age…we could've recovered from that."

His words opened all of the old wounds, not horribly, but enough that she felt the pain of that loss, of then losing him. But that had been her choice, for better or worse.

He set his glass on the counter and stood. "I'm heading to bed. Thanks for the whiskey and…this. Night."

She watched him go and finished her whiskey then turned off the television. She wished losing the baby hadn't driven them apart, that it had instead drawn them closer together. No, that wasn't true. She wished they hadn't lost the baby at all.

Chapter Twelve

"Mom, ARE YOU sure you don't want to come to the movie with us?" Sara asked the following night after Sunday dinner. She and Tori, and all the female SOs were headed to a chick flick, while the guys were going downstairs to play pool.

"No, thanks. Your dad and I have a date with *Sherlock*, thanks to Bex turning us on to the show." Mom smiled toward Bex, who was slinging her purse over her shoulder. She looked pretty great in a white V-neck T-shirt, green patterned skort, and wedge sandals, her hair twisted into a messy bun. A few strands of dark hair grazed her neck. Hayden remembered how soft she was there, how she squirmed when he licked along her nape.

Whoa there, boy. Settle the hell down.

Sara waved at Mom. "Okay, see you later!" The ladies filed out, leaving the men with the parents.

Kyle went to the sink. "We'll help with the dishes."

She waved him off. "No, you won't. Go start your game of pool."

Derek brought his plate to the counter. "You sure? This will go quick if we all pitch in."

Mom shooed him away, too. "No, go. All of you. Except Hayden."

Hayden, who'd been about to refill his beer from the tap, stopped and looked at her. "What'd I do?"

She smiled at him. "Nothing. I just wanted to talk to you for a minute."

With Dad, who'd also come toward the tap to refill his pint glass. Hayden's gut twisted. Here came the conversation he'd been dreading.

Liam nodded toward Hayden. "We'll warm up the table for you."

Great.

Hayden filled his glass and walked around the counter so Dad could refill his. "Can I guess what this is about?"

Mom came and sat on one of the stools at the beer bar. "I'm sure you can. We're just wondering how many more Sunday dinners we can look forward to having you here."

And here came another hard sell.

Dad sipped his beer. "We know you're settled on your decision, but we can't help but see how you've fallen into a routine this week. You've been everywhere—helping me, working up at The Alex, volunteering at the festival booth. We know the pull of the job offer in France, but what about what you've got here? You've got us."

Uh-oh, they were pulling out all the stops with this one—going for his emotions. "Thanks, Dad. I appreciate you saying that."

Dad exhaled. "Don't you feel a little tug to come home? We miss having you around."

Mom's forehead creased, and she threw Dad a worried look. "It's going to be hard for me to watch you go again. Having all of my children here is a dream come true." She ended with a light laugh, but Hayden heard the edge of nervousness in it.

He hated seeing the pain lurking in his mother's eyes. It reminded him of how she'd been after Alex had died. He never wanted to see her like that again. "I'm mulling options."

Mom's eyes lit. "There's a chance you'll stay?"

Damn, why had he said that? Because he hadn't been thinking. He'd just been trying to make her feel better.

He almost said, *there's always a chance*, but he didn't want to get her hopes up even more. And anyway, that was a lie. Some things had no chance—a diseased vine, his and Bex's relationship. Where had that come from? Wasn't it obvious? She was right here in front of him, and she'd invaded his thoughts from the moment he'd seen her on that elevator the day after he'd come home.

Dad set his beer down and braced himself against the counter. "Forgive me for being nosy, but I just have to ask. Is there some reason you don't want to come back?"

He chose his words carefully this time. "I won't lie—things are so different. I had a clear place when I was at Archer. When I was here helping with Alex."

Mom's eyes were full of compassion and maybe a hint of tears. "There will always be a place for you here."

Hayden smiled at her. "I know. And I *will* come home. If not now, some day." He could tell this conversation wasn't going the way that they'd hoped.

Mom seemed to relax, and Dad nodded. "We'll stop bugging you about it," he said.

Mom stood and kissed Hayden's cheek. "Go on downstairs. I love you."

He touched her shoulder. "I love you, too." He cast a glance toward Dad. "And you."

"You too, son."

Hayden practically ran from the kitchen in his haste to get away. When he got downstairs, he saw Kyle lining up shots of Jägermeister on the bar.

Hayden stopped short. "Jäger? Are you guys kidding?"

"We figured you'd need a shot of something," Liam said. "Were we wrong?"

"Hell no. I'm just surprised at your choice of booze."

Kyle poured the last glass. "Found an unopened bottle. Sounded good. What more excuse do we need?"

Everyone snagged a shot. Evan lifted his and said, "To brotherhood."

They all raised their glass and tossed it back. Then they lined them back on the bar for Kyle to refill.

Dylan smacked his lips. "Good shit. One more, and then we play."

Kyle poured, and they all retrieved their glasses.

Liam raised his glass. "To coming home."

Hayden frowned. No one seemed to notice that he drank a bit after them.

Sean racked the balls, and Hayden went to grab his cue. "You have a cue?" he asked Sean.

"Yeah, didn't you know? Tori said everyone agreed to give me Alex's." Sean looked mildly uncomfortable.

Hayden hadn't known. It seemed "everyone" didn't include him. Maybe she'd asked him, and he just didn't remember. *Oh hell, Hayden, stop giving everyone the benefit of the doubt.* Maybe she *hadn't.* What the fuck did it matter now anyway?

His mood seemed to be tanking. Disappointing your parents would do that.

He took a long swig of beer and decided another shot might be in order.

Kyle took his cue from the rack. "How are we doing teams?"

Evan snagged his cue. "Odd number, so someone's going to have more."

Dylan chalked his cue. "Age?"

"Archers vs. non-Archers?" Derek suggested. "I'll be a non-Archer, but that still gives the Archers the four-person team."

Hayden had a thought. "Sextuplets and non-sextuplets." He looked at Derek and grinned. "That'll give us the advantage."

Derek smiled broadly in return. "Brilliant."

Liam shook his head. "That's fucked up."

"Why, because we have Dylan, and he's awesome?" Hayden glanced at Sean. "Sorry, I don't know how well you play."

"Pretty well, provided I have the right cue." This earned snickers from a few of the others, and Hayden knew immediately what had happened.

"You got stuck with The Humiliator, didn't you?"

"Just for one game, thank God. Then I got Alex's."

Hayden understood now, and he approved. Sean was a good guy. Hayden couldn't think of a better person to inherit Alex's cue.

"Since you have four, one of you assholes gets to break first," Kyle said. "Make it good."

Derek gestured to the table. "Go on, Dylan."

He stepped up and broke, knocking the five down. He studied the table for his next move. "Three in the corner there." He did exactly as he said and continued for three more shots.

When he barely missed with the eleven ball, the rest of their team groaned. Dylan held up his hand. "My bad. I think I need another shot of Jäger."

He went to the bar to pour another, and Hayden joined him while Evan took his turn.

Dylan filled two of the shots and handed one to Hayden. "Interesting way to split the teams."

Hayden shrugged before tossing the liquor back.

"Hey, I know how it feels to be the odd guy out, remember?"

Of course he did. He'd felt ostracized in *two* families, while Hayden had just one. "But you're good now, right?"

It was Dylan's turn to shrug. "Sure. As good as you can be. I mean, I can't change the past, but I don't dwell on it anymore."

Liam joined them. "Hayden is *not* the odd man out." He poured a shot for himself and emptied the bottle. "Well, shit, when did a fifth get so small?"

"When you're pouring for seven, dick-for-brains," Kyle answered. "I don't think there's any more Jäger. Have to move on to something else."

Behind the bar, Dylan turned to survey the liquor cabinet.

"Where's the single malt?" Sean called out.

Dylan pulled out the bottle Hayden and Bex had been drinking from last night. "Single malt for Sean. What else?"

"Oh hell, get the Patrón," Liam said just before he threw back his shot of Jäger.

Dylan grabbed the tequila and set it in front of Liam. "We're going to have to pour you into your car later so Aubrey can drive your drunk ass home."

He picked up his beer with a smile. "I'm pacing myself."

Kyle cleared his throat. "Evan scratched. Whose turn?"

"I'll go," Sean said, leaving his just-poured glass of whiskey on the bar.

Hayden finished his beer then went to the tap to draw another.

Kyle came up to the bar, eyeing Hayden's quick refill. "Whoa. That must've been some convo upstairs."

"Oh, you know, 'Why aren't you coming home?' No pressure."

Kyle winced. "Sorry, man. I know what that's like, believe me."

Hayden wanted to say he really didn't, that their situations were completely different. Hayden hadn't run away, hadn't pissed off half the family. But he didn't want to be a dick. He thought for a moment. Liam totally would have said that to him. So would Alex.

"You don't know shit." The words fell out of Hayden's mouth, and once they did, he felt good.

Liam slapped his arm around Hayden's shoulders and gave him a firm squeeze. "That's my little brother! I've got your back."

Hayden flinched. "Really?"

Liam frowned slightly and withdrew his arm. "What? Too much? We're all having fun, right?"

"Sure, fun. I was just starting to think you'd cast me in Alex's place."

Liam looked confused, which only sparked Hayden's ire. "What do you mean?"

"Now that Alex is gone, you need someone to pair up with, right?" Hayden stared at him a second before drinking his beer.

Liam's eyes flickered with surprise and then understanding. "I guess so," he said quietly. "Sorry."

Hayden wished he hadn't said anything, especially not tonight. He'd been looking forward to a night with his brothers. Like old times. Except it wasn't like old times because Alex wasn't there. He realized that's what felt different. They were all together at last, but not. And they never would be. "I miss him."

The game stopped, and everyone gathered around the bar again.

"I miss him, too," Liam said, dropping onto a stool.

Kyle shook his head, a faint smile tugging his lips. "He'd hate this. He'd tell us all to stop crying in our beer and play the damned game."

Evan poured a shot of tequila and held it up. "To Alex."

Everyone scrambled to arm himself with a beverage and joined in. Their drinks were followed by a moment of silence.

Kyle looked at Liam. "What was in your letter?"

Liam laughed, but it was hollow. "I didn't get a letter."

Kyle's eyes widened. "Dude, I know you had this weird love-hate thing, but that's cold."

"It was a video. He went skydiving and filmed it."

Hayden was shocked to hear this. He'd lived here, seen Alex pretty much every day, but he didn't know anything about that. "No shit?"

Liam nodded. "He's the reason I do that stuff. He asked me if I'd jump out of a plane and record it so he could experience it vicariously. After that he kept coming up with ideas, and I kept doing them. I guess I kind of liked it."

Light laughter filled the room. "Yeah, kind of," Evan said.

"Was that it?" Hayden asked, wanting to hear more about this video. "Just him jumping out of a plane?"

Liam stared at his now-empty pint glass. "Oh no, there was much more to it than that. You don't think he'd let me off that easily, do you?"

Dylan took the glass from Liam's hand and refilled it from the tap. "Was it bad?"

"It wasn't good. Like Kyle said, we had this love-hate thing. He, uh, he called me that night."

Sean leaned forward, his gaze intense. "Like he called Tori? What did he say?"

"He was drunk—or so I thought. I guess he was drugged up from what he took. He told me I could come home." Liam looked at Sean, his eyes dark. "I'm sorry. I know Tori wishes she knew why he called her, but I don't know either. And frankly, I'm glad she didn't answer. I did, and the guilt...well, let's just say that no one wants that."

"I think we all have guilt, for one reason or another," Kyle said, grimacing.

Hayden didn't. Well, he did, but his anger had overtaken that. He'd altered his life to be here for his brother. Maybe he would've left with Bex. Maybe he and Bex never would've even come back to Ribbon Ridge after college. But he'd insisted on standing by Alex, and for what? For Alex to throw that gift back in his face by killing himself. But he never said that to anyone. What would be the point?

Liam looked at Kyle. "What was in your letter?"

Kyle huffed out a breath and ran his hand through his blond hair. "Honestly, he absolutely nailed me. Called out my failures but also praised my abilities. He told me exactly what I needed to hear when I needed to hear it."

"That's a credit to Aubrey," Liam said. "Alex left her a letter too—along with all of our letters—instructing her when to deliver them. Some of his directions were kind of vague."

"What about you, Evan?" Kyle asked. "What was in your letter?"

"I, uh, it sounds like it was different than yours." His eye contact was always sketchy, but right now, he wasn't even looking in their vicinity. "He started a book and asked me to finish it."

"What?" This question was asked by several people, including Hayden. That was something else he hadn't known. That Alex had shared these things with his other siblings but not him burned.

Liam looked astounded. "He wrote a book? I had no idea."

Okay, so Alex hadn't told everyone everything. He'd been really good at keeping secrets, apparently. But hadn't his shocking suicide illustrated that?

"What's it about?" Kyle asked, rapt.

"Two brothers. It's...complicated." Evan fidgeted with his pocket.

Hayden threw him a lifeline. "Tell us some other time, when we aren't all half-drunk."

"Did you finish it?" Dylan asked.

"Uh, yeah." He shrugged. "I'm trying to figure out what to do with it."

Kyle shook his head again. "Damn, Alex certainly pulled the wool over all of our eyes, didn't he?" He looked over at Hayden. "What about your letter?"

Hayden froze like a deer in a pair of headlights. "Pretty basic. 'Sorry I killed myself. I love you. Et cetera.'" Or so

Hayden imagined. He'd never actually opened it. He'd been too pissed. Aubrey had given it to him a couple of days after she'd shared Alex's trust with them. She'd only said that Alex had asked her to give it to him away from anyone else, so that he could open it alone.

Hayden had promptly stuffed it in the glove compartment of his car and forgotten about it.

Not completely, of course. He'd thought about it from time to time, but since it had been here in Oregon and he'd been in France, he'd put it out of his mind again. And again.

Now he wanted to read it. He wanted to feel that familiar anger. *Why did you abandon me when I stuck by you?*

Kyle poured a shot of tequila and tossed it back. "Sucks that he's gone."

Liam pressed his lips together. "Yes, it does."

Sean let out a low whistle. "Wow, you blokes sure know how to piss all over a good time. Next time you invite me for pool, I think I'll watch *Titanic* instead. Far more cheerful."

Everyone stared at him for a minute, and then laughter erupted. Even Hayden cracked a smile, despite the emotion swirling inside him.

Dylan rubbed his hands together. "All right, whose turn was it?"

"It was mine," Sean said. "But I actually scratched so it's someone else's go."

Liam took his turn next, and the mood turned more jovial. The drinking continued and after a while, they simply couldn't play anymore. Hayden had actually stopped drinking a bit ago, but he was pleasantly shitfaced. Not so far gone, however, that he didn't remember Alex's letter and the fact that it was in his car, which was parked outside and wouldn't be as soon as the girls got home and poured their respective guys into their vehicles to drive them home.

Hayden stood from the couch where he'd collapsed a little earlier. "Unlike you losers, I can stagger up to bed. Do yourselves a favor and don't drink anymore."

Kyle saluted. "Yes, sir."

Evan waved a hand from the corner where he'd retreated close to an hour ago. He was undoubtedly the most sober of all of them. "Night, Hay."

Everyone else shouted "Good night" or "Sleep tight," and he thought he even heard "Don't let the bedbugs bite."

He made his way upstairs and stole outside. His Honda Pilot, which he'd let Kyle continue driving since he thought he was going back to France, was parked near the closest garage, and it was unlocked. He opened the passenger door and popped the glove compartment. After a minute of fishing through random crap, he found the envelope with his name on it. Alex's handwriting stared up at him, and Hayden glared back.

He folded it and stuffed it into his pocket, intending to tell anyone he encountered that he'd stepped outside for fresh air on his way up to bed.

But he didn't meet anyone. Once he was in his room, he closed the door and flopped onto his bed, his head crashing into the pillows. He really ought to drink some water unless he wanted a bitch of a hangover tomorrow. He pulled the envelope from his pocket and tossed it aside then got up and went to his bathroom to drink three glasses of water in quick succession.

When he retreated into his room, his gaze fell on the envelope. It was facedown, so that the seal seemed to call to him, "Break me."

He snorted and picked it up. Sliding his finger into the corner, he tore it open and pulled out the single sheet.

Dear Hayden,

I suck. I know how much you gave up for me. Who you gave up. And I'm sorry. You should've left when Bex asked you to. You guys belonged together, and I selfishly kept you to myself. What a dick, right?

I don't know if you're mad at me or not. You've got the kindest heart of any of us. I swear you have every decent gene from Mom and Dad. I know I didn't get any of them.

I hope you'll chase your dreams now that I'm not here to hold you back. I imagine you will be the best, most celebrated winemaker in the entire Willamette Valley, maybe even the country. If anyone can do it, it's you.

I wish I'd told you what I was planning. I wanted to. Of everyone, I wanted to tell you. You deserved my honesty. But I'd already burdened you enough.

You have my utmost admiration and appreciation. You are the grit among us, the glue that keeps us all together. That may not seem rewarding or satisfying, but it's necessary. This family needs you, and I know you'll always be there.

All my love,
Alex

Well, wasn't that fucking fabulous? Even in death, Alex was making him feel like he was some sort of guardian angel, or worse, an insurance agent. That without him, things would go to shit.

But they hadn't. Hayden had left, and everyone had managed just fine. Swimmingly in fact.

Screw you, Alex.

He crumpled the letter and threw it to the floor before falling back onto the bed. He stared up at the ceiling, his insides roiling with emotion. He wished he hadn't known about Kyle's letter or Evan's book or Liam's video. It all made him feel so secondary. Sure, he was needed—wasn't that what he wanted?

Maybe it wasn't. Hell, he didn't know what he wanted.

He wanted this winery, but tonight he'd remembered what it was like to be the guy who didn't quite fit in. And now he felt that more keenly than ever. He was single, unattached to any of the Archer businesses, and he didn't even have a place to live in Ribbon Ridge that he could call his own.

The house was quiet. At least from up here. His parents were on the other side of the house on the main floor, and the guys—if they were still here—were two floors below him.

Then he heard voices and the door to the outside opening and cars starting. The girls must've come back, which he'd somehow missed, and now everyone was taking off.

That meant Bex was back. Down the hall. He listened but heard nothing. Silence returned. Minutes passed.

Then he heard it. Muffled footsteps followed by the slight creak of her door.

Before he thought better of it, he bolted from his bed and strode to her room.

He didn't bother knocking, just went inside and closed the door behind him. He paused, watching her as she turned in surprise.

She'd tossed her purse on the dresser and her hands were on the hem of her shirt, like she'd been about to take it off.

He thought of her without her shirt, a view he'd seen and appreciated many times. But he hadn't come here for that. Had he?

Why had he come?

"Hayden." Her brow was furrowed, her green eyes luminous, like pale jade. "What's wrong?"

Did he look like something was wrong? "I just read my letter from Alex."

Shit, where had that come from? He hadn't meant to say that.

"What do you mean?"

"Never mind." He started to turn, but her hand on his wrist stopped him.

"Don't go. I want to listen. What letter from Alex?"

Her touch seared through him, aroused him in ways he'd thought long buried. "Forget I mentioned it."

Her tone was soft, pleading. "Hayden, let me help you. Please."

He pivoted back around, and she dropped her hand from his wrist. "Alex wrote us all letters, or in Liam's case recorded a video, which Aubrey had to deliver to all of us at various, predetermined times based on his wishes. I got my letter pretty much immediately, but I didn't read it until tonight. Want to know what it said?"

She was utterly calm in the face of more emotion than he'd shown in years. Maybe forever. "Yes."

"That I should've gone with you. That you and I belong together. That he was a selfish dick for manipulating me to stay." He hadn't used those words precisely, but that's what he'd done with all of the little comments about how helpful Hayden was and what a great brother and son he was to stay in Ribbon Ridge working at Archer. Hayden had felt needed and wanted, but now he just felt handled.

She lifted her hand to her mouth. Her eyes were wide. "I...I don't know what to say."

Hayden knew he was still tipsy, but he didn't care. Now that he'd let loose, he couldn't seem to stop it. "Then don't say anything." He took two steps toward her and slid one hand around her waist and the other along her neck. Then he kissed her, his lips gravitating to hers like a leaf falling to the ground. Soft, gentle, a whisper.

His mouth moved over hers, so familiar and yet different. He stroked the soft underside of her jaw and pressed his fingers into her waist. It was the Bex he remembered and a woman he'd just met all in one. He was mesmerized.

Her hands splayed against his chest, and for a moment he thought she meant to push him away. But she dug her fingertips into his shirt and pulled him into her. He parted his lips at the exact moment she parted hers. Their tongues met, and fireworks exploded.

She moaned softly as she twined her arms around his neck, tugging him down so she could deepen the kiss.

He hadn't meant for this to happen, but he wanted it. He wanted her.

Palming the back of her head, he swept his tongue into her mouth, licking and tasting, devouring. And she kissed him back, her body arching up into his, her breasts pressing deliciously against his chest.

His thoughts from earlier assaulted him. He dragged his mouth from hers and kissed along her jaw, moving to nibble her ear. Then he tipped her head to the side to give him access to her neck. Just as soft and sensitive as he remembered. She shivered when he tongued her flesh.

He slid his hand up under the hem of her shirt and squeezed her side, careful to use firm pressure so as not to tickle her. He remembered so many things about her, but wanted to discover new ones.

"Hayden." She gently pushed at his shoulders.

It took him a moment, but he pulled back. "What?"

"You've been drinking."

"So?"

She looked at him intently. "Are you sure this is what you want?"

"Absolutely. I'm not that drunk. Not so far gone to have regrets." He splayed his fingers beneath her shirt, feeling her heat. "Right now, you're the only thing I know, without hesitation, that I want. That I *need*."

"We shouldn't..."

"Why not? We're grown-ups. I want you. You want me." But maybe she didn't. Maybe she was trying to politely end this. "You *don't* want me."

She closed her eyes briefly then her hands were around his neck again, and she was on her toes. "I want you so bad. Right *now*. Right *here*."

He stared into her eyes and let himself be lost. "Then I'm yours."

Chapter Thirteen

BEX KNEW THIS was a bad idea. He was drunk. Emotional. Upset. And she was totally taking advantage. Except she'd tried to tell him they shouldn't. Maybe she should try harder.

Oh, but his lips on hers were so heavenly, the feel of his warm neck beneath her fingertips divine, the scent of him exhilarating—pure Hayden—a smell she hadn't realized how deeply she'd missed until now. She never wanted this moment to end. And yet, she had to make it stop.

She pushed at his shoulders gently, but firmly.

He looked down at her, the stark desire in his gaze robbing her of thought. "What's wrong?"

Yeah, what the hell was wrong? With *her*? She mentally shook herself. "You've been drinking. I know you said you aren't that drunk—"

"I'm not really drunk at all, actually. I stopped drinking over an hour ago, and I had a ton of water. You know me. You can tell when I'm shitfaced." His mouth ticked up into an almost-smile, and her knees turned to mush.

"That's true," she murmured. He wasn't shitfaced. And like he'd said, they wanted each other. They were consenting adults.

He stroked his hand along her spine, from her nape to the small of her back. Then he caressed her there, his fingertips grazing the top of her backside. Every touch brought her further under the spell of the moment. "Don't you want to know if it's as good as it used to be?"

She practically melted against him. She'd thought of that very question so many times over the past two weeks. And she absolutely wanted an answer.

"Yes."

His mouth was on hers before she finished enunciating the S. She was transported back in time to when she'd felt happy and loved. He felt like…home.

He pulled away, and she just knew this had been too good to be true. He couldn't really want her. Not after all this time and everything they'd been through.

He frowned at her. Her chest tightened. She resigned herself—

"I can't do this," he said.

She stepped back from him, but he didn't let her go. His hands were still wrapped around her waist.

"No," he said. "I can't do this here. In my sister's room." He stuck his tongue out as if he'd had to eat fried liver. "Come on." He took her by the hand and led her from the room. They walked down the hallway, and she knew where they were going.

The wistfulness she'd felt intensified the minute she stepped into his bedroom. Everything about it was the same—the bed, the dresser where she'd kept a few items of clothing stashed, the desk, the poster from the beer and wine festival they'd attended. Memories, good and bad, assailed her. But mostly, she just wanted him to touch her again, to take her back to what she realized now had been the best time of her life.

So far.

He'd opened the door for her and now came in behind her. She heard the door close then felt the whisper of his breath against her neck as he pushed her hair aside. "Been a long time since you were in here, Sexy Bexy."

He hadn't called her that in forever, of course. It had started out as a flirtation when they'd first dated. Later, after they'd been together awhile, he'd called her that only in bed, and never more than once. She'd later come to realize it had been his shorthand for saying "I love you" before they'd both worked up the courage to actually utter the words.

She closed her eyes and forgot about time and place for a moment. She focused on the heat of his body pressed against her back, the soft press of his lips on her exposed flesh. A shiver tickled her spine and her breath caught. His tongue, hot and wet, traced her nape.

"Just like I remember," he whispered.

His hand snaked around her waist and held her tight against him while his other hand came up and cupped the underside of her breast. He went slow, his touch gentle, seeking. She kept her hands at her sides though she longed to touch him. For now, she would let him explore, allow her body to respond.

He closed over her breast, bringing his thumb and forefinger together at the tip. It wasn't enough. There were too many clothes separating them. She pulled up the hem of her T-shirt, but he stilled her hands with his own.

"Let me." His words caressed her flesh just before he kissed her neck. It was hot and wet and sent shocks of pleasure straight to her core. She stifled a moan as his hands pushed her shirt up over her breasts.

She expected him to pull it over her head, but he left it scrunched up, her bra exposed. He slipped his hands inside her bra and pushed the cups down, freeing her breasts. But not quite. They were sort of trapped there between the garments.

"I always loved your breasts. So soft. Just the perfect size for me." He caressed her with both hands, rhythmic strokes that set her hips to moving. He pulled at her flesh then used his thumb and forefinger again. But this time was so much better and she couldn't keep the moan from escaping. "Your nipples are a shade darker. A dusky rose instead of that pink I remember. Do they taste the same, I wonder?"

"You'll have to find out." Her answer came out breathy and needy, and she couldn't have cared less.

He chuckled softly. "Now, that's a dare if ever I've heard one. But then you always were a daredevil. Like the time you broke into one of the offices on campus—I can't remember which one—so we could make out."

She recalled that night vividly. "I think we did a little more than make out."

"Like tonight? Or is this going to stop before it even gets started?"

She pushed back and felt his erection against her ass. "You're being a real tease, you know that?"

"You like it when I tease you. At least you used to. Maybe you've changed. Maybe you'd rather I throw you on the bed and screw you senseless."

Yes, please.

Pathetic as it sounded, she'd take him any way she could. "We've done that, too." Her voice was thread-thin.

His hands continued their torture, caress, pull, soft pinch. "Which do you prefer? Slow and seductive or hard and fast?" Then a hard pinch.

She gasped. "Both?"

He walked her to the bed, his body gently pushing her from behind. He tapped her back so that she bent down, her breasts swaying. "We could do it like this." He ran his hand over her backside before slipping it between her legs. His touch grazed over her, neither firm nor light, but enough to make her already quivering body scream for more.

She parted her legs in silent invitation.

"Mmm, yes. But I think I'd rather see your face." He tugged on her shoulder until she was upright once more then turned her around. His eyes were hooded, his lips parted.

She couldn't stand it another second. She put her hands on his chest and fisted his shirt. "I don't care what you do, so long as you do it *now*."

She cupped his face and kissed him hard, her lips grinding against his just before they each sought the other's tongue. Giddiness cartwheeled through her. She'd never imagined she'd feel this way again, that she'd be in his arms. And until last week, she hadn't realized she'd wanted it. Missed it.

He gripped her hips and rocked against her, his pelvis meeting hers. She clutched at his neck as her joy catapulted into desperation. At last, he pulled her shirt over her head, breaking their kiss briefly. Then he made short work of her bra, tossing it from her body with effortless care. It was like they'd done this before. But of course they had.

She'd kicked her sandals off back in Tori's room, so she had on only her skort and panties, whereas he was wearing everything. Except shoes. She tunneled her hands under his shirt, her fingertips skimming over the muscles of his back. He definitely felt bulkier—just as he looked. She couldn't wait to see what he looked like shirtless.

With a quick tug, she pulled his shirt over his head, baring his chest. But before she could survey her prize, he held her arms up and lowered his mouth to her breast. He covered her with wet heat, drawing a long moan from her throat.

He let go of her arms. "Tastes just like I remember."

She dropped his shirt and thrust her fingers into his hair, urging his mouth to take her harder and deeper. He licked at her and devoured her flesh, his hands cupping her.

She realized she'd started repeating his name over and over and stopped before she sounded like she was completely losing her mind. Which she totally was.

He moved one hand down her abdomen, his fingers skidding over her flesh and then finding the heat buried between her legs, beneath her skirt. He fondled her through her clothing, pressing on her clit until she cried out his name. She gripped his head even tighter.

He kissed his way down her stomach as he pulled at the waistband of her skort. With a rough yank, he pulled the garment down her legs then did the same with her panties.

He clasped her hips and knelt, licking a path toward her core. "God, I just want to—"

He pushed her back onto the bed—not hard, but she was startled. She'd thought he meant to do something else.

She looked up at him as he shucked the rest of his clothing. Yep, his chest and abs were more defined than they'd been five years ago. A sparse trail of light brown hair led her vision south to his cock. *That* hadn't changed. She was suddenly overcome with a need so strong, she started to shake. Had he felt the same? Had that been why he'd changed course?

"I can't wait. I've waited long enough."

His words bored a hole into her heart. She wanted to ease the pain she'd caused him. "I don't want to wait another second."

He grinned down at her. "I'm afraid we have to. I need to get a condom." He turned and went into the bathroom.

Ah yes, that would be good. They'd gone without before…she didn't want to think about that right now. There'd be time for reflection and analysis later. Now, she wanted to live in this glorious moment.

When he returned, he was sheathed and ready. He knelt between her legs on the bed. They locked eyes as he clasped her thighs and kneaded her flesh. He spread her legs a little wider. "If memory serves, you like it when I touch you here." He softly stroked her outer folds. "But even more here." He thumbed her clit, sending jolts of pleasure through her. "But most of all, you liked it when I touched you here." He slid his finger inside her. She was slick and he went in easy. He pumped once, twice, and then pierced deep, curving his finger until he found her G-spot. She closed her eyes in ecstasy. "Wait, I forgot about this spot."

He put his mouth on her breast again, suckling her while he fucked her with his hand. With two fingers, he stroked her hard and fast. She brought her legs up, bending her knees. Her hips rotated and lifted off the bed. Then his mouth found her clit and he sent her over the edge.

Her orgasm obliterated everything but the feel of his hand and mouth and the sound of her cries. She was blissfully broken, and she didn't think she ever wanted to be put back together again.

Except he did—put her back together again. He brought her back to reality with gentle licks and soft strokes.

"Hayden." His name tore from her mouth like a plea. She pulled at his hair, urging him to move up. Then she kissed him, openmouthed and hungry. His tongue speared into her as he framed her face with his hands.

His hips ground into hers, and she rose up to meet him. She reached between them and found his stiff cock. The condom jolted her for a moment, and she briefly entertained the idea of taking it off and sucking him bare. She wanted to, but it would have to wait for another time. Would there be another time?

She closed her hand around him and stroked him from base to tip.

"Bex." He practically groaned her name into her mouth. "I *really* can't wait anymore now."

She guided him to her entrance. His fingers met hers as he opened her then pushed inside. He moved slowly, filling her—not just physically, but emotionally. She'd had no idea how much she'd missed him.

Once he was settled inside, he gazed down at her. "I forgot how well we fit together."

She clasped his waist and his ass. "So did I."

"Let's see how well we move." He slid out and then in, slowly, methodically at first, and then gaining momentum. She locked her feet behind the small of his back.

"Oh, I remember *that*," he said between gritted teeth. He pumped faster, driving into her. She dug her nails into his ass. "And that. God, *that*."

He twined one hand in her hair, pulling gently as he kissed her deeply. His flesh pounded into hers, the delicious friction feeding another orgasm. Her senses exploded, but she didn't want to fly away. Not quite yet.

She reached between their bodies and found his balls, massaging them and then closing her thumb and forefinger around the base of his shaft. She squeezed—not too tight, but just enough to elicit a low moan from deep in his chest.

"Bex!" He battered into her, crying out as he came.

She let go then, and another orgasm engulfed her body. She'd always enjoyed sex with him, but this was something different. Maybe it was because she was older, more experienced, but she felt every sensation in her bones, along her nerves, within her heart.

She was in such trouble.

When their bodies had stilled and their breathing slowed, he kissed her temple before leaving her. After a quick trip into the bathroom, he came back and pulled the covers back. "You can stay, if you want."

She did want.

She rolled to where he'd exposed the sheets then tucked herself under them, scooting back over. She patted the mattress that they'd shared so many times before.

He climbed in beside her and it was like no time had passed at all. She curled onto her side away from him, and he spooned her from behind. His hand came possessively around her waist. She smiled.

His fingertips fluttered against her. "So was it as good?"

She answered without hesitation. "Yes."

But that wasn't the truth. No, the truth was that it had been better.

BRIGHT SUNLIGHT FILTERED through the blinds on the windows on either side of Hayden's bed. He stretched then nudged a foot.

Holy hell. *Bex.*

He turned his head on the pillow. She lay next to him, her dark hair framing her beautifully sculpted face. There were no dimples now, just smooth flesh, pink lips, and ink-black lashes fanned against her cheeks.

There was a small scar on her forehead—from the chicken pox she'd had when she was five. He stopped himself from touching it, from gathering her close, from making love to her again.

He pushed up and got out of the bed. Hurriedly, he grabbed his clothes and went into the bathroom. His morning wood seemed far more inconvenient today, which was insane since unlike most days, he had a willing partner in his bed.

Would she be willing? Or would she wake up with precisely the same what-the-fuck freak-out that he'd just had?

He went through his morning ritual, but didn't jump in the shower. He ought to go back and wake her. Tell her that it had been a mistake.

Except he wasn't sure it had been. Even if he never spent another moment alone with her—which was unlikely given her current job and her apparent closeness with several members of his family—maybe last night was supposed to happen. One last night together. A farewell.

He knew it wasn't that. It hadn't felt remotely like a good-bye. More like a new beginning.

And what the hell was he supposed to do with that? He didn't *want* to start over with her. It had taken so long to untangle himself from her. He didn't want to be bound in her web for a single moment.

Wait a second, a voice in the back of his head said. *You slept together. Once. It felt good, right? When you left Ribbon*

Ridge, you said you would put yourself first. And you deserve that. What's wrong with living in the moment? You've been doing it the past year, and it's worked out great so far.

Yeah, it had. He braced his hands on the counter and exhaled, pushing the stress from his muscles. One of the things he'd promised himself when he'd finally left Ribbon Ridge was that he'd stop overanalyzing. He'd always considered every decision he made so carefully, thinking of everyone and everything so as to make the best possible choice that would benefit the most people. Alex's death had been the wake-up call he'd needed to pull his head out of his ass.

Pushing away from the counter, he left the bathroom. Bex was up and already half dressed. She was just pulling on her skort and now grabbed her T-shirt. And just like that, she was all covered up, though her hair still looked like she'd just enjoyed a good lay.

"Hey," he said, tamping down the awkward silence that seemed to envelop the room.

Her cheeks were faintly pink. Was she embarrassed? "Morning."

Words failed him for a moment. What did you say to your ex the morning after a nostalgia screw? He still suspected it was more than that, but he wasn't going there. Not today. Not with her.

"I'm, uh, sorry about last night," he said.

She winced, and he instantly felt bad.

He stepped toward her. "No, not like that. I have zero regrets." He smiled at her. "I just hope you know that...well, it was one night."

She nodded quickly. Maybe too quickly. Her feelings weren't his problem. Just like his feelings hadn't been *her* problem five years ago.

"I get it," she said. "I had fun. I hope you did, too."

Fun. That was probably undervaluing it, but he wasn't going to tell her that. Whatever emotions were swirling around in his slightly hungover brain were better left unexplored.

"It was great. Thank you."

She nodded, and again the awkwardness in the room seemed a living, breathing thing. And for that he felt bad. They'd developed a good rapport the past couple of weeks. They'd become something he'd never expected—friends. But maybe that was the issue. Maybe they couldn't really do that. Maybe there would always be a lingering attraction, dormant feelings, baggage.

That was too bad because he'd always liked Bex. Love affair or not, he'd liked her. That was probably another reason why he'd taken so long to get over her.

She moved toward the door. "I need to get showered and get to work. See you later."

"Yeah, see you later."

She left, and he immediately turned and went back into the bathroom. He turned on the shower, intent on scrubbing away the vestiges of last night. He could still smell her, like she'd permeated every part of him. Part of him didn't want to wash that away. But it was for the best.

An hour later, he pulled into the driveway at Quail Crest. He'd called Amos French and asked for a meeting.

He parked the car and got out then walked around the house to the backyard, where Amos had said Hayden could find him.

The day was bright and hot, the sky a brilliant blue. Hayden had put on his hiking boots with his shorts because flip-flops were not appropriate vineyard attire. Shorts weren't usually either, but he wasn't going to be trimming bushes or anything, just walking. Or hiking, since the elevation here was pretty steep.

Hayden caught sight of Amos's white hair over near the shed. "Amos," he called.

Amos turned and waved. "Just you this morning?"

Hayden nodded. "I know you're looking to list the property maybe today or tomorrow, and I was hoping I could persuade you to hold off."

Amos was holding a baseball cap and put it back on his head. It was black and orange. Hayden grinned. "You're a Beaver."

"Hell yes. You?"

"Hell yes."

They both laughed, and Amos gestured for Hayden to follow him. "Walk with me."

They strolled into the vineyard. "These are my oldest vines," Amos said. "Is it funny that I'll miss them?"

"Not at all." In France, the vines were precious. Like family, almost. And why not? You invested your time, your energy, your heart and soul in an operation like this. It was much more than a garden. With a vineyard, you were cultivating something lasting, something strangers could enjoy and fall in love with. There was a poetry in it. Or maybe Hayden was just a hopeless romantic. He'd been called that before. By Bex.

Amos looked over at him, squinting. "Why do you need more time? You guys struggling to get the money together? I would've thought you could buy this on your own, what with your name."

Yes, the Archer name was synonymous with real estate and wealth. "I probably could, but I'm only buying a quarter. It's not the money." Jamie and Cameron were ready to sign. Luke was nearly there. Like Hayden, there was something holding him back from committing, but he wasn't saying what it was. Hayden wondered if there was a woman, but Luke hadn't said a word. For all they knew, he was as romantically untethered as he'd always been.

Amos stopped and pivoted toward him. "Then what is it?"

Hayden looked out over the valley, at Ribbon Ridge below. He'd lived here his whole life. The past year felt like some sort of dream—both because he'd been doing what he'd always wanted to do and because he'd been away from his family, his home. It was as if he'd been living in a bubble. A great bubble, but bubbles didn't last.

"I don't know if I'm ready to come back," he said finally, turning his head to look at Amos. "I've been pretty happy on my own the past year."

Amos nodded, his gaze knowing. "Spreading your wings."

"Exactly."

"You know, you can do that here."

Hayden opened his mouth to respond, but closed it again. He could... Just leaving Archer had been a huge step, and no matter what he did, he wasn't going back to that.

"I can, but maybe it feels like a regression?"

"Only in your head, I think. Families do a number on us—good and bad. I grew up with eight brothers and sisters."

"Wow, that's more than me."

Amos chuckled. "And none of us were twins or anything—there's quite an age range. My oldest brothers are gone now." He looked out over the distance for a second then glanced at Hayden. "I know you lost one, too."

They fell silent. Hayden succumbed to thoughts of Alex and that damned letter he'd read last night. The letter that had led him to Bex. He'd done a good job of banishing it from his mind, instead focusing on the Bex complication and now this. What would Alex tell him to do? he wondered. He realized he had no idea. He thought he'd come to know Alex better than anyone, that they'd developed this close bond. What a load of shit. He'd been no closer to Alex than to any of his other siblings.

Hayden jerked his mind back to the present. Alex didn't deserve his time. "Maybe I should know this, but are you from Ribbon Ridge?"

Amos shook his head. "No. I lived in Forest Grove until I retired and bought this place. I worked for Intel back in the eighties, retired early." He waggled his brows at Hayden and gave him a sly smile.

Hayden laughed. "Well played, sir. Was your family close?"

"We were, but we spread out. A few of us are around here—close enough to spend holidays and whatnot together. But my closest brother—we were only eighteen months apart—lives in Florida. We haven't lived in the same state in fifty years, and yet we're still thick as thieves. Home and family are a state of mind. Geography's got nothing to do with it."

Hayden's confusion must've reflected on his face because Amos clarified. "What I'm trying to say is that regardless of where you go, family's family. If there's something causing you trouble, it's going to be trouble no matter where you are."

Hayden began to understand. "You're telling me that I shouldn't let my family influence my decision."

"Or whatever it is. I used family as an example because that's something we have in common." He cocked his head to the side. "You said it felt like a regression. Why? Answer that and maybe you can figure things out."

Why *was* it a step back? Because he'd moved forward, pursued his dream, left his younger self behind. The things that were here now—his family business, his family, The Alex, Bex—were all the things he'd moved on from. But Amos was right. If the next step in his journey was to start this winery, the geography didn't matter. So what if it was Ribbon Ridge?

Because it would be complicated. He'd be the extra Archer again, the afterthought. And then there was Bex, who shouldn't have been a problem, but after last night, he had to think extra hard about it.

Amos started walking again. "Looks like you've got a lot to think about."

What had Hayden told himself that morning? That he overanalyzed everything? Screw it. He wanted this vineyard, and he *did* miss Ribbon Ridge. He'd figure the rest out. Or move up here into this house and ignore everybody except his business partners.

He took long steps to catch up with Amos. "We'll buy it. Don't list the property."

Amos stopped and turned. "Are you sure?"

"Absolutely. Do you want me to give you an earnest-money deposit right now?"

He laughed. "Once you make up your mind, you're ready to go, aren't you?"

Hayden smiled. "I'm trying to be." He just had to make sure Luke was in, and if he wasn't…well, they could find another vineyard manager. But no, he'd talk Luke into it. If he could commit, so could Luke.

Amos offered his hand to Hayden. "All right then. Have to say that I'm happy to see it go to you guys."

Hayden shook his hand firmly. He still felt a grain of uncertainty, but attributed it to his family issues and Bex. Starting this winery filled him with nothing but excitement and joy.

Maybe if he focused on that, it would spread to the rest of his life, too.

Chapter Fourteen

HUNGRY FOR LUNCH, Bex drove into Ribbon Ridge. Today was one of her two nonbrewing days this week so she was taking advantage of the opportunity to leave the brewhouse. It was much easier to wallow in her humiliation and disappointment away from The Alex and its hive of Archers, who only reminded her of what a moron she was for thinking she could rekindle something with Hayden.

She drove past The Arch and Vine. *Yeah, not going there either*, she thought.

Instead, she turned up Second and parked on the street. She got out and locked her truck then walked toward the little Mexican restaurant with the best salsa she'd ever had. Muy Loco was a Ribbon Ridge treasure even if it looked like a dive.

As she neared the door, her phone chimed. She pulled it out and read the text.

Emily: I'm so sorry, but the apartment isn't going to be ready tomorrow as planned. The flooring was supposed to arrive today, but there was a problem and it's going to be another week. You know you can stay with us as long as you like!

Her shoulders slumped. She'd been hoping that her nights sleeping down the hall from Hayden were numbered. Damn it. As soon as she ordered lunch, she planned to scour Craig's List for any rental in a thirty-mile radius.

She stepped into the cool, dim interior of the restaurant and froze. The place was tiny, with maybe ten or twelve tables. Seated toward the back at a rectangular table were Sean, Derek, Aubrey, and Alaina. They weren't technically Archers—well, she supposed Alaina was by name at least—but they were close enough.

And they'd already seen her, which meant she couldn't turn around and escape.

Alaina waved from the bench seat attached to the wall. "Hey, Bex. Come sit with us!"

Bex had no choice but to walk over. Maybe she could just order takeout.

Derek jumped up and grabbed a chair. He brought it to the end of the table between him and Alaina. "Here." He held the chair for her.

"I was going to get something to go," Bex said weakly. "I have work…"

Aubrey, who sat on the bench beside Alaina, smiled at her. "Oh come on, sit. You can spare a few minutes, right?"

Bex looked at the four people and wondered how they'd come to have lunch here together. That at least had to be a good story. And she could use a distraction. "Sure." She sat down in the chair, and Derek scooted her in. "What are you all doing here?

They exchanged glances and smiled. Aubrey laughed. "Would you believe we're a club?"

Bex hung her purse over the back of her chair. "Uh…" She couldn't think what kind. They weren't Archer spouses or SOs. Some of them were, but that didn't account for Derek. Plus, they'd be missing Dylan and Maggie. But then they were both crazy busy up at The Alex. "What sort of club?"

"I guess our official name is the Only Child Club," Sean said.

The server arrived with a large tray bearing their lunches. She made eye contact with Bex and smiled. "Can I get you something?"

Bex still wasn't sure she was in the mood to hang out, but she was starving. She'd at least order, and if she wanted to leave, she'd ask for a box. "Yes, I'd like a chicken tostada salad, pinto beans, please. And I'm good with water."

The server distributed the plates. "You got it. You all be careful, plates are hot." She disappeared into the kitchen.

Bex looked around the table. Yes, they were all only children, including her. "Is that why you invited me to join you? Because I'm an only child, too?"

Alaina cut a piece from her enchilada. "Actually, I was just being nice, but yeah, you could totally join."

Bex surveyed the group again and frowned. "I hate to break it to you, but there's a key component missing here. I'm not married to an Archer." She looked at Aubrey. "Or engaged to one."

Derek shrugged. "I'm not either." He flashed her a grin as he picked up a taco.

"Ha ha." But Bex smiled anyway. Okay, this was actually making her feel a little bit better.

The server briefly returned with Bex's water and a napkin-rolled set of knife and fork.

"But you were almost married to an Archer, right?" Aubrey asked.

And there went her escalating mood right back into the drain. "Not really."

Aubrey winced. "My bad. Sorry."

Alaina looked at Bex, her gaze lingering. Then she went back to attacking her enchilada like only a pregnant woman could. Bex picked up her napkin-wrapped utensils and pulled them apart. As she laid the napkin in her lap, she let her fingertips slide over her belly, thinking fleetingly of the baby she'd lost.

She didn't want to go down that path. Not today when she was feeling emotionally vulnerable thanks to last night's catastrophe. And not in front of these people. So she changed the subject. "How'd this club start?"

Sean and Alaina exchanged looks. "It's kind of funny, I guess," Sean said. "Alaina and I have been friends for a while. We met in LA."

Alaina sipped her water. "Sean's the reason I came to Ribbon Ridge. I needed a place to hide out, and he offered up the Archers' garage apartment. I met Evan when I set off the fire alarm."

Again, Bex couldn't resist a smile. "You did what?"

"I tried to cook bacon. Luckily, Evan came to my rescue." The love in her gaze was almost palpable. Bex's heart twisted.

Sean swallowed a bite of his lunch and wiped his mouth with his napkin. "Anyway, we were having lunch one time—this was after Alaina and Evan got engaged—and Derek happened upon us. Just like you did today. We'd been talking about how to navigate this huge family when we were both only children."

Derek drank from a bottle of Dos Equis. "So I offered to be their guide."

"How helpful of you." Bex narrowed her eyes at him. "Where was this club when I was living in town?"

"It was different then." He arched a brow at her, and his mouth curved up. "There was a much smaller number of Archers."

She rolled her eyes. "I see. For the record, that's a lame excuse."

Aubrey shared a sympathetic glance with Bex. "Totally."

The server brought Bex's lunch then looked around the table. "How is everything?" Everyone offered positive comments, and the server left.

Bex picked up her fork. "That's it? That's how the club started?"

Sean nodded. "Pretty much. When Liam and Aubrey got engaged, we invited her to join us. We meet every few weeks."

"Yeah, see, I can't join." She displayed her unadorned left hand to the group. "Not engaged."

"Well, you can be our special guest today," Aubrey said. "You have a lot of experience with the family that might be useful."

Alaina polished off the last of her enchilada and started in on her chile relleno. "Especially with Hayden. I don't know him very well."

Bex ate a bite of salad, glad that she couldn't respond immediately. Or maybe she could avoid responding altogether. She wasn't sure she knew him anymore either. His aloofness this morning had been a shock. She hadn't expected him to fall to his knees and profess his undying love, but she'd hoped for something more than just a one-night stand.

"Derek knows him better than I do," Bex said after she swallowed. "You guys worked closely together at Archer for a long time."

Derek nodded. "That's true. He was COO to my CFO for four years. He and Alex and I were sort of the three musketeers for a while." Derek looked down at his plate briefly. "Now it's just me. I miss them." He smiled sadly.

Alaina reached across the table and touched his hand. "I'm sorry. I didn't mean to open up a can of worms."

"It's fine," Derek said. "It's not like we can't talk about Alex. It was hard at first, but it's become a lot easier. It helps to have this amazing legacy about to open."

"I'm sorry I didn't get a chance to know him," Sean said.

Alaina withdrew her hand to her lap. "Me too. You knew him, right, Bex?"

"I did." He'd had a very dry sense of humor, and he was wicked smart. And attractive, despite his illness. He was thin and always seemed to look a bit sickly next to his healthier brothers. She knew that bothered him and that it bothered the others that he looked physically different. She didn't really want to talk about her time with the Archers. At least not today. "Aubrey, you got to know him well, I imagine."

Aubrey washed down a bite of her chimichanga with a drink of water. "Yes. He hired me to set up his trust. He told me his life expectancy wasn't great, and he just wanted to be prepared." She shifted on the bench, and Bex sensed her discomfort.

Bex wanted to hug everyone at the table. "His suicide was just as shocking to you then as to everyone else." She'd been devastated when she'd heard. For herself and the relationship she'd had with Alex, but mostly for the Archers, for Hayden. She'd called him and left a voice-mail, but he'd never returned her call. She'd taken that as a clear message that their relationship—even as friends—was completely gone. Knowing what she knew now, that he'd been hung up on her, she realized that her call might have just complicated his grief. He was despondent, and here was his ex calling and dredging up old feelings. No wonder he hadn't called her back.

Aubrey exhaled. "It was. The whole thing was an ugly mess. Last year was tough for the whole family."

Sean shook his head sadly. "Almost broke up my marriage. Tori was a wreck."

Bex thought of Tori and how she'd been less visible on social media last year. Despite that, Bex hadn't picked up on the depth of Tori's emotions. Now she felt like a terrible friend. "Is that right?"

"Yeah, but we pulled through." Sean smiled. "It's all good now."

Derek lifted his beer bottle. "To everything on the up-and-up. This year is like a total flip what with all the weddings and a baby." He grinned at Alaina.

They all joined in the toast and drank. The conversation continued and when the bill came, Derek picked up the tab. Bex protested, but he said it was his turn to pay for lunch.

"But I'm not even in the club," she said.

"Doesn't matter." He looked around at the other three. "Does it?"

"Not to me," Alaina said. "I think almost married to an Archer counts for sure." She winked at Bex. "I need to use the restroom. Don't wait for me." She waved before taking off to the back of the restaurant.

Aubrey smiled at Bex as she stood up from the table. "I'm glad you could join us today. I'll let you know when we meet next. Us only children have to stick together. Plus, you and I have some crazy parent stories to swap, I think."

Bex had enjoyed lunch, and was glad for the pick-me-up. She'd needed it. "Definitely. Thanks."

Derek touched her arm. "See you, Bex."

Sean kissed her cheek. "Bye." She looked at him, surprised. He laughed. "I'm from Europe. We do that. Also in Hollywood." He chuckled on his way out.

Bex didn't leave with them. She wanted to get a giant Diet Coke to take back to work with her. She flagged the server and put in an order for a to-go cup.

While she was waiting, Alaina came from the bathroom. It was still a bit strange to see this mega movie star in such an everyday place. But why should it be? Alaina was just a person. A super famous person. Her dark blonde hair was pulled back from her face, and she wore very little makeup.

She smiled at Bex. "I said you didn't have to wait, but I'm glad you did."

The server came back with Bex's drink. Bex tried to pay her, but the server only smiled. "Pay for it next time."

"Thanks, I will. With tip!" Bex sipped her drink as she turned with Alaina toward the door.

"You headed back to work?" Alaina asked.

"Yes. I need to check the gravity in the tanks this afternoon and prep for tomorrow's brew cycle."

Alaina sighed. "I miss beer. Rob's making me a small batch of nonalcoholic."

"Aw, that's so nice. And so Rob."

Alaina pushed open the door, and they stepped out into the heat of the afternoon. "You know him pretty well?"

"I interned with him for six months after college, so we worked together. Plus, I was with Hayden for three years."

Alaina pivoted, and they stood beneath the overhang of the building in the relative cool of the shade. "That's a long time. What happened? If you don't mind my asking."

"I don't mind. It's just…It was a long time ago." And she'd been thinking about it more lately than in the previous five years. "We were really young."

"College, right?"

"Pretty much."

"I worked with a writer in my early twenties who said young love was the deepest. Granted, that was the point of that particular film, but I think he meant that emotions are maybe rawer when we're young."

Bex agreed with that. Except her emotions felt even more vulnerable now. She sensed something wrong with Hayden, something she wanted to help with, but couldn't. Because they weren't a couple, and they never would be.

"Is it awkward being back here together?" Alaina asked. "You guys seem to get along great. Very adult of you."

Bex laughed. "Yeah, right. It's a bit weird sometimes." Like when you wake up in bed together and realize it had been a mistake. "But we're managing."

"That's good, especially since you're living in the same house right now."

Crap, Bex still needed to peruse Craig's List. She was doing that first thing when she got back to the brewhouse.

Alaina's gaze softened. "I hope you'll join our group. I like you—you're cool. It sucks that you aren't going to be an Archer. Sure we can't fix that?"

Bex tried not to be flattered that Alaina Pierce—Archer, whatever—said she was cool and failed miserably. But her question gave Bex pause, and not just because of her now-complicated relationship with Hayden. As much as she loved the Archers, she'd found them overwhelming when they were all together. That hadn't happened very often when she'd lived here, but now it was the norm. She *was* an only child. Of parents who didn't give a rat's ass what she was doing. She was quite used to being on her own and answering to no one. Having a family meant having responsibilities that she wasn't used to and wasn't sure she could handle.

She cocked her head to the side. "What makes you think I want to be an Archer?"

Alaina shrugged. "I don't know. I get a vibe from you, like there's unfinished business for you here. With Hayden. But maybe I'm wrong."

No, she was completely right. Bex knew that sharing a baby with him, even though they'd lost it, would tie them together forever. At least in her heart and mind. For the first time, she considered confiding in someone. Alaina would get it. She was pregnant herself. And she likely valued discretion more than anyone Bex knew.

"You're not wrong."

Alaina's eyes lit. "Oh, well then. Let's make this happen."

Bex laughed, but there was a bit of unease in it. She suddenly regretted saying anything. She couldn't do anything about it—about Hayden. Last night, they'd had sex. He'd said it was a one-time event. It was pretty clear to her where things were headed: nowhere. She was glad she hadn't mentioned the baby. What a stupid thought that had been.

"There's nothing to make happen. Not anymore." She hastened to soften her refusal. "But thank you."

Alaina narrowed her eyes briefly. "I'm not sure I buy that. If I've learned anything in my life it's that if you want something, you have to fight for it. I clawed my way out of a cycle of drugs and poverty. *I* did that." She smiled warmly and touched Bex's arm. "Don't be complacent. Life's too short."

Fight for what she wanted…What did she want? Did she truly want Hayden back? To what end? Were they going to get married this time? Would there be another baby? Her brain sputtered and started to shut down. Emotional overload. He was over her, and she needed to let him go.

Bex fished her sunglasses from her purse and put them on. "Thanks, Alaina. I appreciate it."

"I'm glad you found us today," she said. "See you next time!" She turned and walked in the opposite direction from Bex.

Bex went to her truck and set her drink in the cup holder before climbing inside.

Next time. There wasn't going to be a next time. She wasn't a part of the Archer family or their club, and she never would be.

Chapter Fifteen

THE NEXT MORNING, Hayden walked into Stella's, one of three coffee shops in Ribbon Ridge, but the only one that was just a coffee shop. Books and Brew was also a bookstore, while Beaker's was a drive-thru and maybe didn't technically count. He glanced around but didn't see Cameron. Hayden had texted him yesterday to talk about buying the vineyard, but he'd been in the Bay Area for the day on a sales trip.

Hayden walked to the counter to order and smiled at the owner, who'd established the shop close to twenty years prior. "Good morning, Stella."

She grinned at him as she pushed her wire-rimmed glasses back up her nose. White hair pulled into a bun, Stella had a generous heart and a mouth like a sailor when she was fired up about something. "Morning to you, Hayden Archer. I'd heard you were back in town, but I wouldn't believe it until I saw you."

He hung his head sheepishly. He'd tried to make contact with as many denizens of the town as he could in the two or so weeks that he'd been home. "Sorry, I've been in a couple times, but you were out."

"A gal's gotta take a vacation now and again. Don't you worry—you're still my favorite Archer." She winked at him. "You want your summer regular, or have your tastes changed since you went to France?"

"If you think I could come to Ribbon Ridge and *not* have one of your iced mochas, you're insane. I can't get anything close to what you make over there."

She chuckled. "You always knew how to flatter a girl. Speaking of that, I heard your ex was back in town, too. She's working up at the new hotel?" Stella was also a bit of a gossip.

Hayden handed her a five-dollar bill, and she made change, which he promptly dropped into her tip container. "Yes, she's the brewer. I'm surprised you remembered her. We dated a long time ago."

Stella moved to her left and started making his drink. "Of course I remember her. She's a lovely girl." She clucked her tongue. "I was really hoping you'd get married. Ah, well."

Hayden clamped his teeth together in annoyance. Five years and people were still pairing them off? Intellectually he understood why. They'd been together three years. They'd moved in together. They *had* been on a path to happily-ever-after. But that just went to show that you could never predict what would happen, no matter how good or right something felt.

The door to the shop opened, and Cameron walked in. He was dressed for work in khakis and a light blue polo shirt. He pulled his sunglasses off and nodded as he made eye contact with Hayden.

Stella shook her head, but smiled. "Uh-oh, here comes trouble."

Cameron joined Hayden at the counter. "Always. What're you making this loser, Stella?"

"Iced mocha. I'd ask if you want your usual, but you don't have one. What's your poison today?"

"I have to go with an iced espresso. Large, please. I got in late last night so I need some extra caffeine."

Stella finished Hayden's drink and gave it to him then looked at Cam. "What was her name?"

Hayden laughed, and Cam grinned. "Very funny. It was an airplane actually. Mechanical difficulty, so my flight didn't get into Portland until after midnight, and then I had to drive home."

That trip took a good hour and a half, and that was without traffic.

"You *do* need caffeine," Hayden said.

Stella whipped up his espresso then charged him for it. "I'm heading out in a bit, but if you need anything, my granddaughter Grace will be here. She's in the back washing some dishes."

Hayden blinked at her. "Your granddaughter's old enough to work here now? Isn't she, like, twelve?"

Stella laughed. "Honey, she's seventeen now. She's going to be a senior at West Valley."

"Wow, time flies." He turned with Cam to sit at their usual table in the corner. "I was only gone a year."

"A little more than that."

"Still. Sometimes I can't help but feel like life has moved forward at an astounding speed, and I've been standing on the sidelines."

They sat down, and Cam sipped his coffee. "Seriously? How can you possibly feel like you were standing still? Every time I talked to you in France, you had a dozen things going."

That was true. "Maybe it's just being back home again. Everything here seems vastly different."

Cam set his drink and sunglasses down and sat back in his chair, stretching his legs out in front of him to the side of the small table. "Probably because it is. All your siblings are home now, dude. And married or getting married. It's creepy as hell, right?"

Hayden snorted. "I don't know if *creepy* is the right word."

"Come on. Evan's going to be a dad? Liam's engaged *and* moved home? If that's not creepy, what is it?"

"How about *unexpected*?"

Cam grinned as he picked up his coffee. "That's nicer. Also accurate." He sipped his drink then set it back down. "I'll tell you what else is unexpected—you *not* living here."

"Well, that's what I wanted to talk to you about this morning. I told Amos yesterday that we'd buy the property."

Cam's eyes widened. He sat up sharply and leaned forward over the table. "You did what?"

"I committed. We just have to get Luke to agree." Hayden took a drink of his mocha. "If he doesn't, we could find someone else to manage the vineyard, but I'd rather not."

Cam pressed his lips together and sat back from the table again, his gaze determined. "He'll agree. Let me talk to him. I'll call him as soon as we're done." His mouth broke into a wide smile. "Dude, this is *awesome*! I have to tell you, ever since we started talking about it, my job has become more and more mundane and awful. I can't wait to leave. If you'd said no, I was seriously thinking about what else I might do."

Satisfaction warmed Hayden's chest. He was glad this decision helped his friend. "Now you don't have to." He used his straw to stir his drink. "We need to talk about timing though. Luke won't be free until November probably. I think we can close on the property by the end of August, but harvest won't be until September, maybe into October."

"And the profit from those grapes will be Amos's, not ours."

"Yep, so we can start moving forward on infrastructure right away, just nothing with the vineyard until after harvest."

Cam smiled. "It's actually great timing then for Luke."

Just about perfect, really, provided he was ready to leave his current job. "Yeah, that's what I'm thinking."

"Have you told your boss in France that you aren't coming back?"

"Not yet." Hayden had relegated Antoine—and disappointing him—to the recesses of his mind. He'd been too focused on Bex and this business that he'd decided to pursue. "I'll take care of it. Also, let's wait to announce this until after the soft open next week. Everyone's caught up in that, and I don't want to steal any thunder."

A faint smile teased Cam's lips. "You're always so thoughtful of everyone."

Yep, that was Hayden. Nicest guy ever. And what did they say about nice guys? He pushed that irritating thought away. "So you'll talk to Luke and let me know?"

"ASAP. Did you talk to Jamie?"

Hayden sipped his mocha. "No. I wanted to tell you first."

"I appreciate that." He picked up his coffee and drank for a moment. He slowly put it back on the table, scrutinizing Hayden the entire time.

Hayden grew suspicious. "What?"

"You don't seem as excited as I would've expected. This is a huge deal. Winemaker at your own damn winery. Dream come true, right?"

Hayden shifted in his chair, uncomfortable that Cam had picked up on the disquiet he was trying to shield. But what should he expect from his oldest and best friend? "Definitely."

"Then what gives? And no, I'm not going to ignore this…funk or whatever it is. Is it the family? I know you feel disconnected, but that will fade when you get used to the new normal."

The new normal. He'd liked the old normal. But had he been satisfied with it? *No.* The problem was that he wasn't sure he could be satisfied with this either.

Cam narrowed his eyes at Hayden. "Or is it Bex?" Hayden must've reflected something in the affirmative, though he couldn't imagine what that was. Cam frowned. "I was worried about that."

That rankled him. Bex was the past. Oh yeah? Then what had he been doing having sex with her? Hayden sat back and folded his arms over his chest. "*What* were you worried about?"

"Her screwing with you."

"She wouldn't do that." Bex was a lot of things, but she wasn't vindictive. Besides she was the one who'd left him. If anyone were going to "screw" with the other, it would be Hayden. "Come on, you know her."

"Yes, but I'm *your* friend. And the one who picked up the pieces she left behind."

He *had* done that. For far too long. "It's no big deal."

Cam's eyes widened. "Shit, something happened." He leaned forward, his gaze intent, his voice low. "Did you have sex?"

Hayden said nothing.

"You *did* have sex." Cam blew out a breath. "You better watch yourself. I get what you're saying—she's not out to screw you over or use you or anything—but she broke your heart once. You'd be a fool to let her do it again."

Yes, he would. But he couldn't deny that he'd relished having her back in his arms. He'd barely slept last night. In fact, he'd had to get up after trying to sleep and change the sheets on his bed because they'd smelled too much like her. It had been pure torture. Even then, with her scent gone, he could still feel her touch, taste her kiss.

"Although, I suppose there's no harm in sex for old time's sake. Or if you're just horny since your fuckbuddy's in France. Just so long as you keep things physical. Trust me, you don't want more than that. I speak from experience."

"I know. You've spent the last five and a half years as a total manwhore." That was perhaps overdramatizing it a bit, but not much. Cam's heart had been more than broken—it had been carved out with a spoon and set on fire. Hayden knew it was in there somewhere, but it was going to take a very special woman to find it again. "But it was just one night with Bex."

"Hey, you can have more than one night—I do from time to time—you just have to keep it casual. Like with the girl in France." He paused in lifting his cup from the table. "That's how it is with her, right?"

"Yep." By mutual agreement. Bex, on the other hand…Since they'd split up, the thought of her with someone else had made him feel terrible. Not jealous exactly—though there was that too—but unsettled.

Deep inside he still felt that way, he realized.

Then don't look deep inside, moron. You've gotten pretty good at that.

Cam sipped his espresso. "Glad to see you're looking out for yourself. I'm still your wingman, whenever you need me."

"Thanks." Hayden glanced at his watch. "I need to go."

Cam checked his watch, too. "Yeah, I've got a meeting. I'll call Luke on the way and let you know how it goes."

Hayden stood with his drink. "Cool."

Cam stood as he sucked the rest of his espresso down. Then he poured the ice into the waste bin and tossed the cup in the recycle bin.

"You're done already?" Hayden asked.

Cam shrugged. "Hey, I was desperate for caffeine. Like I said, I was up really late. I might've left out the part where I hooked up with the flight attendant after we landed."

"Stella was right." Of course she was.

"Hey, we sat on the runway in Frisco for like four hours. She was flirty."

Hayden shook his head, smiling. "You're a regular James Bond."

Cam grinned as he slid his Tom Ford sunglasses back on, making him *look* like James Bond. "Minus the assassin part."

Hayden opened the door and stepped outside. "Yeah that. See you later."

"See ya."

Hayden went to his parents' Prius. He should probably decide what to do with his car that Kyle was driving. Unlike the house, Hayden kind of wanted his car back now that he was going to be living here. Kyle would be fine with that.

Since he was selling his house to Kyle, he also needed a place to live. His parents' house was fine, but not for a permanent residence. Even after Bex moved out.

Which brought him to his appointment—a rental that had just come on the market yesterday. An older house with two bedrooms, it sat at the base of the hills on the edge of downtown. The drive there took about four minutes.

He parked across the street. The house had good curb appeal—blue, with shutters and a small, white porch. Too bad it didn't stretch the length of the front of the house. The second story had a wide bay window in the front.

He walked up the front path and climbed the three steps to the porch. The front door was ajar. Presumably the rental agent was waiting for him inside.

He stepped over the threshold and was instantly greeted by a middle-aged man with very little hair and a broad smile. "You must be Hayden." He offered his hand. "I'm Theo."

Hayden gave him a brief handshake. "Nice to meet you. Thanks for coming out to meet me here this morning." The rental agency was based twenty minutes away in McMinnville.

"No problem. I have several showings today. Lots of interest, but then the rental market here is pretty tight."

"That it is."

Theo's phone, which he was holding in his other hand, rang. "Excuse me for a minute. Go ahead and look around." He answered the phone then stepped outside onto the porch.

Hayden toured the ground floor. The front of the house boasted a decent-sized living room, a smallish dining room, a half bathroom, and an eat-in kitchen, which had been remodeled within the past five years. It was nice—nothing spectacular—but perfectly acceptable with a granite tile counter and white cabinets.

He went back to the entry where the stairs led to the second floor. He climbed up and turned to the left where a hallway stretched from the front bedroom to the back, with a bathroom in between.

Bex stepped out of the bathroom, and his mind just stopped.

She wore jean shorts and a purple T-shirt, just an ordinary outfit, and her hair was pulled into a ponytail. She shouldn't have looked stunning, but to him, she'd never looked better. His body reacted, hardening with desire and pulsing with need.

Damn it all.

Her eyes flickered with surprise. She blinked. "Hayden, what are you doing here?"

"Probably the same thing as you. House hunting."

More surprise in her gaze, but something else, too. Alarm? Excitement? Maybe both. "Wait, does that mean you're staying in Ribbon Ridge?"

"I'm exploring my options." He wasn't going to publicly commit until after they'd made this vineyard purchase official. He stepped past her and tried to ignore her alluring scent, the one he'd banished from his bed the night before. "How's the bathroom?"

"Nice. Updated."

He walked inside. It wasn't particularly spacious, but it had good amenities. "Two sinks is cool." He walked to the window on the outside wall.

"What about your house?"

He turned. She'd moved to the threshold. Her brow was wrinkled with confusion. "Didn't you know?" he asked. "I'm selling it to Kyle."

The disappointment in her eyes reached into his soul and squeezed. His emotions tried to break free, but he wouldn't let them.

"I *didn't* know," she said softly. She stepped into the bathroom. "You loved that house."

"I did, but it's sort of his and Maggie's now." And it had way too many memories. It was bad enough that he was staying in his room at his parents' house where there were also memories, including a new one from two nights ago.

God, he wanted to touch her again.

"So you need a new place to live." She took another step inside. "I need a place to live too, and I like this house."

He arched a brow in challenge. "I see. We're going to have to fight for it?"

She narrowed her eyes. "What do you have in mind?"

He surveyed her and was again struck by her beauty. He was just going to have to accept that he would always be attracted to her. "Arm wrestle?"

She laughed. "Right. No."

"Tickle fight?"

She gasped. "That's playing dirty, Archer. You know I can't stand to be tickled."

Tickled no, but stroked in a very specific way? That drove her wild. And just thinking about it was driving *him* wild. He really ought to go.

She put her hand on the doorknob and gave him a saucy, borderline seductive stare. "I could lock you in here and run downstairs to close the deal."

He reached over her head and shut the door, moving close enough that she had to flatten her back against the wood. "I don't think it locks from the outside. But look"—he turned the lock in the knob—"it does on the *inside*."

She looked up at him, her lips parted. "Hayden, what are you doing?" Her voice had dropped two octaves, and its throaty breathiness only fueled the fire in his belly.

He watched her pupils grow larger. He tucked an errant strand of hair that had dislodged from her ponytail behind her ear. "Playing dirty, apparently."

"This isn't a good idea. You said—"

"Screw what I said." He lowered his head and kissed her.

Chapter Sixteen

THE MINUTE SHE'D seen Hayden in the hallway, her body had screamed for his. But she knew nothing would happen. He'd made that clear.

Then he'd walked past her, and she'd practically bitten her tongue to keep from saying something flirtatious, or outright asking him to reconsider his one-night rule.

Then he'd mentioned a tickle fight, and she'd known he would never do that to her. That he'd meant something else entirely. So she'd let herself flirt a little by threatening to lock him inside. She'd never imagined he'd take it a step further. She couldn't believe he was kissing her.

And it felt divine. She'd woken up early this morning from a hot, sensual dream in which he'd made achingly slow love to her in his house. The house he'd just told her he was selling to Kyle. That made her sad.

The hell with sad. She didn't want that emotion right now. She wanted desire and anticipation and pleasure.

His kiss wasn't soft or gentle, but hard and demanding. His body pressed into hers, pinning her against the door. His hands were on her hips, kneading her flesh through her shorts.

She slid her hands up under his shirt and ran her nails lightly over his back. He thrust his pelvis into her, connecting just enough with her clit to send a wave of need pulsing through her.

She moaned softly into his mouth, and he pulled away, saying, "Shh. You don't want Theo to hear, do you?" He moved his mouth to her neck, nibbling and licking at her flesh.

"We're not really doing this, are we?"

"Sometimes you talk too damned much." He kissed her again, his mouth hot and wet, his tongue spearing into her as his hips slammed into hers.

He brought his hand up under her shirt and cupped her breast, squeezing her through her bra. Then his hand was inside, plucking at her nipple, driving her frantic with want.

She clutched at his back, her nails curling into his flesh. She widened her legs, silently pleading with him to ease the ache between them.

He still understood their language. His hand glided down over her belly and unfastened her shorts. Then he plunged into the garment, his fingers finding her heat.

"Damn, Bex. You are so wet."

"Because you are so damn hot. *We are in the bathroom of a random rental house.*"

"What's your point?" He picked her up by the waist and turned, setting her on the counter between the two sinks. He cupped the back of her head with one hand and kissed her again.

What *was* her point? She gave herself over to him, spreading her legs so he was nestled right between them.

He let go of her head to pull her shorts and panties down her legs. Together, they managed to get them off one leg before her impatience won out and she tugged him forward once more. All the while, their kiss blazed on—hot and sultry, amping her desire.

He tore his mouth from hers. "You know, I could do this all day, but we should hurry before Theo comes looking for us."

She snagged her lip with her teeth, almost afraid to ask this question. "Do you have a condom?"

His lips curved up, slowly at first, and then spread into a Cheshire cat grin. "That would be a real bitch if I didn't, now, wouldn't it?" He pulled his wallet from his back pocket and withdrew a condom.

She took the package from his fingers and tore it open. "When did you become such a hardcore tease?"

He tossed his wallet on the counter and unbuttoned his shorts. "You don't like it?"

She pulled the condom out and dropped the wrapper. "You're different." With her free hand, she shoved his underwear down inside his shorts and stroked his cock. Smooth and hard, she ran her fingers up and down his length. "I like it. *A lot.*"

She moved faster, loving the feel of him.

"Now who's the tease? Bex, you need to hurry."

She flashed him a not-sorry smile. "Sorry." She ran her thumb over the tip, capturing the moisture there before stretching the condom over his length.

She'd barely covered him before he slipped his hand beneath her ass and scooted her to the edge of the counter.

"Wrap your legs around me and hold on tight," he growled.

She tilted her hips up and did as he said. The anticipation she'd been looking for rocketed through her. "Is this the part where you screw me senseless?"

He guided himself into her, slowly, but then he plunged forward, filling her completely. He kissed her deeply, his tongue mimicking the thrust of his cock as he drove into her. She heard his hand slap against the mirror as he braced himself. Then he let loose and did exactly what she'd said.

He pulled his mouth from hers as they moved together. Their pants filled the small room, but they fought to be as quiet as possible. At least it was a struggle for her. She wanted to moan and yell and tell him how good he felt.

She squeezed her legs around his hips, urging him deep, while she clawed at his back through his shirt. She was mindless with need, pleasure beating through her. His speed and depth were relentless, pushing her to the edge. Then he brought his hand around from her backside and found her clit, stroking her over the mountain and down the other side into sheer bliss.

Her orgasm exploded through her, and a cry started in the back of her throat. He kissed her again, stealing any sound she'd been about to make.

A moment later he came too, his body thrusting deep into hers. She swallowed his grunt and held him tight, her heels digging into him as she pinned him against her.

He broke the kiss once more, panting as he fought to regain his breath.

A soft knock on the door made them both freeze. "Hello?"

Bex widened her eyes and mouthed, "Now what?"

Hayden shook his head and put his finger to his lips. "I'll be out in a sec, Theo."

Hayden pulled free from her body and went to the toilet to dispose of the condom.

Bex slid from the counter and pulled her clothes back on.

After flushing the toilet and readjusting his clothing, Hayden turned and pointed to the bathtub. "Get in," he mouthed.

Bex stepped in as Hayden went to the door. Just as she was about to pull the shower curtain closed, she saw the condom wrapper on the floor. "Hayden!" she hissed softly.

He turned, and she pointed at the wrapper.

He bent and picked it up then shoved it into his pocket. He threw her a sexy grin before turning back to the door.

Struck with an impending case of serious giggles, Bex slapped her hand over her mouth as she pulled the curtain closed.

"Sorry, I had to use the bathroom." Hayden said. Then all she heard was muffled voices and retreating footsteps.

She waited a minute then left the bathroom, picking her way down the stairs quietly. The front door stood partway open, and she saw Hayden and Theo talking on the porch.

She walked toward them and pulled the door wider so she could step outside.

Theo turned. "Oh, there you are. I wondered if you'd left." He frowned. "Did I miss you upstairs?"

Hayden arched a brow at her.

Bex smiled at Theo. "No, I was in the backyard. There's a lovely pear tree."

"Yes, and strawberries, though they're done now." Theo looked between them, his brow creased, but didn't say anything more.

"Thank you for meeting me," Bex said. "I'll make a decision as soon as possible and let you know."

Hayden stepped off the porch. "I'll do the same. Thanks, Theo."

"If you both decide you want it, you'll have to duke it out."

Bex walked down the steps to the front path where Hayden stood. She made eye contact with him but quickly looked away before she broke out laughing.

"Oh, I'm sure we'll find a way to make peace," Hayden said.

Had they? His words filled her with hope. But what had changed since yesterday morning?

Theo chuckled. "Sounds good. I look forward to hearing from you!"

Hayden waved as they strode, side by side, to the sidewalk. Once there, he glanced over at her. "Well, that was a new one."

Bex finally let her giggles go. "I'm sorry," she managed between fits. "But that was close. The condom wrapper..." She wiped at her eye.

Hayden grinned then looked up and down the street. "Where are you parked?"

She pointed to the next block over. "Up there."

They crossed the street since they were both parked on that side. Once they reached the other sidewalk, a sliver of discomfort edged through her good mood. She longed to ask what had happened to change his mind since yesterday, but was afraid to tempt Fate.

"Listen, I'm sorry about that," he said. "I got a little carried away."

"I'd say we both got *a lot* carried away." She laughed nervously. "Can't say I minded, though."

He looked at her, his gaze assessing. "Clearly I didn't mind either. Just the same, we should probably be careful."

She nodded. "Absolutely. Wouldn't want to get caught."

He seemed to be struggling to keep a straight face. "Definitely not. That said, it's possible it could happen again. You know, if we happen to meet up in another rental property."

"In the bathroom," she added.

He set his hand on his hip. "I'd be open to the kitchen. Or even a closet."

"Or a laundry room. Washers are supposed to be fun."

He laughed. "But then I don't think you'd need me."

She wanted to say, *I'll always need you,* but didn't. They'd made some progress today, even if it was very small. She didn't want to jinx it.

"I need to get back to the brewhouse," she said at last, not wanting this wonderful interlude to end.

"Yeah, I've got some things to do. And listen, please don't mention that I was here to anyone. I haven't decided if I'm going to stay in Ribbon Ridge, and I don't want to get my parents' hopes up."

She completely understood. "Mum's the word."

He smiled. "Thanks. See you later."

"Bye." She turned and walked to her truck. By the time she got to it and turned around, he was already pulling away from the curb. She climbed into her truck and fired up the engine. The air-conditioning blasted into the heated interior, blowing the wisps of hair that had escaped her ponytail during their quickie.

She let her head drop against the steering wheel and groaned softly. What on earth were they doing?

He'd wanted only one night, but then jumped her bones the next time they were alone. They had heart-to-heart, meaningful conversations, and he shared things with her he hadn't shared with anyone else. She was falling in love with him all over again—she was sure of it— but she'd decided she ought to leave him alone now that he'd finally moved on with his life.

Alaina's words from yesterday haunted her. "If you want something, you have to fight for it."

Bex wanted Hayden. More than she'd ever wanted anything—including him five years ago. When she'd broken his heart.

She raised her head and looked at where he'd been parked. She knew she'd hurt him when she'd left, but she hadn't realized how deep the wound had cut. If she had it to do over again, she'd…she'd what? She'd do the exact same thing. She'd felt like she couldn't breathe here, especially after they'd lost the baby.

If she had it to do over again, she'd leave. Which meant she'd put him through that hell again.

But she wasn't going to do that, not *this* time. She cared too much for him. Maybe if she could get him to open up and talk about how he'd felt after she'd left…

Somehow she wasn't sure he'd do that. He seemed to be burying his feelings quite deep these days. Like he was suppressing something.

But if he was really here to stay, and it looked as if he was, she'd have time to figure it all out. She'd peel back the layers and get to the heart of what had gone wrong. Then they'd fix it and start fresh.

Wow, she'd never believed in fairy tales, but that right there was a full-blown Disney story. *One day at a time, Bex.* Right now, she'd focus on just fighting for him—showing him that she cared, that she wanted him, that she wasn't the same girl who'd left him. She wanted a second chance.

And she just might want forever.

ON SATURDAY, TWO carloads drove to Slide Mountain for their group hike. In Cam's Range Rover, there was Jamie, Hayden, Sean, and Tori, while Liam and Aubrey had ridden up in Bex's truck. Kyle and Maggie planned to drive up to the campsite later for dinner and to sleep over. They'd determined there was an old logging road that led most of the way to the campsite, which sort of defeated the purpose of hiking everything in. Still, they were doing their best, with Kyle bringing the rest.

Evan and Alaina had opted to stay home while Dylan and Sara were busy working at The Alex, and Derek and Chloe had made prior plans. They'd all fervently tried to convince them to come, but Dylan had staunchly refused. The soft open was Thursday, and he was determined to make sure everything was done on time.

Cam parked at the trailhead, while Bex pulled in next to him. They all bailed out of the cars and grabbed their packs.

Hayden couldn't help but watch Bex as she slung her pack on her shoulders. She wore olive green ripstop shorts and a fitted light gray T-shirt. Well-worn hiking boots encased her feet, indicating she'd been doing this awhile since their breakup. She hadn't been a hiker back then. What had prompted her to start? Where had she gone? Had she done this with a boyfriend?

A streak of baseless jealousy shot through him, and he cautioned himself to take a step back. Since their crazy quickie at the rental house, they'd slept together twice, hooking up in his bedroom late Wednesday and Thursday nights. Neither one of them had gotten the rental house—someone else had offered above market—so they were stuck living together. For now. The garage apartment was supposed to be ready later this week when the flooring arrived. Still, she wouldn't be far away...

Again, he urged himself to take it easy. It was one thing to enjoy this...fling or whatever it was, but it was another to take it too seriously. For now they were enjoying each other. Laughing, teasing, having a great time. They hadn't talked about anything deeper than what felt good, and right now that was fine with him. He wasn't sure he ever wanted to rehash the past. At least not more than they already had.

Bex looked around at the group. "Everyone ready?"

They answered with nods and yeps, and Liam clapped his hands together. "Let's go!"

"You still want to lead, and I'll bring up the rear?" Bex asked him.

Of course Liam wanted to lead.

"I'm good with that," Liam said. He tugged at Aubrey's hand. "Come on, babe."

Hayden was tempted to hang back with Bex, but decided that would be a bad idea. They'd be likely to flirt, and he didn't want to do that today in front of everyone else. He sensed they'd all start hardcore shipping them as a couple, and he didn't want to deal with that.

So he started out at the front of the pack, just behind Liam and Aubrey. After a while, the group shook out a bit based on speed, and soon Hayden and Liam were alone in the lead.

Hayden glanced up through the canopy at the bright blue sky. It was cooler here in the forest, but still quite warm as they hiked in and out of small breaks in the trees.

"Such a great day for this," Liam said.

"Definitely." Hayden looked over at his brother, knowing this was something he'd love, but thinking it was a bit sedate compared with skydiving and heli-skiing. "Have you really toned down the extreme stuff?"

"Yep." He tossed Hayden a glance. "Hard to believe, right?"

"Honestly? Yeah." For as long as Hayden could remember—close to a decade anyway—Liam had been taking on one extreme sport after another. "I guess we have Aubrey to thank for that?"

"For sure. And my therapist." Liam threw him a wink.

Hayden practically tripped over a rock. "Your *what*?"

Liam chuckled. "My therapist. Come on, we're all seeing mental health care professionals now thanks to Alex, aren't we?" He adjusted his pack. "Maybe not all of us, at least not right now. But Mom has, Kyle sees someone— particularly regarding his gambling addiction—and Tori was seeing someone after she and Sean got back together."

Hayden had known about Mom, but that was it. Shit, he'd been so far removed from his family that he was pretty much completely out of the loop. But that was his fault, right? He'd pulled himself out and focused on himself for once.

"I had no idea."

Liam shrugged. "Yeah, well, it's not exactly cocktail party conversation."

Hayden smirked at him. "And that's our primary mode of communication?"

"Good point. But you've been off doing your thing. Why would any of us burden you?"

Because we're family? Hayden thought about when he'd been the one at home, providing support for both his parents and Alex. He'd kept an open stream of communication with everyone about pretty much everything. Yet it seemed they hadn't done the same.

"You aren't a burden," Hayden said quietly. "Neither was Alex."

"I didn't say he was a burden, but you can't deny his actions fucked us all up." Liam paused, turning to look at Hayden. "Alex and I had an incredibly twisted relationship. He hated me because I was healthy, and I hated him because he wasn't, and I felt guilty. But we also loved each other. More than anything. Still, we found it best to live apart, so I went to Denver. Like I told you, the sports were all for him."

"That's...cool? I mean, I'm glad you had something you shared." Of course they did. They'd been identical twins. They'd shared a closeness the rest of them never could.

"Yeah, I guess, but twisted as fuck, too." He shook his head and continued on.

Hayden fell into step beside him. "So you stayed away because he wanted you to?"

"It was pretty mutual, but yeah. He told me right before he died that I could come home."

"Wow."

"But I still resisted. When I came back for Evan's wedding and ended up staying to help with the zoning appeal case, I felt...strange. Like I didn't belong. Like everyone had found their place, and I never would. Not in Ribbon Ridge anyway."

That's exactly how Hayden felt. Maybe he and Liam *could* form a bond.

"It's not like you," Liam said. "You come home, and it's as if you never left. You've been really instrumental in helping Kyle figure out the wine situation. He said you had a few leads on a sommelier?"

Is that how they saw him? They had no idea how detached he felt. Maybe he should try telling them. "Yeah, hopefully they'll pan out. But you're wrong about me. It *isn't* like I never left. I did leave. I left Archer, and I don't plan on ever going back. And I don't have a permanent role at The Alex like all of you."

Liam looked at him sideways. "You *could* have one. Why don't you take the sommelier position? And you know you can have any management responsibility you want."

Except for the ones his siblings had taken. No, he wanted his own project. The winery would be his—or at least, it wouldn't be any of theirs. "Kyle hasn't offered it to me," Hayden said as they cleared a small ridge and emerged into the sunlight. They both pulled sunglasses over their eyes.

"He would, but I don't think he realizes it's a possibility," Liam said. "Is it? I thought your job in Burgundy was a done deal."

He'd certainly led them to believe that, so that was on him. It was also no longer the case at all. He and the Westcotts had put an offer in on Quail Crest, which Amos had accepted. Soon, Hayden would have to share the news because they needed to get started on mapping out infrastructure. For that, he'd need Tori to design the winery, and he planned to contact the engineer who'd worked on The Alex, Cade D'Onofrio.

Hayden didn't want to spill any of that yet though, so he said, "I'm mulling my options."

Liam looked over at him in surprise. "You are? That's great. Mom and Dad will be thrilled. Did you miss Ribbon Ridge?"

More than he'd realized. "Did you, while you were in Denver?"

"At first, yeah. But I built a pretty good life for myself, and I just got it in my head that I would never come home. You're not doing that though." He cocked his head to the side. "Or are you?"

That hadn't been his intention when he'd left, but he couldn't deny that there was a competitive drive in him to prove he was as capable and successful as his siblings had been away from Ribbon Ridge. Which was perhaps a bit messed up. Maybe he needed therapy, too.

"No. I plan to come home."

Aubrey caught up to them and snagged Liam's arm. "You guys were getting pretty far ahead, and we're stopping for a break."

Liam stopped and turned. "Oh, sorry. We just got to talking." He grinned at Aubrey and kissed her fast and hard. He snaked his arm around her waist and drew her close. "How are you doing?"

She smiled up at him. "Good. I've had a great view." She tapped him on the ass, and Hayden decided it was time to leave them alone.

He walked over to a fallen tree and took a long drink of water from his hydration hose. Everyone caught up, and Tori joined him. "Hey, you and Liam were really cruising."

"Apparently. We'll slow down." Hayden glanced over toward Liam and Aubrey, at how close they stood together, and guessed Liam would be hiking with her the rest of the way. It was just as well. He didn't want to field any more questions about his plans.

"It's okay. We're all ending up at the same place."

Bex finally entered the small clearing along with Jamie. She laughed at something he said.

"How are things with you and Bex?" Tori asked, drawing Hayden to turn his head toward her.

He blinked, glad that he was wearing sunglasses so that Tori couldn't see that he'd been staring at his ex. But maybe she'd figure that anyway based on the direction he'd been looking. "Fine, why shouldn't they be?"

"No reason. It seems like you guys are friends. That's great."

"We're adults, you know. And we broke up a long time ago."

Never mind that they were having sex.

"Sure. It's just great to see." Her brow creased briefly. "I worried about it, to be honest. We thought long and hard before offering her the job."

"But didn't bother discussing it with me."

Her lashes fluttered, and she winced. "Sorry. We should've. In hindsight."

Great, he was *hindsight*. That always felt good.

Shit maybe he *did* need therapy. Especially if he was going to be living back here. He'd spent so long— his whole life, really—burying his feelings of exclusion and inadequacy. Inadequacy? Is that how he really felt?

Maybe. He thrust the emotions away. Today wasn't the time to finally search his soul.

Tori touched his hand. "I missed you when you left. We had a good thing going with The Alex. You, me, Derek, and Sara. I liked working together."

Hayden felt a rush of delight. "Yeah?"

"Yeah. But Kyle stepped in all right. Still, I look forward to you coming back."

"And doing what?" Hayden was curious if she'd bring up the sommelier thing too or something else.

"Whatever you want. We all own an equal share." She adjusted one of the straps on her pack. "My day-to-day stuff is over now, and I have my own fledgling business to tend to, so I'm keeping my input somewhat limited. Mostly, we're all just doing our part to execute the soft and grand openings. Then the staff will sort of take it away."

"Doesn't it feel bizarre to turn it over to people outside the family?"

"Well, Kyle's there full-time, and Liam has a pretty strong hand on the management side. The hotel manager is reporting to him."

Sounded like they had things pretty well covered. "I have no idea what I would do."

"You could be the sommelier." There it was. "At least temporarily."

"Maybe."

She took a sip of water and cocked her hip. "Why not? You love wine. It would be great to have you back."

He tried not to sound exasperated. "I want to *make* wine, Tori, not just recommend it."

She sighed. "Right. Sorry." Her eyes lit. "You *could* make wine here. Buy some grapes. Set up a facility at The Alex. We have room. I could design it for you."

Why hadn't they ever come up with that plan before? Because Hayden was an afterthought. *Hindsight*. He always had been. "I'll take that into consideration."

Her eyes lit. "I'm serious. This is a great idea. You should totally do it."

"Do what?" Cam asked, joining them. Jamie followed on his heels.

Tori pivoted to include them. "I just had the best idea. We can build a winemaking facility at The Alex for Hayden to make a house label."

Jamie's brow scrunched as he looked at Hayden. "You want to build the facility there?"

Oh shit, he thought Hayden had told Tori about their plans. He shook his head. "It was Tori's idea for me to *buy* some grapes and make wine. She offered to design a facility at The Alex." He caught Cam subtly elbowing his younger brother.

"That's not a bad idea," Cam said, going along with him. "You thinking about it?"

"I'm thinking about a lot of things. Excuse me for a minute." He turned and walked off into the woods to relieve himself. He supposed he ought to come clean about their winery plans. What was he waiting for?

He didn't know.

When he came back, Cam was waiting for him. "Sorry about that. Jamie feels like a douche."

"It's okay. I can see why his brain went that way. It did sound like I'd told Tori about the winery."

Cam stared at him. "I know you wanted to wait until after the soft open, but I'd kind of like to go public. It's pretty much a done deal."

It was. And telling his family would mean they'd stop asking about his plans. Then he'd have to talk to Antoine...and Gabrielle. He felt bad about that, mostly for turning down Antoine's offer. Gabrielle would be fine.

But what would it mean for him and Bex? He glanced toward her. She stood talking to Aubrey and Liam. With both of them living in Ribbon Ridge, they'd have to figure out what the hell they were doing. Or put a stop to it.

Cam frowned. "You're looking at Bex. You guys still sleeping together?"

"Yeah, but don't worry, I listened to everything you said. We're just having sex." Fun, amazing, mind-blowing sex.

"Good. Is it a secret?"

"We're not advertising it. Can you imagine what my family would say? Shit, they'd probably throw a god-damned party."

"So what are you going to do? You can't keep this up forever." He put his hands on his hips. "Unless you want to." The bitter tone of his voice indicated how he felt about that possibility.

Hayden couldn't say he felt much better. Being with Bex this week had felt familiar, comfortable. He could see himself settling into a routine with her. But he didn't want that, did he?

Why did it suddenly seem as though the cushioned haze he'd built around himself over the past five years was about to burst? He needed to get his head on straight.

"Let's tell everybody," he said. "You want to do it tonight at the campsite?"

Cam blinked at him. "Really? Yeah, that'd be great."

"Then let's do it."

"Sweet." He clapped a hand against Hayden's bicep. "I'm so excited about this, man. More excited than I've ever been about anything."

"I am, too." But there was still something holding him back, something irritating the back of his mind. Something that kept him from diving in and completely losing himself in the lure of the future before him.

Maybe because there was too much of his past holding him back.

Chapter Seventeen

WHEN THEY STARTED up again, Bex was surprised to find herself alone with Hayden at the back. Had that been by design? She'd taken her pack off when they'd stopped and now had to readjust it a little as they got moving.

"You got all that?" he asked her.

"Yep."

"That's quite a pack. I'm sure it weighs more than mine."

"I doubt it. We spread the stuff out pretty evenly last night." She and Liam had taken on organizing the gear. "It just looks bigger because I'm smaller than you."

He nodded. "That must be it."

"You don't have to hang back here with me," she said, still wondering why he was.

He cast her an amused glance. "Are you trying to get rid of me?"

"Not at all. I'm just wondering about your motives."

He laughed. "I need a motive? What, do you think I'm going to whisk you off into the trees and seduce you?"

That sounded heavenly. "No, but don't let me stop you."

He kept his face straight ahead, but she saw him smile. "I wanted to know how you got into hiking in the first place."

"Oh, that's easy. A friend I worked with at the brewery in Bend invited me." She left out the part where she'd been a walking zombie for a few months after leaving Ribbon Ridge. The invitation had come at her lowest point, when she'd been certain she'd never be happy again. "Jill's an avid hiker and she took me under her wing." That day had been the best Bex had felt in ages. For the first time, she'd felt the return of peace. Of hope that stretched beyond making it through the workday or sleeping through the night.

"So that was it?"

"Pretty much. I was hooked." She'd gone every week-end and after a few months had done an overnight. "Jill and I did part of the Pacific Crest Trail a couple of years ago. That was amazing."

He tossed her a look of admiration. "Oh wow, I had no idea. That's so cool."

"Thanks. I'd love to do the whole thing someday. Maybe when I retire."

"Bucket list?"

"Sure." They'd talked about their bucket lists when they'd been together. His had included making wine in France, while hers had included making beer in Germany. "Seems like you're crossing things off yours," she said.

"Am I?" He was quiet a moment. "Oh, right. We talked about that. What have you done?"

"Nothing that we talked about. I don't know that I've really thought about it until now." No, she pretty much lived for each day because that's what you did when you had parents who didn't plan or organize, when you weren't sure what was happening that weekend, let alone what might be for dinner. The usual answer to both questions had been *figure it out yourself.*

"I'm surprised you didn't take off for Germany. Or did you have something keeping you here?"

"Just work. And money. We don't all have trust funds," she said without heat. "I've been saving to go to Oktoberfest in Munich. Maybe next fall."

"So you were working and hiking the past five years. Anything else?"

She sipped from her water pack. "That's about it. I tried living in Seattle to see if Debbie and I could have a better relationship as adults."

He let out a laugh. "I can just imagine how that went over. Your mom's a piece of work."

Hayden had heard the stories of course. How she'd put a thirteen-year-old Bex up in a hotel during one of their scheduled visitations because she was hosting an elegant party and having a guy sleep over. She didn't think it was appropriate to have her daughter there. But instead of planning her party around their weekend, she'd just done what she'd always done—her own thing.

He looked at Bex askance. "I'm surprised you tried that."

"I guess it was on my bucket list, though not officially. I'd hoped we'd establish some kind of closeness, but I've given up now."

He slowed his gait for a moment. "I'm sorry."

She shrugged. "It's okay. It's hard to miss something you've never had." That wasn't precisely true, but she didn't miss having a connection with her mother the way she missed having one with Hayden. She'd had that once, and she wanted it again. She hadn't realized how much until she'd come back to Ribbon Ridge. And it wasn't just about him. It was about the entire package. She'd kept his family at arm's length before, but now she found she wanted to open up, even if she was having trouble. Like with Emily and with the Only Child Club members.

"What about you?" she asked. "What were you up to in Ribbon Ridge before you went to France?"

"Same old, same old. Working for my dad, hanging out with Derek and Alex. And Cam, of course."

She imagined the four of them leaving a stream of broken hearts in their wake. "Did Cam convert you to the dark side?"

This drew a puzzled look from Hayden, but then realization dawned. "You're asking if I turned into a man-whore." He shook his head. "No. At least, I don't think so. Ask Derek. I think we kept our heads on straight."

"So there's a teensy potential?" Why was she asking? Did she really want to know?

"Bex, are you fishing for information about who I slept with when we weren't together? If you want to know, I'll tell you, but it's not a short list."

She stumbled but caught herself. Her chest ached. Why had she pursued that topic? "No, I don't really want to know, sorry."

He stopped and looked at her, his gaze full of concern. "You okay?"

"Yeah, just hit a rock with my toe."

"Be careful. You're supposed to be the expert."

She laughed. "Thanks. Even experts can trip."

"We're all just a step away from total disaster, aren't we?"

His tone was light, teasing, but she wondered if there was something more to his statement. Was he a step away from disaster? She couldn't shake the sense that he was holding something back, that he wasn't really at ease. She began to wonder if this had anything to do with her, or if there was something else going on with him.

"So when do we get to taste your beer?"

She almost wanted to steer the conversation back to him, but she was the last person to press someone to reveal emotions. "The first batches should be ready Monday. One's a loganberry ale."

"Sounds great. What're you calling it?"

"I asked Evan for suggestions. He came up with Legolas. Because he's an archer, and it sounds kind of like loganberry."

Hayden laughed. "And it's from his favorite book and movie series of all time."

She grinned. "True, but I still like it."

"I like it, too."

"The other's an IPA, but it doesn't have a name yet." She'd thought of a few, but nothing had stuck. "I designed it with hints of pine and spice. We'll see how it turns out."

"How about calling it Hot Prick?"

This time her stumble was much bigger, and he had to reach out and grab her. She laughed hard. "Are you serious?"

His eyes glinted with mirth. "Hey, we get away with calling our stout Shaft."

"True, but Hot Prick is maybe a little over the top. How about Spice Whirl?"

He laughed. "As in the Spice Girls movie? That's lame."

He was right, but she pretended to be offended anyway and failed miserably as she laughed with him. "Hey, I *loved* that movie when it came out."

"So did my sisters. But I doubt that's your audience. I'm still voting for Hot Prick. Or how about Zestactular?"

She narrowed her eyes, still laughing. "That's ridiculous."

"It's better than Spice Whirl."

"I think you're right. Hot Prick is better. Why don't I just go with a dirty theme? Instead of Legolas, I'll call that one Twig and Berries."

It was his turn to burst out laughing. "Brilliant. You need a honey beer that you can call Sweet Lick."

She dabbed at her eye as her laughter continued. "You're terrible. What about one I can call Goldenrod? It'll be a wheat beer."

He laughed with her, bending at the waist. "Pink Lips. Something with cherries. Better yet, Pop My Cherry."

She gulped air. "Hey, when I was in Eugene I got away with naming one Beaver Beater."

He stopped, his hand catching hers so she stopped, too. He laughed harder. "You didn't. No, of course you did. Those Duck-loving assholes."

She loved that he was touching her. "They especially loved it since I was a Beaver. They thought it was a funny joke, and that I was just being a good sport. I laughed the entire time."

"Come on, they got the double entendre, right?"

"Of course they did, but since it was a Beaver slam, they didn't care."

He took a deep breath as he wiped his eye, unfortunately letting go of her hand in the process. "This is kind of turning me on."

"Me too."

"I suppose stopping for a quickie now would be a bad idea," he said, finally reining in his laughter.

"Probably. We can sneak away later after everyone's asleep."

"We're keeping it a secret then?" He nodded. "I'm on board with that."

That he asked gave her pause. Was there a chance they could go public? She'd like that. She'd love to be with him outside of the bedroom. The past five minutes were a prime example of how much she enjoyed his company. He'd always made her laugh, made her feel like the most important person in the world, something she'd never experienced before. Or since.

Damn, she'd been a colossal fool.

She was suddenly overcome with love for him. Had it always been there, or was this a new, slightly different emotion? It was both, she realized. She'd loved him before, of course, but this was deeper, richer. Not because of him—he was the same man she'd fallen for in college—but because of her. *She* was different. More able to love, perhaps more able to *be* loved.

She looked ahead and saw Sean and Tori holding hands, recalled Aubrey and Liam embracing when they'd stopped earlier. She wanted that with Hayden. But she also knew it was too soon to expect it. That was okay because she was willing to wait. Slow and steady won the race, right? She'd be patient and love him. He deserved that and so much more.

She smiled at him. "Probably best to keep things uncomplicated."

He turned from her. "Yep. We should catch up." He started up the trail then after a moment called back, "You coming?"

She'd gotten caught staring at his backside and thinking about sneaking into the trees later. "Yes. Right behind you."

THEY'D REACHED THE summit and set up their rudimentary camp. Kyle and Maggie had arrived around six thirty, toting a wagon full of food and drink. Kyle's campfire cooking skills proved as sophisticated as in a professional kitchen. With the beer and wine flowing, it was a very pleasant evening, maybe the best Hayden had enjoyed since he'd been home.

They sat around the fire, the sun finally going down, everyone in low chairs that Kyle had also brought during a second trip to the car with the wagon. Cam sat to Hayden's right and gave him a questioning look. They'd looped Jamie into their plan to share the big news tonight.

Hayden answered with a subtle nod. "So, Cam and Jamie and I have some news," he said loudly.

Kyle finished stowing some cooking items in the wagon then came to sit down. "Hey, same-sex marriage is legal, but polygamy is still out."

Laughter erupted around the campfire. Hayden smiled and shook his head. You could always count on Kyle to inject humor into pretty much every conversation. It was a gift. And sometimes a curse when you wanted to be serious. Fortunately this wasn't one of those times.

"Very funny, but that's not quite it," Hayden said when the laughter had died down. "We're starting a business together—with Luke. A winery."

This was met with whoops and exclamations and Tori jumping out of her chair and practically tackle-hugging Hayden's chair into the dirt.

He patted her back, grinning. "Thanks."

Liam sat forward in his chair. "Details. Spill."

"There's not a whole lot to share just yet. We're buying the Quail Crest vineyard, and we'll hopefully be in production next year."

Kyle drank from his beer—he'd brought bottles from Dad's home brew stash. "How long have you been keeping this secret?"

Hayden bristled. "It wasn't a secret. We were getting our ducks in a row. It happened pretty quickly. Just the other day."

"This is so great!" Tori yelled into the sky. "We're all going to be home now. Do Mom and Dad know?"

"Not yet. I'll tell them tomorrow."

Liam sat back in his chair. "We won't steal your thunder, bro. They're going to be stoked."

Hayden nodded, glad that he would make them happy. That's all he'd ever wanted. But then that had been his problem, hadn't it? He'd been so busy caring about everyone else that he'd forgotten about himself. But he was over that. This was the Hayden show now.

"So, Tori, let us know when we can get together and talk architecture plans," Cam said.

"Oh, *yay*! I can't wait. Oooh, you *could* put the facility at The Alex. But that means trucking the fruit over."

"Nope, not doing that," Hayden answered. Even if it hadn't been a logistical headache, he didn't want his new venture commingled with his family's. Not in any way, shape, or form. He was good paying them to provide services—such as Tori doing the design—but at the end of the day, it was his thing with the Westcott boys.

"What are you calling it?" Bex asked.

He smiled, thinking she had to be recalling their conversation earlier. He thought of several inappropriate responses, but kept them all to himself. "We haven't decided. West Arch or Arch West are in the running though." They'd wanted to somehow combine their names if possible. "I'm partial to West Arch myself."

"West Arch *Estate*," Jamie said. "Sounds cooler."

"Congratulations, you guys," Kyle said, raising his beer. "A toast to the new Gods of Wine Country."

"Bollocks, I think you just came up with a new show," Sean said. "I'm pitching that to Alaina tomorrow."

Everyone laughed while Hayden exchanged looks with Jamie and Cam.

Cam turned his head toward Sean across the fire. "Seriously?"

Sean nodded. "Sure, why not? We chronicled the building of The Arch and Fox, why not West Arch Estate? I think it's a great premise."

"That title is the bomb," Kyle said. He turned to look at Sean. "How come the title of my show isn't that cool?"

Hayden didn't remember the title of Kyle's show, but knew it didn't contain the word *god*.

"I dunno," Sean said, shrugging exaggeratedly. "You just came up with this one. You had total input on yours, *and* you approved it."

Liam sucked in a breath and gave Kyle a condescending head shake. "I think you just got burned, son."

Kyle grinned. "I think I did."

The conversation focused on the winery for a few more minutes before turning to something else. Then someone suggested s'mores and they broke out the supplies.

Hayden found himself next to Bex as they speared marshmallows on their roasting sticks.

"Congratulations on the winery," she said. "I'm so happy for you. It's a dream come true."

"Yeah."

"That's a big one on the bucket list."

"Maybe the biggest." Right after falling in love and having a family. But those had fallen to the bottom after she'd left him.

As good as he felt tonight, there was a splinter in his brain from that afternoon when she'd said that it was best to keep things uncomplicated. He'd wanted that too—at first. But now he had to admit that while hooking up with her this week, the feelings he thought he'd buried were maybe resurfacing.

He told himself to watch out for the Bex who'd broken his heart—the woman who kept her emotions at bay. They'd been close, but he realized now that he'd always been waiting for her to completely lower her guard. It had taken a full year to get to the "I love you" stage, and he'd been the first to say it after months of not wanting to put it out there for fear she didn't reciprocate the emotion. Then later, after she'd lived in Ribbon Ridge awhile, he'd seen how she was with his family. She'd kept herself detached—not aloof really, more like protected. But he'd been so in love with her, he'd fooled himself into thinking she'd lower her guard, as she finally had with him. But then they'd lost the baby and she'd completely shut down, which had made him think she'd never really been truly vulnerable at all.

When he thought of how quickly and completely she'd frozen him out, he grew even more uncomfortable. That had entered his mind earlier, during the hike after they'd talked about sneaking off. But as usual, he'd avoided letting himself delve too deeply. That was an old hurt, a profound one. It was best if he left it buried in the past, and it was the primary reason he shouldn't be dawdling with Bex in the present. They had no future together. Not in the bucket list sense. Been there done that, and it had been a total fail.

Any further conversation between them was interrupted by the arrival of Maggie. Hayden went and roasted his marshmallow. When they were done with s'mores, they kept the fire going until after midnight when the yawns started to outnumber the words spoken.

Hayden was tired too, but the southern regions of his body were still hoping to meet Bex in the woods. He knew he had to put a stop to their shenanigans, but not tonight. Tonight he was buzzed and happy, and he just didn't give a damn.

The plan was for everyone to sleep under the stars near the fire. They began to spread out their bedrolls, and soon people filtered off to take care of whatever business they needed to before bed.

Hayden waited a long time. So long that he dozed off for who-knew-how long. He jerked awake and found that the fire was nothing but embers. The sounds of sleep reached his ears, and he wriggled out of his sleeping bag.

He looked over toward where Bex was bedded down, but her bag was empty. Shit, how long had she been gone?

He tucked a small flashlight into his pocket and looked around the campsite, but didn't see her in the near darkness. There was only a sliver of a moon tonight but thousands of stars brightening the sky. Still, he relied on the dying fire to cast its glow.

The logical place to search would be the thick trees to his right. That would provide the most cover for what they had planned. He slipped into the forest and was plunged into darkness. He pulled out his flashlight and set it on its lowest setting, a sort of milky white shadow that stretched only a few feet in front of him.

Narrowly missing a rock, he stepped over it and whispered, "Bex?"

Nothing but forest silence.

He kept going, careful to pick his way over the uneven ground. "Bex?"

Another few feet, and he finally heard an answer. "It's about damn time."

He found her standing near a grouping of large rocks. Her hair was down, the dark locks caressing her neck. The temperature had dropped some, but it was still well over sixty degrees, and she wore that same fitted gray T-shirt. But she'd changed her hiking shorts into a pair of very short pajama-type shorts, like the ones she'd been wearing the morning he'd run into her at The Alex. He lifted his gaze to her face. She'd worn very little makeup today, but she didn't need it. Her lashes were always dark enough to make mascara redundant, and her lips were lush and pink enough to make lipstick unnecessary.

"What took you so long?"

For some reason, he focused on that very question, on the years they'd been apart. He wanted to turn that question around on her. What had taken her so long to come back? But it didn't matter just then. The only thing that mattered was taking her in his arms.

He turned off his flashlight and thrust it into his pocket then closed the distance between them. Sliding his hands around her waist, he pulled her against his chest, their gazes connecting for a split second before he kissed her.

He splayed his hands over her lower back, holding her tight as he lanced his tongue into the sweet heat of her mouth. Her fingers wound in his hair and she met his thrusts with her own, kissing him with fierce abandon.

Their hips met, grinding against each other. He dug his fingers into her back, wanting more, needing everything she could give.

She raked her hands down over his shoulders and along his abs to his waistband. There, she unbuttoned his shorts, working her hands inside and cupping his ass as she thrust against him. He felt her heat against his raging cock and couldn't wait to be inside her.

He interrupted the kiss. "Condom's in my front pocket."

"Not yet," she said into his mouth before reclaiming the kiss. Her hands kneaded his flesh. Her touch was firm and demanding, and he was absolutely on fire for her.

"You better make it fast," he managed to say.

She pulled her lips from his and kissed his throat, her tongue and teeth leaving a trail of need as she moved down to the neckline of his shirt. "I just...I just need to taste you. Haven't done that..." Her words disappeared as she knelt before him.

Overheated, he ripped off his shirt. She splayed her hand over his abdomen, her fingertips sliding over his muscles. Then she moved down, gripping his hips briefly before she tugged his clothing down to his ankles. Her breath drifted over his cock, arousing him to a near-painful state.

He tangled his hand into her hair and guided her head forward. "Don't make me come."

"Why not?"

"Because there's no way I'm not fucking you."

She wrapped her hand around the base of his shaft and sucked the tip into her mouth. Stars danced behind his closed eyes. She'd always been good at this. Good? She'd been spectacular. No other blowjob in his life had compared to her. No other sexual experience had. Period.

Her other hand curved around his ass, holding him fast as she sucked him hard. He had no choice but to thrust into her mouth, encouraged by her fingers digging into his flesh. Her tongue slid along his length, her lips closing over him as she moved up and down. She squeezed his balls, lightly, but enough to force a groan from his throat. She took him deep, her throat opening.

Motherfucker, he was going to completely lose control. She either didn't notice or didn't care. Her mouth moved faster, the sounds of her lips and tongue in the ebony night creating a symphony of seduction that he was powerless to refuse. He was going to come.

Then her mouth was gone, and cool air stole his orgasm before it hit. He sucked in air, trying to calm himself before he shot his load into nothingness. That would be a damned shame.

"Holy shit, Bex." She'd gotten better, and *damn it* he did not want to know how. Maybe, just maybe, he'd forgotten how good it had been.

"*Now* I'll get the condom," she said, her voice husky and darker than the woods around them.

He felt her take it from the pocket of his shorts wrapped around his ankles. Then he heard the sound of the plastic opening. Next he felt her fingers stretching the latex around his heated flesh. Lust pulsed through him, and he kept his hold on her head, urging her, guiding her, needing her.

When he was sheathed, he knelt. His knees caught the edge of something soft. A blanket maybe. He kissed her hard and fast, his tongue licking at her mouth. "You thought ahead."

"Of course." She sounded breathy, excited. It fueled his desire.

"Turn around."

She did as he said, moving forward on the blanket. He did the same so that his knees were completely on the soft cotton.

He yanked her shorts down her thighs, exposing the creamy paleness of her ass. His eyes had adjusted so that he could make out just enough to appreciate the view. Not that he hadn't committed it to memory years ago.

He pulled the shorts down farther, working them past her knees and taking them off one leg entirely, careful to move them past her hiking boot. She opened her legs and arched her back, offering herself to him. He shoved her shirt up so he could see her back.

He traced his fingertips down her spine. "I've always loved your back."

"I know." She reached back and grabbed the shirt, pulling it over her head.

He hadn't noticed before, but she wasn't wearing her bra anymore. He reached around to stroke her breasts. They hung hot and pendulous, the tips hard and pointed. He cupped one and squeezed the nipple. She moaned, her backside moving backward.

"I thought you wanted to make this quick." Her voice was breathy, starkly seductive.

"It would be a hell of a lot easier if you weren't so damned sexy."

He slipped his hand between her legs and found her moist heat. She was so ready. He was beyond ready. He thrust his finger inside her, eliciting a sharp gasp and a quick snap of her hips.

"Hayden, please."

"Hold on, baby, I'm coming."

He reluctantly let go of her breast to guide himself into her slick channel. He went slow, sheathing himself inch by delicious inch. Apparently impatient, she pushed back and took him as far as he could go, his balls slapping against her ass.

She cast her head back and moaned again. *"Yes."*

That was enough to drive him directly to the edge. He clasped her hips and let himself go, ramming into her with deep thrusts. She met every single one of them and he had to fight not to come too soon.

Then her hand was around his balls, pulling and stroking. Her thumb and forefinger ringed the base of his shaft and held him tight while he plunged into her. God, he loved when she did that. He hadn't realized how much he'd missed her touch.

Her muscles began to contract around his cock, and he gave up the fight. White-hot pleasure slammed through him and sent him careening into oblivion. He gripped her tight, holding on for his life as his orgasm ripped him apart from reality.

He worked to catch his breath as he slid from her body. "God, Bex, that was amazing." He considered the condom and what to do with it. Guess he'd just have to take it back to camp and get it far enough into the garbage bag that no one would notice.

She was quiet, her head down on the blanket. She'd brought her knees up so that she was more compact. If they were anywhere else, he would think she could just roll to the side and fall asleep. That sounded fantastic.

He stood and set the condom on the rock while he pulled his clothes on. "Bex? You okay? That was amazing, right? If you tell me it sucked, I'll have to get professional help. On second thought, don't tell me, even if it *did* suck."

She rolled over and pulled up her shorts. Then she pushed her hair back from her face and looked up at him. "That was more than amazing."

He held his hand for her and helped her up. "Excellent." He felt great. Fucking *fabulous*. "We should get back."

She bent to pick up the blanket then handed him something. "Here. I brought a paper towel and a baggie for the condom."

Wow, she'd *really* planned ahead. He appreciated it, but was also concerned that there was now an expectation.

A routine, even. And that wasn't good. Maybe it was time to back off.

He took her hand as they made their way back to the campsite. He used his flashlight again, but turned it off well before they emerged from the trees.

As they reached the edge of the clearing, a figure came toward them. His gut clenched at being found out by Liam or Kyle, who would undoubtedly flip him shit. Or Tori, who would be insanely happy and probably tell their mother. But the silhouette was too big to be her. In the end, it was Jamie.

Hayden had dropped Bex's hand the minute he'd seen the shape. "Hey, Jamie. I found Bex stumbling around in the dark."

"I didn't think I'd need a flashlight," she said. "Thanks, Hayden." She walked to her sleeping bag.

"Got mine," Jamie said, heading into the trees.

"Be careful." Hayden turned and took care of disposing of the condom before going to his bag. He slipped inside and stared up at the sky. The stars were so brilliant out here away from any city lights. A flash caught the corner of his eye—a shooting star. Weren't those supposed to signify good luck or something?

Or he was supposed to make a wish, maybe?

What would he wish for?

He thought of his bucket list conversation with Bex and realized he didn't know. It seemed his life was falling into place. But instead of brimming with optimism, he felt apprehensive, like he was on the cusp of something that would bring it all crashing down around him.

After all, it had happened before.

Chapter Eighteen

BEX WAS GLAD that she and Hayden had ridden back to Ribbon Ridge in different cars. It had been hard enough to stop herself from gravitating toward him during the hike back down the mountain. She wanted to hold his hand, laugh with him, claim him as hers.

But she couldn't. Not yet. Now that he was staying in Ribbon Ridge, maybe she'd have a chance. She was certainly going to try.

Both vehicles drove to the Archer house to unload. Rob and Emily greeted them and provided assistance then everyone went their separate ways, leaving Bex and Hayden alone with his parents.

They went into the kitchen, where Emily poured them iced tea, complete with colorful straws. "How was it?" she asked.

"A lot of fun," Hayden said. "And I shared some news that might be of interest to you."

Emily handed him his glass, her eyes widening. She flicked a glance at Bex, and Bex had a horrible feeling she was expecting an announcement to do with her. "What is it?"

Rob joined them at the island, his gray gaze expressing rabid curiosity. "Do tell."

"I'm starting a winery with the Westcott brothers. We're buying Quail Crest. I'm making the wine, Luke's managing the vineyard, Jamie's doing the numbers, and I guess that means Cam's managing the rest of it."

Rob and Emily exchanged the briefest of glances, but Bex caught it. Rob grinned and slapped his son on the back. "This is fantastic news. The best. Come here." He hugged Hayden tight. "It'll be good to have you home."

Hayden gave his dad's back a thump. "Thanks."

"My turn!" Emily squeezed between them and gave Hayden a warm hug. "You've made my day. No, my year." She stepped back and cupped his face, smiling up at him. "I'm so happy."

Hayden smiled back, his love for her evident. "I'm glad."

Rob leaned against the island. "I'm sure Antoine will be disappointed, but I think this is the right decision for you."

"I hope so," Hayden said.

Bex expected him to toss her a look, as if she might be a reason that this could be a bad decision, but that was her hang-up. Since learning of his decision last night, she'd been consumed with thoughts of "now what?" They had this sexy fling going, but could it be more? She wanted more, but wasn't sure he shared that sentiment. She hoped he did—he was certainly physically engaged.

"So where do you plan to live?" Emily asked. "Maybe you should change your mind about selling your house to Kyle."

Hayden let out a chuckle. "Yeah, that'd be real nice of me. No, that ship has sailed."

Bex could interpret that two ways—he was just talking about the house or he was talking about her. When he'd bought that house, they'd lived in it together for six months. Then he'd gone on to live in it for several years, during which time he'd been hung up on her. She had to think the house reminded him of her. It would absolutely remind her of him. In fact, she'd sort of wanted to visit Kyle and Maggie so she could see it after all this time.

"Well, you can stay here as long as you want, of course," Emily said.

"Thanks, Mom. I'm looking at places." He took a long drink. "Mmm, you always make the best tea. I'm going to take a shower." He took his glass and left.

Bex picked up her drink. "I should bathe, too. Thanks for the tea."

"Wait just a minute?" Emily asked. She looked over at Rob, who gave her an infinitesimal nod.

Bex immediately sensed something was up. "Sure. Is this about the garage apartment?"

"No, we're still waiting on the flooring. Sorry." Her forehead creased but then she smiled as she came around the island and sat on a stool. Rob stayed on the opposite side of the counter.

Bex felt as though she ought to sit, too. This seemed like a serious conversation all of a sudden.

"We're so happy Hayden's moving home. Aren't you?"

She tensed, wondering where they were going with this and feeling uncomfortable with the invasion. Probably because she had something to hide—her feelings for Hayden. "I've only ever wanted him to be happy."

Even when she'd left him in broken pieces, she'd wanted him to find happiness. She'd just thought that she wasn't the right person to give it to him. Did she think she was now? Had she changed or matured or whatevered enough to be The One? She wanted to be, but she didn't know. That was life, however—taking risks when you had absolutely no clue how it would work out.

"Us, too," Rob said. "He's happy with you."

Shit, what did they know? "I'm not sure what you mean. We aren't together anymore." Unless you counted a week of hooking up.

Emily gave her a knowing smile. "It's okay, dear. We're not stupid. We live here, too."

Hell's bells. They knew. Great. What the hell was she supposed to say to that? And why were they bringing it up? They weren't high schoolers or even college students. "We aren't together-together. At least not right now."

But she wanted that. They'd had such a great time on the hike yesterday. She wanted more days like that. She wanted forever.

"It'll get there. We just wanted you to know that you have our full support. We're just so glad it's working out, that he's home now."

There was something in the way she kept glancing at Rob, in her tone—like this was some sort of plan. Bex thought back…Rob had been the one to convince her to take the job here. The garage apartment was never ready…*holy shit*. They'd orchestrated this entire thing.

Bex turned her head to look at Rob. "Why did you want me to come back here?"

To his credit, he didn't look at his wife. "You're one of the best brewers I've ever encountered. I always regretted not having a job for you here." *Now* he sent Emily a look. It was almost apologetic. Wait, had Emily been angry with him for not giving Bex a job? Maybe she thought that's why Bex had left. Ergo, if there'd been a job, she would've stayed, and she and Hayden never would've broken up. "This job at The Alex was meant for you," he said.

Bex's hand shook so she didn't pick up her glass. Instead, she leaned down and took a long pull of the icy liquid while she tried to organize her tumultuous thoughts. When she looked at both of them, she worked to keep her face and voice as pleasant and even as possible. "I want to be clear about something. There were a lot of reasons that Hayden and I broke up—none of which are really anyone's business but ours. Whether I had a job here or not, there were…other things." Like this right here. Meddling was something she had no experience with, and was quite frankly happy to live without. The Archer family was huge and complicated and just way out of her comfort zone. "Please don't think that just because we're…falling into old habits that we're *together*. We're not."

"We understand," Emily said.

Bex wasn't sure she did. What mess had she gotten herself into? The reasons she'd left Ribbon Ridge rose in her mind—she'd been overwhelmed by this family, its closeness and interdependency. This time around, she'd thought she'd begun to feel more comfortable, like she might just open up and let them deeper into her life. But it wasn't the same. She wasn't *with* their son like she'd been five years ago, no matter how much they wanted her to be. She asked herself if she could let them in if she *was* with him, and didn't have a clear answer.

She did know, however, that they were a package deal. If she wanted Hayden—and she did—she'd have to find a way to be comfortable in this family. Five years ago she'd been young, immature, and probably unreasonable. She'd loved Hayden so much and had wanted him to herself, away from his family. But he'd chosen his family over her. She realized now that things were rarely that simple.

Sometimes, she wondered what would've happened if they hadn't lost the baby. She probably would've married Hayden, and they would've lived here in Ribbon Ridge. He wouldn't have pursued his dream of making wine, or maybe he would have. There was just no way of knowing. She only knew that at the time she'd wanted out. She inwardly winced and suddenly wanted to be alone. *Needed* to be alone.

Bex stood. "I'm going to keep this conversation between us. I'm not sure what the future holds, but you can't assume Hayden and I will be together."

Emily's face fell. "You aren't going to leave again, are you?"

"Emily, let her go." Rob looked at Bex. "Maybe we made a mistake here. We thought...we thought there might be a chance for you two. If not, we're sorry. We'll get the apartment fixed up as soon as possible."

Bex was still going to amp up her rental search. "Thanks."

She turned and left the kitchen, going up the back stairs. She walked past Hayden's room and heard his shower running. A vision of him nude, water streaming over his body, flashed in her mind. Longing swept through her, but she kept walking.

She never should've jumped back into bed with him. Especially when she was falling back in love—if she'd ever really fallen out of it.

Letting herself into Tori's bedroom, she closed the door and sank onto the bed. She focused on unlacing her boots and kicking them aside. Then she pulled her socks off and let herself fall back onto the mattress.

The same question rang in her mind: Now what?

She hoped Hayden never found out what his parents had done. If he knew his family had tried to manipulate him, he'd be crushed. She remembered what he'd said about Alex after reading his letter. He'd felt manipulated by his brother, so this would be especially harsh.

Did any of his siblings know about Rob and Emily's plan? Had they been in on it, too? Bex didn't really want to know. As it was, she now wondered if she really was that great of a brewer in Rob's eyes or if he'd just been trying to get her to come back.

What she didn't understand was why they'd thought there was any chance of her and Hayden getting back together. Was it because he'd apparently been hung up on her for so long? She sat up, thinking of what Rob had said, *he's home now.* That's what they'd wanted most—not Bex. If she could be the one to bring him home…

She felt sick. She could only imagine how Hayden would feel, and her heart broke for him if he ever found out.

It might be best for everyone if she left. They'd find another brewer. If she and Hayden didn't get back together, she didn't think Ribbon Ridge would be big enough for both of them.

HAYDEN WORKED ALL day Monday at The Alex, helping Maggie with the garden, interviewing sommelier candidates, and troubleshooting phone issues in the hotel. Everyone was working like crazy, and they were almost ready. He was pleasantly exhausted when he walked into the kitchen at his parents' house, intent on grabbing a beer before heading up to his room to veg out for a bit before bed.

He'd seen Bex's truck outside the brewhouse when he'd left. She was working as late as anyone. He knew she'd kegged her new beer today. Kyle had tasted it and said it was amazing. Hayden had wanted to go over and try it, congratulate her, but then Antoine had returned his call, and Hayden had delivered that bad news.

Mom came into the kitchen just as Hayden was filling his pint glass. She paused upon seeing him. "Oh, I

didn't hear you come in, dear. Did you just get home?"
She glanced at the clock on the microwave.

"Yep. Long days in this final stretch."

She grabbed a water bottle from the cupboard and
filled it from the purifier on the fridge. "You're all working so hard. I'm so proud of all of you. Is Bex back yet?"

Hayden shook his head. "She was still working when
I left."

Mom put the top on her water bottle. "It's nice having
her back, don't you think?"

Hayden's natural defenses kicked up, suspicious
of where she was going with this and not at all sure he
wanted to tag along for the ride. "Sure."

She walked to the edge of the island and leaned her
hip against it as she sipped her water. "You seem to be
getting along really well." There wasn't a question, but her
tone was definitely questioning. Like she was digging for
information.

Hayden sipped his beer. "Mom, Bex and I broke up a
long time ago. We're friends now. Nothing more." Unless
you counted the hot sex.

Mom exhaled wistfully. "A mother can hope, can't
she? You two were so wonderful, and seeing you together
again makes me wonder what might have been. Is it terrible that I hoped you'd be married?"

And that was about all of this conversation Hayden
could stand. He walked past his mom on the way to
the pantry for a snack. "It's not terrible, but it's also not
happening." He kissed her cheek to soften the blow, but
didn't look back as he rounded the corner to the pantry.

He perused his choices, listening for Mom's footsteps along the hallway toward her room. Satisfied that she was gone, he finally let out a breath and allowed the tension in his shoulders to fall away. He knew his mother had always liked Bex, but was this something more? Had she figured out they were having sex? Yikes, that would be awkward.

He heard the exterior door and popped his head out to see Bex stepping inside. Seeing her in the flesh after dwelling on her the past several minutes made his heart rate speed up. "Hey."

She looked at him, surprise glinting in her pale green eyes. "Hey."

"Long day," he said, leaning against the doorframe with the beer in his hand.

"Yes, I'm wiped." She nodded toward the pantry. "Foraging for dinner?"

"A snack. You hungry?"

"Not really."

He glanced down at his glass. "Beer?"

"Thanks, but I'm good. I just had a pint before I left."

"Your new stuff?" he asked. "Kyle said it was awesome."

She tried to suppress a smile and failed. Her adorable dimples flashed for a brief moment, and Hayden wished he saw them more. Like the other day on their hike, when they'd been practically ever-present. "That was nice of him. I guess it is pretty good."

"I'll make a point to stop in and taste it."

"How was your day?" she asked. "Seems like they keep you pretty busy up there. I thought I saw you digging holes, and then Kyle said you were conducting interviews."

"Yeah, whatever they need."

"You've always been that guy—the one who fixes everything."

He had. Kind of dumb that he'd come to resent that because the truth was that he enjoyed being that guy. He liked feeling needed.

"Very dependable," she added.

He snorted. "Tell that to my boss—*former* boss—in France. I told him I wasn't taking the job. He wasn't happy. A little pissed, truth be told, but he understood and eventually wished me the best of luck."

The same couldn't be said about Gabrielle. She'd called precisely five minutes after he'd hung up with her father. That had gone considerably worse. She'd been *very* pissed. It seemed she thought they had more of a relationship than he did. He'd been so confused. She'd specifically told him on several occasions that they were not a "thing." Still, he'd apologized profusely and hoped she'd be okay.

Standing here with Bex, he thought about taking her with him to France when he went back to collect his things. They could stop over in Germany—it wasn't Oktoberfest, but she'd love it anyway.

Wait, what the hell was he doing? Planning a future with her? No, no, no. That wasn't happening. They'd fallen into some habit last week, but it couldn't last.

She pivoted. "Well, I'm going to turn in."

There was something off here. She seemed...removed. But maybe she was just tired. He touched her arm and instantly regretted it from a self-preservation perspective as heat threaded through him. "You okay?"

She turned her head, her green eyes wide and luminous as she looked up at him. He saw vulnerability in their depths and questioned his sanity. He wanted her, he didn't want her. He didn't *want* to want her. Yeah, that was it.

"I'm fine. I'm just…*Hayden*." She exhaled softly.

He didn't know what she meant or what she was thinking, but he set his glass on a shelf in the pantry and moved toward her. He cupped her face, tracing her jaw with his thumb. She closed her eyes briefly and tipped her head, nuzzling into his touch. Her fingertips found his abdomen and pulled gently at his shirt. He lowered his head and kissed her, their lips meeting softly.

He pulled back and looked down at her. She gazed up at him, and he wasn't sure she'd ever looked at him like that—with such emotion. It completely swept him off his feet. He kissed her again, angling his head and pulling her against him. He curved his hand behind her nape and licked at her lips until she opened for him. She clutched at his sides and kissed him back fervently, their tongues tangling with urgent need. He suppressed a groan, loving the feel of her, wanting all of her.

He lifted his head. "We should move this upstairs." Before his mother came back and squealed with joy upon finding them in an embrace.

She splayed her hands over his chest. "Wait." Something about the way she said the word made him pause. The bliss pitching through him faded. "What are we doing?"

Uh-oh. Not this conversation.

He stepped back and picked up his beer. "I was getting a snack."

She frowned at him. "That's not what I meant."

He clutched his beer like it was some sort of talisman against the intimacy of the conversation she seemed intent on having.

She moved closer. "I want…I want to be with you. More than ducking upstairs before someone sees us."

Fuck.

What had happened to uncomplicated? "Why are you bringing this up now?" He glanced around, half expecting his parents to pop out of the woodwork. "Here?"

"Because I can't keep doing this without saying something. Every time we're together, I…I want more." She touched his free hand. "Don't you? The way you touch me, the things you say…It seems like maybe you do."

So she didn't want uncomplicated. She wanted something else entirely. Something he wasn't sure he was ready to give her. And he honestly didn't know if he ever would be.

He pulled his hand away. "Let's get one thing straight. The man I am today isn't who I was five years ago."

She blinked at him, realization crystallizing in her eyes. "I guess you aren't."

"I don't want a relationship right now. Not with anyone." He didn't want to hurt her, but he also had to be honest. "I like being on my own."

She took a moment to seemingly process what he said before tentatively asking, "Is that because it took you so long to get over me?"

Damn, he wished she hadn't known that. "Who told you that?"

"Does it matter? It's true, isn't it?"

Completely. But that was *his* pain. And he'd finally conquered it. He didn't need her dredging it up again. "You know what doesn't matter, Bex? Everything that happened after you left. You gave up any right to know what I did or what I felt."

She winced. "I know. I'm so sorry. Tell me what I need to do to make it up to you."

God, how many times would he have crumpled under those words? If she'd come back to him and said them anytime before Alex had died, he would've gladly given himself over to her. But not now. He didn't want to revisit that ache any more than he had in the past five minutes. "There's nothing you can do. I've moved on."

"What about the past week? It hasn't meant anything?"

It had meant more than he wanted to admit. He'd started to feel…something he didn't want to. "It was great, but I think it's done now. I don't want to go back, Bex. Only forward."

She moved closer to him, so that he could feel her heat. "We *could* be forward. Not the old us, but a new and improved us. I love you, Hayden. I don't think I ever stopped."

Her words sliced into him, flaying the old wound. A part of him would always love her. He couldn't help that. He could, however, protect himself from further heartache.

He stepped back from her, intent on fleeing upstairs to his room. "That's too bad, because I did."

Chapter Nineteen

BEX SAT IN her office in the brewhouse and blinked at her computer screen after zoning out for the umpteenth time. She'd spent most of the night tossing and turning, her mind and body a twisted knot of stress and regret. She never should've told Hayden she loved him. The look in his eyes had been enough to make her wish she could take it back. But she couldn't. Just like she couldn't wipe away the pain she'd caused him five years ago.

She'd wondered if Ribbon Ridge would be big enough for both of them, and she had her answer—no. She'd been a fool to think she could come back here and live in the same town as him and his family. Worse, to think she could *work* for his family.

Then again, she hadn't anticipated the impact of coming back. Of being with Hayden. Seeing him had rekindled feelings she'd thought long buried. About him and the life they could've had. A life he no longer wanted.

Yeah, staying here would pretty much be a huge middle finger in his face.

Which was why she had to leave.

She'd texted Tori and Sara and asked them to come to her office at noon. She'd brewed another batch of beer in a kind of haze, feeling sad that she wouldn't get to do this for very long and hoping she could find another job relatively quickly.

Tori and Sara came into the brewhouse together. Bex stood from her desk, where she'd been nervously tapping her foot, and called for them to come on in. She had just two other chairs situated around a small worktable.

She tried to infuse as much cheer into her voice as possible. "Hi, have a seat."

And apparently failed spectacularly. Tori immediately frowned. "What's wrong?"

Sara took one of the chairs and looked from Tori to Bex. "*Is* something wrong?"

Bex took a deep breath. "I need to give you my notice. I'll do it in writing, but I wanted to tell you both first."

"*What?*"

They said the word in unison, both of them sitting forward in their chairs, their faces reflecting shock and surprise.

"What happened?" Tori sat back, her eyes narrowing. "Is this Hayden's fault?"

Bex shook her head vehemently. "No. It's mine. I thought I could come back here, but I was wrong." Maybe she was as emotionally stunted as she'd always been. No, that wasn't it. For whatever reason she was different now. She realized she was going to regret not having the chance to be a part of this crazy, complicated family, that somewhere along the way she wanted the closeness they all shared. Maybe it was the Only Child Club or the camaraderie, or yes, even their parents' meddling. What she wouldn't give to have two parents who cared as much as Rob and Emily did. But if she couldn't have Hayden, she couldn't have his family either.

Sara's brow puckered. "I don't understand. Why can't you be here? I thought you liked it here. I heard you all had such a good time last weekend on the campout."

Bex thought about spilling everything—found that she wanted to for the first time—but she didn't for Hayden's sake. In the end, it was far easier to bury everything. "It was really fun, but…but I just can't stay."

Tori crossed her arms over her chest. "I don't get you. You left town practically overnight five years ago, breaking our brother's heart. Now you come back, and you're going to bail again?"

Put like that, Bex sounded like an awful person. And right now, she felt like one. But she was really trying to do the right thing, particularly since she was the one who'd screwed it up in the first place by coming back. "Why were you all so forgiving after I left? I don't understand why you stayed friends with me."

"Yeah, you broke his heart, but maybe he deserved it." Tori shook her head. "I don't know what went on between you. I love my brother—and I'll choose him over you in a heartbeat—but I grew to love you, too."

Sara's eyes were kind as she looked at Bex. "I think in our minds, you were already our sister-in-law. When you left, you broke up with all of us."

Bex's heart twisted. She loved them, too. All of them. "I'm so sorry. Things were...I can't tell you everything, I'm sorry." She winced, but let the words come. "I did break up with all of you. Frankly, you were all part of the problem."

Tori's eyes widened, and Sara's brow wrinkled with confusion.

"I don't understand," Sara said. "You didn't like us?"

Bex was really screwing this up, too. "I liked you very much. I loved you, even. But I come from a tiny family. Actually, I barely come from a family at all. You're scary as hell."

Tori uncrossed her arms, and her shoulders relaxed slightly. "I get that. You're not wrong."

"No," Sara agreed. "Why do you think we all left town?"

Wait, what? Bex blinked at them in surprise.

"We needed space," Tori said. "Just to spread our wings a little, to find ourselves, I guess." She glanced at Sara, who nodded in response.

Bex wanted to say that Hayden hadn't had that chance. That his not taking it was a key point of their breakup, but that was between them. Just like the baby. If he wanted to share any of that with his family, that was his decision, not hers.

"So that's why you're leaving?" Sara asked. "You just can't tolerate our crazy?"

Bex laughed, glad for the humor. "You're not crazy. Just a bit overwhelming. But yes, I don't really fit here." Although she desperately wanted to. Wasn't irony a bitch?

Tori pursed her lips. "You're so full of shit. This isn't about us. This is about Hayden. I saw the way you were looking at each other when we were camping, and Jamie said he saw you guys coming out of the woods. Late."

Sara sucked in a breath. "You guys aren't—?"

Bex shook her head firmly. "No, we aren't." *Anymore.* "We are no more together now than when I got here." That was certainly the truth.

Tori rolled her eyes. "Whatever. I'm not buying it. Just please tell us if we're going to have to pick up the pieces again." She looked at Bex intently.

"No," Bex said quietly. At least not where Hayden was concerned. Bex, on the other hand, might need a mop to clean up the mess of her heart.

Tori's gaze softened. "You're still in love with him."

She shouldn't confirm that. It wasn't their business. But the pull to strip away her armor and reach out to them was too overwhelming to ignore. She nodded.

Tori scooted forward in her chair. "That jackass. What did he do?"

Bex blinked, coming out of her stupid lovelorn haze. "*Nothing.* He did absolutely nothing. I've put him through enough. I'm leaving because it's best for him."

Sara looked confused again. "I don't understand. Does he know how you feel?"

Again, she probably ought to file this under "none of their business," but she didn't want them talking to him about it. *At all.* And yeah, it felt good to share this with them. Like they were the sisters she'd never have. Which they totally were. "He does, and he…" Bex shook her head.

Tori exhaled, looking defeated. "That sucks. I would've thought he'd be open to getting back together."

"Because he was hung up on me for so long?" Bex asked.

Tori nodded. "You knew about that?"

"Not until recently. If I'd known…" What would she have done? She had no idea, and she never would.

"Are you sure he won't come around?" Sara asked. "You guys were pretty great together."

She'd thought so too this past week, but it didn't matter. "No, that ship has sailed. His words."

Sara got up and went to Bex's chair to hug her. "I'm sorry, Bex."

Bex stood and hugged her back. "Me too." She smiled sadly.

Tori joined them. "This sucks. You were supposed to be our sister."

Bex blinked back tears. She suddenly wished she hadn't shared so much. This was more painful than she'd imagined. She didn't want to go back to being alone. To being lonely.

The tough part of her—the girl her parents had conditioned to suck it up—swallowed the crushing emotions and cleared her throat. "Do you want any recommendations for my replacement? I could give you a few names."

Tori shrugged. "I guess. What are you going to do in the meantime? Is the apartment ready yet? Can you at least move in there for the next few weeks?"

Bex didn't plan to tell them the full story regarding Rob and Emily's role in everything. "No, I'd rather find somewhere else. Away from the house entirely."

"Come stay with us," Sara said. "We have a spare room. The main bathroom is in desperate need of updating, but it works. Dylan plans to get to it this winter when things slow down a bit."

Bex stared at her. "You guys got married like two weeks ago. No way am I staying with you."

Tori looked at her sister. "Seriously. Dylan would shoot you."

Sara giggled. "Okay, maybe. But she needs a place to stay, and your loft is too small."

"True. I wish our house was done, but that's months off." Tori pressed her lips together for a second then her eyes lit. "Duh, Evan and Alaina. They have scads of space. I'll call her now." She pulled her phone from her pocket.

Bex wasn't sure. "I don't want to be a nuisance— they're newlyweds, too."

"With an *estate*," Tori said. "I'm pretty sure you'll have your own wing. Don't stress."

It was more than that. "I don't want anyone to know about Hayden and me. I'd rather they think poorly of me—that I decided this job wasn't a good fit."

Sara blinked at her. "No one's going to believe that. They'll figure it out, but we'll do our best to downplay everything. Okay?"

"Yeah, trust us," Tori said. "The hard part will be Mom and Dad. I think they were hoping you'd get back together."

They'd done a little more than hope, but she wouldn't tell them that. She also wasn't going to worry about their reaction to her leaving.

"So, we're good?" Sara asked, drawing her back to the present.

"Definitely. You'll always be my friends. I love you both."

Tori smiled. "Even though our family's nuts?"

A loving family, even a crazy one, was still a damn sight better than what Bex had. And while she didn't agree with Rob and Emily's methods, she knew their hearts were in the right place. Anyway, none of it was her issue anymore.

"Even though," Bex said.

"'K, I'm calling Alaina right now." Tori pulled her number up on the phone and moved from the office into the brewhouse.

Bex thought of how awkward the next few weeks would be, but she wasn't going to leave them hanging. She'd stay until they found a replacement. Her mind was already working on whom she could recommend.

Tori came back into the office. "Done. Alaina says to come by whenever. She's texting you the code to their gate."

"Thanks, I appreciate it. Now go, I have beer to tend." She needed to keg a batch of Robin Hood ale.

They hugged her again then left, and she marveled at the complexities of family and friendship and how lucky she would've been to share both with those women. But Bex had never been lucky, had she?

HAYDEN TOOK ONE last glance in the mirror. He smoothed his hand over his hair then turned and walked through his bedroom to the hallway. He looked to the left, but Bex wouldn't be there. She'd moved out last night, going to stay with Alaina and Evan until they found a new brewer for The Arch and Fox. Then she'd leave Ribbon Ridge. Again.

He wanted to feel triumphant, like he'd somehow come out the victor this time around, but there were no winners here. If anything, he was angry for putting himself into a position where they'd had to go through this again, albeit on a much lesser scale.

He couldn't really compare this to before. That had been far more complicated with her wanting him to leave Ribbon Ridge, him refusing, the baby... No, this was easier. Or at least it should be on paper. Why then was he tied up in knots?

Because he'd started to allow the old feelings back in. Stupid, stupid, stupid. Yes, she said she loved him. Now. But for how long? When she got tired of Ribbon Ridge again, which he fully expected her to, what would happen then?

Just like five years ago, she was doing him a favor by leaving. Yep, a big fat favor.

He turned sharply and went downstairs. His folks were already over at The Alex—they were staying in the penthouse suite tonight—so he just had to drive himself.

He stepped out into the driveway and saw the contractor walking from the garage apartment toward his work truck.

The contractor noticed him and changed direction. "Hey, is Emily or Rob here?"

"No, they aren't. I'm their son Hayden." He offered his hand. "Can I help?"

The contractor shook his hand. "Maybe. I had an emergency come up and can't finish tomorrow. Do you think that will be a problem?"

Now that Bex was gone, there wasn't any rush. "No, I'm sure it's fine."

The contractor visibly relaxed. "Great. I didn't think it would be an issue since your mom kept putting me off, but I wanted to check and make sure."

Hayden's neck pricked. "What do you mean she kept putting you off?"

"She kept rescheduling the install."

Ice formed in Hayden's belly. "I thought the materials were on backorder."

The contractor looked thoroughly confused. He shook his head. "No. We had everything we needed."

"Ah, my misunderstanding." *Completely.* "I'll let her know you won't be here tomorrow."

"Thanks. I'll finish up Friday. See you." He turned and went to his truck while Hayden strode to the garage where they kept the Prius.

Hayden backed out and drove through the porte cochere, his mind churning. His mother had clearly lied about the apartment. The only thing he could come up with was that she'd wanted Bex to stay in the house. And why would she do that, other than to have her close to Hayden?

He drove up to The Alex and pulled into the lot, parking in front of the restaurant, where they were holding the family-only party tonight. They were celebrating this monumental achievement, Alex's legacy.

Opening the door, he stepped out into the warm evening. He took a deep breath, inhaling the scent of freshly mowed grass and sweet flowers. A light breeze stirred his hair, and he closed the door. The office trailer was gone. It had been removed last week some time.

Everything looked ready—the landscaping, the lighting, the signage. They'd done it. He felt a pang of regret and envy. He'd left only to have everyone come home and work together to execute this accomplishment.

He'd always thought he was the glue holding the family together—like Alex had said in his letter—and that if he left, something might fall apart: his dad, Alex, Archer Enterprises. But it turned out they didn't really need him at all. In fact, maybe his absence had made all of this possible.

That was absurd. It was Alex's absence that had done that. The same way it had spurred Hayden to do what he needed to chase his own dreams.

He walked into the restaurant and saw that several tables had been set into a large ring so that they would all sit together. There were flowers and candles set at intervals.

But no one was in the restaurant, which was strange since he'd seen everyone else's cars outside. Or most everyone else's; he hadn't exactly taken inventory while he'd been reflecting.

Liam came in bearing two baskets. "Hayden, you look spiffy."

Hayden looked at his older brother. "You're wearing an apron."

Setting the baskets on the table, he shook his head. "Yeah, Kyle drafted me, can you believe that?"

"No. No, I can't."

"Hey, did I hear my name?" Kyle came in, also carrying a couple of baskets. "Stop talking smack about me."

"You wish," Liam scoffed with a smile.

Hayden wasn't in the mood for joking. "Hey, can I ask you guys something? Did you ever post the brewer job anywhere?"

Liam and Kyle exchanged looks. Kyle answered, "No, but we should've so we could have a backup candidate since Bex is leaving."

"Like we told you, we went with Dad on this one," Liam said. "Our bad."

Kyle put his hands on his hips. "I'm just surprised she's leaving. She was so excited, and her first brews are fucking killer. Pisses me off."

Hayden still hadn't tried them, but his mind was focused on what he was becoming more and more certain his parents had done. "So hiring her was really Dad's idea."

"Yeah, but don't blame him," Kyle said.

Oh, he sure as hell would, just not for what they thought.

Kyle pivoted. "I need to get back to the kitchen. Dinner will be up in a few. Liam, you can hang here if you want."

Just as Hayden was wondering where everyone else was, they began filtering in from the back hallway. Conversation filled the space immediately. Everyone carried pints of beer, the glasses stamped with the new Arch and Fox logo.

Dad saw Hayden. "You're here. We're just trying Bex's new IPA." He turned. "Bex, you have a pitcher, right? I'll grab a glass." He moved toward the bar.

Then Hayden didn't see anything else but a dull haze of red. Bex was here? "I thought this was a family-only event," he said.

Someone touched his sleeve, and he blinked, turning his head to see who it was.

Sara looked up at him. "She was in the brewhouse."

So they'd had to include her? Well, they'd all been raised to be polite. Too bad he wasn't feeling the least bit amenable right now.

Bex came forward and set the pitcher on the table. "It's there if you want it. I'm going to go." She turned and went back the way they all came.

Heedless of his family, he followed her from the restaurant, trailing her into the brewhouse. He could see that she hadn't been invited—or that at least she hadn't planned on coming. She was still wearing work clothes while they were all dressed up. "So this is how it works now? You blow into town, insert yourself back into my family, and now you're off again?"

She turned at the doorway to her office, her features inscrutable. "It doesn't work like that at all."

He stopped a few feet from her. "That's right, your intent was to get back together with me, and when that failed, you decided to leave."

She pressed her lips together, her face pale. "That was *not* my intent. I was offered a job, which I wanted very badly, and after *great* consideration, I took it."

He snorted. "What sort of consideration? Tell me, did my dad talk you into it?"

Her lashes fluttered as her eyes widened briefly. She looked away, but it was too late. He'd seen the damning evidence in her guilty gaze.

"Congratulations, Bex," he said softly. "You've breached the inner circle, and you didn't even have to marry me to do it. All my life, I've clawed my way to the center of this family, never quite getting there. It's always been Alex and his illness or Liam and his death wish or Kyle and his addiction. I could go on, but you know what I mean. You've lived here. You've seen how it works. In fact, you were smart enough to want me to leave, to break free." He laughed harshly, emotion tearing from the well he'd built deep in his chest. "I guess I should've listened to you."

She took a step toward him. "Hayden, your family loves you."

"Like you do? I'm not sure I can tolerate all of that *love*. Especially when it comes with lies and manipulation."

Her eyes lit with some emotion he couldn't discern or maybe didn't want to. "I didn't lie to you or manipulate you."

"Do you deny that you came back here because my parents talked you into it?"

She looked him square in the eye. "Yes. Truly. They only wanted you to be happy—"

"That's such bullshit. You were supposed to be *my* soul mate, *my* partner, my *refuge*. But now you're with them."

She stared at him, and he realized he sounded overemotional, but that's because he was. "Hayden, you can't possibly think it's like that."

He felt completely exposed, just like five years ago. God, he hated that. He'd never wanted to feel that way again. "I don't know what to think."

"Hayden?" His mom's voice echoed through the brewhouse. He didn't turn, but saw her from the corner of his eye. She wasn't alone. Dad was with her. And behind him came the rest of his family—just his siblings, not their partners. "Are you all right?"

Bex edged backward. "I'll go."

"Why?" Hayden spat. "I'm sure they'd like you to stay." He turned then to look at his family. "You brought her here, right? Don't you want her to stay?"

He saw the guilt in his mother's eyes and had a moment's remorse. He shrugged it away. She'd chosen to set this in motion. Let her deal with how it played out.

"We want *you* to stay, Hayden," Dad said. "That's all we've ever wanted."

Mom came toward him, her hand outstretched. "The whole family, here in Ribbon Ridge. *Home*."

Hayden stared at them a moment, finally comprehending. He backed up and his mother stopped, her hand falling to her side. "I get it now." He flashed Bex an apologetic glance. "Guess we were both fools. They used you to get me home. They figured with you here in town, I'd stay." He looked back at his parents. "Didn't you think about what would happen next? That she'd leave, that I'd—" *be broken again*.

He snapped his mouth shut. He wasn't doing this.

"We just wanted you to come home," Dad said, his voice thick with emotion.

"I get that. How come it was okay when they all left?" Hayden flung his hand toward his siblings, who were standing around Dad like a security detail. How fitting that they were all over there, a unified force, while he was alone. "What schemes did you hatch to lure them home? That's right, *none*. You let them go and do their thing. Why didn't you let me do the same?"

Mom's brow furrowed. "You did. You went to France. You left Archer."

"That's not what I'm talking about. I stayed here when they all left. Don't you remember, Mom?" His eyes found Derek. "I know *you* remember. We talked about it plenty—how it was up to you and me to be here and work for the family company. But it wasn't the same for you as it was for me. You *wanted* to be here. You wanted that job, that opportunity. I wanted to make wine. I wanted to leave with *her*." He pointed toward Bex, but didn't look at her. He couldn't. He'd never admitted that—not to her, not to himself. He'd wanted to leave, but he hadn't thought he could.

Liam came forward, his eyes dark. "I get it. We abandoned you."

"And Alex. Don't forget that you abandoned him too, and don't think he didn't know it." He looked at each of his siblings, registering their stricken, wounded expressions. But he didn't care. He never imagined he'd unburden himself, and now that he was, he couldn't seem to stop.

"That's a low blow," Tori said, wiping her eye.

"It's not a blow, Tori, it's the truth," Hayden said. "What choice did I have when I was the youngest, the only one who was left? Do you think I was going to turn to Alex and say, 'Hey, I'm taking off, too. Enjoy your oxygen tank'?"

Mom brought her hand to her mouth. "Oh, Hayden. I didn't know you felt like that."

"I doubt any of you know how I feel about a lot of stuff, but that's how it is over here in the cheap seats. There are all of you—the precious sextuplets—and there's me. You all have each other—Mom and Dad, Liam and Alex, Kyle and Sara, Tori and Evan. Who does that leave me with? *Nobody.*" Thankfully he'd found Cameron, a true best friend, and later Bex. But then she'd left, and he realized now that it had been the catalyst for all of this. From that moment, he'd felt like he really didn't belong. Then Alex had shown him that not only did Hayden not belong, but that his love and support weren't enough.

He waited for someone to tell him he was wrong, but there was just silence.

He had to get out of there. Not just the brewhouse, the whole damn town. "I'm going back to France to tie up loose ends. And when I get back, I want you all to leave me alone. Understand?"

Dad came forward and put his arm around Mom's shoulders. "Son, don't go."

"I have to. And you need to let me."

He turned and left, walking by Bex on his way and not sparing her so much as a glance.

Chapter Twenty

BEX WATCHED THE door from her office to the back parking lot close as Hayden left. Her heart pounded in her chest, and she blinked back tears. He'd *wanted* to leave with her. She finally understood the hold his family had over him—it was more than love or loyalty. He'd been looking for the way he fit in, the role he was supposed to play, and he'd thought he'd found it by staying home and being the anchor.

"Bex?"

She turned back to the Archers and saw Emily coming toward her, wiping at her eyes. "I'm so sorry for what we did."

Had they really brought her here only to keep Hayden home? "Did you want us to get back together, or was that just something you said?" Because if they'd used her as a lure and then expected that she and Hayden *wouldn't* get back together, that was pretty damn cold.

Emily winced. "I *did* want that." She looked back at her husband, who came forward to join her. "Rob did, too."

Bex shook her head, emotion roiling through her—confusion, anger, despair for Hayden. "I don't understand. I broke up with Hayden five years ago and left. Why would you think we could possibly get back together?"

"We knew Hayden still loved you," Rob said. "And we hoped you might still love him, too."

She couldn't shake the fact that their primary goal had been to get Hayden to stay in Ribbon Ridge. Maybe if Rob had said, "We believed you'd be happy together," she wouldn't feel so... disgusted.

She went into her office and grabbed her purse, intent on trying to find Hayden to tell him... what, that she understood? That she'd been right to try to get him to leave five years ago?

Tori came in behind her. "Hey, Bex, you can't go after him. Not right now."

Bex kept her head down. "I know."

Everyone else crammed inside, with Rob and Emily hanging back near the doorway.

"We'll let him cool off," Kyle said, sounding way more serious than normal. "We'll talk to him later."

This lit a fire in Bex's gut. She looked up at Kyle, at all of them. "What will you say? 'Sorry you feel left out'? Or maybe, 'We never realized you felt that way'? Think long and hard before you stick your feet in your mouths. Help him figure out where he belongs—*show* him he's a vital part of this family."

She wished she could tell them exactly what to do, but she didn't know. She only knew she wanted to take his pain away.

Tori's face was pale and tense as she nodded at Bex. "We will."

Bex turned and left. As soon as she stepped outside, she gulped air. After a moment, her heart rate began to slow, and she felt a little better. Instead of going to her car, she walked to the bench that she could see from her office window and sat down.

The garden around her was alive with beauty and scent. The sun was heading toward the horizon, the sky beginning to dazzle itself for the sunset. She just wanted to sit for a minute and think. No, she actually *didn't* want to think.

Footsteps on the crushed-shell path forced her head up. Liam came toward her. "Can I sit?"

She wanted to say no, but she didn't. Instead she said nothing.

He sat anyway. "The shitty part is that he doesn't feel that different than a lot of us do. Trying to find your place in such a big group is hard."

She didn't look at him. "Didn't seem that tough for you."

"Actually, I was hesitant to come back to Ribbon Ridge permanently, even with Alex gone. Did you know I stayed away because of him? We had this mutual agreement— I could pretty much have the entire world, but Ribbon Ridge was his."

She glanced at him then. "This is why I left five years ago. Or at least, one of the reasons. You people are crazy."

He smiled briefly. "Probably. *Definitely*. I saw that everyone had come home, found their niche, fell in love...I couldn't see myself doing that. So from that perspective I understand where he's coming from. I tried to bond with him over it, in fact, but I think he thought I was trying to fill the void that Alex left behind. He said something to that effect, but I didn't realize how serious he was." He looked at her sadly. "The reality is that no one can fill that space."

She agreed with him wholeheartedly.

He leaned back against the bench and stretched out his legs. "And I don't know, maybe subconsciously I *was* doing that." He fell silent for a minute then straightened, pulling his legs up. "We were all pretty messed up after Alex's suicide."

She turned her body to look at him. "How was Hayden?"

Liam blew out a breath. "The truth? I don't know. I was too wrapped up in my own shit." He cast her a self-deprecating glance. "That's not an excuse, by the way. It just is what it is. I think we all could've done a better job of supporting each other, but we sure made it damn hard. Tori closed herself off completely. Kyle tried to bottom out with his gambling addiction. Sara threw herself into a relationship—which thankfully worked out. And Evan...well, we could learn a lot from Evan." He finished this with a smile.

"I think finding out how Hayden has dealt with this is important. Your mom spent time with him in France.

Maybe she can shed some light. Maybe together—as a family—you can figure out how to bring Hayden into the fold."

Liam cocked his head to the side, his blue-gray eyes focused with laser-sharp intent. "You say that like he was never *in* the fold."

Bex lifted a shoulder. "I don't know that he feels like he was. When we were together, he made offhand comments about being the 'oops' kid, the afterthought, the one most likely to be forgotten at the grocery store."

Liam grimaced. "I know. We made those same jokes. I never realized they were cutting deep."

"Then, when I suggested we leave Ribbon Ridge together—spend a few years finding ourselves—he was adamant that he couldn't, that he was needed here. I think *he* needed to be here." And how she wished she'd realized that. He'd spread his wings when it had been the right time for him. But maybe that was why they hadn't worked five years ago. They'd been in different places. Maybe now they could work. She honestly didn't care where they lived. She'd follow him to the ends of the earth to be with him.

Problem was, he probably didn't want her to.

Liam turned away from her and stared straight ahead. "Any ideas on what we do now?"

She wished she knew. "Not really. I don't think I'm much help to you."

He gave her a sideways look. "You're that certain he's over you?"

"He told me so."

The corner of Liam's mouth ticked up. "Remember, he's a guy. We're not so great at realizing shit that's right in front of us, especially when we're doing our damnedest to keep people at bay. Which, I think, has been Hayden's goal all along. I think you hit the nail on the head when you asked how he dealt with Alex. His death changed all of our lives, but we've all managed to find our way home—and I mean that in the emotional as well as physical sense."

She thought she understood. They'd all found their footing again, while Hayden was still floating out there. "You're saying I shouldn't give up?" She thought of Alaina's advice to fight for what she wanted.

Liam stood. "I wouldn't. If Aubrey woke up tomorrow and told me she didn't love me anymore, I'd do whatever I could to change her mind. After I got out of the fetal position, that is."

Bex smiled in spite of her black mood. There, sparking in the back of her despondent mind, was the faintest bit of hope. "Thanks, I'll think about it."

He nodded. "And hey, don't be a stranger—however this all falls out."

If she and Hayden were truly done, she didn't think she could keep up any relationships with these people. It would be too hard, too painful. The old Bex, the one for whom emotional outreach was difficult, would turn tail and run. But now she wanted to try.

And maybe she and Hayden weren't done. Maybe he could find his place—with her. She wouldn't know unless she gave it a shot. It was time to take the emotional risk.

What did she have to lose?

HAYDEN WAS ALREADY on his second beer and third shot of tequila by the time Cameron showed up at Ruckus, the dive bar on the outskirts of town. He sat at a table in the corner and vaguely wondered if he ought to eat something to soak up the alcohol.

Cam sat down and stared at him. "Shit, what happened to you?"

"Not much. Just told my family to fuck off basically."

The server came over, and Cam ordered a beer and some sliders. "I'm guessing you need to eat," he said.

Hayden waved his hand. "Whatever."

Cam settled back in his chair and got comfortable. "What'd they do?"

"Typical family garbage—they tried to use Bex to get me to move back to Ribbon Ridge."

Cam snorted. "Did they forget you guys aren't together anymore?"

"I guess."

Now Cam frowned. "Except you did fall right back into bed with her, so maybe they know more than you do."

Hayden glared at his best friend. "Fuck off."

Cam held up his hands. "Sorry, I wasn't trying to be a dick. My bad. But I did tell you to steer clear of her."

"So you did." Hayden took another drink of beer, wishing he'd listened to Cam's advice. Why had he even needed it? Bex had left him a broken mess five years ago. He should've been able to get over her and never look back. Instead, he'd carried a torch and now had to question if he'd *ever* really gotten over her at all.

Hayden kept his gaze fixed on his beer on the table. "I never told you why she left."

The server dropped off Cam's beer, and he took a sip. "Sure you did. She wanted you to move out of Ribbon Ridge so she could have you all to herself. Your family gave her hives or something."

"They made her feel *claustrophobic*." Looking back, given his own experiences, he couldn't really blame her. That might not have been the best word, but he couldn't think of one to describe the feeling that came from being the object of extreme meddling. "But that was only part of it."

Hayden's gut clenched. Did he really want to share this? On the way over, he'd been thinking of how good it felt to just unload everything. Why not this, too?

"She was pregnant." He picked up his beer and took a long pull.

Cam had also taken a drink and worked not to spew it everywhere. He ended up coughing.

"Sorry," Hayden said.

Cam clacked his pint glass on the table. "*Dude.* What happened?"

Hayden peered at him over his beer. "We didn't plan it, obviously."

"Can't imagine you did."

"She was about six weeks along when we figured it out. Threw us both for a loop." His mind went back to the stress of that time. They'd been fighting about leaving Ribbon Ridge, and he'd been afraid the end was in sight. Then she'd gotten pregnant, and the tension had shifted. "It wasn't that we didn't want it. We just hadn't expected it."

Cam was watching him intently. "Were you happy?"

"Scared to death is probably a better description, but yeah, I wanted to have a family with her."

"I can't believe you never mentioned it. All those times we talked about her—how you wished it had worked out and didn't think you'd ever find another woman like her...and you never told me."

Hayden gave him an apologetic look. "We'd agreed to keep it between us. I took that promise seriously."

Cam shook his head. "So wait. Back up. What happened to the baby?"

"She lost it."

Cam exhaled sharply. "Sorry, man."

He could end the story there. That was enough, wasn't it? Except it wasn't. His guilt didn't want to be silent anymore. It was apparently tired of festering deep inside him. Hayden turned his pint glass on the table, the smooth glass rubbing against his thumb and fingertips. He stared into the pale amber liquid. "Do you remember when I ran my old Jeep off the road?"

"Of course. You loved that car, and it had to be totaled."

He'd bought that car when he'd started college. It had been old and beat up, but perfect for off-roading and camping, things he rarely did, but always wanted to be prepared for. After the accident, he knew it would remind him of what they'd lost, of what *he'd* caused. "It wasn't totaled actually. I just didn't want it back so I sold it. Bex and I were arguing one night on our way back from

Portland. It was raining. I slid on that S-curve on Bell Road, and we went into the ditch."

Cam's eyes widened. "*Shit*. She miscarried."

Hayden drank a good third of his beer. Almost time for another. And maybe a fourth shot. Or was it a fifth? Whatever.

Cam reached across the table and clasped Hayden's forearm. "No wonder you were so beat up."

"Yeah, I guess. We never told anyone what happened. She spent the night in the hospital, but she had a minor concussion so that's what everyone knew." Hayden, on the other hand, had walked away pretty much unscathed. At least physically. "She said she couldn't stay, and she left town a week later."

Cam frowned. "She blamed you for what happened."

Hayden stared at his beer. "Maybe. I don't know. I just know that *I* blamed me."

"I never understood why you weren't mad at her for leaving. I got that you were hurt, but not like torch-the-earth mad."

Hayden squinted at him. "Like you were with Jennifer?"

"You are *not* supposed to say her name," Cam practically growled before taking a long hit of his beer.

Jennifer had been Cam's college girlfriend. She'd lived in Portland, but she and Cam had kept up their relationship after graduating. Or so Cam had thought. He'd come to find out that she had another boyfriend, one who asked her to marry him with a giant diamond and a brand-new BMW. Since Cam had been about to pop the question himself, the betrayal had cut hard and deep. He hadn't been the same since, and Hayden doubted he'd ever trust another woman, especially to get married.

Hayden didn't blame him. Looking back, he'd had a hard time trusting anyone too, and as a result, hadn't been open to any lasting relationships. He hadn't gone about it in the same way—Cam still fervently and consistently refused to date anyone seriously while Hayden had quietly kept his romantic interactions short and sweet.

"Look at us, a couple of guys who just can't trust women," Hayden said.

"Amen, brother." Cam picked up his glass and tapped it against Hayden's before taking a sip. "I'm glad to hear you're done with her for good. I was worried for a minute there, especially when Jamie said he saw you coming out of the woods holding hands at the campout. You know what they say, 'If you give a girl your heart, she'll stomp it into the ground.'"

Hayden chuckled. "That's *your* saying, douche bag." He'd never thought about that happening to him again, maybe because his heart had never really been available. Because it had belonged to Bex all along. He probably would've gotten over her—he'd been getting there when he came back for Sara's wedding—but then he'd seen her again. Spent time with her. Went to bed with her. Laughed with her.

But now she was gone. Or would be soon. Unless he stopped her.

"She told me she loved me."

Cam's brows arched. "Do you believe her?"

"Damn, you're such a cynic. Why would she lie?"

"Maybe your parents put her up to it? You said they brought her here to get you to move back home."

Hayden was pissed at them and probably would be for a while, but he didn't think they'd go that far. But, hell, how could he really know?

He finished his beer. He didn't know if he could risk any of it again—his family, Bex, any sort of close relationship. He was better off on his own, away from people and situations that might hurt him. "Cam, I'm going back to France."

Cam had finished his beer and now slammed the empty glass on the table. "*What?* What about our winery, dick-for-brains?"

Damn, the alcohol was catching up with Hayden. "Sorry, not for good. I need to go and get the rest of my stuff, move out of the house, all that shit. And Gabrielle wants to talk to me in person."

Cam grinned. "Excellent plan. Get right back on the horse. Then when you come home, we'll hit the town." He rubbed his hands together. "Just like before you left."

"Sounds great." It didn't really. Not now anyway. But it would. Hayden was bound and determined to come back to Ribbon Ridge with his head on straight and a new lease on life. Without his family breathing down his neck. Without Bex. "Just do me a favor and let me stay with you."

"Tonight?"

Hayden nodded. "And when I get back. Then when Amos and his wife move out of the house at Quail Crest, I'll take that until I find something."

"You might have to share it with Jamie. He's itching to get out of our parents' house. When are you going to France?"

Hayden looked at his empty beer glass and decided it was a metaphor for exactly how he was feeling right now. Shit, but he was a melancholy drunk tonight. "As soon as I can get a flight."

you might have to share it with Jootse. HES wining
to get out of our present house. When are you going to
France?

Chapter Twenty-One

Burgundy, France

Bᴇx ɴᴇᴀʀʟʏ ʟᴏsᴛ her nerve at the waist-high wooden
gate in front of Hayden's house. She chided herself. She
hadn't come this far to turn back now.

Taking a deep breath, she opened the latch and
walked through. The house was beautiful—two stories
made of stone with mullioned windows. Situated a mere
ten-minute walk from the main street of the village, it
was everything she'd imagined a cottage in Burgundy
to be.

And it came with the love of her life.

She only hoped he didn't throw her out as soon as she
arrived.

Steeling her resolve, she walked to the front door and
knocked. It wasn't latched and swung open, creaking

softly. She peered inside and gingerly placed her feet over the threshold.

Laughter drifted from the back of the house. She took another step then stopped short as a stunning blonde walked into the main living area. Her head was turned away from Bex, her arm stretched out behind her because she was holding Hayden's hand.

His lips were curved into a half-smile. Bex felt like she'd been kicked in the gut and wished she could melt into the floor.

The blonde turned her head and nearly let out a little shriek at seeing Bex. She came to a stop as Hayden walked up beside her.

Bex's chest cinched. He looked so unbelievably handsome in a blue heathered V-neck T-shirt and khaki shorts. His pale blue eyes fixed on her, but she couldn't read them. He could be ecstatic to see her or pissed as hell, and she wouldn't know. Wait, there was surprise, too. At least there was that.

He let go of the blonde's hand. "Bex, I didn't know you were coming." He flicked a glance toward the gorgeous woman to his right. "This is Gabrielle. Gabrielle, this is Bex. She's, uh, a friend from back home."

Gabrielle came forward, her hand extended. "I'm pleased to meet you." Her accent was thick, but her English was good.

Bex shook her hand. "Hi. I hope I'm not interrupting."

Gabrielle tossed a seductive look at Hayden. "Not now. Maybe later." She laughed as she turned back to Bex, flicking her long, shiny blonde hair over her shoulder. "You came as a surprise?"

"Yes. I'm, uh, just passing through." That was partially true. If this plan went south, she was going to Germany and drinking all the beer she could find.

"How charming." Gabrielle's dark eyes narrowed, and Bex had the sense that she found it anything but.

Bex looked at Hayden. "I can come back later." *Or not at all.*

No, she hadn't come this far to give up.

"That's not necessary," Hayden said. "Gabrielle was just leaving anyway."

Gabrielle went to him and said something in French. Bex didn't understand a word. She'd taken three years of Spanish in high school and had forgotten most of it, not that it would've helped in the slightest.

Hayden responded in her native tongue, and Bex wanted to melt into the floor again, but for very different reasons this time. Good Lord, that was sexy. If she managed to win him back, she was going to ask him to say something to her in French every single day for the rest of their lives.

Their conversation went on, in slightly hushed tones, for a few minutes. Hayden flicked a glance toward Bex then put his hand at the small of Gabrielle's back while they walked to the front door together. Bex stepped out of the way, going to the fireplace and pretending to take great interest in the books and small figurines situated on the oak mantel affixed to the stone.

"Good-bye, Bex," Gabrielle called.

Bex turned and waved. "Bye, it was nice meeting you."

Gabrielle smiled, but it didn't quite reach her coffee-colored eyes. "Enjoy your trip...wherever."

Hayden closed the door behind her then turned a curious eye toward Bex. "This is unexpected."

"Yes. I'm sorry. I didn't mean to take you by surprise."

He arched a brow at her, his hand still on the door. "Really? I have a cell phone you could've called. Or texted."

She inwardly winced. But he didn't sound mad. Just...surprised. And maybe a *little* annoyed. She really couldn't tell. Oh hell, she was tied up in knots and had been the past three days since the blow-up at The Alex. "Should I go? You look, er, busy."

He moved away from the door and took a few steps toward her. "Gabrielle? I'm not busy with her."

Bex's heart leapt. Maybe he meant just for the moment, but she'd take that. For now. "Oh, good."

He crossed his arms over his chest, looking utterly bemused. "Why are you here? Are you really just passing through?"

"Yes, actually. I'm going to Germany." *If you decide once and for all that you really don't want me.*

He narrowed his eyes. "This is hardly 'on the way.' You should've flown directly to Berlin or Munich. Unless my parents asked you to come."

"They did not." Although, they knew she was here. She'd had to arrange coverage at the brewery—Rob and some of the other brewers for the other pubs were making enough beer for The Arch and Fox and Archetype.

"I'm here because I want to be. Because I wanted to make sure you're okay."

He dropped his arms to his sides and walked to the wide front window that looked out over the small front yard. "That was quite a scene before I left. Are my parents all right?"

"I think so. You haven't spoken to them?"

"They've left a few messages, sent texts. But no, I haven't responded." He turned his head to look at her briefly. "And yes, I realize that makes me an asshole." He went back to looking out the window.

She took a few small steps toward where he stood. "No, it makes you human. They feel terrible. They love you."

He pivoted. "I know. But I think you'll agree with me when I say that sometimes love isn't enough."

No, it wasn't. She'd loved him five years ago when she'd left, but she didn't think she'd been the right person for him. She didn't fit with his family and then when she'd lost the baby, it was as if life was telling her to get away. She'd do things differently now, but that's because *she* was different.

"Can I...that is, will you accept my apology?"

His brow furrowed, and his lips parted. "For what?"

"For leaving you. For thinking you chose your family over me. For not sticking by you when you needed someone."

He let out a sound that was part laugh, part harrumph. "I did choose my family over you. For what good that did me."

She came to stand in front of him. "No, it's not quite like that, is it? You didn't choose them; you did what you thought needed to be done. You stood by Alex, your father, your commitment to Archer. I understand what you were hoping to gain." She didn't want to come right out and say that she knew he'd been seeking his place or approval or validation—whatever the right word was.

He stared at her, his eyes taking on a sheen that might've been appreciation. "You do understand. Thank you." He moved away from her. "Where are you staying?"

She watched him walk past the front door to a dining area with a long farm-style table with benches on either side and chairs at each end. "I have a room in town at a little bed-and-breakfast."

He picked up a glass from the table. "Maison Dominique?"

"That's the one."

"That's a great place." Holding the glass, he turned back toward her. "Anne-Marie makes the most amazing bread and pastries. Be careful or you'll gain five pounds overnight."

She widened her eyes and let out a quick laugh. "Yikes, I'll watch myself."

"How long will you be here to check up on me?"

A voice in the back of her head told her to make her case, to fight for him. Wasn't that why she was here? She gave him a look that she hoped was half as seductive as Gabrielle's had been. "That depends on how long you'll let me."

They stood there staring at each other, a polite starch in the air around them. *Fight, Bex*, the voice said. "I came to see if we were really over. I know you said you didn't love me anymore, but I was hoping that maybe you might. Or that you could maybe just fall in love with me all over again. I think that's what happened to me when I came back to Ribbon Ridge. I'd forgotten how much I adored being with you, how fast you make my heart beat when you walk into a room, how kind and generous you are—even when you're hurting. How could I ever have thought you'd chosen your family over me when every day you showed me how much you loved me and how deeply you longed for a future—a family—with me? Amid my own insecurities about joining your family and then the angst of the baby, I lost sight of the simplest things right in front of me. Sometimes love *isn't* enough, but we had more than that, didn't we?"

"I thought so, but when you left, something inside of me snapped. You were the one person I felt connected to. I'd had to go outside of my family to find it. *You* were my family, Bex, and you left. I'm not sure…I don't know how to regain that trust. With you, with my family, with anyone."

She heard the despair in his voice, but there was longing, too. He wanted to find it. And that gave her infinite hope.

She took his hand and brushed her thumb over his knuckles. "Then let me earn your trust. I didn't come here to talk you into coming home. I didn't come here to seduce you. I came here to truly see if you were all right, and yes, to plead my case." She allowed herself to smile. She wanted to show him the joy she felt at just being here with him. "But I'm patient, Hayden, and I will wait for you for as long as it takes. I don't care where you go or where you end up, I want to be there with you. If you'll let me."

THE STROKE OF her thumb lulled him into a sort of trance as his mind devoured every word she'd said. God, he loved her so much. He'd never stopped. He just didn't know if he could take the risk of surrendering to that emotion again. But she was here, and she wanted to earn his trust. Maybe he should let her try. It wasn't as if he were blameless.

He let go of her hand. "Hang on." He turned and went into the small kitchen to set the glass on the counter. When he went back to her, she hadn't moved. In fact, he wasn't even sure she'd blinked.

"Do you want to go for a walk?" he asked.

Now she blinked. "Sure. Yes."

Together they went to the door, which he held open for her as she stepped outside. The afternoon was bright and hot. He grabbed his hat from the hook by the door and crushed it on his head. "You should have a hat," he said, joining her on the path.

She looked up at him, squinting. "Should I?"

"Or sunglasses. There's a shop in the village. Come on." He opened the gate for her and watched her walk through. She wore a short, blue-and-yellow sundress and flat, strappy sandals that made her ankles look unbearably sexy. All of her was unbearably sexy. From her pale jade eyes to the scrumptious dimples he'd seen very little of today to the curve of her hip and the sway of her backside as she sauntered in front of him.

He strode up alongside her as they walked along the edge of the road toward the village. After a moment, she sent him a tentative glance. "Can I ask you about Gabrielle? She seemed irritated that I was there. Maybe even a bit jealous."

And Bex *sounded* jealous. He liked that. "She'd like there to be more between us than there is. I thought we were on the same page before I left to go home, but somewhere along the line she developed stronger feelings for me. I didn't get the memo."

"That sucks. For her, I mean." Now she sounded pleased. He liked that, too. "What were you talking about in French?" she asked.

"Sorry about that. I didn't mean to be rude, but I didn't think you wanted to hear her call you a shameless tramp in English."

She laughed. "Wow. What else did I miss?"

"Just her asking what I saw in you."

Bex turned her head and looked up at him, her dimples creasing into her cheeks and making it damn near impossible to keep his hands to himself. "What did you say?"

"I told her to look at you, and that it should be obvious what I saw in you."

She sucked in a breath. "You *didn't*."

"Okay, I told her you were my sisters' friend and she had nothing to worry about." That was true. He'd sensed a potential catfight and had wanted to prevent it.

Bex looked forward once more. "Oh." Now she sounded disappointed. And he didn't like that. "You never told her about me?"

"Nope. I worked really hard to get you out of my system. Talking about you to other women wouldn't have helped with that. Trust me, I know. I did it a lot at first."

She winced. "Sorry." She inadvertently kicked a rock with her toe, sending it skidding into the middle of the road. "I did the same thing."

That made him feel better. It made him feel pretty damn good actually. "Is it bad that I like hearing that?"

"No worse than me wanting you to tell Gabrielle that I'm the woman you were having sex with last week."

Now it was his turn to laugh. "Fair enough." They were nearing the village, but he was enjoying their conversation so he slowed his gait. "You had a hard time after you left Ribbon Ridge?"

She nodded. "I did. I still loved you. I just didn't want to be in that town or with your family or with you after what happened."

It was like a cloud had moved over the sun, but the day was as bright as ever. "The baby."

She stopped beneath the shade of a tree and faced him. "Hayden, I know I said I didn't blame you, but I did. Subconsciously. I didn't realize it at first. I feel so ashamed." Tears welled in her eyes, and his heart twisted in a way it hadn't for five long years.

He put his hands on her biceps and held her. "Hey, don't be. I blamed me, too."

She sniffed. "It's more than that. I was…relieved. Sad, but also relieved. We hadn't planned that baby, and I wasn't ready."

He realized then that his guilt had stemmed from the same feelings, not just the fact that he'd been driving the car, though that was still a big part of it. "I know. I wasn't ready either. I guess the universe knew what needed to happen."

She blinked and brought her hand up to wipe away a tear that was stuck to her lashes. "That it wasn't our time."

It wasn't our time. Did she mean they were meant to break up and find each other again? He didn't know if he believed that.

He stroked his fingertips along her upper arms. "You okay?"

She nodded, sniffing again. "Sunglasses might be good since my eyes are probably red now. I have a pair at the B and B. I don't know why I left them there. In a hurry to see you, I guess." She offered him a fragile smile.

If things were different, if he hadn't been experiencing this incredible emotional turmoil where she was concerned, he'd pull her into his arms and kiss her. He wanted to see the strong, happy Bex he loved.

But wasn't sure he trusted. Not yet.

"The hat shop is just up here." He took her hand without thinking. Should he let go? He peered over at her, but she didn't look at him. He thought he saw the hint of a smile tugging at her lips.

He decided not to question every damn thing and just walked with her to the shop. Once inside, the shopkeeper greeted him in French, and he introduced her to Bex in

English. They chatted about what sort of hat would look good—Hayden playing interpreter. The shopkeeper left them alone while Bex tried about twenty different ones—small hats, fancy hats, wide-brimmed floppy hats, straw, knit, and even one with a bird on it. "How *Portlandia* of you," he said, laughing.

She pursed her lips and cocked her head to the side, modeling for him. "From what I hear, I think Maggie's mom would like this."

"Didn't you meet her at Sara's wedding?" At her nod, he asked, "And you saw what she was wearing? Apparently we should've been grateful that she'd at least donned a bra."

Bex giggled as she took off the hat. "I see your point. The bird might work, but the little net is maybe a bit too fancy for her."

Hayden snorted, enjoying himself immensely. "Just a bit."

The shopkeeper came back to check on them. "Did you make a decision?"

Hayden picked up a soft, woven straw hat with a two-inch brim around it. *"Celui-ci."*

Bex turned from the mirror as she smoothed her hair. "What did you say?"

"I said we'd take this one. It's my favorite."

She beamed up at him. "Mine, too!" Her smiled faded. *"Merde."*

The shopkeeper had taken the hat from Hayden to ring it up, but shot Bex a surprised glance before she continued to the register at the back of the store.

Bex cringed. "What did I say? I thought it was like saying darn or something."

"Technically, you said 'shit.'"

Bex clapped a hand over her mouth then giggled. "Well, *merde*. Sorry, I got so wrapped up in you speaking French, I wanted to give it a try. Maybe you can teach me a few words."

"Really?" He gave in to the impulse to flirt with her. "Or do you just want to hear me speak French?"

Her eyes widened briefly then narrowed to a seductive slant. "Every. Single. Day. Please don't stop." Her voice took on a breathy quality that sent a wave of heat rushing over him.

He worked to pull himself back from the brink of desire. "Why did you swear?"

"Oh! I don't have my wallet." She blushed and looked away. "It's also at the B and B. And before you tell me I shouldn't leave that sort of thing lying around in a foreign country, I know." She returned her gaze to his, and he couldn't ignore the heat in their depths. "Like I said, I was in a hurry."

He needed to get out of here before he did something foolish, like kiss her senseless in front of the shopkeeper. "No worries. I'll take care of it. My treat."

Her shoulders came up in a quick shrug. She smiled, her dimples carving deep into her cheeks. "Okay. Thanks."

He went to the counter and paid for her hat then they left the shop, turning down the street toward Maison Dominique, where she was staying.

"This has been an interesting afternoon," she said.

He had to agree. They'd shared some enlightening things. He felt better about what happened five years ago than he ever had. Better than he'd ever thought possible. "Yeah. Thanks." He didn't really want it to end, but he had a few things to do that afternoon. "Do you want to come for dinner later?"

She looked momentarily surprised, but nodded. "I'd love that. What time?"

"Seven?"

"Sounds great. Can I bring anything?"

He'd been about to say no, but they'd just come to the entrance to her B and B, and the delicious scent of Anne-Marie's fresh bread filled the air. "Yes, a loaf of Anne-Marie's bread. And if you can't get one, don't bother coming."

She laughed. "I'll steal one if I have to."

He gave her a nod of approval. "Just don't get caught."

She paused in the doorway and gave him a saucy look. Beneath it, he sensed a warmth and an anticipation he felt in himself. At least, he thought he sensed it. He hoped he wasn't wrong.

"See you later." She went inside.

He turned to head back down the street toward his house. He didn't know what he was doing. All he knew was that it felt good, and he'd spent far too long feeling bad.

Chapter Twenty-Two

BEX SET HER fork down on Hayden's table. "I can't eat another bite. I had no idea you were such a good cook. I mean, I knew from experience that you *could*, but you've gotten really good." She resisted the urge to add that he'd gotten really good at a lot of things—including his ability to make her feel like a girl with her first crush.

He sat at the head of the table while she perched on the bench to his right. "Thanks. It wasn't much. Just fish and greens. And they paled in comparison to Anne-Marie's bread."

Bex eyed what was left of the loaf. Not much. Anne-Marie had also insisted on sending her with a small chocolate gateau with whipped cream. Bex was going to have to wait a bit before she could attack it, but she had every plan to.

"I guess we're waiting on the cake?" Hayden asked.

Bex nodded. "I think I have to."

Hayden finished his wine and picked up the bottle. "A little more?"

Her glass wasn't quite empty, but the wine was phenomenal. He'd said that he'd picked it up that afternoon from the winery where he'd interned. "Yes, please. This is almost as good as our pinot back home."

Hayden laughed. "Almost. I won't tell Antoine you said that. He'd be mightily offended." He poured for her then emptied the rest of the bottle into his glass.

Bex picked up her wine and took a sniff, savoring the aroma. "Are you sure this isn't poisoned? I can't imagine he was too happy that you aren't coming back. Or maybe Gabrielle decided to spike it with something."

He laughed again. "What, like she roofied me?" He shook his head. "I think I finally got through to her."

Bex sipped her wine then set the glass back on the table, keeping her finger around the base of the stem. "You spoke to her this afternoon?"

"I had to. I went in to get the rest of my stuff, and she was there. She understands that a relationship just wouldn't work out."

"There's no chance she could have talked you into staying?" Given the way he'd left Ribbon Ridge the other day, Bex would've thought it was possible.

"None. I'm too excited about Quail Crest. Besides, I don't love her. I never did."

Bex tamped down the ridiculous wave of giddiness that crested through her. "What about your family? You said you wanted them to leave you alone when you go back."

He frowned into his glass. "Yeah, I did say that, didn't I? I was angry. Hurt. I won't ignore them. At least not permanently."

"Good. I don't think that strategy would work for you as well as it works for me and my parents."

The edge of his mouth slanted up. "Is that what you do? I know they ignore you, but you've always tried to watch out for them, particularly your dad."

"I have, but I've pretty much given up on my mother. And my dad's got Joss. I don't have to like her. If she makes my dad happy, that's great."

He pinned her with an earnest stare. "I always felt bad for you, you know. I wanted you to experience how good a family could be. Too bad they scared you off."

She laughed softly. "No, it wasn't that. I was…over-whelmed." She thought back to the first Christmas she'd spent with them and how they'd given her gifts and included her in their traditions—she'd even had her own stocking. Then they'd talked about the next year and that's when she'd maybe felt a little fear. It was a lot to take in for a girl who hadn't had a visit from Santa since she was eight. The last "real" Christmas she remembered had been with her paternal grandparents when she was ten, before they'd both moved to assisted living facilities.

"And you're not now?"

She thought about her answer. "I won't lie. I wasn't very happy with your parents when I figured out what they were trying to do. I had no idea they were using me as bait to get you to stay in Ribbon Ridge." She flinched. "That sounds terrible."

"It *was* terrible." He looked at her intently. "You had no idea?"

She shook her head. "No, I didn't. I put it together the day we got back from the hike. Maybe I should've told you, but I didn't want you to be hurt."

His gaze warmed. "I appreciate that. I'm sorry I thought you were in on it."

"It's okay. I get it. Their hearts were in the right place." She thought of her parents and could only imagine her mother cooking up a scheme to keep her away, not get her to stay. "It's good to be wanted, isn't it?"

He studied her, seeming like he was trying to understand what she meant—that he should be glad for their love and concern, even if it could be smothering at times. "Yes and since I'm the only kid they pulled something like this with, I guess I should be flattered." He said this with a bit of humor, and she couldn't help but smile. This was the Hayden she loved. The man who always— eventually—found the bright side.

She put her hand on his forearm. "*That* is an excellent perspective. Very adult."

He looked at where they touched, and the air seemed to shift. Electricity crackled around them. She half expected him to pull away from her and was thrilled when he didn't.

"They just…I know they love me, that they just want me to be happy, but I can't help feeling…" He withdrew his arm from beneath her hand and picked up his wine-glass. "Never mind."

She could practically watch him bury the emotion bubbling just beneath the surface. "You've gotten really good at that," she said, putting her hand in her lap. "Hiding your emotions. And don't tell me you weren't because I'm the queen. You were a lot more open when we were together—I think that's one of the things that drew me to you. Maybe subconsciously I wanted to be like that. Now, I *know* I want to be like that. Even so, it seemed you worked hard to…I don't know, put on a front maybe? For your family."

"I've changed a lot since then. So have you."

Yes, he had. He wasn't the same person, and maybe that's why she'd fallen in love with him so hard and fast again. Harder and faster than the first time. Not because he was burying his emotions, but because he was confident and independent in a way he hadn't been before. Plus, he spoke crazy-sexy French.

She took a drink of wine for courage. "I have a theory." He arched a brow at her and she held up her hand briefly. "Bear with me. Please. I've been wondering how you've been since Alex died, how you've coped." She thought of her conversation with Liam. It had helped plant this idea in her mind, and then their conversation that afternoon under the tree had crystallized it. "I imagine it was extremely difficult."

His gaze hardened a bit, and she worried she was walking down a road and might not like the destination. "What's your theory?"

"I look at us now—where we are, what we're doing, *who* we are—and I can't help but think things were meant to happen as they did. Losing the baby was awful, but it set things into motion that led us here. Alex's death did the same thing. You applied for that internship when he died, didn't you?"

He turned his head toward the living room and was quiet for a long time. She watched the muscles of his throat work, his Adam's apple move as he swallowed.

When he looked at her again, his sky blue eyes were cool, his expression tense. She longed to stroke his cheek, kiss his mouth, draw the pain from him like a balm.

"Yes." He cleared the cobwebs from his throat. "Yes. I'd given up my future plans to stay in Ribbon Ridge—for dad and for Alex. When I talked about making wine, Alex told me I should start a label on the side. He never once encouraged me to leave Archer or follow my dreams. In fact, when I told him I was considering leaving Ribbon Ridge with you, he asked me not to."

Bex hadn't expected this. Her insides coiled with apprehension. She didn't know what to say, so she said nothing.

"How could I leave him after that?" Hayden shook his head, his lip curling. He took a drink of wine and set his glass down hard enough that the ruby liquid sloshed and nearly spilled. "He was a selfish prick. And he knew it. In his letter to me, he apologized. He said he should've told me what he was planning. But hell, Bex, what would I have done with *that*?"

His eyes were so full of pain she almost couldn't bear it. But she didn't know if he wanted her comfort. "I don't know," she said softly. God, she sucked at families. What was she supposed to say? "You would've figured it out."

He laughed, but the sound was hollow. "Right, because I'm the 'good' son. He told me that too in the letter. Or a version of it anyway. No pressure."

"Hey, I didn't mean it that way. I just meant that you're...I don't know, you have your head on straight. It was one of the things I liked most about you when we dated. Life could be crazy, but Hayden would always be there to keep me safe."

"Until I ran us off the road."

Oh no, he was in a really dark place. She couldn't stand it anymore. She scooted to the edge of the bench and touched his arm. "Don't do that. It was an accident. And I have to believe it was meant to be. I should've stayed. We should've worked through the miscarriage together."

He smiled sadly. "But then your theory would be blown. Your leaving was meant to be, too."

He was right. "Yeah, I guess so. Anyway, I'm okay now. But are you? Please don't hide your feelings away. I can see that you're hurting. Maybe it would help to talk to me."

"Isn't that what I've been doing?" He took a drink of wine. "I'm not trying to be obtuse. I understand what you're saying. I was so mad at Alex. I'm still mad. I should probably work through that."

This was progress. Hope and joy unfurled inside her. "Probably. But there's no rush. There's no time frame on healing." She wanted to say one more thing and then she'd shut up. "I think you could rely on your family to help you through this. You aren't alone."

"I know that *here*." He pointed at his head. "But here"—he laid his hand over his heart—"I seem to have forgotten how to listen to this."

Bex knew instinctively that was her fault. Or at least in large part. "You'll find it again. Your family will help you. Whoever you fall in love with will help you." How she wished that could be her.

She stood abruptly. "I should go. I didn't mean to take us down this dark path." She laughed uneasily.

He got up. "Why are you leaving?"

Because she didn't want to rush anything. She wanted to give him time and space, show him that he could trust her to be here for him. Always. "I'm just going back to the B and B. I'll stay around as long as you want me to." *Please let me stay forever.*

He walked her to the door. "Thanks for being so…patient. And supportive. I really appreciate it."

She stood on her toes and kissed his cheek, her lips caressing his warmth for a precious few seconds. "Good night."

Bex walked out into the sunset and hoped she was doing the right thing.

HAYDEN FINISHED HIS wine then cleared the dishes from the table. He set everything in the sink to soak and stared out at the backyard with its tangle of rose-bushes and planter boxes of herbs. A giant oak tree stood in the corner. He'd wanted to put a swing on it, but hadn't gotten around to doing so. Now he never would.

There were a lot of things he'd never do—climb Mount Everest, go back to working for the family company, hug his brother Alex again. But there were things he would do, things he *should* do.

Such as try to find a way to forgive Alex.

That was the heart of the matter, he realized. Why he'd felt unsettled. Why he'd locked his emotions away. It wasn't Bex. It had never been Bex. But Alex's death had helped him finally banish his feelings for her, too.

Until she'd come back and reawakened them. He didn't know if he'd fallen in love with her all over again or if he'd just never stopped. And he didn't care.

He hadn't taken risks before. He'd played it safe—staying in Ribbon Ridge, acting the part of the consummate people-pleaser. And he'd seen how that had worked out for him.

He'd decided a few weeks ago that he was going to please himself. That he was finally the priority—his dreams, his life, his happiness. He realized all those things were Bex. She was here, asking him to love her, and he just had to say yes.

He turned from the sink and strode to the front door. He rushed outside and jogged to the gate. He looked down the road, but it was empty. Throwing open the gate, he ran through and took off toward the village. When he finally saw her—she was almost to the tree they'd stopped under that afternoon—he broke into a sprint.

He was nearly upon her when she turned, her lips parted, her eyes widening in surprise. He clasped her waist and lifted her against him as he kissed her. His mouth found hers with an eager precision. Desperation ripped through him. He held her fast, lifting her feet from the ground, never wanting to let her go.

She kissed him back, her arms wrapped around his neck, her body pressing into his.

He tore his mouth from hers. "I love you. I know there are no guarantees, and I'm willing to risk it. Just, well, please don't leave me again."

He felt wetness on his cheeks and realized she was crying. "Bex, don't cry, sweetheart." He set her down and swiped his thumb over her cheek.

She smiled up at him, her dimples working overtime. "I love you too, and I will never leave you again. Ever. Not unless you tell me to. And even then I'll refuse."

He kissed her again, more softly this time, his lips and tongue flirting with hers. When they came up for air again, they were both breathing heavily. He rested his forehead against hers. "I propose a new pact. No regrets. I like your theory."

She nodded. "No regrets."

He swept her into his arms and she giggled. "You're carrying me back to the house?"

"Too caveman?"

"You didn't throw me over your shoulder." She giggled again. "I'm worried you'll wear yourself out."

He looked down at her as he walked. The setting sun cast a golden glow, making her even more beautiful than she already was. "I'm a big, strong guy. I thought you liked all my new muscles."

"I love your new muscles." She ran her hand over his shoulder and bicep with lingering appreciation. "But I'd rather you reserve your energy for other activities."

He gave her a seductive stare. "I promise you that I'll have plenty of energy to last all through the night." He felt her shiver.

"Show me." She kissed his neck, her tongue sliding over his flesh.

He was glad he'd reached the gate.

He bore her up to the house and carried her over the threshold. The door was barely closed behind them before she slid from his arms and tugged him toward the stairs. "Where's the bedroom?" she asked huskily.

"Who needs a bedroom?"

She narrowed her eyes at him. "I don't *need* anything. Except you. However, I'd like a nice, soft mattress and access to wherever you keep your condoms."

He walked slowly, teasing her with his hesitance.

She let go of his hand and pulled her dress over her head, leaving her in nothing but white lacy undergarments. His mouth went dry.

He walked faster, stalking her to the stairs. She started up and turned, going backward.

"Careful," he growled.

She put her hands behind her back and unhooked her bra then tossed it at him. "You, too."

The undergarment dropped to the hardwood stairs as they reached the top.

She broke eye contact to find her bearings, and he made his move. He wrapped his arms around her thighs and boosted her up over his shoulder caveman-style.

"This what you wanted?" he asked, carrying her to his bedroom on the other side of the upper floor.

She ran her hands down his back and pulled his shirt up to expose his flesh. "Mmm. Hurry."

He quickened his pace and went straight for the bed, an ancient four-poster that squeaked horribly. He dropped her on the mattress with a loud creak and whisked her panties off, leaving her completely and gorgeously nude.

He dropped to his knees on the floor and clasped her ankles, pulling her hips to the edge of the bed. He quickly divested her of the strappy sandals and cast them aside. Then he ran his hands up her legs, skimming her heated flesh, pausing at her thighs, to push them apart.

He stroked his thumb over her flesh, knowing she'd jerk, and he wasn't disappointed. "You're so predictable."

She sat up, bracing herself on her elbows, and looked at him, her eyes slitted with desire. "You want unpredictable?"

"I want anything and everything you have to offer." He stared at her, holding her captive with his gaze as he pushed a finger inside her. Her eyes closed briefly, and her lips parted to release a breathy sigh.

He thumbed her clit and thrust his finger in long, slow strokes. She was hot and wet, and he didn't think he could do this for very long. Not if he wanted to make love to her. And he wanted that more than he'd wanted anything.

But first he wanted to push her over the edge. He knew her orgasm would be that much better when he made love to her. And he loved that he knew that about her.

He used his thumbs to part her flesh. She rotated her hips, seeking him. "I want to remember everything about you." He licked her, and she cried out. "I want to learn everything that's new and different." He suckled her clit, and she wound her fingers in his hair. "I want to go to bed every night with you by my side and wake up every day exactly the same way." He plunged his tongue into her and she thrust against his mouth.

With fingers and tongue, he coaxed her higher. With each jerk of her hips and pull on his hair, he felt her move closer to her orgasm. He found her G-spot and pressed. Her muscles contracted and moisture flooded his mouth.

He didn't wait for her to recover, but stood and tore his clothes off. He went to the nightstand and found a condom. After he'd donned the sheath, he joined her on the bed. She'd managed to situate herself against the pillows, her head cast back and her eyes nearly closed.

"I think you got better at that," she said, her voice low and dark. "And I don't want to know how."

"I wasn't a monk. Sorry. And I can't imagine you were a nun." It was strange, but he was simultaneously jealous and turned on by that. Jealous of the men she'd been with but excited for the new things they'd both bring to the bedroom.

She looked up at him and pulled his head down. "Okay, lover boy, show me what you've got." She kissed him, tasting of wine and need and everything his life had been missing.

He guided his cock to her entrance, and she wrapped her legs around him, welcoming him into her. He slid in deep, his body thrumming with need. When he was fully seated, he just stopped for a moment. Pleasure and joy crested through him. He was right where he wanted to be. He was home.

He braced himself above her and brushed her dark hair back from her forehead. She opened her eyes, her green eyes finding his and filling with emotion.

He stroked her temple. "I love you so much."

She skimmed her hands along his back. "I love you, too."

He kissed her again and began to move. The friction was immediate and intense. He couldn't hold back. He drove into her with hard, fast strokes. She met him, her hips snapping against his. "Yes, Hayden. *Please.*"

He buried his face in her neck and lost himself in her.

She clutched at his back and brought her knees up. He caressed the back of her thigh and wrapped his hand around her knee as he slammed into her. She cried out over and over again, and the bed creaked and squeaked, maybe alerting the neighbors who were a good hundred yards away.

She dug her nails into his back. "Come with me, Hayden. Please. I can't wait." She gasped, tensing as her orgasm hit.

He was nearly there. One more thrust. His balls tightened and he came, shouting her name over and over.

It took several minutes for him to return to reality. With great effort, he got up and went to the bathroom. When he came back, she was under the covers and had pulled them back invitingly.

She nodded toward the window where the curtains were blowing in the breeze. "I didn't realize the window was open. Oops."

"I think between us and the noisy bed, the state of the window is moot. But I frankly don't care if all of Burgundy heard us."

She smiled as he climbed into bed beside her. He drew her close and kissed her. "Were you really on your way to Germany?"

She snuggled against his chest, wrapping her arms around him. "Only if you told me to leave. I figured I'd go as long as I'd come all this way. Plus, I'd planned to drown my sorrows in beer."

"Then let's go. I have to finish packing and arrange to ship some stuff home. After that, I'm all yours." He shook his head. "Not true. I'm actually yours starting right now. Or an hour ago." He grinned, happier than he'd been in a very long time. "Whatever. I'm yours."

"Are you going to call your family?"

He looked at her. "Do they know you're here?"

She grimaced. "I'm afraid so. They're kind of a meddlesome bunch."

He liked that she said that with humor. "They are." He sighed. "But they're all I've got. And I'm guessing they're waiting with bated breath to see what happens."

"I'm sure."

"Maybe we'll keep them wondering. We'll just show up for the grand opening of The Alex in a couple of weeks."

She laughed and lightly tapped his arm. "You're mean. The old Hayden never would've done that."

He arched a brow at her. "There is no old Hayden. I'm still me. I'm still the frat boy you fell in love with."

She looked at him with love and joy. "You're still the one—and you always will be."

Chapter Twenty-Three

Ribbon Ridge

HAYDEN PULLED THROUGH the porte cochere in the rental car they'd picked up at the airport and parked near the back door to the house. After the last couple of weeks in Europe with Bex, he felt more like himself than he had in years, maybe in forever.

Bex reached over and clasped his hand. She gave him a warm smile. "Ready?"

"For anything with you next to me."

She leaned over and brushed her lips against his. "You say all the right things, Hayden Archer."

He captured her mouth in a searing kiss, taking strength from her love. "Okay, let's do this."

He jumped out of the car and walked around to help her. Hand in hand, they made their way to the back door, and he paused briefly, thinking that just inside were all the people he loved most in the world—aside from the one beside him.

He opened the door and stopped. The hooks that had been on the wall since they were children had been moved higher and reorganized. There were more hooks— ones for Dylan, Maggie, Sean, Alaina, and Aubrey. Alex's wasn't there anymore.

Hayden's gut clenched. He glanced down the hallway to his right toward Alex's bedroom. Had they changed that, too? He didn't want to look.

He didn't think they'd be in the kitchen—there were too many of them now—so he led Bex to the great room. As they neared, he heard conversation. It stopped as soon as he and Bex came into view.

Mom jumped up from the couch, her gaze expectant. "Hayden. We're so glad to see you." Her gaze dipped to where he held Bex's hand then rose again. "We're glad to see you too, Bex."

Hayden looked around at everyone. "Let's just get this part out of the way. Bex and I are together. We're engaged, actually. We're moving into the house at Quail Crest. But tonight we're staying at The Alex."

"We all are, loser, it's the grand opening." Leave it to Kyle to try to lighten the mood. It seemed to work as everyone stood and came toward Hayden and Bex, congratulating and hugging them.

After several minutes, everyone resituated themselves, but Dad lingered near them. "Son, I hope you know how sorry we are. We shouldn't have meddled. We just thought that you and Bex belonged together."

"Clearly we think so, too," Hayden said wryly then took Bex's hand again, giving her fingers a squeeze. The engagement ring he'd bought her in Germany twisted on her finger. They really needed to get that sized, but on their drive through town he'd seen that a jewelry store had opened up on the main street. Life was always changing, and that wasn't a bad thing.

He looked toward his mom, who stood beside his dad. "You changed the hooks."

"We did. The family's growing." She smiled at Bex. "I'll order yours today."

Bex's dimples made an appearance. "Thank you."

Hayden looked around the room at his siblings and their significant others and felt the love in the room. He also felt a tense expectation. "I know I said I wanted you to leave me alone when I came home, but you don't have to. In fact, I'd rather you didn't."

Kyle stood next to a chair where Maggie was sitting. "Good because we actually didn't have any intention of listening to you. See, the sommelier I hired while you were gone is kind of a tool so I'll be needing you to fill in again. I know you've got winery planning to do, but dude, I *need* your help."

Hayden nodded, a smile tugging at his lips. "I can do that."

Sean sat on one of the couches next to Tori. "And I've got a proposal written up for filming the winery start-up. I'd love to meet with you and the Westcotts early next week."

Hayden felt Bex squeeze his hand. "I can do that, too."

"I've got a skydive session all set up for this Sunday afternoon," Liam said. "Everyone's going. Except Aubrey and Alaina. They're going to watch from the ground."

Hayden glanced at his parents. "Wait, Mom and Dad are going?"

Dad nodded. "Actually, I am. And your mother is still thinking about it."

Holy shit. Hayden never would've guessed their mother would jump out of a plane.

"You up for it, Bex?" Liam asked.

She grinned. "Definitely."

"And Bex, we just can't find a brewer we like as much as you," Tori said. "Any chance you'll come back?"

She squeezed Hayden's hand again. "In a heartbeat. Thank you."

Hayden decided it was time to unburden himself—in a more positive way than last time. "I have some work to do here…and I'm going to need your help. See, Alex died on my watch. I know we all feel variations of guilt, but I really felt like I didn't deserve to be here. So I left. Plus, I was mad at him. Really mad. I'd situated my entire life around being here for him." He looked toward Bex. "To the point that I messed things up for myself."

Kyle stepped toward him. "You deserve to be here as much as any of us. More, really. I, uh…" He glanced away. "I envy the years you had with Alex. You say you messed things up, but nowhere near as bad as I did. I won't speak for anyone else."

Sara stood from the couch where she was sitting. "I may not have messed up, but I'm so sorry you felt left out.

It never occurred to me. I always thought I was the out-sider. Or Evan." She looked at Evan, who nodded.

Evan stood then, too. "I'd say you're nuts for think-ing you were somehow excluded, but we all have our own unique perspectives. I can see how you felt that way."

Tori joined the little semicircle that was forming in front of Hayden. "I completely blew it. We were all such jerks, always making stupid comments about you being the 'oops' kid." She grimaced. "I'm sorry."

Liam moved in beside Tori. "You may not believe this, but I envied you sometimes. I thought it would be nice to not be associated with this group, to be on my own."

Evan nodded. "Especially during the show...to not have the focus on you...I would've traded places with you in a second."

Hayden was absolutely floored by everything they were saying. Emotion welled up inside him, and he was surprised he could find his voice. "I'm sorry you had to put up with the show at all."

Evan shrugged. "Mom and Dad came around and put an end to it."

Everyone exchanged looks, and it seemed this was news to at least some of them.

Dad stepped into the circle. "See, you aren't the only ones who make mistakes."

Mom took Dad's hand then Hayden's. "And we'll all do it again, I'm sure. I'm just glad we have each other to work through them." She looked around at her children, at her husband. "We do have each other, don't we?"

Hayden thought of what he'd told Bex in France, about not trusting them. But the truth was that he hadn't trusted himself. He'd screwed up with Bex, felt like he'd failed Alex, and the result had been a man who'd felt completely disconnected.

He took Liam's hand, and Liam took Tori's who took Evan's who took Sara's who took Kyle's who took Dad's. Hayden looked for Derek and made eye contact. "Um, hello?"

Derek jumped up and wedged himself in between Kyle and Dad. "Sorry, I was getting kind of choked up over there. That you all welcomed me into your family has always been the greatest gift I will ever receive."

"*Our* family," Mom said softly. "It's our family. We might have lost one, but look at all we've gained."

Everyone's significant others joined them, sliding into the circle and widening it so they filled the room. Hayden squeezed Bex's hand, so happy that they'd found their way back to each other.

The quiet in the room was incredibly peaceful. Then Evan spoke.

"I like to think of Alex like a pebble dropped into a lake. The ripples he caused were far-reaching—some large, some small, but all of them important. Whether it was bringing Kyle home to meet Maggie, hiring Aubrey so that she would meet Liam, dreaming up The Alex so that Sara and Dylan would find each other, and so on. Only you can say what his impact has been for you, and I suspect in many ways he isn't done. That is his legacy. This is his love."

Everyone was silent for a long moment.

Kyle sniffed and wiped at his eye. "Evan, if you'd told me that you'd be the one to think of exactly the right thing to say at the right moment, I would've said you were batshit crazy."

The tension and the melancholy gave way to laughter and joy. Hugs were exchanged again, and Hayden blinked back his tears.

"Enough with the sappy stuff," Hayden said. "We can't show up to the opening of our own hotel and restaurant looking like we cried our eyes out."

Liam's eyes found his. "So we're all...good?"

Hayden absorbed all of the love around him and looked at Bex, his heart bursting with joy. "We're family."

Epilogue

November, Ribbon Ridge

BEX STOOD IN the corner of the waiting room sipping her coffee. The place was full to bursting with Archers and had been for hours while they awaited the birth of Alaina and Evan's baby. Aubrey joined her, stifling a yawn since it was well past midnight.

"If this goes on much longer, they'll need to bring us blankets and pillows," Bex said.

Aubrey nodded. "No kidding. I just hope Alaina's doing all right. I know first labors can be long, but this marathon might deter the rest of us from getting pregnant."

Bex chuckled but didn't voice her differing opinion. She and Hayden were getting married in March, and they were ready to start a family as soon as possible.

"So I guess we're not having our Only Child Club lunch tomorrow," Bex said. Alaina had gone into labor eight days before her due date. Bex had been welcomed into the club with open arms, and last month she'd invited Hayden, saying he deserved an only-child status as much as any of them. Hayden had appreciated her inclusion but said he didn't qualify. He'd found his place in his family and wore it like a banner.

"Guess not," Aubrey agreed. "We'll be too tired anyway. I imagine we'll all be stumbling through our workdays as it is."

Tomorrow was a brew day for Bex, but she thought she might have to readjust her schedule. Maybe she'd take the day off and just work on Saturday. That way she could finish painting the bathroom she'd started last weekend. She and Hayden were updating the house on Quail Crest. Someday it would become the tasting room, and they'd build a new house nearby, but they hadn't found property yet. Right now, they were both too focused on their jobs and, more important, each other.

Crystal Donovan, Alaina's best friend and the only person allowed in the birthing room besides Alaina, Evan, and the medical staff, came running into the waiting room, her face beaming. "It's a girl!"

Everyone shouted with joy and exchanged hugs and laughter.

Crystal finished hugging Emily. "They're getting cleaned up now and you can all go in to see them in a few minutes."

Hayden found Bex and kissed her temple. He held her close, whispering, "Maybe that'll be you next year. I'd like a baby girl with dark curls and jade green eyes."

She snuggled against his chest. "If it's a boy, we'll just try again. And again. You know I'm not having just one." She wanted her children to have what she hadn't—a large, loving family.

He laughed softly. "I know."

A few minutes later they were all ushered into Alaina's birthing room. They barely fit, but no one wanted to take turns. Evan stood next to the bed holding his daughter. Alaina looked exhausted but happy and still more beautiful than anyone had a right to be.

Emily went to her son and asked softly, "May I?"

Evan handed her the tiny bundle and glanced briefly around the room. "We're naming her Alexa."

Emily looked up at him, and from where she stood, Bex could see the sheen of tears in her eyes. A sheen that was reflected around the room.

"That's perfect," Emily said, dropping a kiss on her granddaughter's forehead.

Everyone took turns either holding Alexa or cooing over her, but they kept the visit brief to let the new family rest. Kyle rubbed his hands together and surveyed the room. "Who's next? Don't look at me and Maggie. We're still newlyweds." They'd been married all of about six weeks.

Tori slowly raised her hand, her gaze fixed on her husband. "I guess it's us."

This was met with gasps and a squeal from Emily. "Really?" she asked.

Tori nodded as Sean pulled her against him. "I'm not that far along. Probably late June."

"Good thing your house is going to be done soon," Dylan said with a wink. He was overseeing the work, and it was due to be done in just a few weeks—in time for Christmas.

Tori looked at Hayden. "And don't worry, this won't impact the new facility at West Arch. It'll be up and running before the next harvest."

Hayden smiled at his sister. "I'm not the least bit worried, sis. We Archers know how to get things done."

They did. Whether it was building something, working together, or opening their home and family to everyone they met, the Archers were a special breed. And Bex felt so honored and happy to be a part of them.

"Come on, let's clear out and give these people some much-needed rest," Liam said, prompting them all to say good-bye and take their exits.

Bex and Hayden left the room hand in hand. She felt the silver ring on his hand—the one she'd given him years ago and had only recently engraved with the words *family is love.*

They made their way down the corridor and said good night to the others as they left the hospital. It was freezing cold so they hurried to his Pilot, which he'd regained from Kyle. He fired up the heat and the seat warmers.

"It's so great that they named her after Alex," Bex said.

"It is." Hayden had been seeing a therapist this fall and had made great progress working through his anger and grief regarding Alex. He wasn't mad at him anymore, and he'd gained a better understanding of bipolar disorder and how it had affected Alex in particular.

Maggie, since she'd treated Alex, had actually been a huge help. "I wish Alex could've seen her."

Bex reached over and touched his arm. "I know. I do, too. And maybe he can."

Hayden cast her a warm smile. "I'm so glad you knew him, that I can share memories with you."

"I am, too." Alex was one of the things they talked about in Only Child Club since Alaina and Sean hadn't known him. The rest had told enough stories that they felt like they did, however.

By the time they reached their house on Quail Crest, it was two in the morning. The sky was clear and full of stars, reminding Bex of that night on Slide Mountain. She'd wanted so badly to be exactly where she was right now—at Hayden's side with their future stretching before them. Full of anticipation and hope. And love.

He took her hand again as they walked toward the house but stopped short and pointed at the sky. "Did you see that?"

She shook her head. "No, what was it? A satellite?"

"A shooting star." He pulled her into his arms. "I saw one this summer when we were on Slide Mountain. I thought about making a wish, but at the time I was certain nothing I ever hoped for would come true."

"And now?"

He smiled down at her. "I made a wish."

She curled her hands around his neck. "What was it?"

He kissed her lips softly. "I don't think I'm supposed to tell you."

She arched a brow at him, burrowing closer into his warmth. "So we're keeping secrets now?"

"Bex, you ought to know by now that my heart, my soul are completely open to you. You have me lock, stock, and barrel." His eyes were clear and blue as they gazed into hers. "The wish wasn't for me. It was for Alexa. I hope she knows a life as rich and loving as I have. As *we* do."

Bex's heart was so full of love for this man. "You are the most generous person I know. I'm the luckiest person."

"No, *I* am. It took me a long time to realize it, but I'm so fortunate to have this life, this love. I might not have been planned or expected, but the best things in life rarely are. Just goes to show that if you open your mind and your heart, you never know how things will turn out. And maybe, just maybe, you'll get a happily-ever-after."

He kissed her again, and she knew she'd found hers.

The end

Have you read the entire Ribbon Ridge Series?

If not, be sure to check out all of
Darcy's contemporary romances featuring
the Archer family!

Where the Heart Is
(Derek and Chloe)

Only In My Dreams
(Sara and Dylan)

Yours to Hold
(Kyle and Maggie)

When Love Happens
(Tori and Sean)

The Idea of You
(Evan and Alaina)

When We Kiss
(Liam and Aubrey)

Available now!

Acknowledgments

I AM ESPECIALLY grateful to my editor, Nicole Fischer, for her excellent insight with this story and these characters. This was an emotionally tough book to write, and it wouldn't be where it is without her help.

Thank you, Cyndi Barber, for arranging an amazing day at WillaKenzie Estate. Special thanks to Ronni Lacroute for taking time to talk with me. I especially loved watching the new tanks being unloaded via crane and of course the delicious harvest lunch. Sometimes the writer life is really hard, but I try to be up for the challenge!

Hugs to Rachel Grant for brainstorming naughty beer names with me. Our IM conversations could be their own book.

Thank you to Justin Azevedo at McMenamin's Wilson-ville Brewpub for the incredible tour and information about brewing. I had a great time and now want to make my own! And of course name it inappropriately.

I want to give a special nod to two very important people. First, to my beautiful friend Dominique Dobson, who was suddenly faced with an unimaginable situation. Your grace and courage will inspire me forever—I love and miss you something fierce. Second, to my dear friend Jenni Miller-Duhl, who was shocked with tragedy. You have always been a model of motherhood and a study in taking the high road. I feel so fortunate to have you both in my life. To quote the theme song from *The Golden Girls*, thank you for being a friend.

Thank You!

Thank you for reading *You're Still the One*! It's been a wonderful journey to write about the Archers. They feel like family to me, and I hope to you, too. Thank you to everyone who's sent me notes about the characters and stories—you've touched me with your support and feed-back. And don't think this is the end! While this is the last of the Archer siblings' books, I have plans for many more stories set in Ribbon Ridge about people you've already met. If you're guessing the Westcott brothers are next, you're correct!

Ribbon Ridge is a fictional town based on several cities and towns dotting the Willamette Valley between Portland and the Oregon Coast. It's pinot noir wine country, very beautiful and picturesque—and a short drive from where I live. My brother actually dwells right in the heart of it in a tiny town with no gas station or grocery store (he recently informed me they now have a smallish grocery store/carniceria). There is, however, an amazing antique mall in an historic schoolhouse.

Reviews help readers find books that are right for them. I hope you'll consider leaving an honest one on your preferred social media or review site.

Be sure to visit my Facebook page for the latest information and to say "hi," follow me on Twitter (@darcyburke), check out images of the northern Willamette Valley and other things that inspired this series on Pinterest, and sign up for my newsletter so you'll know exactly when my next book is available.

Thank you again for reading and for your support!

About the Author

DARCY BURKE is the *USA Today* bestselling author of hot, action-packed historical and sexy, emotional, contemporary romance. Darcy wrote her first book at age eleven, a happily-ever-after about a swan addicted to magic and the female swan that loved him, with exceedingly poor illustrations.

A native Oregonian, Darcy lives on the edge of wine country with her guitar-strumming husband, their two hilarious kids who seem to have inherited the writing gene, and three Bengal cats. In her "spare" time, Darcy is a serial volunteer enrolled in a twelve-step program where one learns to say "no," but she keeps having to start over. She's also a fair-weather runner, and her happy places are Disneyland and Labor Day weekend at the Gorge.

Give in to your Impulses . . .
Continue reading for excerpts from
our newest Avon Impulse books.
Available now wherever ebooks are sold.

SERVING TROUBLE
A SECOND SHOT NOVEL
By Sara Jane Stone

IGNITE
THE WILDWOOD SERIES
By Karen Erickson

BLACK LISTED
A BENEDICTION NOVEL
By Shelly Bell

An Excerpt from

SERVING TROUBLE
A Second Shot Novel
by Sara Jane Stone

Five years ago, Josie Fairmore left timber country
in search of a bright future. Now she's back home
with a mountain of debt and reeling from a loss
that haunts her. Desperate for a job, she turns
to the one man she wishes she could avoid. But
former Marine Noah Tager has never forgotten
their one wild night and the only thing he desires is
a second chance with his best friend's little sister.

She tried the door. Locked, dammit.

Ignoring the warning bells in her head telling her to run to her best friend's club and offer to serve a topless breakfast, she raised her hand and knocked.

"Hang on a sec," a deep voice called from the other side. She remembered that sound and could hear the echo of his words from five long years ago, before he'd joined the marines and before she'd gone to college hoping for a brighter future—and found more heartache.

Call, email, or send a letter. Hell, send a carrier pigeon. I don't care how you get in touch, or where I am. If you need me, I'll find a way to help.

He'd meant every word. But people changed. They hardened. They took hits and got back up, leaving their heart beaten and wrecked on the ground.

She glanced down as if the bloody pieces of her broken heart would appear at her feet. Nope. Nothing but cement and her boots. She'd left her heart behind in Portland, dead and buried, thank you very much.

The door opened. She looked up and . . .

Oh my . . . Wow. . .

She'd gained five pounds—well, more than that, but she'd

lost the rest. She'd cried for weeks, tears running down her cheeks while she slept, and flooding her eyes when she woke. And it had aged her. There were lines on her face that made her look a lot older than twenty-three.

But Noah . . .

He'd gained five pounds of pure muscle. His tight black T-shirt clung to his biceps. Dark green cargo pants hung low on his hips. And his face . . .

On the drive, she'd tried to trick herself into believing he was just a friend she'd slept with one wild night. She'd made a fool of herself, losing her heart to him then.

Never again.

She'd made a promise to her broken, battered heart and she planned to keep it. She would not fall for Noah this time.

But oh, the temptation . . .

His short blond hair still looked as if he'd just run his hands through it. Stubble, the same color as his hair, covered his jaw. He'd forgotten to shave, or just didn't give a damn. But his familiar blue eyes left her ready to pass out at his feet from lack of oxygen.

He stared at her, wariness radiating from those blue depths. Five years ago, he'd smiled at her and it had touched his eyes. Not now.

"Josie?" His brow knitted as if he'd had to search his memory for her name. His grip tightened on the door. Was he debating whether to slam it in her face and pretend his mind had been playing tricks on him?

"Hi, Noah." She placed her right boot in the doorway, determined to follow him inside if he tried to shut her out.

"You're back," he said as if putting together the pieces of a puzzle. But still no hint of the warm, welcoming smile he'd worn with an easy-going grace five years ago.

"I guess you didn't get the carrier pigeon," she said, forcing a smile. *Please let him remember.* "But I need your help."

An Excerpt from

IGNITE
The Wildwood Series
by Karen Erickson

Weston Gallagher is falling hard—
for the wrong woman.

One night of passion has haunted him for years.

Now he's got a second chance to get the girl of
his dreams . . . but there's just one problem:

She hates him.

A knock sounded at his door, startling him and he climbed off the couch to go answer it, pissed that it was most likely Holden ready to convince him he should go out to the bars. He didn't bother looking through the peephole, just unlocked the door and swung it open, launching right into a speech for his little brother.

"I already told you I didn't want to go out tonight," West said, the rest of the words stalling in his throat when he saw who was standing on his front doorstep.

It was Harper, wearing a black trench coat on a warm June night, her long auburn hair extra wavy and flowing past her shoulders, a secretive little smile curving her very red lips.

"You did?" She blinked up at him, all wide-eyed sexy innocence. "Maybe I should go then?"

She started to turn and he grabbed hold of her arm, halting her progress. "Don't go." He sounded eager. Way too eager. Clearing his throat, he started over. "Sorry. I just thought—I thought you were Holden."

"Oh." She turned to fully face him once more and his gaze dropped to her feet, which were in the sexiest, shiniest black high heeled shoes he'd ever seen. "So you don't mind that I stopped by?"

He looked up, their eyes meeting. "Not at all." What was she up to? Her eyes were heavily made up, as were her ruby red lips. And her hair was downright wild . . . all he could think of was fisting it in his hands and tugging her head back so he could plant a long, deep kiss on those juicy lips.

"It's sort of late." She blatantly scanned his mostly naked body, her glossy lips parted, her pink tongue touching just the corner of her mouth. Her gaze lingered on his chest and arms, cataloging his tattoos. She seemed fascinated with them and he was half tempted to flex his muscles just to see if her eyes grew hungrier . . .

Which they seemed to do, without any encouragement on his part. If she didn't stop looking at him like that he might get a freaking boner and that probably wouldn't be good. "Were you in . . . bed?"

The provocative way she just said it made him aware of her close proximity. How her hands tugged on the ends of the belt wrapped tight around her waist. The hollow of her throat was exposed, as was a bit of her chest. She looked practically naked under that coat.

Hmmm.

"No, I wasn't in bed." He paused, wondering what the hell she was up to. Whatever it was, he could appreciate the way she was staring at him, and he was damn thankful she'd come by. He figured he'd blown it for good with Harper. "You want to come in?"

"I would love to." She smiled and he stepped out of her way, the scent of her surrounding him as she walked by. He shut and locked the door and followed her as she moved deeper into the living room. Grabbing the remote from the side table, he turned off the TV, the sudden silence amplifying every move she made.

"So I have a proposition for you," she said, turning to face him once more. "One I'm hoping you'll agree to."

In the hushed quiet of his house, she looked a little less sure, a little more nervous. A lot more like the Harper he knew. He wanted to reach out and reassure her but he also wanted to hear what she had to say first.

"Really?" He rested his hands on his hips, noting the way her gaze dropped to linger on his stomach. He felt downright exposed, what with the way she studied him. Not that he minded. "What is it?"

She bit her lower lip as she contemplated him, her straight white teeth a bold contrast to the deep red coating her lips. "Last night, when we talked, you said you weren't boyfriend material."

He winced. Did he really need a reminder of the stupid things he'd said?

"And I told you I wasn't looking for a relationship, which is true. I don't want one. But I do want *something* from you, West." She reached for the coat belt, slowly undoing it. "I'm hoping you want the same thing."

An Excerpt from

BLACK LISTED
A Benediction Novel
by Shelly Bell

Years ago con artist Lisa Smith fell in love with
her mark, then vanished without a trace . . .
but now he's found her and he's not going
to let her slip through his fingers again.

An Avon Red Romance

He sucked in a breath, the tightening in his chest becoming more pronounced as he watched her glide across the dance floor with a glass of champagne in her hand. She'd changed since the last time he'd seen her. Gone was her halo of white blonde tresses that spilled down her back and those round silver irises that looked at him with what he'd believed was love. Like a chameleon, she'd adapted to her environment, her chestnut hair cut into a sleek bob and an air of sophistication clinging to her designer-clad body.

With a smile on her face, she had everyone at this wedding fooled, but he knew the truth. She was a con artist who had stolen millions from unsuspecting men and women. At the drop of a hat, she could become someone else, fade into the crowds until she turned invisible, only to return moments later as someone new. And no one would ever guess the truth. She'd mastered the art of disguise, her ability to convince someone of her love and devotion worthy of an Academy Award. Just when she had you wrapped completely around her finger, she'd disappear without a trace, taking your money and your heart with her.

But she'd grown careless when she'd allowed herself to be

photographed, the picture on the front page of every major newspaper. She'd been in the background, barely discernable to most. But not to him. Never him. He'd know his chameleon anywhere.

She had no idea he was watching her.

Stalking her.

Hunting her.

His chameleon had forgotten to use the reptilian sense that warned her of impending danger. She might believe she was a predator, but she was now the prey.

His prey.

Sweat dripped down the back of his neck and black spots flickered in his vision. He shook his head as if clearing the cobwebs from his mind. Didn't she understand he needed her? After everything he'd done for her, she owed him. It was time for her to repay her debts.

Time and fate had kept them apart for far too long. But now that he'd found her, he was never letting her go again.

She loved to play her games.

He smiled.

A game was what they'd play.

Walking away from her friends, Lisa Smith took a sip of wine and headed toward where she'd last seen the caterer. Not spotting him, she stopped and scanned the crowd.

"Lisa!"

Lisa turned and caught sight of her friend Rachel Dawson walking toward her with two men by her side.

It took only a moment for it to register.

The long blond hair she loved to tug on during rough sex.

The stubble lining his jaw that used to scratch the skin of her inner thighs as he worked her over with his mouth.

The roguish and lighthearted appearance he maintained in public and the dark dominance that lurked beneath the surface.

It was him.

He was here.

Her *Master*.

He had found her.

She blinked a few times, trying to see if maybe she was imagining that the man she'd run from five years ago was suddenly only feet away and talking with her friends as if he knew them. Which was impossible, right?

Her heart galloped a wild beat and the sounds of the crowd disappeared under the roar of her pulse.

She wanted to run *from* him.

She wanted to run *to* him.

All the sorrow and regret she'd buried deep down inside came rushing back with a force that nearly bowled her over. And when the ghost from her past stood right in front of her and looked at her like a stranger, the glass of red wine slipped from her shaking hand onto the green grass, the liquid pooling beneath her heels.

Seemingly oblivious to her shock, Rachel smiled, a twinkle of mischief in her eyes. "I'd like to introduce you to Logan's friend, Sawyer Hayes. Sawyer, this is Lisa Smith."

"Hello," Sawyer said cordially, standing so close she could feel his body heat radiating off him and smell a scent that reminded her of the best days of her life. "It's nice to see you again, Annaliese."

Her mind was a jumbled mess.

Like she was prey caught in the sights of a hunter, she became entrapped in his eyes.

She couldn't breathe.

Couldn't speak.

Couldn't move.

"You know each other," Rachel said, her brows wrinkled in confusion.

"You could say that," Sawyer said slowly, still holding Lisa captive with his eyes. "She's my wife."